To [signature]

A Few
TABLES
Away

GLENHAVEN BOOK ONE

DEB ROTUNO

Mooches — [signature]

RR Books

Published by RR Books
www.rr-books.com

First print edition, October 2019
First published in ebook format, October 2019

The characters and events in this book are fictitious.
Any similarity to real persons, living or dead,
is coincidental and not intended by the author.

The Count of Monte Cristo was written by Alexandre Dumas
The Secret Garden was written by Frances Hodgson Burnett

ISBN: 978-1-69544-287-0

Library of Congress Cataloguing-in-Publication Data

10 9 8 7 6 5 4 3 2

Cover Design & Interior Book Design by Coreen Montagna

Printed in the United States of America

*To everyone who has found their strength
in unlikely places, things, or people.*

Chapter One

EVAN

"That asshole's tryin' to kill us with homework," said a male voice from behind me. "I'll never get all this reading done."

"Stop goin' out every damn night," the girl with him countered.

He cursed under his breath because she was either right or he liked her enough to shut up. I turned just enough to see it was a guy from my Lit class who spent more time on his phone than taking notes.

The dining hall was loud, filled with chatter, phones ringing, and TVs blaring in the top corners of the large space. The entire room made me sweat more than the humidity outside. Before the true panic of being surrounded by so many people I didn't know — didn't *want* to know — set in, I was called up to the counter to order my food.

Despite the blaring sun and the thick, muggy air, I made my way back outside to the tables in the shade. I could breathe better outside. Outside, there was less chance of someone talking to me. Talking led to conversation, and conversation led to someone finding out just how awkward I was. Alone was better. Alone there was less of a chance I could make a fool out of myself.

The caw of seagulls was loud, sounding like rude laughter. It surprised me just how far away from the beach they'd come to steal French fries and leftover bread crusts. Hell, they'd snatch it right out of someone's hand if they had the opportunity.

I set my heavy backpack on the table, followed by my tray. After pulling out my journal and pen, I picked at my food. My phone vibrated in my pocket, and my whole body froze for a moment.

Please, don't be —

But a smile curled up on my face at the sight of the name on the screen, and I couldn't swipe it quickly enough to answer.

"Faith?"

"How's my favorite big brother handling the Sunshine State?" she started immediately.

"You'd better not let Ty hear you say that," I warned her with a chuckle.

"What? That it's sunny? He knows. Oh, and he knows you're my favorite. I tell him every opportunity I get. He said he doesn't care, that he'd squeeze the love out of me."

Laughing, I shook my head at my baby sister. I missed her like crazy, and I missed my big brother, Tyler, too. But I couldn't stay. The very second I'd started applying for colleges, I'd made sure most of them were as far away from my home state of Montana as I could get. Another country would've been better, but the complete opposite side of the US would have to do.

"It's okay. Hot, humid, um…beachy," I finally answered her question, looking at my watch. "Shouldn't you be in class?"

"Half day. Teacher workday or some shit. Thank God! Key Lake High hasn't changed a bit since you left."

I snorted derisively, picking up a fry and dragging it through ketchup. "I'm sure you have it way easier than I did," I mumbled around my food.

She sighed deeply. "Yeah, well…I don't have time for bullshit from those idiots. I've got better things to do than to deal with the petty, small-town people of Key Lake."

"No shit," I murmured, shaking my head at how much stronger my sister was than me. She simply didn't care what people thought—not the school kids; not the whispering, gossiping adults; and especially not our father. Though, the latter ignored her, which was better than how he dealt with Tyler and me. As a kid, I'd have killed to be ignored. "I miss you."

"Miss you too, Evan," she sang back. "I wanna come visit. Can I? Spring break?"

Grinning, I nodded foolishly. "Yeah, Faith, if he'll let you. Sure."

"What he doesn't know…"

"You can't do that. You'll only make shit worse, Rylee Faith," I scolded her, but the absolute terror of Dad setting his sights on Faith was too much to think about. "Ask him first. If he says no, then… the summer, maybe."

"He doesn't scare me."

"Nothing scares you. That's the problem."

She laughed, and it made me smile. It made me homesick, if only for her. Despite the fact that she was younger than me, she was my best friend.

Instead of arguing, she changed subjects. "How's Library Girl?"

Groaning, I set my elbow on the table, reaching up to adjust glasses I wasn't wearing anymore, thanks to Faith. Contacts were fine, but my nervous tic was to adjust the glasses. Now my hand shot to my hair, raking, gripping, and essentially sending it into disarray—worse than it normally was. Thankfully it was shorter now than it used to be.

"Have you even talked to her, Evan?"

"N-N-No."

The sinking, gut-punch anxiousness that hit me was almost debilitating.

"Hey, big brother…" Faith sighed again. "Why don't you write her? You know that helps you."

Nodding even though she couldn't see me, I groaned. "I know. I just…She's…*way* out of my league, Faith."

She laughed. Hard. And at me, for some damn reason. "Oh, *good Lord*, Evan. You have no idea, do you? You have *any fucking idea* how many girls were crushing on you your senior year?"

Scowling, I stayed quiet, wondering if I should've kept my crush to myself, but I also knew full well that Faith could get me to confess just about anything. Prime example was this conversation—the girl in the library who I couldn't help but stare at, wonder about, and essentially drool over. She was beautiful, with a sweet smile and stunning eyes. Never mind that she had phenomenal taste in books.

"Laura, Erin, and Mrs. Wilson said to tell you hello."

"*Mrs. Wilson?* The school office lady?"

She laughed again. "Crushing hard, that old cougar. Says you have the nicest…*manners.*"

"Aw, stop."

"Evan, you're very handsome, and you're smart and sweet. If Library Girl can't see that, then she's a blind bitch and you shouldn't even waste your time."

"I don't even know her name, Faith."

"Doesn't matter. Write it down. You'll feel better. It's how you work, big brother."

"'Kay."

"I gotta go. I've got a date."

"With who?"

"Ron."

"Rylee Faith Shaw! Seriously? He's an asshole. His dad is an asshole. He works at —"

"He works with Dad. I'm aware, but there's a party and I wanna go," she stated firmly.

Shaking my head, I began packing up my things. "Well, text or call when you get home."

"I will, I promise. Love you," she sang before ending the call.

I huffed a humorless laugh, shouldering my backpack and tucking my phone back into my pocket. After dumping my lunch trash, I started across the campus of Edgewater College. It was a small school, private, and not as intimidating as some colleges could be — definitely not as big as UM, where Tyler was going — but I still avoided eye contact the whole way to the library. It had been a toss-up between small school and big. While large campuses would allow me to get lost in the masses, the thought of all those people made me nervous. Edgewater was only slightly bigger than my old high school — maybe twice as many students. It was the center of the small, panhandle town of Glenhaven, Florida. The distance from home had been far more important than the fact that it was near the beach when I was choosing schools.

Bishop Library, where I was headed, was on the east side of the campus, situated beneath the shade of large old oak trees. The front of the building overlooked a small lake at which I rarely looked. Bodies of water were worse than bodies of people. They made me sick, like sweaty hands, nausea, and shallow breathing.

You should really get over that water shit, son.

I shook my head at the jibe I'd heard more times than I could count. Out of sheer belligerence, I stopped on the sidewalk and faced the small lake. The brownish-green water was dotted with ducks, swans, and tall herons, not to mention tall, bright green cattails with their puffy brown tips that were breaking apart in the breeze. I glared at the water with both hatred and fear, the emotions battling for dominance.

Not that lake. Not that one, I soothed myself, only to give up when the thought of going near it crossed my mind.

The air conditioning in the library was almost frigid in comparison to the heat outside, so a shiver practically rattled my teeth when I stepped inside the one place that could ease everything. When I was in the library, nothing could hurt me. When I fell through the rabbit hole of a good story or lost myself to homework and projects, my loneliness and fears and the life I so desperately wanted to leave behind faded away like a puff of smoke, if only for a chapter or two.

My usual table wasn't exactly empty, but at least my end was vacant. I set my stuff down, pulled out my books, and forced myself not to look, but I was a weak idiot and looked anyway.

My heart hurt at the sight of her. Library Girl — as my sister so easily named her. She was just on the other side of another table, her back to the rows of bookshelves as she faced the large open space of the study area. The library wasn't the only place I saw her. She was in my Lit class and my Creative Writing class as well, but Faith had locked in on the fact that the library was where I had developed this stupid, useless crush on a girl whose name I didn't even know.

I sat down in my chair, giving her another glance as I blindly pulled out my notebook and journal. As usual, she was buried in a book, fingers wrapping a lock of her light brown hair around and around, tying it in a loose knot, only to let it fall out to start all over. It was mesmerizing. She was beautiful, with long hair and deep sea-blue eyes, and her eyelashes were insane, especially against creamy skin. She never wore a lot of makeup, but she didn't need it. She dressed casually but not like some of the girls around here and back at home. Some of them showed way too much. No, Library Girl looked like she dressed for comfort, not for show.

The first time I'd ever seen her, she'd been crying, and something about that had bothered me—almost to the point that I forgot my fear and approached her. It wasn't until I realized the tears were caused by the book she was reading that I sat down at the same table. I waited patiently to find out what book it was, if only because I couldn't remember the last time I'd read something that moved me to the point of tears.

"Excuse me," I heard as a shadow fell over me.

I looked up expectantly at a girl in dark glasses I knew from a few of my classes. Rachel...no, Rebecca...No, that wasn't it, either.

"I'm Regan," she introduced herself. "We're in Physics together."

Nodding stupidly, I whispered, "Evan."

Her smile was accompanied by a blush of her cheeks. "Right, Evan. Um, I was wondering...Do you have the notes from the last class? I was out sick, and..."

My eyebrows shot up, but I nodded nervously, reaching into my backpack for my notes. I flipped to the most recent page and handed them over.

"Thanks," she said, smiling my way and pointing to the other end of the table. "I'll be right here. I'm just going to copy them down really quick."

"Okay," I whispered softly, and she stepped away to reveal Library Girl watching us. For the first time, those expressive blue eyes locked with mine, and she smiled softly, though they broke from me to the other end of the table to look Regan's way, her brow furrowing a little.

My heart pounded in my chest, and I dropped my gaze to my journal. Maybe Faith was right; maybe I did need to write it down first. Writing always helped me to sort out my thoughts, align words together better than my mouth ever could. I could almost hear my little sister's laugh at me, but I put pen to paper, hoping that by the time I was finished, I'd maybe have the bravery to give it to her.

As I wrote, I imagined leaving it in her book or on top of her homework. The thought of handing it to her sounded juvenile and silly, not to mention practically impossible, considering I didn't think I'd be able to form a complete sentence around her.

While writing, I glanced up to see her attention back on her book, so I finished out the letter.

Dear Library Girl,

I call you that because I don't even know your name, but I see you. I see you every day.

I saw you my first day on campus. Beautiful and popular, surrounded by friends some days and alone others. You seem comfortable in either state.

I saw you the day you were crying over a book. It was silent and sad, with trembling lips and the softest of sniffles, because you either didn't want anyone to know you were crying or you didn't want to disturb the quiet of the library. You're here as much as I am, so I can't decide which it is.

It took what seemed forever to catch sight of what you were reading, and when I did, I checked it out of this library. I'll admit it was sad, but I don't remember if I cried. I did, however, start to pay attention to what books you're reading.

It was then that I truly started to see you. Really see you. But I wanted more. I needed to know more, but I wasn't even sure how to sit near you, much less speak to you.

Because as much as I see you, I'm certain you don't see me. Most people don't, and those who do bring with them unwanted attention. I've spent most of my life trying to be invisible, and now it's pure habit.

You're too pretty, but not the kind of pretty built on makeup or expensive clothes. You're the kind of pretty that comes from the inside. It's made up of kind smiles for strangers, teases to friends, and the obliviousness of falling into a good book.

I guess I hope that you'll see me one day, but I'm not holding my breath. I'd like to think I'd eventually muster up the courage to speak to you or even sit at your table instead of mine, but I don't know about that either. You're all things sunny here, and I'm not. I come from dark places, fear, and guilt. I'm not sure what you'd think of that.

I want to thank you for all the books I've seen you read, which I've checked out after you. They've been the best recommendations I've ever had.

Love, the boy in the library a few tables away

I sat back, skimming over what I'd written, and not a bit of it was untrue. When I glanced up to Library Girl's table, she was surrounded by a few people, smiling and nodding as she packed up her stuff. One of them was a tall, somewhat good-looking guy, his body leaning toward hers, and she didn't back away. Without a glance back, she left the study area with them.

Frowning, I reread my note before slamming the book closed. Who was I fucking kidding? She was pretty in every way. She was so pretty that she could have any guy she wanted, so why on earth would she even look my way again?

I shoved my journal in my bag and pulled my homework closer. I needed to get some of it finished before my shift at the coffee shop.

Chapter Two

EVAN

"Here you go."

Glancing up from where I was packing up my things in the library, I met Regan's gaze, which seemed bigger behind her glasses, and for a split second my attention drifted away. I wondered if my own eyes looked like that when I had my glasses on. I'd never really thought about it.

"Thank you," she said softly, snapping my attention out of the daze.

"Oh," I said with a polite smile as I took the notebook from her and stuffed it into my bag. "No problem."

"Um…listen," she started nervously, still keeping her voice low, but she fidgeted, adjusted her glasses, and then twisted her fingers together in front of her. "I know we have that project in Physics coming up. We're supposed to…get with a partner or group, and I was wondering…well, if you don't have one already…though I'm sure you do, but I just thought…Forget it."

Her ramble was familiar, and I had sympathy because in all reality, I wouldn't even begin to know how to ask someone to be my partner.

"Yeah, no…That's…That works," I told her. "I'd forgotten about it, actually," I lied. I'd really just planned to do all the work alone. I was used to it from high school.

"Okay? Cool," she said, smiling my way, but her cheeks turned red. "'Cause I don't really know anyone yet."

Smiling, I nodded as I shouldered my bag. "Me, either."

"You have class?" she asked, grabbing her own bag.

"No, work. I'll see you in class next week," I told her softly before heading out of the library.

A glance at my watch told me I had just enough time to head to my dorm room, drop off my stuff, change into my work T-shirt, and walk over to the coffee shop. I honestly didn't have to work—my partial scholarship combined with the college savings account that had been started when I was born paid for school—but I was saving up for a car.

A small jolt of anger charged through me, and I shook my head as I made my way back across the campus. I thought of my car that was parked in the garage back in Montana. It didn't matter that I was nineteen, or that I'd graduated Key Lake High School with honors, or even that I'd gotten into college. William Shaw still found a way to exert his disappointment in me in every way he could drum up. He'd wanted Ivy League; I'd wanted Edgewater, specifically for its location. So he'd decided he couldn't trust me with a car so far away, saying the insurance was too high. The car was in his name, so I couldn't say shit about it. He wouldn't even let my sister drive it. He'd let it rot before giving it to me. Truly, it was one of the more minor things he'd done in order to prove his point.

The dorm was quiet, most people still in class or at work, and when I stepped into my room, I saw my roommate, Brett, was one of them. He was a quiet guy, and he liked his video games, graphic novels, and comic books. We were both tidy, not to mention serious about our study time. We were a good match in that respect, thank goodness. I'd heard stories of when roommate matches went wrong.

I dropped my backpack onto my bed and grabbed my work T-shirt out of the drawer. I tugged off the shirt I was wearing, my gaze falling to my reflection in the mirror. I wasn't in bad shape, thanks to my older brother—and all the walking I did. But using my fingers, I immediately traced the splash of angry, raised skin down my right side, running the length of my ribcage. The scars were ugly, and the reason they were there was even uglier. Because of my fear of water, the mere idea of going to the beach was laughable, so at least I didn't have to worry about taking my shirt off in public. I changed shirts quickly in order to cover the sight, leaving on my jeans because my manager, Wes, didn't care. Sunset Roast was right on the pier, so casual was fine. He wore shorts most days.

Glenhaven was small, so walking from the dorm to the pier took no time at all. That was another reason I'd picked this school. Without a car, I could at least get around on foot without much hassle. There were buses when I needed to go farther than campus, but I rarely used them.

It was midafternoon as I walked up the boardwalk to the coffee shop. As usual, I didn't look toward the beach. While the smell of saltwater and the sounds of waves rolling up to shore were soothing, the sight of endless sea was unnerving. As long as I didn't look at it, I was okay.

The weather in Florida was still warm, though with September almost over, I was told that the heat would lessen soon, that fall would bring less humidity. I was looking forward to the change from what I was used to; it would be interesting to see the holidays wearing short-sleeved shirts instead of heavy coats and even heavier boots. Because there wasn't a chance in hell I was going home for Christmas.

The coffee shop was pretty busy, with plenty of people taking up the tables outside and the sofas and chairs inside. Most of them were probably college students, though there were a few I'd guess were still only in high school. Sunset Roast had free Wi-Fi, so the younger people of Glenhaven took advantage of it.

Wes was running the counter when I stepped through the doors, and he grinned my way. "Ah, there he is. I'm glad we haven't scared you off yet."

Smiling a little, I shook my head. "No, sir."

He snorted, gripping my shoulder. "I'm about five seconds older than you, bud." When I nodded again, he chuckled. "Actually, I'm only a few years older. What are you…eighteen? Nineteen?"

"Nineteen."

"Ah see? I'm almost twenty-two, so…don't 'sir' me," he teased.

Grimacing, I said, "Habit."

"And it's a good one, Ev. But save it for the old lady at the bakery for extra donuts or the old man who runs the flower shop when you need somethin' for your girl."

"I don't...I mean...There's no..."

His brow furrowed at me, but a half smile played on his lips. "Good-lookin' kid like you? Pfft...Shit, you'll be knockin' them off with a stick before your first semester is over." I could only stare at him in confusion, which seemed to amuse him more, but he changed subjects quickly. "Oh, hey...I was putting your file together. Come with me. I need to talk to you before you get to work."

I started to panic, thinking I'd done something wrong, but he'd said I'd be getting to work, so I figured I wasn't fired...yet. "What'd I do?"

He led me through the kitchen and down the hall to his office. Papers and files were strewn all over the top of his desk, which made the neat freak in me break out into a sweat and swallow thickly. I shifted on my feet, gazing down at my sneakers as he shuffled through some stuff, only to slap down a manila file folder with my name on it.

"Listen, I was doing the paperwork on you, and I noticed you didn't put down a name and phone number in case of emergency."

"There's no one to call."

Wes stared at me for a moment, and I frowned at his finger pointing to the blank line on the application. He opened his mouth and then shut it, only to say, "Where's home, Ev?"

"Montana. And everyone I know is too far away to do anything about any emergency."

Wes sighed, falling down in his chair. "I gotta have somethin'. Even if it's your roommate."

My nose wrinkled as I shook my head, and I thought it was pretty damn sad I didn't have Brett's phone number, but I didn't think I'd need it.

"Parents? Mom or Dad?"

"No...N-No mother, and my dad wouldn't care if there was an emergency." The truth came flying out of my mouth quicker than I could pull it back in, and Wes flinched. "If I give you my brother's number, don't bother to call if something happens. He'll just...freak out that he can't do anything. Then he'll call my sister, who will... She'll panic. I..."

Something akin to pity warmed his usually jovial, easygoing blue eyes—eyes that reminded me of my Library Girl's—but he nodded, pushing the file toward me. I jotted down Tyler's name and cell phone before looking back at my boss.

"And I thought my family put the *fun* in dysfunctional."

I couldn't help but laugh. "From what I can see, you're pretty normal, so...I probably win."

"Oh, damn." He chuckled, shaking his head as he shut the file and stood. "Unless you're torturing baby animals in your spare time, buddy, I can't see much wrong with you. Shy, sure, but new school, new town...it's expected. Once you get settled in..."

Out of respect, I didn't want to contradict him. I liked him, so I nodded in acquiescence. No amount of "settling in" would make me normal. I was an idiot for moving to a beach town, thinking I could overcome my fear of water. I was scarred, awkward, and preferred writing and reading to interacting with people. I'd spent most of middle school and all of high school avoiding bullies who hated me for breathing and girls who laughed at me, at the stupid shit I'd said...or hadn't said. I'd spent the same amount of time trying to melt into the walls of my own home, hoping every damn day that I could become invisible, because invisible was better than hearing about every mistake I'd made, including the worst one of all. If I could spend the rest of my life behind a computer screen, I'd probably eke out a halfway calm existence. Until then, I had classes and classmates, work and coworkers to contend with for at least the next four years.

Wes waited for me to say something else, only to glance at his desk. "I swear...I don't have time for the filing. My cousin promised me she'd help, but she's got her own first year at Edgewater to deal with...not to mention all her social shit."

Swallowing nervously, I pointed to his desk. "I'm um...I can... help. I'm okay at...organizing."

His eyebrows shot up. "Maybe, but not today. I got a delivery this morning, and I need your help opening boxes and putting shit away while Meg and Susan run the front for a bit."

"Okay," I said with a nod.

Unpacking the delivery from that morning wasn't too bad. Tyler always tried to tell me that any hard job could be turned into a workout, so I pushed myself to lift, carry, and break down boxes. Once everything was put away, Wes put me out front to make the drinks for a bit. Faith liked her Starbucks shit, so it wasn't hard to learn. I knew most of it already; it was just learning where everything was and how it was made.

I passed off the last two cups to a gentleman waiting at the end of the counter after a bit of a rush but looked up when Wes leaned in front of me.

"Not bad, Evan. You kept up okay," he praised me with a nod and a smile. "I'm gonna let the girls go home, and you'll close with me."

I nodded, smiling a little as I cleaned up my messes.

"You wanna watch the counter or take the garbage out back to the dumpster?" he asked me.

"Garbage," I told him. "You want me to…" I gestured to the cans by the front doors.

"Yeah, yeah…and the two out on the deck too. Thanks, Ev."

Nodding, I got to work. After changing out the full bags, I replaced them with new ones and tossed the old ones into the rolling bin before pushing my way out onto the deck. A few tables were still occupied, some with people just chatting, some with groups of loud laughter. I stayed focused on my work, cleaning some of the empty tables along the way.

I pulled the last full garbage bag, dropping it into the bin I was rolling with me. Just as I started to push it around to the back of the coffee shop, a half-empty, partially melted frozen coffee flew across the deck and landed at my feet, sending a splatter of cold, sticky, tan-colored liquid all over my sneakers, the edge of my jeans, and the deck floor around me.

The louder table exploded into laughter, and I glanced up to see a guy getting slaps on the back and praises. I recognized him instantly. He'd been the guy to walk away today with Library Girl.

"My bad," he said through an unapologetic chuckle. "I was aiming for the can, pal."

"S'okay," I muttered, bending down to pick up the cup. I tossed it into the can I was pushing.

Just before I turned the corner, I heard a girl yell, "You did that shit on purpose, you asshat!"

I didn't bother to wait or even to see who said it. I needed to get the garbage finished and get back inside to at least clean up a

little. It was going to be a long few hours in cold, wet, sticky shoes…
and I needed to clean the spill on the deck before someone slipped.

As I approached the dumpster, the back door of the coffee shop
flew open, allowing a bit of light out, along with Susan and Meg. The
latter was also a student at Edgewater, and she had been the newest
employee before I'd been hired. The former wasn't as young — probably in her midthirties. Susan was a little…rough around the edges.
She smoked, which meant she immediately lit up a cigarette once she
was outside, and she rarely took shit from pushy customers.

"You okay?" Susan asked, eyeing my sneakers and then the garbage
can. "C'mon, kiddo, I'll help you." She left the cigarette hanging
between her lips and grasped the other side of the full can. We lifted
together, dumping it all, and then set it back down. She eyed me
shrewdly, saying, "We saw what happened. You aren't even pissed
off, are you? You act like people throw shit at you every fucking day."

I huffed a humorless laugh. "This isn't the worst thing to happen to me."

She pursed her lips in a disbelieving manner. "I can believe that,
but that 'customer is always right' is pure bullshit. And…the asshole's
gone. Dani made sure of it."

"Who's Dani?"

"Wes's cousin," Meg piped up shyly. "She goes to school with us."

Nodding, I pointed to the can. "I'd better get back inside. Thanks."

Susan took a long drag on her cigarette before dropping it to the
ground and smashing it with her shoe. She pointed to my sneakers.
"Use that blue dish detergent and some water. You might be able
to save that shit. Luckily both your jeans and shoes are black, so
stains are…"

Grinning, I nodded again, rolling the can back inside through
the back doors. Once the can was back in place, I grabbed a clean
rag, wet it, and did as Susan said, propping each foot up on a shelf
to wipe them clean. It wasn't perfect, and my new sneakers looked
a little broken in, but at least they weren't ruined.

I stepped out from the back, coming out behind the front counter
to see Wes in a heated, hissed argument. He was standing tall, his arms
crossed over his chest, but I couldn't see the person he was talking
to…until he shifted. He stepped to the side, smiling my way, but I
felt my heart sputter and the tips of my fingers go numb.

Library Girl.

"There he is. You all right, Ev?" he asked, and I could only nod in response, forcing myself to look to Wes. "Fuck, dude…You're white as a sheet."

I had to get my shit together. I shook my head, waving a hand. "I'm okay. It's just…cold coffee." I pointed down to my pants and shoes, shrugging a shoulder. In the great big picture, it wasn't the worst thing. Hot coffee, however, was a bitch when thrown. You can't get the burning wet clothes off and away from sensitive skin quickly enough. I sighed, starting toward the mop.

"I got the deck already." Wes told me, pointing to Library Girl, who had been watching us silently. "Evan, this is my cousin, Danielle. Dani, this is Evan. He just started with me."

Dani was Library Girl. Being face-to-face with her made it hard for me to breathe, but I held a hand out. "N-Nice to meet you."

Her smile was stunning, her blue eyes — the ones I realized were indeed similar to Wes's — so very clear as she slipped her hand into mine to shake it. "Finally, my library guy has a name."

"You know each other?" Wes asked with a chuckle.

"We're in some classes together, but mostly I've seen him in the library," Dani answered because I couldn't find my tongue at all. She turned back to me. "I'm really sorry about Brad."

Grimacing, I shrugged a shoulder. *Brad.* Even his name made him sound like a spoiled, pretentious asshole. Maybe Dani liked guys like that. I tried not to stare at her. I tried like hell not to notice that beneath her tank top was what I thought was a bikini top. I couldn't see her legs from my side of the counter, which was a damn blessing because I didn't think I'd be able to stand, much less breathe. Just knowing her name, standing there talking to her — it all seemed like a dream, like some story I'd made up in my head but was too scared to write down because I feared it would come out like erotica. It was one thing being a guy; it was another being a geek guy *virgin* with an overactive imagination.

She was simply too beautiful to look at, so I turned to start cleaning up for closing time.

I heard Wes leave out the front doors to finish up the deck, but I also heard Dani's steps as she followed to the end of the counter behind me.

"I really am sorry. I saw him do it before I could stop him. I'd just walked up, and...If he bothers you..."

I spun in front of her, and she trailed off. "It's okay. I'm used to it." My voice came out harsher than I'd intended, and I sighed when her brow furrowed. "I...I'd just like to forget it. It's not a big deal." I also hated that she was apologizing for her asshole friend... boyfriend...whatever he was.

Dani nodded, smiling again, which made my palms sweaty, but Wes burst back inside, locking the front doors of the shop. "Cousin, you helpin' me file or what? 'Cause if you aren't, Evan said he'd do it."

"Seriously?" she countered, rounding on him with what looked like a playful angry face. "You're gonna subject him to your...your lazy inability to remember the alphabet?"

I grinned when Wes merely nodded vehemently with a childish smile. "Yup. Sure am!"

"Uh, no. I wouldn't do that to my worst enemy," she argued. "I'll help him. Otherwise, Aunt Tessa will hear about it. You know, your mother...the person you run this place for?"

"Tattletale."

"Sloth."

They fought like Faith and me, like siblings, which told me they were close. I smiled, shaking my head.

"Fine. Tomorrow." Wes looked to me. "Tomorrow is Saturday, Ev. The girls can handle the front. Do you mind?"

I focused on emptying carafes into the sink and cleaning them as I shook my head. "That's fine," I said, sounding much more confident than I felt.

"Awesome!" Dani said, and I shot a glance her way to see if that was sarcasm. Her pretty face was smiling, and she nodded and waved as she started for the door. "See you tomorrow, Evan."

I wasn't sure what I was going to do. I'd be confined to Wes's small office most of the day...with my Library Girl. I was pretty sure before the end of tomorrow, I'd say or do something epically stupid to scare her off.

Chapter Three

EVAN

My head was swimming by the time Wes and I had finished locking up. I took my time walking back to the dorms. The night was muggy, warm, but the sky was clear. The stars were pretty visible and beautiful on my walk.

Just as I rounded the corner of my building, heading for the front door, my phone vibrated in my pocket. Thinking it was Faith back from her date, I pulled my phone out, only to frown when I saw the caller.

"Hello?" I answered, sitting down on a bench in the courtyard in front of my building.

"Where's your sister?" Dad began immediately.

"How am I supposed to know that? I'm across the country," I replied indifferently, which was much easier to do over the phone than in person.

"Because you two tell each other every damn thing, son!" he snapped, making me flinch, despite the three thousand miles that separated us. "You think I don't *read* the goddamn cell phone bill before I pay it?"

I shook my head because I knew this wasn't about Faith. He didn't care what she did, as long as she brought home decent grades and stayed out of his hair. His problem wasn't with Faith, and it wasn't really with Tyler, either. It was with me. However, I'd learned a long time ago that if you gave him something, even something little, he'd back off just a bit.

"Last she told me, she was going out with Ron Lowe," I stated firmly because it wasn't a lie. The party would get her into trouble, but the date wouldn't, especially with that guy.

"Oh," he sighed. "Okay, then. Dr. Lowe's son?"

"Yes, sir."

The line went quiet, and just like always, he shifted his ire to me. "You'd better be keeping your grades up, Evan. If I get a report that says differently, I'll —"

"My grades are fine, Dad," I interrupted before he could threaten to bring me back home…or stop sending my funds for school. "We're just a month into the semester."

"Oh, which reminds me. I've decided to sell the BMW," he stated coldly. "It's not being used, and insuring it is a waste of money."

I closed my eyes in frustration. I loved that car, but in all reality, he'd held it over my head since I was sixteen. He wielded it like a weapon. If I made him unhappy, he took it away. If I dropped a tenth of a point in my GPA, he took it away. If I didn't go to prom, if I burned his toast, if I read a book instead of watching the football game, if Faith or Tyler came to my defense…Once I'd gotten big enough that physically scaring me became almost impossible, the BMW was his choice of punishment. If he sold it, there was one less weapon he could use against me.

"Whatever you feel you need to do, Dad," I stated, shrugging a shoulder that he couldn't see, but it made me feel the indifference I was trying to put out.

"Well, at least you see reason."

I shook my head, almost smiling, because I could hear that my answer had not been what he'd wanted. Apparently he was looking for a fight, and I honestly didn't have it in me to give him one today. He'd have to find one somewhere else. And I also needed to warn Faith before she got home.

"Dad, I gotta go. I've got a lot of reading to get done before Monday."

"Fine, we'll see you at Thanksgiving," he stated.

I opened my mouth to counter that I wasn't going home for the holidays, but I'd save that argument for later, sometime closer to November. I'd use school as the excuse.

The call ended before I could say anything anyway, so I immediately dialed my sister.

"Evan!"

I smiled but decided to get directly to the point. "Brace yourself when you get home. He's prickly."

"He's always prickly. What now?"

"He wanted to know where you were."

"What'd you say?"

"I gave him something to shut him up. I gave him Ron's name."

She sighed, and I could hear the noise in the background. "Fine, I'll head home in a few." The noise died down a bit, and I heard a door slam. "Now...tell me. Was Library Girl—"

"Dani," I said with a grin. "Her name's Dani."

"Shut the fuck up! You talked to her?"

Snorting, I shook my head. "It's kind of a long story. Today's been...weird."

"Tell me. I'd rather hear this. The party was stupid."

I gave Faith the rundown of my day, including the letter I wrote but didn't give, the asshole who threw the drink, and meeting my Library Girl face-to-face.

"You know, I think she was the one who yelled at him when I walked away," I guessed in a mumble.

"So...your bookworm is your boss's cousin? That's fucking awesome!"

Grinning, I broke into a laugh. "I guess, but I think she likes that jerk, Brad."

"Maybe not. She apologized, big brother. If she were into asshats, she'd have ignored what happened."

"Maybe, but now...*now* I'm gonna be stuck in a room all day with her, Faith. What the hell am I supposed to do?" I asked in a hissed panic. "I'm gonna screw this up so bad."

Faith laughed, but it was soft and not really at me. "You...God, Evan, you make way more out of stuff than you need to. I'm telling you, if she's worth any-damn-thing, she'll accept you just as you are, 'cause you *are* a good guy, big brother. Just be you and be honest, no matter what, because you don't want to be a liar. Mom always said—"

"It's much easier to remember the truth than the lies," I whispered with her, closing my eyes. "God, I miss her."

"Me too."

The silence between us was heavy, filled with an old grief. I'd only been twelve when it happened, which meant Faith had been ten and Tyler fourteen. Faith had been home that night with Dad, but Tyler and I had almost died with our mother. I shook my head to get rid of the old memories of screeching tires, crunching metal, and the splash of cold, dirty water.

"Evan...Big brother, come back to me..."

"I'm...I'm okay."

"I know you are, and you'll be even better now that you don't have to hear the shit every day," she stated wisely. "And you aren't here as a slap to the face...You look—"

"Just like her. I know." I smiled, in spite of it all. My whole life, people had told me how much I looked like my mother. Robyn Shaw had given me her hair, her eye color, even her love for reading and writing. I was her made over. And it pissed my dad off something fierce.

"Evan?"

"Hmm?"

"Evan, just...go be you tomorrow. Don't sweat that you think you're different. Don't worry about your past. Go be that funny, smart, sweet guy I love."

After taking a deep breath, I let it out slowly. "I'll try. Love you too."

The next morning, I was a mess of nerves. No matter what Faith had said, I still couldn't shake the fear of working all day with Dani in Wes's office. I was afraid she'd see how weird I was, that my pickiness for organization would make her laugh, and that she'd catch me staring at her. That last one was the scariest because I knew for a fact I wouldn't be able to stop myself. She was just that pretty.

I used my walk to Sunset Roast to try to clear my head, but it didn't work. I thought maybe I should get myself a bike while I was saving for a car. It would come in handy. It didn't need to be expensive; maybe a secondhand from a pawn shop or something. And then I thought about how lame that would make me seem. Not only was I socially inept, but I had no car, either.

By the time I made it to the boardwalk and inside the coffee shop, I'd pretty much come to terms that I was going to embarrass myself in front of Dani in one way or another, so as my little sister would say…

"Fuck it," I sighed to myself, reaching for the time clock and punching in.

"Evan," Wes greeted with a big smile, gripping my shoulder. "My cousin is already here, so I'll let you two just…" His face heated, and he opened the door to his office with a grimace on his face. "Good luck," he blurted out, pushing me inside and starting to close the door.

"Wes Harper, you'll stop right there!" Dani yelled from behind his desk, and when she stood, I could see smooth legs and shorts, so I broke my gaze away quickly.

However, I wanted to laugh at Wes's paling face as he poked his head in the doorway. "Look, Dani, I…"

"Don'tchoo *Dani* me…" She stepped away from the desk and pointed to a few open drawers of the filing cabinets that lined the walls of the small office. "Seriously?"

Glancing at Wes, I walked to the open drawers to peer inside. My stomach knotted at the folders that were completely out of order. There were employee files in with the bookkeeping stuff, banking stuff in with the vendor files, and dated folders were not in order at all.

I looked up to see Dani peering in with me, but then her pretty eyes locked with mine as she shook her head.

"What the hell is wrong with you? Who does this shit?" she yelled at her cousin. "You've made my OCD shoot into orbit, you jackass!"

He laughed, and despite the fact that it was a nervous laugh, he truly was amused with her. "Well, I think you two are probably going to be a bit, so…"

Her nostrils flared as she glared at the door he slammed closed. He'd essentially just locked us in there. I was pretty sure her eye twitched, but I couldn't get past the fact that she'd said she had OCD.

"You too?" I asked softly, pointing to the atrocious filing system.

Her gaze broke from the door to meet mine. "What?"

"OCD?"

She giggled, and sweet God, she was gorgeous when she laughed. "Oh hell yes! Since I was a kid. I mean, I don't flip light switches off and on like three times before bed, but this kind of stuff...Ugh."

Chuckling, I nodded. "Me too. My brother used to turn in homework that was wrinkled and stained, and it drove me crazy. He'd come into my room when we were kids, just to mess it up."

What I didn't add was that Tyler stopped doing that after I got into trouble with Dad for having a messy room. It only got worse when Tyler owned up to the mess; my dad punished us both.

"We'll never, ever get your brother and my cousin in the same room. It'll be anarchy."

A loud laugh escaped me, and I couldn't help it. Her sarcasm was sharp and quick but funny. I caught her stare at me, and her cheeks were flushed pink, but she seemed to shake some thought out of her head as she pointed toward the cabinets.

"I think...maybe we should just empty them, sort the folders, and then refile everything correctly."

"Clean slate," I agreed with a nod, glancing over the drawers. "We're going to need some room...on the desk and the floor. And maybe a permanent marker for labels and such."

Dani smiled, and it was secretive and sexy. She went to a backpack hanging on Wes's desk chair and reached in for something.

She held up a plastic piece of equipment, still wearing that wickedly sexy smile. "Label maker, Evan. I'm not sure I could live without this bad boy."

I was pretty sure my neat-freak side just fell in love with her completely. I had imagined and dreamed for weeks as to what my Library Girl's personality would be like, but the truth was far better than I could've created in my head. She was smart and sassy, but she was kind too. I was beginning to wonder if there was anything that wasn't attractive about her, except maybe her taste in men. And that only served to remind me that she wasn't mine, except in my head.

With a deep sigh, I said, "Okay, let's do this."

"Why don't I take the floor? You can bring me stacks of folders, and I'll sort them," she suggested.

"Then we'll re-label the cabinets and put stuff back," I finished, smiling when she nodded happily.

She paused before taking a seat on the floor, a small, slow smile gracing her features.

"What?" I asked nervously, rubbing the back of my neck.

"You have...the *prettiest* smile, Evan," she stated, and my eyebrows shot up.

My heart sputtered in my chest, and there were shocks in my stomach, never mind the heat on my face, but I smiled again. "Um... th-thank you. So do you," I said softly.

She laughed. "Thanks, but you act like no one's ever told you that."

Turning toward the first drawer, I reached in, pulled out a great number of folders, and stacked them in my left arm, only to do it again. When the stack was about as tall as the length of my torso, I turned to set them down in front of her, but she was still watching me with concentrated interest.

"Seriously? No one's told you? Like...*ever?*"

I shook my head. Her open-mouthed stare made me self-conscious. I shifted nervously on my feet, waiting for her to say something else. She let her gaze drop to the stack, and I darted back to the filing cabinet.

"So..." she said, looking up at me with a smile when I handed her more. "Where're you from, Evan?"

"A...um...a really small town in Montana. You?" I answered her, keeping my eyes on my work.

"Right here. Glenhaven." She smiled again, nodding as she pulled all her hair up into a long ponytail. She started stacks of different folders, creating a semicircle in front of her. "You mentioned a brother...Is that it?"

"Oh, no," I said with a shake of my head, setting another stack into her awaiting hands. "I have a baby sister too. Faith."

"Ah, the dreaded middle kid. Is it true what they say? That the middle child is the most trouble and the overlooked one?"

An ugly, humorless snort rocketed out of me. "Uh, no. Hardly. What about you?" I changed the subject quickly. "Siblings? Parents?"

I couldn't believe, despite how nervous I was being in the same room as Dani, how *easy* it was to talk to her. She made me nervous, only because I didn't want to say something stupid, but I wondered just for a moment if she didn't know how to keep the conversation going.

"Only child, but my parents are teachers. Professors at Edgewater."

My eyebrows shot up at that. "Really?"

"You've already met my dad." She laughed lightly. "Creative Writing."

"What? Your dad is Professor Bishop?" I gasped, smiling a little. He was my favorite instructor so far. He'd given me high marks on my first couple of papers. "And your mom?"

"Mom is head of the art department. She doesn't teach much anymore. She home-schooled me before I started here."

"Makes sense," I said with a chuckle. "Your parents would've made better teachers than the public-school system."

"They thought so," she agreed with a laugh.

I continued to empty the cabinets until they were finished, turning back to Dani to see how the dividing was going. She pointed to the stacks, and I sat down across from her to help finish. Then we took each stack and put them in their correct order. The work was easy, though a bit tedious, and we stayed in a comfortable silence for a bit until I suddenly made a mental connection.

I glanced over at her, and she looked up at me with raised eyebrows as she waited for me. "You…Um…Bishop Library. That's… That's you!"

She grinned. "Well, not *me*, but my grandfather. My dad's dad. He donated the library a long time ago, but…yeah. Dani Bishop."

I sorted a few folders — accounts receivable, accounts payable, vendors, employee files — only to feel her gaze on me again.

"What about your parents?" she asked innocently.

"It's just my dad. He's a doctor — chief of staff."

"Mom?"

My brow furrowed, and I shook my head. "M-My mom died when I was twelve."

"Oh." She shifted a little, placing her hand over mine. "I'm sorry. I didn't mean…"

"S'okay," I whispered, shrugging a shoulder. "How could you know?"

"I know. I just…" She set the stack of folders on the floor beside her and shifted to her knees in front of me. "I don't like that I hurt your feelings." Her clear blue eyes were sweet and sincere. "You must be close to your dad."

Smiling ruefully, I shook my head. "Dani, I moved three thousand miles away from home by choice."

"Oh, Christ, I just keep fucking up more..." She trailed off but put a hand on my shoulder. Her touch seemed to shoot everywhere on me, like a buzzing shock, and I swallowed thickly. "I'll shut up now so you won't hate me."

Grinning, I shook my head. "I don't hate you."

"You might if I keep saying stupid shit." She laughed at herself, which made me laugh with her. "There, that's better. Wow...Evan, that's some powerful stuff, that smile of yours," she said, shaking her head. "You never smile like that in the library."

I sighed, fighting another smile, but she caught my eye roll. My stacks were in order, so I stood to start labeling and putting the folders back in drawers. Starting toward the cabinets, I gasped a little when she grasped my wrist.

"You have no idea, do you?" she whispered, standing in front of me. "All the girls, all the flirting aimed your way...You have no idea. You don't see them...in class, in the library, *borrowing your notes.*"

I huffed a nervous laugh, looking away from her. "Dani, I'm...I don't know what you're talking about. I..." Frowning down at the floor, I shook my head again. "I don't see anything. In high school, I was a pariah. Here, I'm just...me. In the library, I only see...you." It was honest, and I wished I could take that last part back, but her sweet smile told me she wasn't offended.

"Yeah?" she asked in a whisper.

I nodded, shifting my gaze to the floor. "Yeah, sorry."

"Don't be sorry," she said through a giggle that made me start to smile. She grinned again. "Do me a favor, Evan...If you ever figure out the power you have, make sure you use it for good and not evil. Okay?"

I wasn't sure what to say to that. She thought my smile was pretty? I opened my mouth, only to snap it back closed. "Umm...okay?"

She playfully shoved me, and we got back to work, only this time it was filing stuff back, labeling the folders and the cabinets, and putting some sort of order to Wes's desk.

Wes poked his head in the door just as Dani was turning on his computer. Both of us looked up to laugh at his fear-filled face. "I haven't received a stapler to the face yet…"

"You still might," Dani countered, not bothering to look away from the monitor in front of her, which made me grin.

"So I guess you guys figured it out," he finished, narrowing his eyes at his cousin but ignoring her jibe at him. Stepping fully into the room, he gazed around. "Wait, you're done?"

"Yeah, we got you all set up with…" I started for the first cabinet.

"Evan, don't even bother," Dani sang. She pointed to Wes and then to the empty inbox on his desk. "Paperwork. Here. Don't even attempt to do shit about it. If Evan can't find the time to file it, I'll do it, but if you mess up the beautiful work we just finished with, I will personally shave your head in your sleep."

I hid my smile behind my hand because he *was* my boss.

"You think she's funny?" he asked, but I could see he was amused. "Fine. Evan will file for me. Now, get out of here. We're dead today. Go…hit the beach or somethin'."

"Not a bad idea," Dani told him as she picked up her bag and then grabbed my hand. "Let's go, Evan."

I didn't argue with her, simply because I was stunned at the feel of her hand in mine, but once we were through the sitting area and out on the boardwalk, the smells of the saltwater, suntan lotion, and people hit me full force. It was the glittering sight of the water down the long wooden pathway that made me stop, almost making Dani trip.

"I…I'm…" I was shaking my head. "I can't…I just…" My chest constricted, my breathing became shallow, and I licked my dry lips. "I…I'm…I gotta go. I'm sorry."

I turned away from the water. My walk was fast, even when I heard her call after me. I didn't stop. I didn't stop until I heard rapid running footsteps and a flushed Dani was standing in front of me.

"Evan, wait," she panted, and I looked away from her. "What'd I do wrong?"

I was shaking my head before she even finished the question. "Nothing, Dani. You did nothing wrong. It's me. I can't…The beach… the *water*, I just…" When I met her eyes, I expected pity or disgust, but I only found sincerity as she tried to smile my way. "I'm sorry."

"Don't be sorry. Just…tell me you'll be in the library Monday afternoon as usual," she requested softly, looking like she'd be hurt if I said no.

"Y-Yeah, of course."

"Good," she cheered. "See you then, Evan."

She spun on her toes, her ponytail flying behind her, and I watched her walk away. Every assumption I'd made about Dani had been blown out of the water, never mind that even the dumb shit I'd said hadn't bothered her a bit. Shaking my head, I started toward the dorms to get some homework done.

Chapter Four

DANI

My heart was pounding in my chest as I slammed my car door. Unable to stop myself, I looked and immediately found Evan's tall form walking away from the boardwalk back toward the school. I'd just spent the most amazing yet tiring afternoon with him.

If I'd thought he was gorgeous sitting in the library, nothing had prepared me for actually having a conversation with him. I'd been prepared for smart—because my handsome Library Guy studied endlessly—and I'd been right about that. I'd been prepared for aloof because guys with faces that pretty usually knew it, but he wasn't. He wasn't conceited or cocky or anything most guys were. He was shy—painfully so, actually. He'd been nervous, self-deprecating, and holy shit, the smile on that face could light up the entire state of Florida with its power.

Watching his form finally disappear around the corner, I reached for the car's ignition, only to yank the keys out at the last second. I got out of the car and locked it, storming back into the coffee shop.

"Oh, hell," Susan muttered with wide eyes as she watched me cross the sitting area. "What'd your cousin do now?"

"Nothin'."

She grinned evilly. "Not buying it, but if you're gonna kick his ass, he's in his office."

Chuckling, I high-fived her on my way toward Wes's office. When I burst through the door, he glanced up from one of the open filing cabinets.

"Oh, busted. Mess that up again, and I'll—"

"I'm not!" He shut the drawer and backed away like it was on fire. "I just was lookin'!"

I narrowed my eyes at him and then at the stapler I'd threatened him with when Evan and I had finished a beautiful job, which brought me back to why I was again inside Wes's office. I sat down hard in the chair in front of his desk, looking at my cousin.

"What do you know about Evan?" I asked him. I sighed deeply when his fear turned into a slow, crooked smile and curiosity practically oozed out of him. "I'm serious. I…I'm…I think I just really messed up, Wes."

His brow furrowed as he took a seat in his desk chair. "What do you mean?"

"I…I just…I mean, when you said hit the beach, I didn't think twice. I was thinking ice cream at O'Malley's, you know?" I rambled, shaking my head. "But Evan, he…He just about panicked on me at the sight of that water. Who does that? Who moves to a beach town if you're afraid of water? What…What happened to him?"

My cousin was the first to make a joke on just about any occasion, but his brow furrowed as he set his elbows on the desk. "He's brutally shy, Dani. And I think there are some family issues, but he's pretty tight-lipped about it. He busts his ass around here. He's perfectly polite—almost too polite, which you saw thanks to that asshole boyfriend of yours."

"He's *not* my boyfriend, Wes!"

"Whatever. Keep Brad away from my shop and away from *you*." He sighed, shaking his head. "Never seen anything like it. Evan didn't even flinch. He wasn't even mad, Dani."

"I think…I think he's been through something pretty bad," I whispered, and the thought of it hurt because Evan was so sweet and smart, but I'd seen what my cousin was talking about. Evan had simply accepted Brad throwing a drink at him. He'd been more upset that I'd mentioned it again than what had actually happened.

"You like him," Wes stated, and normally he'd tease me about my crushes, but he wasn't this time.

Groaning, I hid my face in my hands. "I...I'm..." I pulled my hands away and met his gaze. "Oh, God! I thought he was this... hot guy who chose to do his homework in the library. I...I just was enjoying the scenery, but working with him today...He's so...sweet. Like *too sweet*. And oblivious. Oh Jesus, he has no idea...And...And... we worked seamlessly together today."

Wes grinned. "I had a feeling you two would hit it off. He's a neat freak like you are." When I laughed softly, he sat back in his chair. "What do you mean, oblivious?"

I giggled, simply because I couldn't help it. "You should see it. Honestly, he's like this...this...magnet for girls. They sit around him in class, they work in the library at different tables, and they ask him for his class notes—all to get his attention, but he doesn't see a bit of it. He has *no fucking clue* as to how handsome he is. None. And some of his reactions today..." Groaning again, I looked pleadingly at my cousin. "I really like him, Wes, but I'm afraid I'm too honest and outgoing and he's way too shy. I don't want to screw it up. I want to get to know him, but I don't think he'll let me."

Wes laughed, his head falling back. "Now who's blind?" He was still chuckling when he added, "That boy was like a puppy for you today. Why do you think I left you two alone?" His humor melted away. "Ah, Dani...He's very timid. Maybe not timid but...*introverted?* Which means he'll never be a party kid or like crowds—hell, I can see that when he's here—and you'll have to be patient. He's obviously better one on one, so...use that."

I started to stand up, but he stopped me.

"Cousin, it wasn't that long ago that you felt like the shy, nerdy kid. Try to remember that."

I nodded and smiled his way. Wes was right about that. Being homeschooled didn't exactly put me in any social scenes, and for a bit, I lived to lose myself in books—which I still did—but Wes had taken over his mother's coffee shop just two years ago, and he'd asked me to help him, so we'd gotten close. Dealing with customers all damn day one summer caused me to shed my shyness, because

I'd had no choice—flirting for tips, dealing with assholes, and even meeting new friends.

"Okay," I sighed with a nod. "I'll try. He said he'll be back in the library Monday, so…"

"I said be patient, Dani. I didn't say to ogle him from afar. He may need a push here or there—just light ones—but if he's as oblivious as you say he is, then you'll have to show him." Wes chuckled again, saying, "You know, I told Evan he was gonna be knockin' the chicks off him with a stick before the semester was out, but I didn't know it was gonna be *you*."

Smirking, I rolled my eyes. "Oh hell no! If anyone is swinging a stick to get girls off him, it'll be me!" I stated, walking out the door, and Wes was still laughing when I made my way down the hall.

Monday's classes seemed to crawl like molasses. Even my dad's class was dreadfully slow, and my attention was drawn more than once to the person sitting across the aisle from me.

Long, strong legs covered in dark denim were spread open to accommodate the small space in front of him. Evan took meticulous notes, and I smiled at the fact that today he was wearing glasses. They weren't the fashionable hipster-like shit—all dark plastic rectangles. They were just simple wire oval frames, and for a moment I wondered if his eyelashes were so long that they brushed against the lenses. From where I was sitting, it looked like they did.

His jaw was sharp, so masculine that it was easy to forget just how unassuming he was. And there was an innocence to him too. Long, nimble fingers toying with his pen, pink tongue dragging slowly across his bottom lip, and short, dark hair giving off the impression of someone's hands having raked through it—and I had to shake my head to clear it of thoughts I shouldn't be having, especially in my dad's class.

I also took note of who was around him. A girl behind him—long blonde hair and big tits—staring at his back like she could force him to turn around; a girl beside him—red hair, pale skin, long legs—who seemed to be lost in fantasies about his hands; and then there was me—boring light brown hair and several inches shorter than the two girls ogling him.

I wanted to take solace in the fact that he wasn't paying attention to the two hot girls, but he wasn't really paying attention to anyone but my dad at the front of the class.

Sighing deeply, I sank a bit in my seat, but when I looked over again, I fought my smile. Warm brown eyes, magnified by clear lenses, met my gaze, but it was that powerful smile that made my heart just about pound out of my chest.

I only see...you.

His words from Saturday afternoon echoed in my head, making my breathing stop momentarily.

"Oh, God, he wasn't kidding," I murmured under my breath as my brow broke out in a sweat.

I looked over at him again, and his brow was furrowed, his head tilted just a bit, like he was asking if everything was okay. I smiled a little with a nod of my head.

When class was over, I packed up my things as everyone made their way outside.

"Evan, Dani...Would the two of you hang back a second?" my dad requested from behind his desk up front.

I stepped into the aisle to make my way down at the same time Evan did. He smiled again, gesturing toward the front.

"Ladies first," he said softly.

"Thank you, sir," I teased him back with a giggle, which earned me the reward of his sweet chuckle. After a step or two, I shot a glance over my shoulder. "Likin' the glasses, Evan."

He groaned, shaking his head and pushing said spectacles up on his nose, which looked like a habit more than something needed. "I ripped a contact this morning," he said through a disgruntled sigh. "I didn't have time to fumble around for another pair."

Grinning, I nodded. We stepped to my dad's desk, and he waited for the last of the students to leave before facing us. His smile was warm as he looked at us, the dimples showing, even behind his beard.

"You!" He pointed to me, raising a teasing eyebrow at me. "Your mother wants you home for dinner tonight, so make sure you're there."

"I'd planned on it," I told him. "Are Wes and Aunt Tessa coming?"

Dad waved a hand. "I assume so. I let you handle Wes."

Grinning, I nodded but eyed his hand when he lifted a thin stack of pages to Evan.

"Evan," he started, handing him the homework. "Here's your work back."

"Sir? Did I do something wrong?" Evan asked, his voice different, unsure.

"Quite the contrary, Mr. Shaw. You exceeded my expectations by a mile. How long have you been writing?" my dad questioned him, and it had been a long time since I'd seen him so surprised.

"Oh, um…" Evan swallowed nervously, giving me a quick glance.

"I can go…"

"No, no, no…It's okay." He turned to my dad again. "My whole life, I think. M-My mother was a writer and an English teacher, so I learned from her. I…I used to make up stories for my little sister when she couldn't sleep or was sick. Fairy tales. My mother taught me to write them down."

"Is your mother published, son?"

"Yes! I mean, she *was*. She's…um, Robyn Shaw…" Evan shifted nervously, and if I wasn't crushing on him before, I was simply done-for now. "Short stories, poetry, and a series of children's books."

However, I gave my dad a stern look and a shake of my head not to push the subject of Evan's mother.

"Well, this is superb writing, Shaw. Almost flawless. Are you…Is this something that interests you?"

"Yes, sir! Very much!" Evan gushed, blushing when I giggled. I couldn't help it. It seemed we'd finally found Evan's passion, his happy place.

"Sorry." I glanced down at my sneakers.

"You keep up writing like this, Evan, and I see you following in your mother's footsteps," Dad praised him.

I glanced up when Evan went quiet. Tears welled up in my eyes at him, at his body language. I could see that no one had ever told him he was good, except maybe his mother, but she'd died when he was a kid. I could see he respected my father's opinion, but he was unsure as to what to say. And I could also see he was just a little heartbroken over his mom.

Slipping my arm into the crook of his elbow, I started him toward the door, glancing back to my dad. "I'll see you tonight, Dad."

"Sure, kiddo," he murmured back, his brow furrowed just a little. "Hey, son…Evan!" When Evan stopped and looked back, my dad added, "Why don't you come with Dani tonight? I'll let her give you the details, okay?"

When Evan looked to me, I asked, "You gotta work?"

"No, I'm off."

"Good, you can come, then," I stated firmly, shaking him a little to let him know that my bossiness was teasing. "When was the last time you had a home-cooked meal?"

He grinned, shrugging. "I don't remember."

"Then you definitely need to come. My mother is really good." Waving a hand to my dad, I tugged Evan out of the classroom. "Library?"

"I, um...I always go to the dining hall first," he said, nervously rolling up the papers my dad had given him. Roll up, squeeze, unroll—over and over. "You...Would you..."

Smiling, I nodded. "Lunch with you? Absolutely!"

He blushed again, letting out a nervous laugh. "It's the least I can do for my behavior on Saturday."

"Evan, stop," I said softly, pulling him to a halt in front of the dining hall. "Look at me. You don't owe me an apology." I sighed, shaking my head and looking away from him for a second. "I'm loud and way too honest, and I tend to do things without thinking. I didn't stop to think you wouldn't want to go with me..."

Evan sighed, his shoulders curling in on him a bit. "I swear it's not you, Dani. Y-You're perfect. It's me. I'm..."

When he trailed off, I could see his struggle to open up.

"Evan, just...tell me *we* are okay."

"We?" he asked, and his voice cracked a little, his eyes widening.

Wes's advice rattled around in my head—to push yet not too hard.

"Yeah, *we*. I mean, I really liked talking to you Saturday. And we obviously have the library in common. I just...I thought..."

Oh my God, if his smile didn't shine brighter than the sun right there on the sidewalk. But he shifted, rolling that homework up over and over, tighter and tighter, until I reached out to stop him.

Finally, he stopped fidgeting and pointed toward the door. "You want something?"

I nodded, and he walked to the door to hold it for me. We stood in line together, but he wouldn't let me pay for my order, and he carried the tray too. But when we aimed for the tables outside, he paused.

"Do you mind? It's just…I like it better…"

Smiling, I shook my head that it was fine, and he led the way to a table just under a large oak tree. He set the tray down, and we divided up everything. He was quiet for a moment, and his paper caught my eye. I could see a bit of my father's red pen, and I reached for the now tube-shaped homework.

"May I?" I asked, holding it up, and he nodded, adjusting his glasses.

Sipping my drink, I unrolled the pages, sinking deep into a short story about a fairy war and the love between a princess and a simple boy, an archer in the king's army. It was short, but it was vivid and colorful, not to mention a touch romantic. It was brilliant.

"Wow," I breathed, looking up to see him more focused on his food than me. "That was amazing!"

"Thank you."

"I want more!" I laughed when he shot his head up to look at me. "Seriously! This could…Wow. Just wow, Evan. Do you prefer fantasy, or do you write in other genres?"

"F-Fantasy mainly," he said with a small smile. "It's what I liked as a kid. That one was for my sister when she was about eleven. She'd caught the flu somethin' awful, and…"

"That's sweet."

He shrugged a shoulder. "She's the…strongest person I know." His phone vibrated across the table, showing a picture of a young girl with the same chestnut hair as Evan. She was beautiful, down to the silly grin on her face. "Speak of the devil," he said with a chuckle. "Excuse me." He swiped a finger to answer. "Rylee Faith, if you're skipping Calculus again—"

She wasn't loud, but I could hear her laugh, and it made Evan smile. It was a different smile—a warm, giving one—but it fell just as quickly as it came.

"No, I know, Faith. I'm aware…He called me to tell me he was selling it. What am I supposed to do? The car's in his name. It's one less thing he can…No, I know that too." He sighed so deeply, it almost hurt to hear it. "I honestly don't care anymore, Faith. I just…can't. And I have to figure out what I'm telling him about the holidays. I'm not going home."

Damn, Evan's voice was firm and I had to admit a bit sexy, but there was a coldness to it too. It was slightly unnerving.

When his furrowed brow smoothed out, he laughed again. "Can't really say, Rylee Faith...No, can't. Gotta go...Love you."

He was laughing when he hung up, but he looked to me with a touch of red to his cheeks. "Sorry."

"She sounds fun," I noted, smiling when he chuckled a bit.

"She's...my best friend. That probably sounds strange, since she's younger than me, but we've always been close. My...My mother said we were twins separated by eighteen months." When I laughed lightly, he smiled and nodded. "She was calling to tell me that Dad sold my car. I guess I forgot to tell her he was planning on it. She was pissed."

"You okay?" I asked him.

He nodded. "Yeah, I'm okay. At least he can't use it against me anymore."

My brow furrowed at that, and I saw that, while he was very close to his sister, his relationship with his father was rather strained. And something told me deep down that I was probably putting that lightly.

"Why would your dad invite me to dinner?" he asked suddenly.

"Oh, probably because of this," I stated, holding up his story. "He usually finds a student once a year who he chooses to guide, to push in the right direction. You don't have to come, Evan, but you're welcome to join us. We're pretty easygoing, but we're loud. We tease a lot, which I'm sure you noticed between Wes and me."

He grinned. "Okay, but I need—"

"Right. Library first. Me too, actually. Then I have one more class. You?" When he nodded, I stood and offered him my hand. "Then library it is. And I can meet you after our last classes to take you to my house."

He swallowed nervously, eyeing my hand, but he took it after shouldering his bag. He threw away our trash, and again, I noticed that he didn't pay a bit of attention to his surroundings—or at least to who was around him, who stared at him with lovesick eyes. And now they stared at me, which would make the library an interesting experience.

"Hey, Evan?" I said, squeezing his hand, and he glanced to them before my face. "Thanks for lunch."

He smiled and squeezed back. "You're welcome."

Chapter Five

EVAN

The feel of Dani's hand in mine was surreal. I wanted it to last longer, but then again, I didn't because I could feel my nerves kicking into overdrive. My palm started to sweat just about the time we rounded the corner for the front of the library.

Pulling my hand from hers, I reached for the door to hold it open and then wiped it down my jeans once she was inside. Suddenly I was a bit self-conscious. Where would we sit? And would it be together? Or were we going to take our normal spots?

Deciding to follow Dani's lead, I felt my jaw drop in surprise when she set her things down in front of the opposite chair from my usual spot. I slid my backpack onto the table, slowly sinking down into my chair.

My surprise had to have been written all over my face, because Dani grinned, tapping the table. "You don't mind, do you?" she asked, and I shook my head.

"It *is* your library," I whispered back, grinning when she broke into a quiet giggle.

"Hush, you," she stated teasingly.

I pulled out my books for the class I needed to work on, but I also pulled out my journal and the book I needed to return. I started to get up to take it to the chute, but Dani wrapped a hand around my wrist.

"I just finished that one…like a few weeks ago," she whispered, smiling over at me. "It was so good. Sad but really good."

I nodded, smiling a little. "Yeah, I um…I liked it." I turned the book over in my hands. "I saw you reading this…the first time I saw you. You…" I shrugged a shoulder toward her table. "You were crying. I…I almost…"

Her brow furrowed a little when I met her gaze.

"Anyway, my curiosity got the best of me. I wish it had ended differently, but it was good."

Smiling, I shrugged again, getting up to walk across the library to the return slot, where I dropped the book in. Then I made my way quickly back to my seat.

"You prefer happy endings, Evan?" Dani asked softly, due to the quiet of the library.

"Well…*yeah!*" I nodded a little and then focused on the books and papers in front of me. "Life is pretty shitty enough, don't you think? People struggle every damn day. They fight with each other and diseases and their careers, and…I don't know. When I read, I want away from all that." I glanced up at her, smiling in embarrassment and adjusting my glasses, but she just smiled back. "I can't help it. My mother said not all stories can end perfectly, but maybe there's a perfect ending for the characters in the story itself. That book…it was sad."

"It was," she agreed in a whisper, pulling out a different book. "This one's not. It's hot."

Laughing, I shook my head. "I think my sister read that one."

"Smart girl," she said, and I raised an eyebrow at the sexy tone of her voice, not to mention made note of the title.

We fell quiet as I worked on my paper for English Lit and she read. People shifted in and out around us for the next two hours. I glanced up when someone dropped their things heavily at the other end of our table. It made me jump a bit, but I frowned at the sight of Regan's anger-filled face, which seemed to be aimed Dani's way.

Dani, however, barely gave her a second glance as she twirled her hair, her book open in front of her. When whispers met my ears, she shot a look over her shoulder too. Finally she looked back to me.

Smirking a bit, she whispered, "Seems I'm not liked much..."

"Huh? What? Why?"

Dani marked her page and closed her book, leaning closer on her elbows. I couldn't help but do the same.

"Why do you come in here, Evan?" she asked, grinning when I raised an eyebrow at her and gestured to all the work in front of me. "And?"

"I...I don't know. I like libraries. They're peaceful. I can lose myself in a book for a little while and block out everything else," I explained.

She stared at me for a moment, her smile small but warm. "Yeah... me too."

"I know. I could tell," I said with a soft chuckle, embarrassed a little with that admission, but Dani had a way of making me say stuff I normally wouldn't.

"But..." she sang softly, still keeping the tone low for where we were. "The two girls behind me probably haven't been in a library since their mothers took them to reading circles for daycare. They sat next to you and behind you in my dad's class."

My eyebrows shot up at that, and I gave a quick glance to the girls she was talking about. They were at the farthest table, facing me. One was rather snobby-looking, with red hair and pale skin. She had the same color eyes as Dani, but they weren't as friendly or happy. The girl next to her was blonde, and her cleavage was practically spilling out onto the table in front of her. While my brother would've totally gone after her at one point in time, all I saw was fake, scary red nails and too much makeup. They reminded me so much of the girls in high school who would laugh at me that I frowned back at Dani, shaking my head slowly.

Dani smirked. "Fair enough, Evan. The other one..." She jerked her chin toward the opposite end of our table.

"Regan?" I whispered.

"Yes, her." She smiled, nodding a little. "She's braver than all of us because she actually approached you."

"She's...She's in my Physics class. She borrowed notes for a day she was out sick."

"Was she sick? Or did you not even notice?" Dani laughed softly as she waited for me to think about it, and I shrugged because I didn't have a clue. "Right. I saw her borrow the notes. I was kinda jealous that she got a smile out of you…until I *really* saw you smile the other day at work."

My face heated, and I shook my head slowly. I took off my glasses and rubbed my face roughly, sliding my hands into my hair. Why would Dani be jealous? My heart sputtered at that thought.

"What do you mean *all of us?*" I asked.

Dani sighed, and I would've thought it was in impatience, but her smile was warm and sweet as always. "You honestly don't see what we see, Evan. Most guys who look like you…What the fuck am I saying? *No one* looks like you. Most handsome guys don't always come across as approachable."

"Most guys are assholes."

Dani giggled, which made me grin when she had to bury the sound in her hands. "Yeah, well…that's true." Her humor faded a little. "Evan, you are very handsome, but you give off a *don't touch* vibe. It can come across as arrogant or cocky, but since I've talked to you, I can see it's a wall you put up. And I'm sure you have your reasons, but it's a touch intimidating."

"I'm sorry."

She grinned, covering my hand with her own. "Don't be sorry."

Frowning a little, I gazed down at her hand on mine, I shifted my thumb so I could feel the smooth, soft skin across her knuckles. It had only been a week since I'd written my letter in my journal to her, talking about how I wished my Library Girl would notice me, how I wondered what she was really like. It all felt like a dream that she was sitting at my table and not her usual one. It felt liberating and freeing to know that she was better, kinder, more beautiful than my imagination ever considered.

Finally, I met her gaze. "The same could be said for you. Apparently I'm not as brave."

"You're plenty brave. You're just shy, and you keep to yourself. There's nothing wrong with that."

I grinned, shrugging a shoulder, but it fell when I heard whispers across the room. "They don't know me."

"They want to," she countered, squeezing my hand, "which is why I'm not liked very much right now. And I'm perfectly fine with that; I have the best seat in the library today."

I huffed a laugh. "I'm…I'm glad you think so." I gave a quick look to Regan, who still looked upset, and then turned back to Dani. "I'm supposed to work with her on a Physics project."

"Lucky girl."

Shaking my head fervently, I said, "No, no…Dani…I don't…" I sighed in frustration. "I *need* to keep up my grades, but I don't…I'm not what they think I am, if what you say is true. My grades come first…but I don't want to hurt someone. She looks…pissed."

"I doubt you could hurt someone even if you tried, Evan. And she's mad at me. Not you. Just stick to the work. It's okay to be friendly. We're doing just fine."

"You don't know me either," I argued, shaking my head and starting to pull my hand from hers. I wanted to tell her I had hurt people, that girls like the ones in the back of the room could be mean and nasty, and I wanted to tell her I wasn't what people saw, but the words wouldn't come.

"But I *want to*," she said so firmly, holding on to my fingers and not letting go.

There was a split second where I wanted to bolt from the library, but I could hear Faith's voice in my head, telling me to suck it up. Even if I called my sister right then, I knew what she'd say. She'd tell me that it was okay to have friends, to let people in, that I was no longer surrounded by rumors and bullies. She'd also tell me I was worrying for nothing because I was in a place where no one knew my past, my family, my *father*.

I took a deep, cleansing breath at that last thought. He couldn't touch me here. Not really. He could threaten or take away funding for school, but he didn't have power over me here. As long as my grades stayed okay, he'd keep to the same old shit.

Dragging my eyes from our hands to Dani's oh-so-pretty face, I smiled and nodded. "Me too."

Her grin was bright and happy and, God, so beautiful. "Good. Give me your phone, then."

"O-Okay." I dragged out the word and reached into my pocket for my phone, which I unlocked before handing it over.

She smiled, swiping her fingers across the screen and typing quickly. She then called her own phone, only to hang up and hand it back.

"There! Now I have your number, and you have mine. I saved myself as a contact. Call me, text me…anytime."

I scrolled through my phone to see she'd put Dani in there with a smiley face emoticon next to it. It made me chuckle, until a shadow fell over us from the head of the table next to us. I glanced up to see Brad standing there, glaring at me and then Dani.

"Where the hell have you been?" he whispered in a hissing tone.

She raised a deadly eyebrow at him, and her humor and patience was completely gone. I didn't have to know her all that well to see that.

"Um, and just when do I have to answer to you, Brad?"

He didn't answer her, merely waved the question away. "There's a party tonight over at the south part of the beach. You goin'?"

"No, I have dinner plans with my family."

"Blow them off. You have to —"

"Okay, first…I don't *have* to do *any-fucking-thing*. Second, I don't 'blow off' my family," she replied so firmly that Brad flinched, which made me smirk a bit. "And speaking of my family, Wes told me to let you know you aren't allowed back at Sunset Roast anymore. I'd take heed to that if I were you."

Brad's nostrils flared, and his gaze landed on me. "I told you I was sorry. You get pissed off that you had to clean?"

I opened my mouth, but Dani beat me to it.

"Actually, we all cleaned up after your fuckery, so…" She stared him down, narrowing her eyes when he went red in the face with anger. "And aren't you in my dad's afternoon class? That's interesting to know, right?" When he didn't say anything, she shrugged, jerking a thumb behind her to the two girls at the table in the back. "Ask them. They'll go with you to the party. I'm almost sure of it."

Grinning, I started packing up to go to my last class. However, I couldn't resist watching him for just a second. Brad eyed the blonde and redhead, a wolfish grin crawling across his face.

"Your loss, sweetheart," he drawled, walking away from us.

Dani locked gazes with me for a moment, raising an eyebrow at me before we both turned to watch him approach the table. It was kind of sickening to see his flirting and them laugh and flirt back. When they all three left together, I grinned at Dani's happy laugh.

"I thought you liked him," I murmured.

"Oh, hell no!" she hissed back. "He's a pompous asshole. And after what he did to you the other night…Oh, I don't think so. Now…" She pointed toward the empty table. "We just killed two — okay *three* — birds with one very jerk-ish stone." She threw her books back into her bag, smiling at my laugh. Nodding at my now-packed bag and then up at the clock, she nodded. "Time for class for both of us, hmm?"

We gathered our things and made our way outside and around the building, where Dani stopped at the split in the sidewalk. "Um, you still want to come to dinner?"

"Yeah…Yes, definitely," I told her.

"Where do you want me to meet you? I live on the outskirts of town, so I can pick you up and take you home."

"Right. You sure?"

She smiled and nodded. "Of course."

"Okay, um…the dorms okay? I can change and drop off my stuff."

"Perfect. Call or text me when you're ready." When I nodded, she smiled and spun around to head to her last class.

I watched her walk away a few paces before turning the opposite direction to do the same.

My Statistics class ran long, which was torture, simply because I didn't particularly care for math of any kind. I could do the work, but it was tedious and boring to me. As a kid, math classes had been a source of many punishments due to my grades. It took forever for me to finally find a way to push through.

Frowning at that, I hurried across the courtyard and into my building, dodging people on the stairs coming and going and ducking when a football was tossed overhead. I walked into my dorm room, giving Brett a quick wave as I set my backpack on my bed.

"I'm glad you're here," he said, and I looked out of my closet to see what he wanted. "Listen, I just changed to the same Physics class as you — a scheduling thing. We've got that group project coming up. Have you started?"

I shook my head. "No, I'm supposed to, though. But I have a partner already."

"We can work with more than one person. I asked Professor Martin today. Can…Can I join you?" he asked, grimacing a little. "I don't know anyone in that class but you."

Glancing his way as I fumbled with a new pair of contacts, I could see we were pretty similar that way, though different in every other way. He was shorter than me, thinner, and he had sandy-colored hair and hazel eyes.

After ducking back into the bathroom, I pulled off my glasses and put in the contacts, saying, "Yeah, sure. We'll talk to Regan after the next class and figure out when we can get started."

"Awesome! Thanks, Evan. I really appreciate it."

"No problem."

I changed shirts, something nicer than the T-shirt I'd been in all day, and I tried to tame my hair but quickly gave up. Then I sent Dani a text to let her know I'd meet her downstairs at the front.

When I stepped back into the room, Brett looked up at me. "That's not work clothes, man. Where you off to?"

"Um…dinner at Professor Bishop's house," I told him nervously.

"Fuck me. Will his daughter be there? 'Cause that girl is *hot!*"

Grinning, I nodded. "Yeah, she's…"

"Uh-oh," he sang. "Go get 'em, tiger."

Rolling my eyes, I shot him a wave and walked back out. I dodged the same people on my way out as I had going in, but when I made it to the sidewalk, my nerves kicked up a notch. I was going to be at the same table as my boss, my teacher, and the girl of my dreams, not to mention others I didn't know.

A little red car was sitting at the corner, and when I looked closer, I could see Dani waving at me from the driver's seat. I slid into the passenger side, still trying to get a grip on my nerves.

"Aww," she sighed, smirking at me when I glanced her way. Her hand tentatively reached up to touch my chin, turning my head a little. "The glasses are gone."

Chuckling, I nodded as my face heated at the feel of her touch on my skin. "Yeah, contacts are easier. My sister used to get really frustrated with my lenses getting smudged and my fidgeting, so she made me get contacts before I left for Florida."

What I didn't say out loud was that Faith had tried so hard to help me prepare for college. She wanted me to be able to start over, be someone different—or at the very least learn to be me without being surrounded by guilt, bitterness, and rumors.

Dani eyed me for a beat more, only to smile and nod. She pulled her hand away and focused on driving. As we got farther from the school, I could see we were still working our way north up the beach. In order to distract myself from the glittering water, I looked to Dani.

"Should...um, should I have brought something?" I asked her.

She shook her head. "Nope, nothing. Trust me, Evan, there will be plenty."

"Does your family do this a lot? Dinner together?"

The concept was strange to me. Tyler, Faith, and I had had to fend for ourselves due to my dad's position at the hospital. He worked long hours and would be on call a lot, so sitting down at the same table was so rare that when it did happen, it was uncomfortable, and it usually ended up in some sort of disagreement—or really, he'd get pissed off at something I said or did. We'd had a woman come in occasionally to clean, but a home-cooked meal mostly consisted of frozen pizzas, boxed macaroni and cheese, or breakfast foods. Tyler and I got really good at omelets and pancakes, and Faith would bake cookies occasionally. But to sit down together—as a family—was a ridiculous idea, especially when I'd rather escape to my room.

"Yeah," she answered, pulling to a stop at a light. "We try, anyway. My dad and Aunt Tessa are close—like you and Faith—which is why Wes and I argue like brother and sister." She grinned at my laugh but went on. "Anyway, Aunt Tessa just turned over the coffee shop to Wes so she can travel when she wants or whatever, but she and Wes live in the guest house. My house is rarely empty. But with the start of my first year at Edgewater, my parents' busy positions at the school, and Aunt Tessa's recent trip, we haven't really gotten together. Tonight is sort of a late birthday...*thing*."

She sputtered that last part, her nose wrinkling a little, which made me narrow my eyes a bit.

"Whose birthday?" I asked, almost knowing the answer.

"Mine." She grimaced, looking my way. "It was a two weeks ago—the first—but we were so busy and Aunt Tessa was in Europe, so I said to wait."

"I really should've brought something, then," I sighed, smirking at her happy laugh.

"Aw, don't sweat it, Evan," she said, poking my leg. "There won't be presents—those are already done. Just my family stuffing their faces."

Grinning, I nodded but gazed out the window at the scenery. The houses were getting bigger and farther apart, with longer, winding driveways. The trees were so old and thick, they blocked out the late-afternoon sun, making it feel later than it actually was, and the canopy of large, fat oaks, tall pines, and the occasional palm tree gave off the perfect tropical feel to everything. Aside from the heat and palms, the woodsy area reminded me a lot of home, even more so when she turned down one of the driveways. Like my house in Key Lake, hers sat on a large piece of property, surrounded by shade trees and green grass. While my house was a touch newer, more modern, hers reminded me of all the movies I'd seen about the South. It was white, with black shutters and a big front porch with a swing on one end. It felt warm and welcoming.

"Wow," I whispered, smiling at Dani's soft laugh. "This is beautiful."

"Thanks. It's been in the Bishop family for years."

Nodding, I looked her way. "It reminds me of *Forrest Gump*."

Her laugh was beautiful and perfect, and she was so gorgeous, my breathing faltered a bit, but she leaned over and kissed my cheek. "Thank you! Most say *Gone with the Wind*."

My whole body froze at the feel of her lips on my skin. I wasn't prepared for it and I didn't want it to end, but I also didn't know what it meant to her. When I turned to face her, we were eye-to-eye.

"Don't be nervous, and don't worry about not bringing anything," she whispered, her brow furrowing a little. "I'm just happy you came."

Smiling a little with nerves, I nodded again, gazing down at my hands as I picked at nothing on my jeans. "Happy belated birthday, Dani. I'll have to get you—"

She shook her head, nudging me a bit. "You don't have to get me anything, Evan, but thank you. I'm getting to know my Library Guy. That's an awesome present."

My head snapped up to meet her playful smile, simply because she'd called me that before. The fact that we had similar names for each other without knowing it was almost scary.

"You ready?"

I laughed, shaking my head, but I reached for the car's door. "Not even a little bit, but…okay."

Chapter Six

EVAN

The sound of birds chirping in the late afternoon echoed all around us as we walked up to Dani's house, though one sound overrode them all. It was eerie and loud, and it sounded like it came from another time and place.

I glanced over to my right to see what it was, and Dani laughed softly. "Sandhill cranes. See?"

She pointed toward the far edge of the yard, where three very tall birds were calling to each other. They were pale gray, with red feathers along the top of their heads. Everything about them was long and skinny—legs, necks, beaks.

"Damn, they're as tall as you!"

Dani grinned and nodded. "They mate for life and raise one baby to adulthood. The shorter guy is their most recent. My mother's painted pictures of them. I'll show you inside."

They called out again.

She smiled again, her lips close to my ear as she whispered, "I love that sound. It's what I imagine pterodactyls sounded like."

I huffed a light laugh because she was right; it was otherworldly. The sound of the front door opening made me jump, but I smiled at Wes's lazy half grin.

"Ev! This is how you spend your nights off?"

Chuckling, I shrugged, but Dani *tsk*ed at him, pushing him out of the way. "Hush, Wes. Dad invited him, but I made sure he came!"

She took my hand and led me inside past her cousin, who was still laughing. He gripped my shoulder but looked to Dani.

"They wanted to eat out back, but I told them not to," he told her, and she nodded. "It's too damn muggy."

I gazed around the foyer, and again, I noticed the difference between my house and theirs. My mother had liked clean lines and light colors, and after she died, those things seemed to represent coldness and loss. But this house was bright and colorful, although not overwhelmingly so. Wood floors with long rugs covered the wide-open spaces. To my right was a large living room, with sofas and chairs and a flat-screen on the wall. To my left was a long table set for six people. But it was the art on the wall that got my attention.

There were sceneries, still lifes, and portraits, not to mention some more modern pieces. And they were all signed L. Bishop, who had to be Dani's mother. However, the large painting in the foyer was of the cranes we'd seen outside.

"You must be Evan," I heard behind me, and I spun to see a woman who shared a lot of her daughter's features—light brown hair, smooth skin, and a very warm smile.

"Yes, ma'am." I held out my hand to shake hers. "Evan Shaw."

She smiled and shook my hand, only to tug me in for a brief hug. "I've heard a lot about you from Dani and Wes…and now my husband. It's good to meet you, honey. Gosh, aren't you a handsome thing?" She cupped my face, and I smiled, not having felt a mother's hug in so long. It wasn't the same as my own, but it was damned close. I couldn't help but smile at her.

"It's good to meet you, Professor Bishop," I said, meaning it.

"Evan, this is my mother, Leanne." Dani laughed a little. "Look, there are two Professor Bishops in this house. Just call them Lee and Daniel."

"God, yes. There's enough name calling in this house between Wes and Dani," added Dani's father, coming into the room. "Good to see you, son. Come on in."

"What's he talkin' about, *Nerdly McGeekerson?*" Wes whispered to Dani.

"No clue...*butthead.*" She narrowed her eyes on him for a second. "You know, cracking a book every year or so wouldn't hurt you."

Wes seemed to take that with a grain of salt and walked away muttering something about hurting his eyes with small print and big words.

I snorted, but Dani pulled me to a stop. "You'll have to forgive my mother. She has a tendency to blurt out whatever she's thinking." She wrinkled her nose adorably. "Sorta like me. We'll either drive you crazy, or you'll get used to it."

Chuckling, I nodded. "It's fine. Really." Actually, it was rather refreshing...and a lot like my sister.

She took my hand again and led me through the house toward the most amazing and mouthwatering smells I'd ever encountered. It beat any restaurant, hands down. I wasn't even sure I cared what they were cooking. The smell alone was maddening, and my stomach almost ached to find out.

The kitchen was huge and wide open, with an island in the middle that was covered in food. It was almost the southern cliché of meals — fried chicken, mashed potatoes, gravy, and fluffy biscuits the size of my fist. There were also fresh vegetables and some sort of cobbler/pie thing on the end. My mouth watered at all of it.

However, my attention was drawn to another woman in the room. She was shorter than Leanne, with a touch of gray in her light brown hair. She was currently cutting up a tomato for a salad in front of her, and her smile was just like Wes's — all crooked and easygoing.

"Aunt Tessa, this is Evan Shaw," Dani introduced. "Evan...Theresa Harper."

"Nice to meet you, Mrs. —"

"Oh, no. Call me Aunt Tessa," she chastised with that same smile. "Mrs. Harper was my mother-in-law, and she was a rather cranky, cross woman...God rest her crusty soul..." As soft laughter rang out in the kitchen, she wiped her hands off on a towel and walked around to me. "My sweet Lord, Dani. Wherever did you find him? He's —"

"The library," Dani interrupted with a laugh, "though he works with Wes."

"Oh? You're at my coffee shop?"

"Yes, ma'am. I just started."

"And my *son*," she drawled, glaring Wes's way as he stole a biscuit. "He's treating you okay?"

Grinning, I nodded. "Yes, ma'am. He's been great."

"Hear that? *Great!*" Wes taunted both his mother and cousin, nodding once firmly.

"Recite the alphabet, genius," Dani sneered.

"Oh, the filing. How bad was it?" Aunt Tessa asked her, and Dani merely shook her head with a scowl on her face. "Sorry, sweet pea."

I chuckled but stayed quiet. If it weren't for Wes's horrid filing system, I wouldn't have met my Library Girl, so I didn't regret the long day spent in his office.

Aunt Tessa patted my shoulder. "It's gonna be a few minutes for dinner. There's one more batch of chicken in the pan." She gestured to the stovetop. "Evan, we don't normally eat such a grand display of artery-hardening food, but it's what Dani wanted."

"It looks amazing," I stated, not caring at all about how bad for me it was. It had to be better than fast food any damn day.

"Don't judge me!" Dani snapped playfully. "C'mon, Evan. I'll show you the house."

The sound of chatter and laughter faded a bit as we walked out of the kitchen. She led me back through the living room but took the stairs this time. The house was truly like stepping into a movie. It was filled with antiques, but it wasn't stuffy at all. The whole place felt lived-in, filled with a warmth that seemed to start at my feet and work its way to my chest, finally spreading to my fingers.

Dani showed me the guest room, the bathroom, and the room she used to work in when she was homeschooled, but attached to the latter was her bedroom. I stopped at the door, not sure I should go in, but she sat down on the edge of a big bed.

I tried my damnedest to keep my thoughts clean, to stay away from wondering things like what she wore to bed or how she looked with her long hair spread out on her pillows. I'd fantasized about it more than I'd like to admit, but all that seemed wrong now that I knew just how sweet she was, how kind and funny and smart she was.

Letting my gaze slowly travel around the room, I took in the neatness, the tidiness that matched my own, but there were plenty of contradictions there. The walls, while painted pale pink for a little girl, had posters of movies and music bands. There were also some paintings that were done by her mother. The bookshelves were overflowing but still neatly organized, packed as tightly as she could get them, leaving a shelf for framed pictures and a few knickknacks.

But the smell of the room made me break out into a sweat. It was the concentrated smell of Dani. I'd caught whiffs of it in the library, in class, and definitely in her car, but it was all here, thick and arousing and beautiful. It smelled clean like soap, but it also smelled sweet like fruit or flowers. If I had to guess — and knowing my sister's room — it was a combination of everything she used: soap, deodorant, shampoo, lotions...all of it. I wasn't sure, but God, I liked it. The smell was comforting and sexy all at the same damn time. I wanted to drown in it.

When my gaze landed on pictures on the dresser, I stepped to look at them, smiling at a young, knobby-kneed Dani.

"Oh, stop it!" she hissed but then laughed. "My awkward phase was...awkward!"

"Wasn't everyone's?" I countered with a grin over my shoulder at her. "At least you outgrew yours."

I turned back to another picture but heard her approach me as I picked up what looked like a family portrait. I recognized everyone in it, despite the fact that Dani and Wes were just kids, except for a man who had to be Wes's father. He looked exactly like his son — wavy hair, smiling eyes, pleasant demeanor.

"Mark. Wes's dad," Dani whispered next to me. "He and Aunt Tessa divorced when Wes was about...oh, fifteen, I think. He moved to Georgia, has a new family, I guess. Wes doesn't speak to him." The question had to have been all over my face, because Dani shrugged. "Why did he leave? I don't know. My dad said that sometimes, people have to start over somewhere new in order to make different decisions."

"I get that, but leaving a wife and kid?" I grimaced, shaking my head.

"My dad gave me that excuse when I was a little girl. As an adult, I think Mark had someone else," she stated but looked up at me with a sad smile. "That makes more sense."

"I guess," I muttered but smiled when Dani slipped her hand into mine again.

"C'mon. You'll like the last room the best, I think."

She led me back downstairs and through the living room again. This time, she took a short hallway to a closed door, opening it for me to go in. My mouth fell open at the sight of that room. It was shelf after shelf of books. Some looked to be as old as the house itself, but there were new titles there as well. One corner was a desk, piled with papers and files. Another corner had a different desk, only it was more like a drafting table, and next to it was an easel. The whole room was a bookworm's dream. Dark woods, nailhead furniture, and thick rugs gave off a feeling of stepping back in time.

"Whoa," I whispered, trying to soak up as many of the titles as I could. Dani's giggle made me smile. "This is…wow."

She squeezed my hand. "Of all my friends, I figured you would appreciate this the most."

My head snapped to face her. "Friends?"

She grinned but bit her lip before standing up on her toes to kiss my cheek. "It's a good place to start, Evan. Is that okay?"

I froze for a moment, my heart pounding too hard to breathe, much less *speak*. So I nodded like an idiot. Honestly, I'd take anything she gave me, but as I gazed into clear blue eyes, I knew I'd never be just friends with her. I wanted more, but I didn't know what to do to go about getting it.

"Good," she sang, grinning up at me. "I'm gonna check on dinner. Feel free to look around in here."

Nodding, I turned to browse the shelves, hearing her footsteps fade down the hall. The eerie call of the sandhill cranes came in from outside, making me smile, and I walked to the large bay window to find them, but I caught sight of her backyard…and froze. Memories and fears rattled around in my head at the sight of the small lake that was situated at the back of their property.

"Gosh, Ev…Could you have waited longer for this book report?" Tyler teased from the passenger seat.

"Dude, seriously? Did you even turn one in?" I snapped at him from the back seat as I sorted through the supplies we'd just bought at the store. "Or were you too busy kissing Ashley to read a book?"

Mom chuckled, shaking her head at us as she turned the windshield wipers up higher. "Hush, both of you. Evan, you've already read the book, so this will be the easy part. It won't take you any time at all."

"Exactly!" I huffed, flicking Tyler's ear from behind.

"You little..."

I heard the click of his seat belt as he started to turn around, but the car swerved and my mother gasped as a dog darted into the road. She slammed on the brakes, causing my seat belt to snap tight. There was a sickening thump before the car started to spin, and it made me sick to my stomach as trees and road blurred by. My brother cried out at the same time the car collided hard into something. I thought it was a tree at first...until my feet started to get wet.

The water was cold, dark, dirty, and it was pouring in from everywhere, despite the windows being up.

"We're sinking!" I yelled but looked up front to see both my brother and our mother out cold. The latter had blood trickling down her face from a cut on her temple. "Mom! Mom!"

She roused a bit, glancing around. "Baby boy...you gotta get out. Get your brother out. I'm right behind you..."

I fumbled for my seat belt lock, and it came undone. I dove over the seat to check on Tyler. Reaching for the window, I pushed the button to roll it down, but the power gave out about halfway down. I was skinny but not that skinny. I kicked at it with my sneaker once, twice, and it broke, leaving shards sticking up that were still attached to the window tint, but I ignored the sharp pain down my side when I swam through it, pulling Tyler behind me. We broke the surface of the water, and he snapped awake.

"Holy hell!" he gasped. "Where's Mom?"

"She said she was behind us," I panted, wincing as I touched the open wound on my ribs.

The car gave a lurch and a great big bubble of air, and I screamed for my mother, starting to head back down after her.

"No, Evan, you can't! You'll get sucked under!"

"What? No! Mom! Mom!"

I gasped when warm hands cupped my face.

"Evan," Dani said over and over. "Evan, look at me." She raked her fingers through my hair. "Oh shit, you're shaking. I'm sorry. I'm...I should've..."

I squeezed my eyes closed, shaking my head. "I'm okay."

"You sure?"

I nodded again. "Yeah. I just…"

"The water?"

My eyes snapped open to see her face, afraid she was disgusted with me—or worse, making fun of me. But she wasn't. In fact, tears were welling up in her eyes.

"You scared me, Evan. One second, you were happy; the next you were zoned out and shaking. You don't have to tell me, but just…let me know you're okay. I should've told you about the lake. I'm sorry."

She wrapped her arms around my waist in a hug so fierce it was almost too tight, but I sighed at the feel of it. It had been so long since I felt that calm after the memory.

"I'm sorry I scared you. I'm okay," I whispered to the top of her head, smiling at how much shorter she was than me. "I-I have a fear of water, Dani, which you've figured out. The…*why* is harder to talk about."

She hugged me closer before pushing back. "Why move to a beach town, Evan?"

Smiling, I shrugged. "Because it was as far away from home as I could get, and honestly, I thought I could fight it. Apparently I'm too weak."

"You're not weak."

"I wish that were true."

She studied my face, but her arms were still around me as she swallowed nervously. "Dinner's ready. Are you…"

"I'm starving," I whispered back, and the urge to kiss her was so damn strong that I started to sweat. She was so close, my arms were around her, and I was still coming down from the adrenaline. I caught a tear that escaped her eye, wiping it away. "I'm okay. I promise."

"Kids?" Leanne called from the living room. "Time to eat!"

"'Kay," Dani answered, taking my hand and leading me to the dining room, where everyone was already seated. They'd left two seats side by side opposite Aunt Tessa and Wes. Daniel was at the head of the table, with Leanne at the other end.

I glanced through the door, only to see a screened patio and another table. Smiling a little, I now knew why Wes had said he'd stopped them from eating outside. For me. In my whole life, no one had cared enough to do that. And no one had ever brought me down from the panic like Dani had; the feelings were almost overwhelming.

"So...Evan," Leanne started, pulling me out of my own head as she passed the mashed potatoes. "Where are you from?"

"A little town in Montana. Key Lake," I told them. "Smaller than Glenhaven."

We all traded stories about small-town life. Wes and Dani ratted each other out about different adventures as kids, and I told a few about my brother and sister. The food was amazing and the conversation so much fun that I'd forgotten who I was sitting with — my bosses, my teacher, and the prettiest girl I'd ever laid eyes on. I made no mention of my parents, which didn't go unnoticed by Leanne, and Dani was right; they were a lot alike.

"What about your parents, sweet pea? What do they do?"

Wes and Dani froze, glaring her way. But I nodded. "My dad's a doctor back home. My mother..." I took a deep breath. "My mother died when I was twelve."

"Oh, darlin', that's...I'm sorry," Aunt Tessa crooned softly. "Did she —"

"That's enough." Daniel's voice was firm but still gentle. "Leave the boy alone."

The table went quiet for a moment, but Leanne turned to Dani. "The art show is coming up. Can you help me again this year?"

"Yeah, sure."

They started talking dates, who would be there, and how the new students this year were really talented, but soon Daniel's heavy hand landed on my shoulder.

"I owe you an apology, son. Your mother's name sounded familiar, so I searched for her online." He kept his voice low and grimaced, shaking his head. "I'm...I...I saw there was an article. I'm sorry about the accident, Evan. Damn shame, really. You're lucky to be alive, buddy. You and your brother."

I nodded, pushing my potatoes around. I didn't feel lucky. I felt like a failure, like I'd let my mother down somehow. Or maybe I'd let my dad down, which was why he hated the mere sight of me. I wasn't sure.

"But I've read your mother's work, son." He grinned, patting my shoulder when I looked back his way. "You're every bit as good as she was…" He pointed his fork at me. "Maybe better. She'd be damned proud. You should be too. We'll see if we can shape you up to be a writer, if that's what you want."

"Yes, sir. I do."

"Well, the talent is there. We'll work on technique." He nodded once to himself but grinned my way. "I'll also tell you who you need for classes next year."

"Thank you, sir. I appreciate that."

"You're a good kid, Evan. I can see that a mile away. If you weren't, then this chatty group wouldn't give you the time of day, but I've heard good things. You're welcome here anytime."

I felt my face heat up, but I thanked him again. Dani's hand slid into mine on my lap, giving a squeeze.

Smiling, I looked her way as she said, "You can stay as long as you like, but I need to help clean up before I take you back to the dorms."

"Okay. Want some help?" I offered.

"Yeah, that'd be awesome. Wes, you too!" she ordered, and he grinned and nodded.

As everyone finished up, Dani and I started to clear the table as Wes put leftovers away. They all were warm and welcoming, but Dani…God, I owed Dani something, anything. She deserved an explanation as to why I was the way I was. I needed to talk to Faith first, but I knew what she'd tell me. She'd say to write it down first, to get it down on paper in order to be ready to say it out loud. That may be true; I'd have to think about it. But for the moment, I was happy being treated just like Wes and Dani. In that house—in fact, for the first time since the accident—I felt like I belonged.

Chapter Seven

EVAN

"There you are," Faith said through a laugh over the phone, and I couldn't help but grin. "He gets a girlfriend and suddenly dumps the rest of us."

I laughed, shaking my head as I walked across campus. "She's not my girlfriend."

"Ah, hell. Don't tell me she's *friend-zoned* you already," she groaned.

"No, no…I don't think so. I mean, it's not…Faith, I've only been talking to her for a few weeks! *Really* talking to her, not just…stalking her in the library," I mumbled.

"But you've had dinner at her house…what? Two times now? She calls you, texts you, not to mention she sits with you in class and at your table in the library," Faith summed up, like she was calculating what that meant.

What the hell *did* that mean?

"Evan, it sounds like she's waiting for you to make a move."

"I don't know how to make *any* moves, much less *a* move."

Faith's giggle was soft and short-lived. "You're asking *me?* Maybe you should call Tyler."

"Shit," I sighed, gripping my hair. "Maybe. But he's gonna give me all sorts of hell, Faith."

I sat down on a bench just outside Sunset Roast. It was truck day, so I knew I had heavy lifting to do once I got inside. But I had a few minutes before I was due in.

"Shouldn't…I mean, before any damn 'moves,' shouldn't I tell Dani? Be honest, Faith. I mean, don't you think she needs to know just how…fucked up I am? She's seen some of it, but…I don't know. I just think I'd rather be honest."

All the humor left her voice. "Are you talking…physically or emotionally, big brother? Because really, I don't think the scars are that bad. I know you caught some shit here, but these people are small-minded assholes, never mind what they thought they knew about our family."

"I know, but I just think Dani deserves to know the truth about me. That's all."

"Can you talk to her?"

I sighed deeply, watching people walk by heading toward the beach or the boardwalk. "She's…*way* more than I expected, Faith."

"Meaning?"

"Meaning she's never once made fun of me or…or…looked down on me, no matter what she's heard or seen. I just…maybe I need to tell it, but I think I need to write it first."

Faith went quiet for a second or two, finally asking, "You really like this girl, don't you?"

"Yes." My answer came easily and assuredly. "I don't wanna screw up, Faith. And…and…I don't want to be something I'm not. I'm… My past makes me…*me*. But I can't play games. I'm not a liar or a good-enough actor to play my bullshit off. I can't hide what I am." I sighed deeply, gripping my hair in my free hand. "I don't give a shit about what most people think. I ignored it in Key Lake, and I don't advertise it, but this is…*Dani* is important."

"I don't want you hurt, big brother," Faith replied softly. "I don't want your heart splattered all over hell and back, because then I'll have to come down there and smack a bitch."

Laughing, I sat forward on the bench and rested my elbows on my knees. "I appreciate that, but I don't think it's necessary. I just have to…find the words."

"I wanna meet these people. They've...You sound...happy."

Smiling a little, I said, "I could be. They're like those silly sit-com TV families—all laughing and teasing and just...accepting. It's different than what we had."

"And for you, better. Mark my words, big brother, getting out of Key Lake will be the best thing that's ever happened to you. Have you talked to Dad about the holidays? No, probably not, or he'd be all stompy and pissy around here."

A laugh barked out of me. "No, but I will. Thanksgiving is one thing. Christmas is another. The dorms close over the holidays."

"Hmm...Well, shack up with your girl."

"Jesus, Rylee Faith! She lives with her parents—*my teacher!*"

She laughed. "It's worth a shot. It'll make it easier to put the moves on her."

"Stop it. I gotta go to work. You have homework. Go. Love you."

"Love you too."

I ended the call before pocketing my phone and walking into the coffee shop. I knew she was right about a couple of things. I needed to talk to Tyler, even to simply check in, but if anyone could help me with all the things I was feeling about Dani, it would be our older brother. I also knew that Faith was right about being happy... or at least *happier*. Without the constant reminder of my mistakes being thrown in my face on a daily basis, I found I could breathe, make clearer decisions, and relax just a little. However, the future conversation with Dani was niggling at me in the back of my mind, not to mention the looming one I'd have to have with my father concerning coming home.

When I stepped into the kitchen, Wes looked up from his clipboard, a smile spreading over his face. "Just in time for the fun shit."

I grinned and nodded, setting my backpack down. Wes had told Meg and me a few days ago that he didn't mind if we did homework during the downtimes as long as we took care of the customers, so I'd started bringing my books and laptop with me to work.

"Lots of homework?" he asked with a grunt as he handed over a box.

"No more than usual," I told him.

"So a shit-ton, huh?"

Laughing, I nodded. "Exactly."

We rotated creamers and milk, unloaded cases of sugar and coffee beans, and broke down the cardboard boxes to take out to the bin. The pastries we sold were brought in every other day from the local bakery, so they needed to be inventoried and rotated as well. After a few hours, I dropped the last of the garbage outside.

While Meg took her break, I watched the front counter with Susan. We had a few people come in, and I was wiping the counter down after the rush when she came to lean against the counter.

"You have an admirer."

My face must've scrunched up in confusion, which made her laugh. "What're you talking about?"

"Curly hair, glasses…sitting along the wall," she said without turning around.

My gaze drifted around the sitting area of the coffee shop, only to lock on to Regan. "Oh, hell…" I sighed, going back to my cleaning. "She's in a couple of my classes. And in my study group."

"She's pretty."

I shrugged. "She's…"

When I trailed off, she finished for me. "She's not Dani." She nudged me a bit.

My grin couldn't be stopped, but I shook my head. "Nowhere close" was all I answered.

"God, you're so fucking cute, Evan, I swear to God." She chuckled low, finally reaching up to rough up my hair. "Dani's a lucky girl. But what will you do about this one?"

"I dunno," I answered honestly. "I've tried to keep to the project in class. Thankfully my roommate is in our group. Brett helps keep things on track." I turned to wipe down the front counter. "I've never had that sort of attention from girls back home, so…"

"I call bullshit," I heard in front of me, and I grinned, tilting my head up to see the prettiest of sights.

"Dani," I whispered, still grinning.

"Knowing you, handsome, I'm willing to bet you just didn't pay attention," she continued, leaning on the counter on both elbows.

Susan cracked up, patting my back. "Now *that's* probably the truth right there." She shook her head. "Take your break, kiddo. Meg's back."

"Okay," I said, looking to Dani. "Did you want something before I..."

Dani merely smiled, shaking her head, and she pointed to the table Meg and I used on breaks. "I'll wait for you."

When I came back with my backpack, she was sitting quietly with a cup of coffee in her hands. Her smile at me made me weak in the knees as I slid into the other side of the booth. I took out my notebooks and journal and set them aside.

"Did...Are you...Did you come to see me?" I asked her, smiling when her soft laugh and nod were aimed my way.

"Well, I didn't come to see my cousin. I can pick on him at home."

Grinning, I shook my head at her sarcasm. "Fair enough."

She pulled my journal closer but didn't open it. "This is beautiful."

My smile was nervous, but I nodded. "Thanks. My sister got that for me before I left home. I'd always used just regular spiral notebooks, but she told me I needed something more...sophisticated." I rolled my eyes at the thought.

"So...are there like a billion stories written down in these?" she asked, and her tone was teasing but sweet all the same, which made me laugh. "'Cause if that's the case, I may run away with it."

"Um...no. I usually type up stories on my laptop. Those are..." I sighed deeply, looking at the leather-bound journal more than the pretty face that made me nervous. "I...I have a difficult time with words sometimes, or...or...really with hard conversations. I tend to write out things I need to say in order to get it straight." I tapped my temple to let her know what I meant. When she looked a bit confused, I added, "Umm...like coming to school here, for example. My dad wanted something closer or something more...Ivy League. I wanted...out." I grimaced at how that sounded, but it was true. "So I wrote down everything positive that Edgewater could bring to the table so that when I finally approached him with my acceptance letter, he couldn't argue...*much*."

"Why would he care? I mean, if you were awarded a scholarship, wouldn't he be happy?"

I was shaking my head before she even finished speaking. "My dad is...strict? He had plans, and I didn't follow them, which made him unhappy."

"Controlling, you mean." She whispered that, looking at me carefully. "Evan, you've said more than once that you moved here because it was as far away as you could get, so I mean, it makes sense. I'm beginning to see that you and your dad don't get along."

"No, we don't." I opened my mouth to say more but snapped it shut again. I wanted to tell her that he blamed me for a whole lot of things, but I didn't. And Wes's voice carried across the coffee shop.

"Dani! Where's the file for—"

"Oh, my sweet hell...If you're filing, nitwit, I'm gonna..." She slipped out of the booth quickly, shooting me a glare when I laughed at them. "Laugh it up, Evan. It'll be you and me fixing his shit again."

Grinning, I shrugged a shoulder. "Worse things could happen..."

"True, but then...there's a shit-ton of better things we *could* be doing besides cleaning up after my alphabet-impaired cousin."

Smirking, I said, "You win."

"Damn straight."

She walked to Wes, who flinched when she snatched a stack of paperwork out of his hand. She was muttering to him the whole way back to his office, and I jumped when she slammed the door.

I shifted my books around but eyed my journal, pulling it to me. I'd meant what I'd said to Faith. I really wanted Dani to know me. I just wasn't sure how to tell her about the ugliest part of me, so I picked up my pen.

To my Library Girl,

You're no longer a mystery to me, and every single fantasy I had of you in the library pales in comparison to the real thing. You're beautiful, yes, but you're more than that. I'm glad to call you a friend, if only because in the short time of knowing you, your friendship has become so very important. You're kind and funny. You're caring and smart. You're all these things I never considered you'd be when I was merely looking at you from the outside of things.

You see me so differently than anyone else. Where I came from, I was an outcast. Aside from my siblings, I was this social pariah. I didn't date. I didn't go to parties. I didn't do anything other than study. But you...You've forced me to see myself, to see what you see. The problem with that, Dani, is that you don't know everything. And I need you to know it all.

I need you to know about me because you deserve the truth. You've seen my fear of water, and you've figured out about my dad, but you need to know the whole story because if you can't handle it, I'd rather know that now.

A shadow fell over the table before someone slid into the booth across from me. I expected Dani but smiled awkwardly when Regan gazed back across from me.

"Hey, Evan," she greeted softly.

"Hey. What's up?"

She looked around and then back to me. Her cheeks were pink, and I felt uncomfortable under scrutiny. I didn't like the attention, but I didn't want to hurt her feelings, either. I wasn't that kind of guy. I knew what it was like to feel something for someone I was sure didn't know I existed. How I'd lucked out with getting to know Dani, I'd never know, but I was grateful, nonetheless.

"Um...I just...I know we have work to do on our project, but..." She trailed off a little, her fingers twisting a bit in front of her. "I just...Well, Brett asked me out and..."

"He did?" I asked, mentally cheering in my head. "He's a good guy, really smart. He's not a jerk. There are plenty of those..."

Regan smiled, but it wavered a bit when Dani slid into the booth next to me. She leaned over, pressing a kiss to my cheek. It wasn't the first time she'd done that, but it never failed to make me freeze just a little and break out into a sweat.

Before I could ask her what that was for, she reached a hand across the table. "Hey, I'm Dani. I've seen you in the library."

"Regan Stone." Adjusting her glasses, Regan shook Dani's hand.

"Oh...the physics project you told me about. How's that going?" she asked, looking between us, but there was a small smile playing on her lips.

"It's good. We're just about finished," I explained but then turned to Regan. "If you want, Brett and I can meet you after classes tomorrow to finish everything up."

"Well, that's...um, we were wondering if it could be Wednesday. There's someplace he wants to go tomorrow."

"Yeah, yeah...whatever. Just let me know. We've got until Friday."

"Okay," she said softly, getting up from the booth.

I turned to Dani to meet her sweet gaze. "What was the kiss for?"

"Originally it was for keeping up with Wes's filing, but when I got out here, I figured you needed help," she answered with a silly grin.

"My roommate asked her out."

"Oh? And she just now told you that?" Dani laughed, shaking her head, but she reached up to brush my hair off my forehead when I nodded. "She was trying to make you jealous."

"Maybe, but it won't work. I'm..." Grimacing, I sighed and started to close my journal, but Dani's hand covered mine. I wanted to say that I only had eyes for one girl—the one currently sitting next to me, all warm and smelling like heaven—so jealousy wouldn't work on me.

"Evan?" she whispered, looking from me to my journal I was closing up and packing away.

"Hmm?"

"Did you say you use that journal to sort out hard conversations?"

"Yeah, it's just easier sometimes. I'm not...always brave enough to just...blurt stuff out."

She smiled a little, but her brow furrowed. "Did...I saw my name, Evan. Were you writing to me?"

Panic hit me hard like a tidal wave, and I squeezed my eyes closed and balled up my fists for a second. My inability to speak aloud was embarrassing, so I waited for the laugh or for her to reach for the journal. She did neither.

"Evan...Calm down, please. Look at me," she whispered, and I felt her hands on either side of my face.

When I opened my eyes, I whispered, "I'm sorry."

"Don't be sorry," she countered softly. "What's so difficult that you think you need to write it first before coming to me? I…I know you're shy, but I don't…Please know you can talk to me about anything."

Swallowing nervously, I nodded. "I know, but I just…"

"Did…Have I done something wrong, Evan?"

My gaze snapped to hers, and I shook my head vehemently. "No! No, not at all. How could you think that? You're damn near perfect."

Grinning, she chuckled a bit. "Uh, no, I'm not. But it's sweet that you think so."

"Well, you are to me," I grumbled, which made her smile all the more.

Her giggle was soft. "Damn, Evan, you make it really difficult not to just…kiss you fucking stupid."

As much as I wanted that, I couldn't do it. I glanced down at my hands in my lap, fidgeting as I realized just how close we were sitting. "You have no idea how badly I want that, but…there are some things about me you need to know before…or…I mean…" Groaning at my inability to fucking talk, I merely shrugged a shoulder.

"And…you were writing it out first?" she asked me, and I nodded. "Every time we've talked, you've done just fine, Evan. You don't…You never need to 'practice' any conversation with me. I'm rather fond of how our talks go."

"Yeah?"

"God, yes! I never thought you'd talk to me to begin with, so this…" She gestured between us, raising a silly but sexy eyebrow at me. "This is awesome."

I smiled, shaking my head. "How do you do that?"

"Do what?"

"Make me feel…normal?"

"You *are* normal, Evan. Shy, nervous, smart, and…*normal.*" She narrowed her eyes at me. "Who the *fuck* has told you you're not normal?"

My shock at her sharp temper caused me to gasp a little, and I couldn't help but think an angry, protective Dani was probably the sexiest, most beautiful thing I'd ever seen.

"Everyone?" I answered with a derisive laugh, though it came out like a question.

She studied me for a moment, looking up at the clock over the counter and then finally back to me. "You're off work in two hours. You have someplace you need to be?" she asked, and I shook my head. "Then I'll be here when you're done."

I started to pack up my things in order to get back to work, but she stopped me again.

"And Evan?" she said softly, sliding out from the booth and smiling at me when I looked up at her. "If you want to write it, I'll read every word without complaint, but I honestly love the sound of your voice, so I'd prefer it if you talked to me. And I'll sit with you all night if I have to."

I stood from the booth, shouldering my backpack to stash it in the kitchen until I was off work. "Is there...Is there somewhere private we can go?"

She smiled and nodded. "I'm sure we can come up with something. Get back to work, Evan. I've got you."

Smiling, I shook my head as a light laugh escaped me. Something told me she meant that, that I could trust her, though it didn't make me any less nervous.

Chapter Eight

EVAN

"Ev, you okay?" I heard behind me as I put away the mop and bucket. I nodded but didn't say anything, reaching for my backpack. When I stood up straight, Wes was still eyeing me, his arms crossed over his chest.

"Did my cousin say something crazy?"

I broke into a laugh, shaking my head. "No, not at all."

"Well, there's a first," he said with a teasing grin.

"No, she's...We need to talk. I'm just...nervous, I guess."

He sobered quickly, walking to me. "Sounds serious..." he started but then trailed off. "Is that why she asked to close up?"

Wrinkling my nose, I nodded. "Yeah, probably. Privacy."

He nodded again. "Try not to hurt my cousin, Ev. Mm'kay?"

I snorted at the ridiculousness of that statement. "Of all the people in this equation, Wes...it's not Dani who'll get hurt. Okay?"

I didn't mean for that to come out so harshly, but it was the truth. I couldn't hurt Dani if I tried. No, this was different. This would put everything in her hands; it would give her the power to destroy me.

"Oh." He inhaled deeply and then let it out, placing a hand on my shoulder. "Then let me give you a piece of advice, and then I'll leave you two to lock up the joint." He waited until I nodded before he went on. "First of all, you and Dani have more in common than you think. Just a few years ago, she was just as...shy and she'd say nerdy, but she wasn't. She's just damned smart...like you. She broke out of that shell, and you will too, Evan. You already have—a little, anyway." He squeezed my shoulder to make sure I was listening. "I get the impression you've seen some pretty tough shit, but you need to know that Dani's not gonna judge you on a bit of it. That's just not the way she works. And..." He grinned, and it was crooked and mischievous. "She likes you, dude, so I'm pretty sure you could tell her anything and she'll take it. She's a pretty tough cookie."

I knew he was right; it was me who wasn't so tough, but I didn't say anything when I followed him out to the sitting area of the coffee shop. Dani was sitting on the sofa in the corner of the room, twirling a set of keys around her finger.

"I've got this, Wes."

"Right. No unsupervised parties, no alcohol, and don't break anything."

Dani grinned. "Sure, *Dad*."

Chuckling, I shook my head at them and took the chair across the table from her as Wes left us alone. Dani followed him, turning the deadbolt on the doors. She flipped the switch, leaving half the lights on. It gave anyone passing by the impression that the place was empty, closed.

I fidgeted nervously with the strap to my backpack, raking a hand through my hair. Bracing myself, I tore my gaze from the little table in front of me to look at Dani, who had slipped quietly back into her spot on the sofa.

"Did you..." I sighed deeply, tilting my head at her. "Did you mean what you said? About staying up all night?" I asked, wearing a smile at the thought of it. "'Cause it might take that long."

Her smile was sweet. "If need be, Evan. I...I wish I could make this easier on you." She offered me her hand on the table, and I placed mine in hers. "I'd say you didn't have to tell me, but then... you seem determined, so..."

I dropped my eyes to our hands, toying with her fingers. "I need to do this. You..." I shook my head slowly. "You make me feel things I've never felt before, Dani. And with that comes the need to be honest with you. Does that make sense?"

"Yes," she whispered, linking our fingers together, "but if it hurts you…"

I laughed harshly, though there was no humor in it whatsoever. "I used to think I couldn't be hurt anymore."

It was cryptic, but it was true. Dani could walk away and I'd live, but it would confirm my theory that I wasn't normal. And I wasn't sure that would stop me from liking her, because I'd truly started to shift from a crush on her to something else, and that was what made me want to be honest with her.

"Evan?" she called softly, and I met her warm eyes. "I'm not going anywhere. I *promise* you. Does what you're about to tell me have to do with why you panicked at my house that night at dinner?" she asked, and I nodded. "Okay, so does this have to do with…with your mother?"

"Yeah."

Her beautiful head tilted a bit, and her smile was small but warm. "And you're scared to tell me?"

"A little," I mumbled, wrinkling my nose. "Your opinion has become…*important*."

She lifted our hands and, much to my shock, pressed kisses to my knuckles. "Then you should know that nothing you tell me will scare me or make me think of you differently. Whatever you say in this…closed-up café is just between us. Whatever has happened prior to this moment has no bearing on this tiny table in the corner of said café. And lastly, my opinion of you is pretty much cemented in stone. I think you're a shy, sweet, smart guy. I think you're the most handsome thing I've ever laid eyes on, and if you don't stop me, I'm gonna embarrass myself by rambling stupid shit."

Grinning, I felt my cheeks flame. "Thanks." I took a deep breath and looked her in the eyes, deciding to just start from the dinner at her house. "Did your dad tell you he Googled my mother's name?" I asked her, and she shook her head. "He did. He said he remembered her name but couldn't quite place what she'd written. When he did, he…he found the news article on her…death—a car accident."

Dani nodded but didn't say anything, so I went on.

Swallowing nervously, I focused on our linked hands. "I was…I don't know. I was a normal twelve-year-old kid." I shrugged. "I had friends and played some sports. I picked on my little sister and bugged my older brother. I procrastinated on homework, watched too much TV, played video games. Normal stuff."

I didn't look at her as I continued. "We're all pretty close in age. Tyler and I were in middle school at the same time, so we knew each other's friends and teachers and whatever. I'd…always been the different one in the family. I liked reading. I liked making up stories for Faith and my mother. Tyler was good at math, and Faith liked science, but I was the…daydreamer." I wrinkled my nose at that term because it had been spat at me more times than I could count—but only after my mother was gone.

"You should know now…I look *just like her*. I have the exact same interests as her. She was a teacher at Key Lake High School—English, of course. Never mind her published work." I smiled a little when Dani nodded, keeping my hand in hers. "My weird hair, my eyes, my smile…all from her. My dad…he has lighter hair and hazel eyes, and my brother takes after him more. Faith…she's…Well, she dyes her hair dark, but her eyes are like his."

"Your hair isn't weird," she interrupted, grinning a little. "I like it."

Shaking my head, I smiled again. "Thanks."

I was quiet for a moment, and she let me be. I needed to get through the wreck. That was it. That was all. But the fear was always there, *right there*, on the surface. Along with that fear came the sense of failure, the knowledge that I should've done things differently.

"I'd forgotten a book report," I whispered, frowning down at the table, but I didn't see the table. I saw the teasing smile of my brother that I was in trouble. I saw my dad's impatience that my mother couldn't finish dinner because she had to drive me to the store for supplies. "I'd…I'd already read the book but had forgotten I needed to make a poster for it. My mom wasn't mad, just…inconvenienced that we had to rush out at the last minute to get what I needed. Tyler went with us. Faith stayed home." Frowning, I licked my lips. "My dad didn't want us to go. He told her to let me suffer the bad grade, but she told him not to worry about it, that we'd be right back."

I met Dani's eyes. "Montana isn't really rainy. Snowy, sure, but not rainy." I swallowed back more nerves. "It's not like here, where it rains in the afternoon but dries up pretty quickly. When it rains there, it makes everything…slick. It was on the way back that it happened. Tyler was happy I was in trouble, but I was giving him shit right back...kinda like you and Wes."

Dani grinned, but it didn't last long. I was pretty sure she could tell what was coming, but I needed to just...*say it.*

"Tyler has always been good with girls, so I was teasing him about not turning in a book report, only kissing his girlfriend. I...I...flicked his ear, and he..." I squeezed my eyes closed. "He took his seat belt off to pound me, but...Mom lost control of the car. A dog darted out, and...she swerved. The tires lost traction, and we skidded off the road and into a...a...lake." I pulled my hands from Dani's, rubbing my face roughly and sinking my fingers into my hair. "I tried...I...I... My seat belt kept me from getting hurt...well, hurt on impact, but... Tyler was out cold, and my mother was bleeding. We were sinking fast. She...she...She told me to get my brother out, so...I was able to open the window some, but the water had killed the car's power, so I had to kick it, break it. I was small enough then that I could climb over the seat to the front and...and..."

I looked to her, but I didn't really see Dani. All I could see was the past. "She said...She said she was right behind us, but when I pulled Tyler up, she wasn't there. She...she..."

Dani got up from her spot and sat in the chair next to me, cupping my face. "Look at me, Evan," she commanded gently, pulling my forehead to hers. I opened to tears and beautiful, sad blue eyes. "I can put the rest together..."

I knew she could, but I couldn't stop now that I'd started. "I tried to go back, but I was too weak and the car was sinking so fast. Tyler stopped me, said I'd get sucked under. I fought him, and I tried anyway, but...I...I'd lost too much blood."

"Blood? I thought you said..."

"The window, the glass shattered, but...the tint held it together, so the shards cut me when I pulled Tyler out." I instinctively reached to touch my side, but Dani's hand covered mine.

"You're lucky to be here," she said softly, squeezing my hand that was still flat along my ribcage.

"That's what your dad said," I whispered back, shaking my head. "We...we were lucky that someone was behind us. They called for help, but I don't remember that. I...I woke up like two days later in the hospital." I reluctantly pushed away from her a bit. "I...can't face water…I can't…really drive in the rain. And…my brother couldn't play sports again because he…he'd taken his seat belt off, so his knee shattered into the dashboard."

I simply stared at her. With tears coursing down her face and her warm gaze my way, she was still the prettiest thing I'd ever seen. Reaching up, I gently swiped away her tears with my thumbs.

"You were so brave." She took my hands in hers again but frowned when I started shaking my head.

"No, not at all. It was…All of it was my fault. My…report, the car ride, teasing Tyler…Not helping my m-m-mom. Every bit of it."

"No! Evan, baby, stop! It's not your fault. You…You…You were *twelve*. Just twelve. A little boy. Nothing about that night was your fault. You have any idea how many last-second homework dashes to the store my parents have had to do? Imagine Wes! Homework? Are you kidding?" she asked, though her voice raised an octave.

I cracked a smile but shook my head again. "Everyone…They told me. She…she drowned. I could've at least *tried!*"

"Who? Who would tell a little boy who'd just lost his mother that it was his fault? Who would be cold enough to do that?" she practically growled those questions at me, her blue eyes fierce and protective.

"My dad."

Dani froze, her face paling as she studied me, and I turned away from her. "He didn't," she argued in a whisper.

"He did. From the moment I woke up in the hospital."

I wasn't going to tell her this part, but she already knew we didn't get along, so she might as well know why. She might as well know everything, even the reason I left Montana and moved all the way down to the Sunshine State. She needed to know my father blamed my mother's death on me, that he used any excuse to tell me, even to this day.

I started shaking my head because I could see it, smell it, hear it all plain as day. I was nineteen, but it didn't take much to make me feel the pain, the fear, the guilt as if it were yesterday.

Beeping and whispers caught my attention, bringing me around slowly. I felt heavy and cold. I also felt pain everywhere.

"Big brother?" I heard beside me, and I blinked over to see Faith. "You awake, Evan?"

"Yeah," I rasped, squeezing my eyes closed. "What...Where's..."

"Hold on! I'll go get Daddy!" she whisper-yelled, and she hopped down from the chair and out the door.

Gazing around, I could see I was in a hospital room. I was in the bed by the door, and to my right was another bed, but it was empty. The door pushed open, and my dad walked in, wearing scrubs and his white coat. His face was blotchy, red, his mouth set in a thin line. He was pissed.

He didn't say a word as he picked up my chart, checked my pulse, and flashed a light in my eyes. Even when he pulled down the covers of the bed and lifted the gown I was wearing, he didn't speak.

Looking down at the bandages once he revealed them, everything rushed back at me. Tears pooled in my eyes, and I flinched when he pulled the wrap and gauze away. When I looked down, the sight made me sick. I looked like I'd been clawed by a tiger or something — long, crooked, angry cuts raked down my side from just beneath my armpit to just above the waistband of my underwear. They hurt, but how I got them hurt more.

"Dad?" I hiccupped through a sniffle.

Without looking at me, he said, "You have a hundred and twenty-two stitches. You might want to keep that in mind before you start to move, hmm?" I nodded, but he wasn't looking my way. "They'll still probably scar, but..." He shrugged a shoulder. "Your brother's in surgery; they're repairing his knee."

"Dad?" I called again, and he looked at me.

"What, son?" he answered firmly. His gaze raked over my face, but then he looked down at my chart.

"What...Mom?"

"Your mother?" he snapped, glaring my way. "Your mother's dead, Evan. I'm pretty sure you knew that."

I turned away from him, a sob escaping me. "Sh-Sh-She said...Sh-She told me t-to get Tyler. Sh-She said she was coming!"

His nostrils flared, his eyes dark as he braced a hand on my bedrail. "Well, she didn't. Had she died on impact, her lungs wouldn't have been full of water. She drowned, Evan. You let your mother drown."

"No, no, no! Dad, I did...I did what she said. I...I...I tried to go back, but everything went black. The car, it..."

"All this..." he spat, sneering at me. "All this over a goddamn book report."

"Th-Th-There was...a...a...dog, Dad! I swear...I tried!"

He huffed a derisive laugh, shaking his head slowly. "You tried?" He laughed again, and it was scary and mean. He'd always been strict but never mean. "You failed, son," he practically sang my way. "You failed, taking away my wife, your mother, and you'll be lucky if your brother can walk. What the hell was he doing with his seat belt off?"

"He...he took it off!"

"Tyler wouldn't do that. He knows better."

I'd never argued with my dad before, and I could barely breathe, much less argue with him now.

"Fucking book report..." he spat out into the room with a slow shake of his head. "That better be one helluva damn report. You'd better get an A on it, no matter how late it is. In fact, you're so worried about your grades, son, you'd better be the perfect student from this moment on... or face the consequences."

Both of us looked up when Faith stepped back into the room, and her gaze landed on me. She barely batted an eye, crawling up on the bed to hug me.

"Faith," he sighed impatiently. "Your brother needs his rest."

My fierce, very small baby sister glared his way. "He's crying! He needs hugs! Mom would hug him!" she stated, and I could see she meant it and wasn't going to back down.

He glared at her but merely sniffed. "Make sure he doesn't rip those stitches."

She nodded, looking to me. "I'll take care of you, big brother. Tyler too."

"Evan, Evan, Evan...Look at me," Dani whispered against my forehead. She'd moved at some point and was standing between my legs. Her arms were practically holding me together. Placing her hands on either side of my face, she tilted my face up. "Look at me."

"I'm—"

Her fingers covered my lips. "Oh, my fucking God...If you apologize..."

I frowned beneath her soft fingers, my gaze raking over her tear-stained face.

"What..." Dani started, but then she stopped.

"Ask me anything, Dani," I said, pulling her fingers away from my lips. "Go ahead."

She pursed her lips together, her nostrils flaring a bit, but she leaned to kiss my forehead. "What…What were those consequences, Evan? Over your grades?"

Shrugging, I looked down at her hand in mine. "Oh, umm, different stuff—chores, like chopping wood or yard work or cleaning the attic. We weren't done until there were blisters. He'd, umm… ground us from TV and video games or make us go to bed without dinner, which rarely happened because he worked nights, so we'd eat anyway. Once we were old enough, he'd take away our cars."

"Did he hit you?" she asked in a whisper.

"No, my dad hasn't laid a hand on me since before Mom died."

"You say *we*. He punished all of you?"

"For grades, yes. We all had to be honor-roll students." I reached up and captured her tears again. "Please don't cry. You're way too pretty to cry," I begged softly, and my fingers trailed across the color that bloomed in her cheeks. "He didn't beat us, if that's what you're asking. If he gets mad enough, he yells, throws stuff. He pretty much ignores Faith, which I envied for years. He thinks I ruined Tyler's chances at baseball, but my brother doesn't care. He's going to UM to be an architect. The older we got, the harder it was for him to punish us because we all make good grades."

"Why do I think he specifically picked on *you?*" she asked.

"He did. I told you…I was different than my siblings, Dani. I'd rather read or write than go to the movies with the kids from school, especially those kids back home. The town is so small, they all heard about the accident, so it went from curiosity to picking on me when I didn't talk about it. I rarely talked to anyone but Tyler and Faith. I wouldn't go to the lake like the rest of them, and soon everyone figured out why, including Dad, which he had no patience for, mind you. My father thought I needed to be more social…or really, keep up appearances, so he'd get pissed when I'd stay home from parties or prom, which resulted in more chores or the car being taken away."

"That's why you told Faith you were okay with him selling it."

"Oh, yeah. He wouldn't let me bring it because he didn't want me here. He tells his friends it's because the insurance would be too much. But he's held it over my head since I was sixteen." Smiling sadly, I looked up at her. "I'm not stupid, Dani. I'm aware that the sight of me reminds him of her, that he needed to place blame somewhere. I learned a long time ago that if I shut up, stayed out of sight, no one—not even my dad—could get to me. Though, that can set him off too."

"It's unfair and so wrong that he blames you. He's the grown-up. You're the kid. Hell, he could've even blamed your mom for not watching the road."

Nodding, I sighed deeply, feeling exhausted. "I know, but he does. Sometimes it's easier to believe he's right."

"No," she stated firmly, almost angrily. "No, he's not right. And I think he's hurt you…"

"Broken dishes and cups of coffee didn't hurt me, Dani. Insults and constant reminders can't hurt me anymore either."

"I can see that they do. You're shaking, baby," she said through a thick, emotion-filled voice, cupping my face. "Why?"

"You…You're the first person I've ever told *anything* to," I admitted softly. "I wanted to be honest with you because you've become so important to me, but I'm scared you can't…That you won't…" I grimaced. "I'm *not* normal, Dani. I don't like parties or crowds. I can't go to the beach like everyone. I'm not…" I huffed a humorless laugh. "I don't even have a car, and…The panic attacks may never—"

"What did I tell you when you started this story, Evan?" she asked, squishing my face a little to stop my rambling. "I told you I wasn't going anywhere." She eyed me for a moment, her lips in a tight line, but I could see she meant it. "I want you to come home with me tonight. Let me take care of you. I promised you all night, and I intend to make good on that. We'll stop by the dorms for your clothes. I'll feed you, you can stay in the guest room, and we'll ride to school together in the morning. Please…"

I smiled a little, shaking my head. "I haven't scared you away yet?"

"Never. I may hold on a bit tighter." She smiled up at me when I stood in front of her.

When she wrapped her arms around me, I pressed my nose to her hair, whispering, "I may get used to it."

"Good! You need spoiling!" she huffed but grinned at my chuckle. "C'mon…I think Aunt Tessa was making beef stew tonight."

She linked our fingers together.

Suddenly, the idea of going to her house instead of my dorm room sounded like the best thing I'd heard in ages.

Chapter Nine

DANI

"You eat as much as you want, sweet pea," Mom crooned to Evan, who was on his second bowl of beef stew. She patted him on the shoulder before taking the seat next to him.

Despite the late hour, my family was still up. Wes was watching TV in the living room, Dad was grading papers in the library, and my mother and Aunt Tessa had been cleaning up the kitchen when I'd walked in with Evan in tow. Not one of them batted an eye when I told them he was taking the guest room for the night; they simply heated up dinner for us and sat us down at the table.

Looking at Evan right then, you'd never know all the shit, the hailstorm of hurt and heartache he'd been through. He never showed it. Before I got to know him, talked to him the first time, I thought it was aloofness, but it wasn't. It was the walls he'd put into place to keep from being hurt, picked on, and it kept him from having to explain himself. As I looked at him sitting across from me, smiling at my mother and aunt fawning over him, I could see he had the ability to shut off the parts of him that had been battered and bruised.

I'd never, ever considered myself a violent person, but as I watched the sweet, beautiful man in front of me, a long list of twisted, vile acts flickered through my head, things I wanted to do to his dad. They ranged from instant gratification to slow, meticulous torture. Shaking my head, I stood from the table.

"I'll be right back," I told Evan but locked gazes with my mother. "I need to ask Dad a question before we head upstairs."

"Sure, baby."

I stepped out of the kitchen and into the living room, where Wes glanced away from the TV. Closing my eyes, I inhaled deeply through my nose, letting it out slowly through my lips.

"That bad?" Wes whispered, turning away from the show he was watching.

I could only nod.

"Everything okay with you two?"

I nodded again. I wanted to shout to the world and back how I felt about Evan, but it wouldn't be today. Finally opening my eyes, I could see my cousin's concern. I teased him — hell, we teased the shit out of each other — but deep down, Wes was a good guy. He was calm and mellow, and he was loyal and kind. He was more a brother to me than a cousin. And at that moment, I could see he was about five seconds from asking whose ass he needed to kick.

Pushing away from the wall, I breathed deeply again, making my way down the hall to the library. Dad's head shot up when I not only stormed into the room but slammed the door behind me. Rushing to him, I fell into his arms.

"Dani?" he whispered, shifting enough so he could hold me. "What happened?"

Tears filled my eyes, and my heart hurt for the boy in the kitchen, but it made me grateful for what I had, where I'd come from, and it made me grateful for my small, loving family. We were loud and crazy, but we'd never hurt each other. *That* was family. Not that poor fucking excuse for a father Evan had.

I pushed back from my dad just enough to kiss his cheek, and then I sat down on the edge of his desk. Wiping away my tears with the back of my hand, I met his worried gaze.

"Evan…" I shook my head. "He…He could've *died!*"

"Ah, so he told you about his mother?" Dad verified, and I nodded. "I get the feeling there's more to it…" He tilted his head at me as he reached up to cup my face.

"His father *blames* him, Daddy!" I hissed in a whisper. I wanted to yell, rage against the unfairness of it all, but no good would come of it, except to upset Evan. *That* I wouldn't have. He'd suffered enough. "He told him that wreck was his fault. Who...who *does* that?"

My dad's face went from calm to dark in the blink of an eye. "Who does indeed?" he asked grimly. "Is the boy okay?"

"Yeah, he's getting loved on by Mom and Aunt Tessa in the kitchen."

Dad grinned. "I'm sure he is, but that's not what I meant, baby girl. I mean...is there a problem at home?"

I nodded. "I think there was, but he came here because it was as far away as he could get."

He nodded, rubbing his temple. "Good." Dad's lips twitched a little. "You like him."

My brow furrowed. "I do. So much, Dad. He's...so sweet, gentle, and kind, *despite* what he's been through, and..."

"He's a good boy. And anyone who can put pen to paper like he does isn't an idiot," Dad agreed with a nod. "Not to mention...well, he's pretty smitten with you too, Dani."

My face heated, and I grinned stupidly. "I want to...lock him up and spoil him rotten and show him this house is what family is, not where he came from, but...I also want to kiss him stupid because I'm falling for him hard."

Dad squeezed his eyes closed and shook his head. "My heart, Dani. If you do, just...let me stay blissfully ignorant, okay?"

Giggling, I kissed his bearded cheek. "Love you, Daddy."

"You're killin' me, kid." He stood and moved in front of me and cupped my face again, dropping a heavy kiss to my forehead. "You are your mother made over. All heart, all honesty, and all goodness, Dani. But you're smart as a damn whip too. I have faith that you know what's right, what's love, and what's not. I've always trusted your instincts on people. You and Wes are pretty sharp about reading bullshit. And when you both rave about the boy, then I know he's worthy."

Smiling, I nodded. "I'm keeping him, Dad!"

Dad cracked up. "Fine, then we keep him." He shot me a wink. "What's one more kid running around here?"

I slipped down from his desk and started for the door.

"Hey, kiddo," Dad called, shoving his hands into the front pockets of his pants. His face was concerned when he met my eyes. "What will you do when Evan has to go home for the holidays?"

I scowled, frowning down at the floor. "I don't know." I looked up at him again. "I can't let anyone hurt him. He's too good."

Dad sniffed and then nodded once. "Well, see what he plans to do. I can't in good conscience send him back to a bad situation if I can stop it. We'll go from there. Okay?"

Nodding, I left the library, only to see Wes smile my way when I got back to him. "Ev's upstairs. Aunt Leanne showed him where everything is, so I think he's taking a shower."

"Okay," I said, heading up the stairs.

The water shut off, and I went into my room to change clothes. Having grown up with Wes around, not to mention some of his buddies roaming about the house, I always slept in shorts and a T-shirt so I could still walk around outside my room. Once I was dressed, I opened my door to see if Evan was out of the bathroom, but I came to a standstill at the sight in the guest room.

Across the hallway, the lamp on the nightstand lit up the most beautiful thing I'd ever seen. Evan's hair was still damp, sticking up in every direction like he'd just finished rubbing it with the towel. Standing in just a pair of sleep pants, he seemed to be focused on his phone. His back was to me, and even though he was lean, he wasn't skinny. He was muscle and broad shoulders, narrowing down to his waist. His skin was smooth, a bit pale—but being from Florida, we expected everyone from outside the state to be pale.

My mouth watered as I took in every inch of his back, his ass, his neck. There were freckles across his shoulders and a few down his back; I wanted to count them, kiss them, and claim them for myself. However, it was when he shifted a little that my breath caught in my throat.

His scars.

They looked like a crisscross pattern. They were thin, yet they stood out a shade darker against his skin tone, and they were raised a bit.

Evan jumped a little when he saw me, and I was in the room before I could think twice.

"I'm…I'm…sorry. I thought I closed the door," he rambled softly as he reached for the T-shirt lying on the corner of the bed.

"Mom should've told you that it has to click to stay closed," I whispered, stopping him when he started to pull his shirt on. "You... you're beautiful." It was the truth, and I couldn't stop it from escaping my lips if I tried.

Evan looked confused, glancing down to his scars and then back to my face. But I didn't see the scars. They were there and they were hard to miss, but they weren't what my eyes saw. I saw definition without being bulky. I saw lean muscles and smooth skin that smelled warm and freshly showered. I smelled boy and shampoo.

"They're ugly, Dani..."

Shaking my head, I met his gaze as I asked permission with my eyes. He froze but then nodded quickly, like if he held his breath, this would be over soon. Without taking my eyes from his, I moved slowly, setting my palm flat against his ribcage.

I swallowed the lump in my throat and blinked back the tears threatening to fall, not because I could feel every single slice that had been etched permanently into his skin but because I could feel his fear. I felt it step into the room like a cloaked, hooded figure. It was a ghost standing between us. His body vibrated with it as his hands balled up into tight fists at his side in order to maintain it.

"Evan?" I whispered, not moving a single inch. "Look at me." Sad, wary, deep brown met my gaze, and his jaw rolled with the clench of his teeth. "These don't make you ugly. In fact, there isn't a single fucking thing about you that's *ugly*." I raised my eyebrows until he nodded that he'd heard me. "If I have to tell you every damn day, I will. I spew verbal vomit all the time; I'll just add it to the mix."

There it was. That stunning smile that took my breath away the first time I saw it in Wes's office. It was real, blinding me in its boyish brilliance. Coupled with the tinge of pink to his cheeks, it made him absolutely the most gorgeous thing I'd ever seen.

I hadn't removed my hand from his side, but as I gazed up at him, I knew I was completely head over heels for him. Just...*done*. And as much as I wanted to blurt that out, I bit my tongue. It wasn't the right time, and he'd just told me the story of how the scars beneath my fingers came to be. I would imagine he felt a bit...exposed. Regretfully, I pulled my hand away from his warm skin.

With a sigh and a smile up at him, I said, "I...I wanted to thank you, Evan."

"For what?"

"For trusting me enough to tell me that story tonight." I nodded when his brow furrowed in confusion. "It was probably the hardest thing to do, but I feel honored that you chose me."

"I meant what I said, Dani," he said slowly, like he didn't understand what I was saying. "You...You've become important to me. I thought...maybe...if I was honest..."

"Withholding something painful isn't *lying*, baby," I countered when he trailed off a little. "But I am..." I balled my hands up and then folded my arms, laughing a little at myself. "God, Evan, you make it so hard to stop myself from just...holding you, squeezing you, kissing you!"

His eyes widened and his cheeks flushed, but that grin of his just made my self-control start to completely unravel. In order not to rush at him, I started to turn.

"I'll let you get some sleep..." I muttered, starting for the door.

"What...Um, Dani?" he called so softly that I could barely hear him, but when I turned to face him, his face was even more fearful than before. "What if...What if I don't want you to stop?"

Closing my eyes, I smiled when I said, "Jesus, Evan...you need to be sure. If I hurt you, or pushed too fast, too soon...I'm willing—"

"You won't," he argued gently, and it came from right in front of me.

He'd moved closer, so when I opened my eyes, I was staring straight into smooth skin and collarbones and pec muscles. I dragged my gaze up his unbelievably attractive neck, along his sharp jaw, to his nervous gaze. Dark...so dark, and wary.

"Though..." He huffed a laugh, looking down. "I don't know what I'm doing, so..."

Oh my damn...I wasn't sure he could get any cuter, but he just had.

Smiling, I cupped his face, making him look back up to me. "Kissing is easy, baby. It's like...breathing."

He grinned. "Yeah?"

"Oh, yeah." I nodded, stepping closer to him, and he tossed the shirt in his hand back to the bed in order to set his hands respectfully on my waist. "You sure? There's no turning back after this, Evan. I may have to kiss you all the time." It was a tease, but holy shit, it was probably the damn truth too. Just standing that close to him was a rush of adrenaline and hormones and everything beautiful he carried with him.

"I don't want to go back."

Something about that whispered, firm statement sounded enormous coming from him. Like he meant us and life and his hometown. All of it. All of it in one big declaration.

Making sure he was looking at me, I decided to copy what he'd said earlier—not once but twice he'd said it. "Evan, you've become very important to me too, so I'm going to ask you again...Are you sure?"

He nodded vehemently. "Yes."

Smiling, I nodded with him. "Okay, then close your eyes, baby."

He did as I said, with complete trust, though I could feel him shudder a little beneath my touches to his face. Lord, his eyelashes were long and dark, resting against his skin. Lifting myself a bit on my toes, I slowly, softly pressed my lips to his.

I kept everything light and slow, pressing my lips again. I wanted to show him how I felt, show him how beautiful I thought he was, so I started to move—top lip, bottom lip, turning my head just a little. I pulled back just a bit, smiling at his heavy breathing, the adorable way he licked his lips, but his eyes were still closed as he rested his forehead to mine.

"More?" I whispered close to his mouth so he could feel me.

"God, yes."

I wanted to giggle at his eagerness, but he was the one to start forward this time, and I moaned against his mouth when our lips met again. Over and over, lips tasted and teased, and I couldn't stop myself when my tongue joined the dance, and when I thought he'd panic, he didn't. He welcomed me, turning his head at the same time he flexed his hands, pulling me flush to him.

For someone who said he didn't know what he was doing...My toes were curling into the carpet, my hands were now slowly slipping into his hair, and my body wanted to feel every inch of him pressed against me.

When his tongue met mine, I moaned shamelessly again, and with one last sweep of my lips across his, I pulled back in order to catch my breath.

Those long eyelashes swept up, and his eyes were even darker than before, like warm chocolate. His chest heaved with his breathing, and he was quiet for a moment as he continued to hold me close.

"Wow," he said, which made me grin. "Is it always like that?"

"Um, Evan…I've never been kissed like that in my life!" I said through awe and need because I wanted more, but I wouldn't push.

He smiled, crooked and easy, but he shook his head. "Don't tell me about other kisses…"

Laughing, I pressed my lips to his quickly but then pulled away. "That's another story for another day." When he looked at me worriedly, I added, "But I *will* tell you."

He nodded, finally reaching for his shirt and pulling it on. "Dani…what's that mean? That kiss?"

I knew what he was asking, so I smiled up at him. "What you want it to mean, Evan?"

"Everything."

He didn't quite meet my eyes when he said it, but my heart just about burst out of my chest with his sincerity.

"Good," I said, grinning at him when his eyes shot to mine. "Because it does mean everything."

His face reddened a bit, but he nodded with the happiest smile yet. "Good."

Evan

"Pick your poison, son," Dani's dad said, gesturing to the kitchen counter when I came in with my things for school. "There's plenty, so help yourself."

"Thanks, Pro—"

"Daniel, son. Inside this house, I'm just…Daniel." He corrected me gently, his lips twitching a bit above his beard, which made me smile.

"Thanks, Daniel."

He nodded once before sipping his coffee. Dani, Leanne, and Aunt Tessa were sitting at the table. The two older women were chatting softly, but I could see Dani wasn't exactly talkative in the mornings, which I found interesting. She was blindly scooping cereal into her mouth as she read a book cracked open on the table. She was dressed for school, but her eyes were still bleary, tired.

Memories of the night before came crashing down on me. Everything about it — telling her my story, the feeling of comfort this house brought, and kissing her. My face heated with that last one. I never once thought I'd ever *speak* to my Library Girl, much less find myself kissing her in her own house.

Turning to make myself a plate of scrambled eggs and bacon, I had to force back the urge to do it again. I *wanted* it again. In fact, the fantasy of spending all day in Dani's arms sounded like fucking heaven, but I knew it couldn't happen. There were classes and homework, not to mention my shift at Sunset Roast.

I took a seat between Dani and Daniel, smiling when she mumbled, "Morning, Evan."

She sipped coffee, going back to her book, but rested her cheek on my bicep.

Leanne chuckled. "It's best to give her at least to the bottom of that coffee mug, sweet pea." When I grinned and nodded, she asked, "Did you sleep okay, honey? The room okay?"

"Oh, yes, ma'am. It was great. Thank you."

"Anytime, Evan."

"You should've told 'im about the door, Mom," Dani told her through a yawn.

"Oh, shit…Sorry about that. You have to click it all the way for it to stay closed."

"Yeah, found that out, but…It's okay." I chuckled before taking a bite of bacon.

Aunt Tessa giggled like a girl but leaned her elbows on the table. "Funny, I don't hear Dani complaining one damn bit."

"And *that's* my cue to leave," Daniel sang sarcastically, making all the women at the table burst into laughter. He drained his coffee cup and said his goodbyes.

Dani stood, but her lips were at my ear. "Oh, hell no. No complaints. You?"

I shook my head but shoved eggs into my face to keep from turning to kiss her again before she left the kitchen. However, the smile on my face might stick all damn day. As I finished my breakfast, I wondered if just a kiss made me this happy, then I couldn't imagine what I'd feel like after sex. That thought made me red in the face and my appetite completely disappear because I had no idea what I was doing. I really needed to call my brother.

A soft kiss was pressed to my temple. "You ready?" Dani asked, suddenly back to the table.

"Hmm?" I looked up at her but then nodded. Turning to Leanne, I said, "Thank you again."

"Evan, when I say anytime, I mean it. You're welcome here whenever and however long you wish," she replied earnestly.

I smiled and nodded, feeling Dani slip her hand into mine and tug me out the door. I just barely was able to grab my backpack before we left Aunt Tessa and Leanne to their laughter. As soon as we were out on the front porch and the front door closed behind us, Dani's lips were on mine. My whole body reacted instantly. My hands cupped her face, my body surged forward, and I found myself pressing her into one of the columns.

I remembered everything she'd said the night before about kissing, and some of it was right. It was as easy as breathing, but it was consuming, it was addictive, and it was amazing. It was also making my body react to her in ways that I'd once thought embarrassing, and I almost pushed away from her, until her fingers hooked into the loopholes of my jeans to keep me close.

I broke away from her mouth, keeping my eyes closed and dropping my forehead to hers. "Sorry. I can't help it. You're way too beautiful."

"Oh, Evan…Thank you, but this is something you never have to apologize for," she said through a sexy giggle, and I smiled when she kissed me lightly again.

"What was that for?" I panted, still trying to calm down, but I hadn't moved from her arms.

"The kiss?" she asked, and I nodded against her forehead. "Because it's gonna be a long damn day before I can kiss you again."

Grinning, I chuckled, but it fell quickly. "Does this mean…"

"Evan," she breathed, pressing her lips to mine so softly. "You said you didn't want to go back."

"I don't."

"Then this...here...is everything. It means I'm yours and you're mine. So if I want to kiss my boyfriend, I damn well will, if he's okay with it."

Groaning, I kissed her again because I felt like I was dreaming. "I'll always be okay with it, and you're right. This'll be a long damn day," I moaned but regretfully pulled back to leave.

We walked to her car, and I slid into the passenger seat, gazing over at her once she was behind the wheel. "I...I don't know what I'm doing, Dani. You should know that. I've never...had a g-girlfriend."

"Me neither."

Laughing, I shook my head. "Dani, I'm serious."

She smirked a bit but cupped my face. "You said the same thing about kissing, baby. And trust me, you picked up on that...*just fine*." She raised an eyebrow at me but placed her hand flat on my chest over my heart, which was still pounding from our kisses. "Just trust this, Evan."

I nodded.

She smiled and then backed up and began the drive to school.

Chapter Ten

EVAN

I couldn't focus on the notes Professor Bishop was writing at the front of the classroom. Instead, my gaze raked along tight, faded jeans and the hand slowly doodling at the top corner of her page. My brain was still scrambled from our kisses. The one from the night before in the guest room of Dani's house, to the one this morning on her front porch, never mind the few minutes we'd lost ourselves in her car when she'd pulled into the parking lot at Edgewater. My thoughts were consumed with her — the feel of her, the taste of her.

Rubbing my face, I forced myself to pay attention to the front of the classroom and take notes on what the next assignment was before he released us for the day.

He shot us a smile and wave as we left the room. Dani slipped her hand into mine as we walked across campus to the dining hall. She stayed quiet, which was a bit unusual for her, so when we were finally outside at our table under the shade, I glanced up at her.

"You…okay?" I asked, scanning my head for something I might have done wrong.

She smiled and nodded, dragging a fry through ketchup. "I'm... perfect. I just...I have a question for you, but I'm not sure how to ask it. Or *if* I should ask it."

Frowning at her, I took a deep breath. "Did I...Is there..."

Suddenly, her smiling lips were on mine. "Hush. You've done nothing wrong, baby. I just..." She pulled back to cup my face. "What are you doing about the holidays?"

"Oh." I smiled a little but shrugged a shoulder. "I'm, um...I don't know. I'm pretty sure I can avoid going home for Thanksgiving, but Christmas is a different story. The dorms close, and then there's Faith...I don't know. I don't want to go, but I'm not sure I can get out of it. I'd be willing to bet my dad's already bought that ticket."

"You can stay with me," she blurted out, grimacing a little, but then she smiled when I chuckled. I loved her habit of just saying whatever she was thinking. "I'm sorry, but I just..." She sighed, her eyes sad and worried. "The thought of sending you home..."

She dropped her gaze to the table, and her hair covered her face, so I reached up to tuck it behind her ear. I needed to see her.

"He can't hurt me, Dani," I stated softly, shaking my head when she looked at me. "He can threaten and yell and say shit, but..." I shrugged a shoulder. "There're only three people on this planet who can hurt me—my siblings and the pretty girl at this table. That's it. He has power over me, but that's because he signs the checks for the part of my schooling that my scholarship doesn't cover, like books and housing. If he took that away, I don't know what I'd do. I don't make enough working for Wes to cover both. I have to appease my father in order to stay here."

Dani's face darkened, but she nodded. "I would never hurt you."

Smiling, I nodded. "I know."

"Do you?" she asked, narrowing her eyes at me and reaching up to toy with the hair in the middle of my forehead. When I nodded again, she smiled, but it fell immediately. "Good, because your dad sounds like a selfish jerk—an abusive, selfish jerk." Before I could argue, she gently added, "You don't have to touch someone to abuse them, handsome. Words hurt. Control hurts."

Nodding, I looked down at the last half of my sandwich, picking at the bread. I knew she was right. Hell, even Faith had lost her temper on our father once or twice, telling him those exact words, but he'd merely smiled at her, taunting her to "prove it." Nothing he'd done to us, to *me*, after Mom died was illegal, just unfair.

Dani cupped my face with her warm hands, making my gaze meet hers. "I want you to remember something for me." Pulling my forehead to hers, she smiled. "You're not that little boy anymore. There's nothing he can do that we can't figure out how to fix — books, housing, whatever. And despite what he's told you, that accident was not your fault. You're not weak; you're stronger than you give yourself credit for. The title of parent doesn't make him right. Just means his sperm got to the right place."

Grinning, I brushed my lips across hers before pulling back. "Yes, ma'am."

We finished our lunch and made our way to the library. Just as I was reaching for the door, my phone vibrated in my pocket. I smiled at the goofy picture of my brother's face on the screen.

"My brother," I told Dani. "I…I actually need to talk to him."

"Sure." She smiled, pointing in through the door. "I'll save your spot."

I held the door for her, answering the phone. "Hey, Ty."

"I was wondering if you'd gotten eaten by an alligator or some shit."

Laughing, I walked away a bit, leaning against the closest oak tree. "No, just busy. How's school?"

"Pfft, you know…Sex, girls, and parties."

Laughing softly, I shook my head. "Right, 'cause Jasmine allows all that to happen."

"Truth." He chuckled low but asked, "I got your text, little bro, so what's up?"

I took a deep breath, bracing myself for an epic amount of teasing. "I…I need your advice."

"Mine? Not the little midget? Must be serious if you aren't talking to Faith about it."

I laughed again. I'd missed my brother because he never took anything seriously — our dad being the only exception to that. "Actually, she told me to talk to you."

"Ah, shit…What'd *Daddy Dearest* fuckin' do this time?" Tyler asked, and even though sarcasm laced through his tone, I could hear him bracing himself for the answer.

"No, no…that's not…Tyler, I need your advice. Seriously."

"What?"

"Two things, really. First, I don't…What're you doing about the holidays?"

"Oh, um…Jasmine and I will be there for Thanksgiving but not for Christmas." My mouth fell open, but he went on. "Jas's family invited me to New York over Christmas break. I'm going. Let me guess…You're doing the opposite."

"Yeah, I think so. I mean, I don't see the point in going for Thanksgiving. It's not even a week, and it's not like we do anything."

Tyler snorted derisively. "I'm surprised you're even considering Christmas, Ev. I would've bet that you'd never come back to Montana."

"It's not for *him*," I snapped, sneering a little. "I want to see Faith. If you're there for Thanksgiving, then I'll go for Christmas just to make sure he doesn't ignore her the whole fucking holiday season."

Tyler sighed, but it came out like a growl. "You know she applied to Edgewater."

"Ah, hell…" I groaned, raking a hand through my hair. "Oh, he's gonna *so* blame me for that."

"Mmhmm, probably, but knowing Faith, she's gonna shrug a shoulder and dare him to stop her. You know, I'm waiting for the day she calls me and tells me he's shot off at the mouth on her. I may have to kill him."

His voice was grim but honest. He'd done his best to step in for me when we were growing up, but Dad had seen through it, making the punishments that much longer. Tyler was so damned big and strong that, by the time he left for college, I had been afraid he'd actually punch Dad square in the face. I was pretty sure the only thing that stopped him was that our father would've taken it out on us once he'd left.

"I can't wait until she's out of that house," I sighed, shaking my head. "I may never go back."

"Don't blame you, Ev. I sometimes wonder if Mom knew, you know? Like maybe she was what kept him reined in, but when she was gone, he just…lost his shit," Tyler said, and again, the old grief fell heavily over us, in spite of the distance.

"She was leaving him, if you listen to the rumors around good ol' Key Lake," I teased, which made him laugh a bit. "I don't know,

Ty. I just…I live with it every day. I don't need him telling me what I've done, how I'm such a loser. I'm aware."

"Fuck him!" Tyler snapped. "You're no damn loser! One day, you're gonna be on the shelves at the bookstore, just like Mom. And I want the first signed copy!" When I laughed, he huffed. "I'm dead fucking serious, little bro. And when he's all old and crusty and rotting away alone in that house, we'll see who the goddamn loser is, okay?"

"Thanks, Ty."

He *tsk*ed a bit over the line. "Now, you said two things…"

I felt my face heat, even more than the Florida temperature around me. "I…uhh…I have…a girlfriend, and I…"

"Shut the fuck up! Go, Evan!"

Grinning, I shook my head. "Shut up. I need…I don't know what the hell I'm doing. I need…"

"Oh. Have you cashed in your V-card yet?"

"Don't be foul. I need your advice, Tyler."

"Okay, okay, okay…Is she pretty?"

"Beautiful."

"Nice, Ev," he said softly. "So what do you wanna know?"

"I…I'm…I'm not like you, Ty. I don't know what I'm doing. It's overwhelming, and…I'm nervous I'm gonna fuck up. I want… everything all at once, but I don't…and she's…and—"

"Whoa, whoa, whoa, Evan! Slow down! I wanna tease the shit out of you, but I can't. I know you, man. You're probably panicking all to hell and back."

"Tyler, don't you dare!" I heard in the background, and I groaned that Jasmine was hearing this shit.

Tyler chuckled but then grunted when she most likely smacked him. "Ow, okay! Damn it. Ev, listen. Just…be honest with the girl, okay? What's her name?"

"Danielle—Dani."

"Okay, well, just be honest with Dani. Chicks dig the whole honesty thing." He hissed the last sentence, making me laugh. "Seriously. They do. And really, your dick may be a virgin, but your eyes aren't. I know that laptop of yours has seen some deviant shit."

Grimacing, I neither confirmed nor denied that fact.

"Look, Evan, girls will let you know what they like or don't like. You can tell, you know? If this girl is worth a damn, then…"

"Tyler, she's…amazing and funny and smart and gorgeous. She's… She knows everything about me, and she's so patient…I mean, I *really* like her."

"Sounds like more than just *like*."

"Yeah."

"Oh."

"Yeah."

Tyler was quiet for a moment, but I heard a commotion on the other end, and then it was Jasmine's voice over the line. "Hey, Evan."

"Hey, Jas," I mumbled back.

I'd met her handful of times. To look at her, it seemed she'd be a cold, snobby girl, but she wasn't. She was very pretty—auburn hair, tall, confident—but she was actually one of the nicest people I'd ever met. She was loyal and completely over the moon for my brother.

"Don't be embarrassed. I want to help, okay? Just…a girl's point of view?" she offered, but it came out like a question.

"Okay."

"Evan, your brother's right. Be honest. But follow your heart. You…You're pretty picky about who you let in, so that right there tells me this girl is special. Go with that. There's no need to rush, but let this Dani guide you. It doesn't have be about *sex*. It can be about expressing how you feel about each other. Your brother wasn't exactly pure when we met, but experience isn't everything. Okay?"

"Yeah, but…"

"Look, I'm all for some porn, but knowing the basics is enough. Truly. How you care about someone will guide you on how good you want them to feel. If you care about someone, you'll want to *show* them, not just…*get off*."

I laughed nervously, running a hand through my hair again. "Thanks."

"Mmhmm…"

"You're a helluva bookworm, buddy," Tyler said, back on the line again. "You can't tell me you haven't read some fuck-awesome shit out there. All that throbbing manhood, quivering what-have-you… His love-rocket exploded into her gaping…Ugh. I can't even."

Grinning, I shrugged a shoulder he couldn't see and said, "Umm, yeah…a bit."

He laughed. "That's my boy. Okay, then you know *what* to do. It's just…scary when your heart is on the line."

"Yeah! Exactly."

"Then be honest. Tell her what you want. Let her tell you. Fuck, little bro, learning is half the fun. And sex *is* fun, so…don't make it out to be more difficult than it is. I know you tend to overthink stuff. Don't do that here. Make sense?"

"Yeah, okay." I took a deep breath and let it out. "Thanks."

"Sure, Ev. No problem. So…I'll call you when I'm home for Thanksgiving, and I'll let you know how the midget's doin'."

"You're taking Jasmine?"

"Yeah, but only because she isn't going home either. Though, I'll probably warn the old man to keep his fucking mouth shut around her. He isn't exactly shy about how he feels."

I hummed in agreement. "Well, don't tell him shit about me."

"Never," Tyler laughed in all seriousness, and then we said our goodbyes and ended the call.

Stepping into the library was a relief from the heat outside, though I had to admit that October was much cooler than it had been when I'd arrived on campus in August. I walked to my usual table, smiling at Dani's things sitting across from me, but she wasn't in her seat. I set my backpack down on the chair, took out the book I needed to return, and dropped it in the chute. When I looked up, I smiled at the sight of Dani turning down one of the aisles.

Just out of simple curiosity, I followed her. She was in fiction, of course, standing on the very tips of her toes as she reached up on a high shelf. I stepped up behind her, grabbing the book she wanted.

"Better?" I asked in a whisper, but I couldn't keep the chuckle back as she spun in front me and took the book I held out to her.

Her grin, her sweet, musical giggle made my damn day. "Thanks," she whispered back, and I started to turn back down the row, but she stopped me. Her head swiveled left and then right, only to look up at me. "Kiss me, Evan."

"Here?"

"Hell, yes, here!"

Something about her tone made me narrow my eyes at her, not because I didn't want to do it but because I really, really did.

"Have you…Have you thought about us…here?"

She bit her lip, her cheeks flushing a touch pink. "M-Maybe."

Giving the aisle one last glance either way, I saw there wasn't anyone near us, and when I faced her again, her lips met mine quickly. Just like on her front porch, I lost myself to her. She tasted like the cherry soda she'd been drinking at lunch, she felt like heaven and all things I never dreamed I'd have, and she smelled like books and fruit and flowers. I wrapped my right arm around her waist, but I had to brace my left on the shelf by her head in order to not slam us into the bookshelf. The last thing I needed was to cause a domino effect with every bookcase in the library toppling over one after the other.

Pulling back, I closed my eyes as I pressed my forehead to hers as we both tried to catch our breaths. "Me too. I've thought about it too."

A sweet little squeak escaped her, and I opened my eyes to see her mouth hanging open and her eyes wide. It made me chuckle a little.

"I may be inexperienced, Dani, but I have an imagination." I pulled back and tapped my temple. "Writer…and bookworm," I said, picking up her hand that was holding the book I'd pulled down for her. "Speaking of…What'd you pick out?"

"Don't judge, okay?" she said with an adorable wrinkle to her nose.

I grinned, turning the book over to read the back. It was a modern romance—the love-hate between two people but with an undeniable attraction for one another. It was as close to erotica as the school's library probably carried.

Handing it back, I said, "Let me know if you like it." When her eyebrows shot up high, I kissed the soft spot between them. "Dani, stop. I can't judge you on anything you read. I've pretty much checked out every title I've ever seen you crack open in this library. You have fantastic taste in books." What I didn't say out loud was that one of my fantasies was simply the ability to discuss said books, so I was pretty damn close to perfect right at that moment.

"Want me to read it to you?" she taunted, and with that, I did spin to leave her in the aisle with a laugh. She rushed to catch up to me. "Could be fun…We could read it together."

I was thinking about the advice my brother and Jasmine had given me—to keep things honest and fun. We walked back to the table, taking our seats, but I pointed to the book in her hands.

"And just *when and where* do you want to do that?" I asked her with a laugh.

Her grin was adorable, if not slightly evil. "We'll figure it out."

Shaking my head, I started to pull my laptop out in order to get to work on the homework her dad had given us today. However, her statement seemed to mean...*more*. Glancing up at her as I turned on my computer, I knew she meant more than just the romance novel in her hands. She meant us, me, my inexperience with all of this. Hell, she probably meant the holidays coming up too, if I was reading her correctly.

Suddenly, the thought of following in Tyler's footsteps came to mind—to bring Dani with me to Montana, for even just a portion of the break. Faith would adore her—they'd probably end up the best of friends—but the mere thought of my father saying something negative, derogatory, or even passive-aggressive toward my girl...That wasn't going to happen. I'd never allow him to hurt her.

"My girl," I whispered to myself in pure adoration and awe at the reality of it. Shaking my head, I focused back on her. "You sure?" I asked, tapping the book in her hands.

"Yes." Her eyes never left mine, and they were warm and sweet, but they were sincere and comforting too.

I couldn't stop my smile if I tried as I shook my head slowly. "Um...okay. Whatever you want, Dani."

She giggled, got up, and pressed a rough kiss to my lips, spinning around to head up to the checkout desk. As I watched her, I caught sight of a few people staring our way—the girls Dani had forced on Brad were two of them. I found that I truly didn't care what anyone thought because the only opinion in the room that mattered belonged to the girl happily taking her seat back in front of me.

"Maybe someday it'll be *your story* you'll read to me," she said hopefully, and there was a touch of teasing there too, but not a harsh tease.

Grinning, I shrugged, knowing full well Dani could ask anything of me and I'd give it willingly, but I wanted to tease her back.

"Maybe." I pointed to the book that she was about to open to the first page. "Don't start without me. Homework first."

Dani groaned but smiled my way. "Okay, okay."

We grew quiet, getting to work, but my mind kept straying to everything that had happened since I'd told her about Mom, the wreck, just...all of it. I knew I needed to speak to my dad, that I needed to get with Faith about some things, but for the moment, I needed this normal, this comfort I'd never had before. But I realized there was something I needed to do.

"Hey, Dani?" I whispered, and she glanced up from her Lit homework. "Thank you."

"For what, baby?"

Smiling, I shook my head but shrugged a shoulder. "For just being...*you.*"

"See? That... *That* shit makes it hard not to kiss you stupid!" she hissed dramatically, smiling when I laughed silently...well, as best I could.

"Homework, pretty girl." I pointed to her books, chuckling a little more when she narrowed her eyes at me.

She went back to her textbook, grumbling, "Long damn day."

Chapter Eleven

EVAN

The sky was a bruised, purplish gray, flickering with bright strands of lightning. It was fascinating to watch from the large windows of Sunset Roast. The rain was so different in Glenhaven compared to back home. It was heavy and harsh, with cold, fat drops that spattered against the glass. It was also interesting to see it roll in off the water, covering the blue sky in its path.

A part of me could feel the old fear at the sight of rain and ocean, but the other part knew I was safe inside the café. I was warm and dry indoors for at least the next couple of hours. October was starting to cool off in Florida, which made me smile at the hoodies and jackets and sweaters I'd seen the last few days.

The café was quiet. We'd had a rush earlier before the rain had rolled in, but now everyone was where they wanted to be in order to wait it out. I finished wiping down all the tables, and I wanted to get a head start on the floors before closing. With no one in the sitting area, it seemed like the perfect time.

It was just Susan and me working. Meg had asked for the night off for a party somewhere on campus—the same party that Brett and Regan were going to, I was pretty sure. Wes and Dani were with

Leanne in the art building, helping her get set up for the art show that coming weekend. I'd offered to help after we'd closed.

I was just about to take advantage of the quiet downtime and work on my Creative Writing paper, but my phone buzzed in my pocket. Pulling it out, I grimaced at the sight of my father's number.

"Hey, Susan?" I called, holding up my phone. "I'll be right out back, okay?"

"Yeah, honey. Do what you do," she said, barely glancing up from the magazine she was flipping through. "Tell Dani I said hey."

I smiled but shook my head as I walked through the kitchen. I *wished* it was Dani.

"Hello?" I answered, stepping out the back door and under the awning that Susan used when she was on her cigarette breaks.

"So your brother will be here for Thanksgiving," he started immediately.

"I can't make Thanksgiving, Dad. I have to cover for someone at work, and I have tests the next week to prepare for, so…" I shrugged a shoulder, steeling myself for his reaction.

Nothing about that was a lie, either. I really would be covering for Meg, who wanted to go home to Atlanta for Thanksgiving. And finals would be coming close by the end of November.

I heard the sigh, and then there was a snort of derision. "Work," he scoffed. "Serving coffee is pretty pathetic, son."

Smiling, I shook my head because I could see he was looking for a fight. He couldn't make me come home for Thanksgiving. Plus, he had forced keeping one's word on us as kids. Lastly, he wouldn't argue studying for tests. Instead of fighting any of that, he was going to remind me just what a piece of shit he thought I was.

"Yeah, well, my boss is pretty cool, lets me study during slow times, and I've saved a little, so it works for me and my schedule."

I stared out across the parking lot, watching the rain's endless drops create circles in the puddles on the ground. My mind sort of shut down when he started his rants. My ears caught a few words—pathetic, weak, pitiful, stupid. I let them roll off me, until he moved on to Tyler and Jasmine.

"He's bringing that whore with him, I suppose," he sighed wearily. "I'll have to watch her…"

Something about that bothered me. Jasmine had been nothing but faithful and loyal to my brother, and she loved him fiercely. She'd only ever been kind to me, which probably meant that Tyler had told her about the accident and Mom, but that didn't bother me at all.

"Jasmine is cool, Dad," I countered, frowning a little. "She really cares about Tyler."

Dad laughed. It was so harsh and so loud that it made me flinch at the humorless tone to it. "Love makes you an idiot, son. Best learn that now. And any bitch who latches on to *you* is just gonna run you the fuck over. You'll probably fall for the first one who gets your dick wet..."

Scowling, I closed my eyes and shook my head slowly in order to bite my tongue. He was goading me. He was testing me, and I knew it. He either knew about Dani, simply from the phone bill or he had overheard Faith, but somehow he knew. The hows weren't important; it was what he'd do with that information.

Panic combined with anger, all meshed into something I couldn't control. It all built up to come out with something that *always* pissed him off. I brought up my mother.

"That's not what Mom always said," I ground out through gritted teeth. "She said love was the best, most important thing in the world. I can only *assume* she was talking about you, but..."

The line went dead quiet. "You know, we're gonna work on that attitude of yours when you come home for Christmas. There's a bunch of shit around here that needs to be done since you left. I've already bought your ticket, so don't even bother to weasel out of it. I know for a fact that the dorms close over the break, so I know you have nowhere to go. And second, we'll also discuss your sister's unreasonable desire to visit you over spring break."

My nostrils flared as I bit down on my bottom lip. He'd just used the *one thing* he knew I couldn't deny — Faith. He didn't punish her like he did Tyler and me. No, he'd simply deny her what she wanted. However, he didn't mention that she'd applied to Edgewater in order to move close to me, so I kept my mouth shut. I had a feeling it would be something brought up once I was back in Montana.

"Fine," I spat, sneering out into the parking lot, where headlights pulled in. "I gotta get back to work, Dad."

I hated that he'd gotten to me, but he always knew exactly how to do it. Pocketing my phone, I glanced up to see Susan standing at the door, lighting up a cigarette and watching the boardwalk for customers from under the awning.

"You okay, kiddo?"

I nodded, shoving my hands into the front pockets of my jeans.

"Helluva fucking call—I could hear them over the line as soon as I got to the door," she mumbled around the filter. "Parent?"

"Dad."

"I can't imagine you doing anything to deserve all that. You're a good kid, so I don't know what had his panties in a twist." She shook her head at my humorless laugh, glancing out into the rainy evening. "My dad was a piece of work too, honey. Believe that. Eventually you have to do what's best for you. Just because he had a hand in making you doesn't mean he's a good person." She slowly turned her head my way, her eyebrow rising up. "Some people are just...toxic. You get me?"

"Yeah," I sighed, shaking my head. "I just...my little sister is still there, so..."

"Ah...gotcha. How old is she?"

"She just turned eighteen."

"Even better," she sighed, smiling my way as she leaned against the wall. She flicked an ash to the ground. "She's legal, so she could haul ass if she needed to."

"She won't. She plays him better than my brother and I do, and he lets her. His beef isn't with her."

Susan shook her head, a smile playing on her face before she took the last drag on her cigarette. "Again, I can't imagine *you* doing anything to warrant that much yelling."

I huffed a laugh. "I don't have to *do* anything."

The sound of a car door caught our attention, and I smiled at the sight of Dani with her hood up on her sweatshirt as she ran across the parking lot. I caught her just as she made it underneath the awning, losing her footing in a puddle.

"Whoa," I said through a laugh as she gripped my shirt, and I glanced over her head to Wes, who was right behind her. "Thought you guys were helping Leanne?"

He merely smiled and shook his head.

"We're done," Dani mumbled into my neck as I held her close, but she shivered in my arms. "I wanted to see you."

"I hate that you drove in this," I muttered without thinking.

Dani pulled back, pushing her hood away from her beautiful face, her brow furrowing a little. "I'm okay, and it was just across campus, baby. Promise." Her body shuddered again as she hugged me close one more time. "I'm sorry that scares you, though."

"Pretty girl, come inside," I whispered in her ear. "I'll make you something warm."

"*You're* warm," she said through an adorable giggle, nuzzling my ear.

I laughed, wrapping an arm around her and lifting her up inside the back door. "In you get. Take that off and put this one on." I grabbed my own sweatshirt that was hanging in the back.

Dani nodded, doing as I asked, and we all went out front. The place was still quiet, though Susan was letting Wes know what we'd done for the day. I quickly made Dani a hot chocolate as she pulled herself up onto the front counter. Something about her in my hoodie made me crazy, but I focused on making sure she didn't catch a chill.

"Here, Dani, drink this," I said, handing her the cup. I started to back away, but she locked her legs around my waist. She sipped the drink, smiling at it, but then reached up to push her fingers through my hair. "What?" I asked at her wrinkled brow.

"What happened? Your eyes look...sad."

I shook my head. "Dad called just before you pulled in." I sighed but smiled at her worried face. "I told him about Thanksgiving. And he assured me I was coming home for Christmas break."

"Mmm," she hummed, pursing her lips. "I don't want you to go."

Her pout might have been the cutest thing I'd ever seen, so I couldn't help but hold her closer. "Dani..."

"I know you *have* to go, but I don't have to like it," she told me firmly, still wearing that sweet pout. "I just...I have a...a...funny feeling about you going. That's all."

Shaking my head, I kissed her—because I could and because she was so damned hard to resist. "I'll be fine," I vowed to her. "And you know I'd never...I'm yours, Dani."

She *tsk*ed at me. "I trust *you*, handsome. I don't like your father."

Smiling, I kissed her again. "We've got time to talk about it. Okay?"

"Yeah. But I'm glad you're here for Thanksgiving. You're coming to my house for that. Promise me."

Chuckling, I stepped back, saluting her. "Yes, ma'am."

"I think it's safe to say her crush on you is over." Dani's lips were at my ear as we started to pack up our things in the library.

My head shot up to watch Regan with Brett, and they looked cozy, happy. Our Physics project was completed and had been turned in earlier that day, but I had a feeling Brett would end up in the library more often than he used to. Regan glanced up, her cheeks reddening, and then went back to Brett.

"Okay, maybe not *completely* over, but somewhat…diminished?" Dani amended with a giggle.

I rolled my eyes to her, raising my eyebrows. "I don't care."

Dani buried her snorting laugh into my upper arm, which made me smile and shake my head. "Did you *ever* care about girls and crushes, or were you always so oblivious?"

Grimacing, I slid my laptop into my backpack and zipped it up. "It was…better if I didn't care, Dani," I stated, standing up and shouldering her bag and mine. "Let's just put it that way."

Dani stayed quiet all the way to my dorm, which was on the way to her car. I was staying the weekend at the Bishop house in order to help Leanne out with the art show on Saturday with Dani and then ride to work with Wes to close Sunset Roast. My bag was packed, but I needed to throw a few more things into it.

As usual, the first two floors were a beehive of activity, though I noticed a few sets of male eyes land on Dani. Her hand was firmly in mine, though, and she didn't seem to pay much of it any attention, which made me chuckle.

"You know," I started, unlocking my room, but I paused before opening the door. "I could ask you the same question, Dani." She tried to look innocent, but I merely shook my head. "Don't even…"

Her grin was adorable as she shrugged a shoulder. "Let me into your room, Evan. I'll answer your question. I've been dying to get in here."

Laughing, I pushed the door open, gesturing for her go on in. "Casa de Shaw-Walker."

I had no idea what made her so damned excited. Brett and I were tidy, and we weren't into the party scene, so there wasn't much to see, except furniture and beds. Though, it was the latter that made me nervous. Dani gazed around as I set our stuff down for a moment, and she smiled at Brett's side of the room, with his video game and sci-fi movie posters. My side wasn't as decorated, but she immediately caught sight of the handful of framed pictures I had on my overloaded bookshelf.

Some were as recent as the last time Tyler was home from UM, so it was the three of us hanging out in my room. There were some that were older, some of just Faith and me being silly, and one of Tyler and Jasmine. But the one that Dani actually picked up was a picture of my mother and me. It had been the summer before the wreck. Faith had taken it, and my mother was laughing and happy... and so was I, I remembered as I looked at it over Dani's shoulder.

"Oh, God," she whispered, looking up at me. "You really do look *just like her*."

Smiling, I nodded and shoved my hands in my front pockets.

"She was beautiful."

"She was...inside and out, actually," I agreed softly. "A very kind spirit. Always."

Dani set the frame back in the exact same place, turning to face me. "Also like you."

Smirking, I shook my head, but I shrugged again. "I don't know about that. She wanted us to always be kind. Faith is very excitable, and Tyler is extremely outgoing—both the complete opposite of me—so she tried to teach us all how to be polite. Just...*nice* to each other and other people. She always told us to be honest, even if it seemed like the hard thing to do. I try to remember those things."

"Those are excellent things to remember, Evan," she stated, glancing around again. "I owe you an answer, don't I?"

Shaking my head, I said, "Not if you don't want to."

"You never answered mine, though," she teased a little.

Deciding to get it over with, I said, "I forced my...my...obliviousness, Dani. It was easier to pretend no one noticed." I gripped my hair for a second, licking my lips. "I...There was a girl I liked—before the car wreck. She...she was quiet, shy like me, but it wasn't as debilitating then as it is now. Before the wreck, there were a bunch of us who just got along, hung out, whatever. But after the wreck, I was out of school for a bit, and when I got back, they...she...I thought she'd started to like me, but..."

Dani cupped my face. "She was...morbidly curious."

"Yeah, and then...being such a small town, kids started to hear from their parents — parents who worked at the hospital, or the police department, and hell, even the tow-truck driver. They started spreading rumors. Some of it was...foul; some of it was not far from the truth. I just...I just shut up."

I shrugged again, grimacing a little at how that may have sounded, but it was the truth. I reached for my packed bag, setting it on my bed in order to add my bathroom stuff.

"Anyway," I sighed, not looking Dani's way, "they started to make fun of or pick on me because I wouldn't say anything. Some...Some of them...they called me a murderer or whatever."

"No!" she hissed, and I looked out of the bathroom at her incredulous expression. When I nodded, she growled out, "Assholes."

"It was to get a reaction, pretty girl," I said through a chuckle. "Nothing more. And back then, I'd already come to terms with it being my fault."

She shook her head. "Not your fault, Evan."

I sighed deeply, dropping my bathroom stuff into the bag and zipping it up. "That's harder to hear when I've heard the opposite — *believed* the opposite — for so long." I set the duffel by our backpacks and then sat down on the edge of the bed.

"It's easier to accept the bad than the good?" she asked, smirking a little when I laughed once and nodded. She came to stand between my legs, reaching up to run her fingers through my hair, something I was becoming truly addicted to, something I found calmed me when nothing else could. "My turn, I guess."

Grimacing, I set my hands on her waist, shaking my head slowly. "Do I want to hear this, Dani? I'm...I don't think I'll be good with hearing about you and other guys. I...Jealousy is new to me."

She smiled, cupping my face to bring my gaze up to hers. "There's not much to tell, baby." She laughed a little. "I was...incredibly shy up to about two years ago. Working at the coffee shop kinda pushed that all away. Being homeschooled didn't give me a lot of social options, but there were homeschool activities and events. I met a few people that way. But you want me to answer the same questions... Did I notice...or *do* I notice guys or whatever? No, I don't. Or at least, I don't acknowledge them. I don't flirt for the sake of flirting, and I'm pretty damn picky. Plus, once I started my freshman year, I kept seeing this...gorgeous thing in my library..."

I chuckled, shaking my head.

"It's true, Evan. This time, it was *me* doing the crushing. My Library Guy is hot, but I found out he's pretty damn awesome too."

When I whispered thank you to her, she kissed me again.

I studied her face, seeing that she was being sincere, but I just needed to know one thing. "Are you..." I swallowed nervously. "You seem more...experienced than me, though. I just..."

Her smile was glorious and sweet and completely warm, not teasing at all, and she brought my lips to hers, kissing me softly before whispering against them. "You said you didn't want to hear about some things."

"Just..." I exhaled roughly through my nose, frowning a little. "Just...the *Cliffs Notes* version."

She laughed, nodding. "Fine, baby. There was a guy...well over a year ago. He was friends with Wes. Peter was his name. We did a lot of things, except for the *one big thing*. He went off to Miami for a job and met his fiancée, Carlie. The end. No broken hearts, no tears, and I adore Carlie, so..." She shrugged a shoulder. "Then you came along, Evan. That's it. Not all that big of deal. No drama. No grand, romantic gestures — not even candlelight...not that I need any of that."

Grinning, I nodded. "Okay."

There was something oddly comforting about knowing we were on the same page, after a certain point, anyway. She leaned into me, setting her elbows on my shoulders, and I couldn't help but wrap my arms around her.

Gazing up at her, I sighed at just how beautiful she was, which came spilling out of my mouth.

"You're so beautiful," I whispered in awe.

"I'd say you were bullshitting me, except you've never lied to me," she countered, and then her lips were on mine.

She took my breath away in every way possible. I held her close, and it took everything I had not to pull her to my lap. When she pulled back, I licked my lips just to keep the taste of her.

"You ready for our sleepover?" She gave me a half smile that reminded me of Wes a bit, and I snorted into a soft laugh.

"Yes, ma'am."

She stepped out of my arms, holding a hand out for me to take. "Good, because we'll pretty much have the house to ourselves. Wes is working, Mom and Dad are at some sort of school dinner thing, and Aunt Tessa won't bug us; she'll probably stay in the guest house. We can do whatever we want."

I laughed nervously, raking a hand through my hair. "And what do you want?"

She gaped at me. "I want to finish our book, Evan! Damn, we're only a couple chapters in. I wanna know what happens."

I raised an eyebrow at her. "Dani, it's not *Sherlock Holmes*; there's no mystery as to how it's gonna go."

Dani's adorably loud bark of laughter was the best sound I'd heard yet. She grinned, biting down on her bottom lip as she tugged my hand. "Exactly!"

Chapter Twelve

DANI

Except for the sound of water running in the kitchen, my house was quiet when Evan and I walked in. Aunt Tessa glanced up from the sink to smile our way.

"Hey, kids," she greeted, shutting off the water and drying her hands. "Don't mind me. I'm going back to the guest house. There's a marathon of *Housewives* of some shit or another. I plan on losing a few IQ points to it but gaining a pound or two with the tub of ice cream I've successfully hidden from my son."

"Sounds like a damn good date, Aunt Tessa," I teased her, kissing her cheek.

"Trust me, it's better than some dates I've actually been on." She shot us a wink and squeezed Evan's shoulder when he chuckled. "There's plenty to eat in the fridge—leftovers, sandwich stuff, frozen pizza—so enjoy. And don't do anything I wouldn't do," she sang on the way out the back door.

"That doesn't leave much," I muttered, smiling when Evan laughed again.

"Why does she keep her ex-husband's last name?" Evan asked out of the blue.

"She'll tell you it's because she didn't want Wes to be different after the divorce, but really, she hates the idea of changing everything back to Bishop. Don't mind her; she's crazy, which explains Wes completely, right?"

Evan grinned and nodded. "She's funny, though."

"She is that." I stood on my toes to kiss his cheek. "You know where everything is, so make yourself at home, baby. I'm going to change clothes."

"Okay," he said softly.

Once I was upstairs, I decided to take a shower. When I was dressed again, I found Evan at the kitchen table with his laptop open and half a sandwich on a plate beside him. I grabbed something to drink out of the fridge and then took the seat next to him. With the most adorable smile, he slowly pushed the plate my way.

"Eat your sandwich, Evan," I said through a chuckle, but he was already shaking his head.

"I only wanted a snack, so...share with me?"

I was pretty damn sure Evan was the sweetest person I'd ever met, and it had nothing to do with the extremely yummy sandwich he'd just given me. It was even more than the hot chocolate and warm sweatshirt he'd given me the other night when the rain had made me cold. It was everything about him. It was his quiet demeanor, his honest nature, and his gentleness. It went beyond polite — which he said his mother had tried to instill in him. It was just...Evan. Even sitting there at my table, typing an outline for his next paper that was due, he radiated a certain sort of comfortable ease, a feeling of being adored, and the knowledge that he'd never, ever hurt me — with either words or touch. He was incapable of the latter. Because if anyone on the entire fucking planet knew how badly words could sting, it was the sweet, gorgeous thing sitting beside me.

And I was completely in love with him.

The urge to tell him was strong, so strong that I almost choked on the last bit of bread I popped into my mouth. Sputtering, I shook my head when Evan glanced up from his typing.

"Dani?"

"I'm o-okay." I chugged some soda, finally smiling at him. "Wrong way."

He grinned, shaking his head. "I won't be long," he promised. "I just...thought of something, and I wanted to get notes down."

"I *will* read without you, Evan Shaw," I teased him as I took the plate to the kitchen sink, giggling when he narrowed his eyes dangerously. "In fact," I started slowly, "I do believe it's in your bag upstairs."

I grinned but then darted out of the kitchen, through the living room, and hit the stairs, taking them two at a time. I heard the chair scrape across the kitchen floor and the thump of heavier footsteps pounding behind me. However, his long legs made it easier for him to catch me, and I squealed when a strong arm caught me around the waist, only to lift me up off the floor.

"Evan!" I cracked up, which made him chuckle.

He set me down behind him, reaching for his bag, and he pulled out the book we'd started. Holding it up, he asked, "Where?"

I took his hand, giving him a tug. "My room. And it's your turn to read to me. I read the start of it!"

He laughed softly, but it was a nervous laugh.

"We could switch off on chapters," he suggested once we were in the room.

"We could," I agreed, pushing him until he sat down on the edge of my bed.

I didn't know how to tell him that I desperately wanted to hear his voice bring life to the romance novel in his hand. I was most likely playing with fire picking that book from the start, but he wasn't complaining. He also didn't seem to understand what he did to me. There wasn't the local southern drawl that Wes carried or the sometimes-harsh northeastern accents I'd heard from others at school. No, his tone was calm and soothing; even when he was upset or bothered, it barely rose to a yell. He was sweet and gorgeous, yes, but his voice was soft, with a bit of rasp to it. When he spoke to me, it was with total honor, and I felt comfortable and relaxed, but I also wanted to hear him read some not-so-respectful things. And Evan had such a respect for the written word that I knew he'd give it his best, no matter the subject.

He flipped through the pages to find where we'd left off and then gazed back up at me with an adorable expression of expectancy.

"Sit back," I told him softly, waiting until he was comfortable at the headboard of my bed before situating myself between his legs.

Leaning down, he brushed the lightest of kisses to my cheek but then pulled my hair away so he could see the book. "Ready?" he asked, and I nodded, leaning back against him.

"Sophia returned to work the following Monday with a new outlook on how to deal with her new, overbearing boss," he started, and it was better than I'd even imagined.

I could barely pay attention to the plot, simply because it was almost sensory overload. His chest vibrated against my back with every word. His breath was soft against my neck as he read over my shoulder, and he smelled like soap and sea air and warm man. He read it better than any fucking audiobook I'd ever bought, despite the fact that the damn thing wasn't exactly Shakespeare. He also seemed to read it like he'd read stories aloud his whole life, and I supposed he had—to his sister and his mother. And that only made me think he'd read his kids to sleep, which caused a whole new set of issues for me.

I shifted a bit, reaching for his free hand and linking our fingers together. The need to touch him was overwhelming. Evan took our hands and wrapped his arm around my stomach to hold me closer but barely faltered in his reading. Though, it was *what* he was reading that caused me to pay attention…to everything.

"Jack found that he could barely breathe. Sophia brought him to the brink of his sanity with what she was wearing, how she walked, and her glare of disdain. He was tired of her being pissed at him, tired of arguing with her when no one else dared to argue. He found it exasperating and a turn-on all at the same time, and no matter how hard he tried to fight it, he couldn't keep his eyes from her lips.

"Reaching just past her, he clicked the lock of his office door and stepped closer to her. His hand flat on the door by her head, he leaned in, inhaling the scent of her. Sophia's breathing picked up, but she didn't move from in front of him.

"'Stop fighting me, Sophia. Stop fighting this,' he said, his lips meeting hers, and at first she pushed at him, but when the stack of files in her hands fell to the office floor, he took the opportunity to move in closer."*

Turning my head just a bit, I took in Evan's profile as he read about a heated kiss going from hate and control to something more, something slightly twisted. What was originally distaste for each other slowly changed into a fiery passion that neither could deny.

When Evan's voice wrapped sensually around words like thighs and nipples and erection, my lips pressed to the tempting skin of his neck, just below the sharp edge of his jawline. His smooth voice pushed the words thong and cock out against my skin, and I literally moaned.

"D-Dani…" Evan murmured softly as I tasted his skin, and it was right then that I felt what all this was doing to him. "I'm sor—"

"Don't be," I whispered, reaching up to rake my fingers through his hair. "Is it the book?"

"God, no!"

He laughed softly, his brow furrowing adorably as he shook his head. I took the book from him, closed it, and tossed it to the other side of the bed. I turned a bit in his arms, looking up at him, but decided to try something.

"You don't like the story, Evan?" I asked him, raising up in order to straddle his thighs. I swallowed nervously at the sight of the bulge in his jeans.

"The guy's a jerk," he replied, shrugging a shoulder.

"He is," I agreed, cupping either side of his face and bringing his lips to mine. "He's really just a spoiled brat used to getting his way."

"Guys like that usually do," Evan countered. "I don't get what women see in it."

Grinning, I shifted closer. "Me, either. Then again, I'm partial to sweet and shy." I smiled at the reddening of his cheeks and his nervous chuckle but decided to taste the other side of his neck. "So it's not the subject you dislike, it's the characters themselves?" I asked against his pounding pulse.

"M-Maybe…"

I smirked down at him as he pulled gently at my waist and tugged me closer, and my breath caught at the feeling of him right where I needed him. I was already turned on from the book, his voice, the close proximity of him, so the feel of his erection pressing into me just right almost made my eyes roll back. The most perfect, most amazing sound escaped him when our hips pressed together. The moan was deep, masculine, and sounded so damned needy that it took all I had not to grind down on him.

I brushed my lips across his, whispering, "So…if you hate them, then what's…" I glanced down to where he was so damn hard against his jeans, which in turn pressed against the thin fabric of my sleep shorts when I shifted again.

His eyes closed and his head fell back to the pillow behind him for a moment. "She's…Sophia…She's described…like *you*—bright blue eyes, long, light brown hair. All I can see is you. Jesus, Dani, please...*please* be still."

"Fuck," I hissed, shaking my head. He really might be the most perfect man ever to breathe air on this planet. "I-I-I...I can't be still. Evan, kiss me."

I wanted to tell him to kiss me in order to shut me up from saying something completely stupid or something inappropriate or how utterly in love I was with him. And while that last thing was an amazing feeling, I knew it was too soon.

His eyes were blazing and heated when he opened them, a warm brown that felt like they were piercing through to my soul. He sat up at the same time I moved forward, and we met in the middle with lips and moans, tongues and a light scrape of teeth. Hands threaded into hair—his and mine. But the slow grind of our hips started to build the most delicious friction. Over and over, my hips rolled, and I knew I was chasing an orgasm. Something about using Evan for that made me feel a little guilty but at the same time made it impossible to stop.

"P-Pretty girl, you...You're gonna make me—"

"Come. I know. Me too."

That caught his attention, and his expression changed from pained or guilty to something akin to awe or determination or maybe even slightly deviant, because his lips lifted on one side in a half smile.

"Yeah?"

I nodded fervently. "Just...*please!*"

I'd never felt more adored or more worshiped than I did right then. Evan's gaze was reverent and beautiful. Even better was the feel of his hands...*everywhere*—my back, my thighs, my ass. The latter was what sent me over the edge, because he seemed to guide me just perfectly over him. My forehead fell to his, both of us slightly sweaty, as my entire being shattered. I gripped his T-shirt at the shoulder with one hand and his hair with the other, and he took it all, watching me shake in his arms.

However, that seemed to be all he needed to let go. And oh God, was he ever gorgeous! His eyes closed, his mouth fell open, and the most satisfied sound rumbled out of him. It took him a second or two to catch his breath, and once he did, he looked slightly overwhelmed, so I wrapped my arms around his shoulders, burying my face into his neck. He did the same, and I could feel our hearts pounding against each other.

"That was...I'm..." I laughed a little against his warm skin. "I never want to leave this spot right here."

He huffed a tired chuckle, but his arms wrapped all the way around me. "Okay."

When I finally pushed back a little, he wouldn't quite meet my eyes. "Evan, baby...look at me." Contrition now replaced the heat I'd seen just moments before. "You did...*everything* right. There's nothing to be embarrassed about here." He nodded, his brow furrowing a little, and I leaned in to kiss the wrinkle it caused. "Best orgasm I've ever had."

"Yeah?" he asked, looking rather proud of that statement.

"Oh, yeah," I sang back in a whisper against his lips. "And that was fully clothed. I may not survive it when we're naked." Grinning, I couldn't help but giggle when Evan's cock twitched a bit at that statement. "Well, *someone's* looking forward to that."

"Dani..." He laughed, his forehead falling to my shoulder as he hugged me closer. "Is...Is that what you want?"

I kissed the side of his head, but I wanted to see his face, so I pulled at him until he sat back a bit. "What do *you* want, Evan?"

"You." He shrugged a shoulder. "I...That's it, Dani. Just you."

I kissed his lips, feeling the sting of tears at just how sweet that was. "You *have* me, Evan. I'm not going anywhere."

He smiled, and it was that breathtaking smile. "Good, but um...I probably need to..."

"Oh, right. Reality versus literature. They never talk about sticky underwear in romance novels."

Evan laughed, his cheeks reddening. "Or bodily functions, either," he added, lifting me off his lap as I laughed. He slipped off the bed but bent down to press his lips to mine. "By the way, Dani...You were...beautiful, and that's the reality."

"I...I'm..." I sputtered, because damn, he made it difficult not to just blurt out how I felt about him. "So were you," I teased back in order to stop myself, and I giggled when he rolled his eyes and left my room to clean up.

EVAN

"Ev, you sure I can't give you a ride out to the house?" Wes called as he locked up Sunset Roast. "Seriously…it's not a big deal."

"No, I'm good. My roommate has to catch a late flight out of Panama City, so he said he'd drop me off. I still have to shower and throw a bag together anyway. Tell Dani I'll be there in about an hour."

We'd just busted our asses giving the floors of the place a power washing. The café would be closed the next day for Thanksgiving, but we'd be open super early for Black Friday. Dani had invited me to stay the whole weekend, and it worked out that Wes and I could ride into work together for a couple of shifts.

I shot him a wave as I started toward the dorms. I'd been looking forward to the holiday weekend like crazy. Every time I stayed at the Bishop house, it was getting harder and harder to leave. It wasn't just Dani, though she was the major part of it, but it was that house, that *home* specifically. Leanne and Aunt Tessa treated me like they did their kids. Daniel was amazing to sit up late with and talk to, chatting about books and writing and the options I had. I felt welcomed there, like a member of the family. There was a part of me that should have been sad about that, about the fact that I felt more welcome in their home than the one I'd left in Montana.

And then there was Dani. If her parents knew she sneaked into the guest room when I stayed over, they never said a word. Though I got the impression from Daniel that being surrounded by women made him happier to be ignorant of some things.

The thought of my girl put a stupid smile on my face as I hurried up the stairs to my room. She was all things sexy and sweet and kind, and holy shit, she was patient with me. Between school and work, our time was precious, though we still met in the library between classes. The rare occasion that I'd stay over, we'd lose ourselves in the dark of the guest room. The mere thought of it had my dick twitching.

Ever since we'd lost ourselves in her room that first time reading together, we'd come a bit further. I wanted her to the point of madness most days, but my shyness would sometimes overwhelm me.

The first time I'd touched her breast—even over her clothes—I'd thought I was fucking dreaming.

I walked into my dorm room, shooting a wave to Brett, who was battling aliens on his TV. "Let me grab a shower and throw some clothes in a bag, and we can go."

"Yeah, dude. No problem. *Die, asshole!*" he yelled at the screen.

Grinning, I shook my head and locked myself in the bathroom. Turning on the water, I stripped out of my work clothes. I caught a glimpse of myself in the mirror, my gaze immediately locking on to my scars—the same scars that used to disgust me, made me feel ugly and guilty, now didn't bother me so much. At least, not as much as they used to. All I could see was Dani's fingers on them the last time we'd been alone. She'd never, *ever* made me feel self-conscious about them, even the first time she'd seen them, touched them, and that was when we'd first kissed. She never looked at them with derision; she only saw *me*. Just watching her fingers trail along each scar, only to move on to my stomach, my pecs, and eventually ghosting down to where I'd been hard for her behind my pajama bottoms...

The memory of it alone had me throbbing as I stepped under the shower spray. My forehead hit the tile with a dull *thunk* when I couldn't help but take the pressure off. My hand wrapped around my dick the same way she'd touched me. I'd never felt anything like it in my life, though I was trying like hell to replicate it. She'd kissed my lips, whispering to me, telling me to come, to *let her* make me come. She'd encouraged me to touch her, and just the feel of her body close to mine, the weight of her breast in my hand, and the taste of her kisses had made me lose it all.

"Christ," I hissed, my eyes rolling back into my head as I came hard in the shower. I could practically hear my brother in my head telling me to "take care of business" before seeing Dani because he said it took the edge off. I hoped he was right.

I finished my shower, dressed quickly, and packed my stuff. The ride out to the Bishop house was pretty quick, but the second Brett saw it, he snorted into a laugh.

"Wow," he said through a chuckle. "Now that's some fitting shit for that pretty thing of yours."

Smirking, I gripped his shoulder. "Have a good Thanksgiving, Brett."

"I'm sure you will," he taunted, raising his eyebrows up and down.

Shaking my head, I grabbed my stuff and stepped out of the car. I waved to him as he backed out, but my smile couldn't be stopped when I caught sight of the front porch.

I walked to her, loving the fact that she was just a step or two taller than me, and her lips met mine sweetly.

"Hey," I whispered, smiling up at her.

"Hey yourself. Ready for lots of food and crazy family members for like four days?"

Grinning, I chuckled. "Yes, ma'am, I am."

Chapter Thirteen

EVAN

"There he is!" Leanne sang when Dani and I walked into the kitchen to find the place was buzzing with activity. "I was beginning to worry. With the crazy drivers out there and it being a holiday week-end...Well, anyway...glad you made it, sweet pea."

My brow furrowed, but I leaned into the kiss she gave to my cheek. "My roommate was saving the universe from aliens controlled by a kid in Dubai."

Wes cracked up, glancing up and over his shoulder from the counter. "Nice."

"Well, good. Better video games than idiot drivers," Aunt Tessa said, hugging me from the side with her free arm. The other hand was holding a casserole dish full of what looked like homemade scalloped potatoes. "I'm glad you're here. I could use another strong back. And you'd better bring your A-game appetite tomorrow, kiddo."

I pushed up the sleeves of my shirt and nodded. "Yes, ma'am."

I tried to focus on the tasks they needed done and not the fact that they'd been worried. I'd been just over the hour I'd told Wes I'd be, but I wasn't used to any adult worried about me. Back home, it didn't matter, simply because I'd never gone anywhere but school, and usually my siblings—one or the other—had been with me. I was pretty certain my dad didn't give a damn.

"C'mere, you two," Leanne called, pointing to Dani and me. "You guys can work on these green beans."

She sat us down at the kitchen table, a ginormous pile of fresh green beans in the middle along with a colander.

When I looked to Dani with confusion, she giggled, leaned over, and kissed my lips. "Like this." She snapped off the ends and then broke the bean in the middle, dropping it into the colander. "They get rinsed before cooking."

"Okay." I nodded, getting to work, but glanced up at her. "How many people will be here tomorrow?"

Dani grinned. "Just us, but everyone likes something specific as a traditional food, so we tend to go overboard. And sometimes neighbors or friends will come over to watch football with Dad, but they bring dessert or their own beer or whatever. Don't worry. It's just us, and it's very informal."

"She's right," Aunt Tessa added from across the room. "So don't feel embarrassed if you fall asleep in front of the TV. We all do it."

Laughing, I nodded. "Fair enough."

"You can scratch, burp, and fart all you want, Ev," Wes piped in, wearing a shit-eating grin.

"Umm…" I glanced at Dani, who was glaring at her cousin like he was a disgusting bug. "Okay?"

"God, Evan, you're way too polite sometimes," Leanne said through a laugh, kissing the top of my head on her way by.

I looked to Dani, saying, "Wes isn't that different from Tyler."

Dani giggled again, a sound I absolutely loved to hear. "Will you miss them tomorrow?"

Scrunching up my nose, I snapped a few more beans and nodded my head. "Yes, I miss them, but it's not like we had this," I said, pointing to all the food being put together behind me. "We'd go out for dinner. There's a café in Key Lake that serves Thanksgiving stuff—turkey, stuffing, cranberry sauce. That sort of thing. My dad preferred to work, so it was usually just the three of us."

The kitchen went quiet, and I grimaced toward Dani, who leaned over to kiss my lips. "Don't you dare apologize," she whispered for only me to hear. "Going out to dinner would be a helluva lot less work."

Her sarcasm brought *tsks* from the women and a muttered, "No shit," from Wes.

I grinned and nodded, but I could feel the acceptance around me like one of Leanne's hugs. Even more, I felt Dani's ability to always just...*get it*. Or, at least, she got *me*. Dani had an amazing talent that took the things I thought made me different and spun them into something better.

"Ah, good!" Daniel sang as he walked into the kitchen. "Evan, you made it okay. *And* they've already put you to work, I see."

Grinning, I nodded and snapped the last bean, and Dani got up to take them to the sink.

"Hey, Ev! Help me out really quick," Wes called, and he was struggling with a turkey that seemed to be the size of Dani. When I got to him, I shifted the pan so he could take the bird out of its wrappings. He glared at it. "That fucker's gonna take forty forevers to cook."

"That's why it's going in at the ass-crack of dawn," Aunt Tessa said, leaning to my ear. "Just be glad it's not your alarm going off at like four in the morning to deal with this bird."

Chuckling, I nodded but helped Wes turn it different ways in order to rub spices on it. It wasn't long before Leanne called us ready for the next day. Most everything was prepped to simply be set into the oven at various times. There were still some things to make in the morning, but nothing major, according to the women.

Wes joined Daniel in the living room for sports news. Aunt Tessa and Leanne sat with them but were discussing the coming Christmas break and what they wanted to do for dinner Christmas Day. The thought of being away from the Bishop house made me slightly sad. The thought of being away from Dani for those few weeks made my chest hurt.

I tried to remind myself that I needed to see Faith, that I had to appease my father in order to keep him funding my schooling, and I needed to remind myself that the dorms were closed during the break. As much as I was welcomed in the Bishop home, I couldn't force myself on them for the holidays. However, none of those reminders made my anxiety level lower. I simply didn't want to go home.

It was when I was sitting on the edge of the bed, my hair fisted in my hands, that I heard Dani step into the room and the door click closed behind her.

"Hey…What's wrong, baby?" she asked softly, walking to me, and I found myself surrounded by her arms, with soft kisses pressed to my cheek.

Swallowing thickly, I lifted my gaze to hers. "I…I…I don't want to go home for Christmas."

"Then don't." She smirked proudly and adorably, like she'd solved the problem.

I huffed a light, humorless laugh. "I *have* to, Dani. I just don't *want* to."

"I know," she said softly. "And I wish…" She trailed off, but I waited patiently. "I wish…" She laughed a little. "God, Evan, I wish for a lot of things. I wish I could keep you right here. Always. I wish I could go with you, wrap myself around you like a shield. I wish your sister could come here instead. I wish you never had to go near your dad again. He doesn't deserve your loyalty, your obedience, or your fear. Fuck, he doesn't even deserve your hatred; even that's too much credit for him." She cupped my face, bringing my lips to hers. "But mostly, I wish you understood just how fucking amazing you are, how strong you are, how smart and sweet and kind you are."

"I'm not," I countered. "I don't feel it, anyway."

Her face was solemn, sincere as she took in every inch of mine. "Take your shirt off, baby," she requested, and when my hands hesitated at the hem, she helped me lift it up and off over my head. "You've never lied to me, Evan, so I'm going to ask you if you trust me."

"Yes."

"Good," she replied, coming back to stand between my legs. "Then I want you to remember something, commit it to memory. Write it down in your journal. Tattoo it on your skin. Something, *anything* to help you remember…You didn't do anything fucking wrong, Evan. You were just a kid. You were brave and strong. You did exactly as your mother told you, and you saved your brother's life. Now, all that being said…If others can't understand that, if they don't see that, then it's *their fucking problem*. Not yours."

I opened my mouth to argue, but she straddled my lap and sat herself down, gripping the back of my neck to make me listen.

"If you want to take the responsibility of procrastinating on your homework, then okay, I can give you that. Personally, I think it's a childhood rite of passage to be lazy with school stuff, but that's my opinion. *But*…you weren't in control of the vehicle, you weren't the owner of the dog that darted out into the road, and you weren't in control of the goddamn weather, Evan. It was an accident.

"Somewhere, deep inside here—" she tapped my temple, only to place her hand on my bare chest "—and here, you know this. You know all of this. What you don't know is that you've already paid enough for a forgotten middle school English assignment. You're done. Finished. No more. Not at school, with me, or inside this house." She placed her hand flat over my scars, meeting my gaze. "A hundred and twenty-something stitches, your brother's busted knee, and the loss of the only parent who gave a shit…You're done, baby. Seven years is enough."

When I dropped my gaze down to our laps, she lifted my face up by my chin. "Dani, I…"

Shaking her head, she said, "When you go home, I need you to remember this shit. I want you to feel it. If you want, I'll call you every damn day you're gone and remind you. I want you to understand that when he's pissed off and yelling or making you feel low, it's *his* problem, not yours, and you no longer have to listen to it."

"You don't know him, Dani…"

"I don't *need*, nor do I *want* to know him. What I know is no real parent would say or do the things he's done to you. They wouldn't alienate their baby in the family or in society. They wouldn't punish them for *fucking surviving*." She raised an eyebrow at me. "I don't give a damn about his funding for your school. That's what student loans are for, so fuck him and his checkbook. I care about *you*. That's it. Where some people would've allowed this shit to destroy their soul, your soul is perfect and beautiful and loving, and I think you're amazing. So even if you don't believe it yourself, I'll believe it enough for the both of us."

"I…I…" I sputtered, pulling her closer and closing my eyes.

I wanted to tell her I cared about her too. I wanted to scream that I loved her, that I was so in love with her I could barely see straight. But the panic seized up my throat and stole my words. I wanted to tell her that she was more than anything I thought I knew when I first saw her in the library, that she'd become my whole world, but more than that, she'd given me a sense of real family—how things *should* have been.

"I've said too much, Evan," she surmised. "I'm sorry."

I huffed a laugh, letting my forehead fall to hers. "No, never, pretty girl. You always say just the right things." I opened my eyes to see her clear, worried ones. "I should probably thank Wes for his messy filing system. I owe him for shoving me into a room with you."

Dani cracked up into the most adorable snorting giggle. "Don't you dare! I thought about that too, but it'll only encourage his behavior." She pressed her lips to mine. "We'll just keep that to ourselves, yeah?"

"Okay."

Grinning at her, I now understood what she'd meant time and time again when she'd threatened to kiss me stupid, because at that moment, I wanted to devour her. I wanted to touch her, please her, show her how I felt, because words were failing me.

I'd read stories where the sexual tension in a room was described as a crackling spark, where the lovers could feel it on their skin, in their hearts, crawling in and around them. I'd never believed a damn word of it until that moment. My lips barely brushed across Dani's, and it seemed like we were sharing the same breath. The hairs on my arms seemed to stand up with it.

"Evan..."

I nodded, unable to address Dani's question. Because my name had come from her like she was asking something. What made my whole being snap to attention was her touch to my skin—across my shoulders, down my arms, back up my chest and around my neck—and her lips met mine almost roughly.

I lost track of anything outside of her lips on mine. It seemed my body took over, and somehow we'd managed to entangle ourselves in the middle of my bed. The feel of her fingers on my skin, her legs wrapped around my thighs, and her tongue touching, twisting, tasting with my own—it was all I could see, feel, hear.

Rolling just a little, I pushed back to see her beneath me, and I swallowed nervously. She was simply beautiful. It didn't matter that she was in her normal nighttime shorts and T-shirt and she rarely wore makeup, but seeing the flushed look to her cheeks that I'd given her made me start shaking my head slowly.

"I...Dani, I want..." My gaze trailed away from her perfect face, and I couldn't stop from reaching out to trail my fingers across that blush, down her neck to as low as the T-shirt would let me.

She glided her hands up either side of my ribcage, finally cupping my face. "Evan, look at me."

My eyes snapped from where her nipples were hard and pressing against the fabric of her shirt back to hers.

"When we're here, like this, I want to hear you, no matter what you're thinking. It's just me. And believe me, whatever it is that's going through that gorgeous head of yours, I'm probably all for right about now."

Grinning, I nodded. "I want to…touch you."

"We are touching," she teased a little, leaning up to kiss me. "Where, baby? Tell me."

"Everywhere."

She sobered a bit but then reached down to take off her shirt. I'd touched her skin, her breasts beneath her clothes, but I hadn't actually seen her. The trust she had in me was amazing, but her patience was endless, because she knew I needed a second.

Her skin was beautiful, smooth, with light tan lines that could be seen in the areas where a bikini would cover her. Her stomach was flat, but she wasn't super skinny, just perfectly curved where it looked so good on her. Her breasts, though, were mesmerizing. They weren't big, but they weren't small either, and the nipples were hard, which made me meet her gaze.

"You're so…beautiful."

I shook my head in awe as, with a shaky hand, I reached out to cup her. Her slight intake of breath made me look back at her face, but her back arched a little as my thumb brushed across that tightly peaked nipple. Lightly, I trailed across her chest to the other one to do it again, and I received the same reaction. Feeling braver, I left my hand flat, gliding down the middle to her stomach, smiling when it tensed beneath my touch.

"Ticklish?" I asked in a whisper.

"Evan," she whispered back, but a giggle laced my name. "Yeah… Yes! Okay…a little."

She writhed slightly as I skimmed up her side and then back to her chest. My hand wandered closer and closer to the waistband of her shorts, across her hip, and when I hesitated just a little, Dani's hand covered my own, slipping us down between her legs. I gasped at the soft, sexy moan that escaped her, watching her face as she pressed my hand, my fingers where she needed them. I could feel the heat, so much heat, coming from her that I couldn't help but lean down to kiss her.

When she pressed down on my hand again, I broke from our kiss to watch what she was doing but then looked back to her face.

"Dani…show me what to do, what you like."

She nodded, guiding our hands back up, and then she locked her gaze on my face as we slipped beneath the edge of her shorts. I wasn't prepared for the feel of her. I'd read about it, and my brother had been right about my computer and what I'd watched, but the reality was so different. What was hot or sexy in fiction was emotionally overwhelming in person. I wanted so badly to make her feel good, to give her what she'd given to me more than once.

My forehead dropped to her temple when she guided my middle finger around. I wasn't completely ignorant as to what it was—her clit—and she swirled our fingers around, gliding back down to her entrance.

When I moved my hand on my own, Dani's head fell back a bit as she hissed, "Oh, Christ…"

Pressing my lips against her cheek, I whispered, "Here?"

She nodded vehemently as her hips started to rise up off the bed. I was on my own when she pulled her hand away in order to hold on to my shoulder.

"Right there!" she breathed, grasping my face and holding me tightly. "Don't stop, don't stop. Please…"

I did exactly what she told me, and I watched her entire being with fascination—her breathing, her tense muscles, and her barely there kisses, not to mention the place where my hand disappeared into her shorts. There was warmth and wetness and heat. There was smooth skin and hair, but mostly there was twitching beneath my touch, and soon it started to seize up all around me. All of it, including my name being breathed against my lips, made my dick throb behind my sleep pants. She was gorgeous, but she was sweaty and smiling lazily too. It was the best thing I'd ever seen.

Smiling at her, I asked, "You okay?"

"Oh, God, yes," she sighed, reaching for me, for the edge of my pants, and I swallowed thickly when she touched me like I'd tried to recreate in the shower earlier. "So hard, Evan."

Nodding, I fell back to the bed, and she shifted with me, looming over my face while she worked me over with her hand. I wanted to speak, but I couldn't. I'd been so hard for her while touching her that her hands were rendering me speechless. I couldn't think, especially when she pulled my pants down just enough so I could see what she was doing to me. She pushed away, keeping her gaze on me, but my breathing picked up more and more as her mouth neared the tip of my dick.

"Oh, shit, Dani…If you…I won't…" I barely made sense to myself, so I had no idea if she understood what I was trying to tell her.

Her smile was soft and sweet, but her breath ghosted across my skin when she replied, "The whole point is to come, baby. It's okay."

It didn't take much to make me lose my mind. Her mouth was wet and hot, and her tongue was evil, I was pretty convinced. And as soon as she started to sink down over me, I had to fight not to explode immediately, though I didn't last as long as I'd hoped. However, it was longer than it had been in the shower.

I tried to push her back, but she kept going—up, down, swirling her tongue over and over—until I felt the telltale shocks in my belly, the tightening of my balls, and my breathing stop. My eyes rolled back, and I lost it completely. I felt a little bad when, after giving me a moment, she took a second to put me back into my pants.

"Damn, I feel boneless," I said, grinning when she crawled back up my body to snuggle closer, and I noted that the feel of her bare chest against mine was amazing and comforting. But I rolled to face her. "I…You…You're the best thing to ever happen to me," I whispered to her, suddenly too serious, but I couldn't help it.

Her smile was sweet, but her eyes watered a little.

"Seriously, you are. I…I was freaking the hell out, but suddenly you're half-naked in my bed, and I've forgotten what the hell I was panicking over."

Her laughter was adorable and musical, and she kissed my lips. "Then my work here is done, handsome." She pulled back a bit, reaching up to rake her fingers through my hair. "I'm…I don't want to go back to my room just yet. Can we read together just a little while?"

"Oh, yeah, definitely." I reached for our latest book we were reading together. We'd finished the romance and moved on to a classic. Dani had never read any Alexandre Dumas, so we were slowly working our way through *The Count of Monte Cristo*.

She put her shirt back on, but we settled into our normal reading position—with her between my legs and me reading over her shoulder.

"*Chapter thirteen,*" I read to her. "*An Italian Scholar. Dantes threw himself into the arms of his new friend...*"

Chapter Fourteen

EVAN

"Go, go, go!" Wes and Daniel whisper-yelled at the football game, and it ended in groans of disappointment when the player was tackled.

Dinner had been amazing, and I was so stuffed I could barely keep my eyes open. Dani and I had stayed up late. My face heated with the memories of what we'd done. We had also ended up reading into the wee hours, and I was pretty sure it was because neither of us had been willing to be separated just yet.

The kitchen was cleaned up, leftovers put away, and Aunt Tessa and Leanne were out back on the porch with hot cups of coffee.

However, it was the sleeping girl with her head on my chest who kept me right where I was on the living room sofa. I didn't give a damn about the football game, and it wouldn't have taken much for me to fall asleep with her, but I was enjoying the simple act of holding her.

"You know, Ev, you *can* move her," Wes said softly with a chuckle to his tone.

"No, no…" I laughed, shaking my head and running my hand down her hair. "She's fine."

Daniel snorted, drained his beer, and stood. "I'm not sure she's ever made it past halftime, but you don't have to be her pillow, son."

Grinning, I shrugged. "She's helped me more times than I can count, so assuming the role of the pillow is an easy thing," I stated honestly.

Wes chuckled and Daniel squeezed my shoulder as he left for the kitchen to grab another beer. My eyes started to drift closed as the game's white-noise came back on. My nose was nestled in Dani's hair, and her hand was gripping the sleeve of my thermal shirt. The weather outside was bright, clear, and crisp. To me, it wasn't cold, but to the native Floridians, it was perfect Thanksgiving Day weather.

Sounds and light started to fade until the feel of my phone vibrating in my jeans pocket shocked me back awake. I shifted as best I could in order not to disturb Dani. And I smiled a little at the sight of my brother's face on the screen.

"Hey, Ty," I answered softly, and I had to pull the phone away from my ear due to the yelling and noise coming through the damn thing.

"I'm so fucking done, Evan!" he growled over the line.

I glanced up to Wes, motioning to help me with Dani. I carefully slipped out from the sofa, and Wes settled her onto a pillow before I stepped out the front door onto the porch.

The yelling didn't stop, but I could barely understand what he was saying. "Ty! Tyler, slow down. What happened?" I asked, gripping my hair as I paced back and forth.

"What do you *think* fucking happened? He's such an ass, baby brother. And without you there, without being able to keep you under thumb, he's taking his fuckery out on everyone else. Oh, I knew...I just fucking *knew* he'd set his sights on Faith eventually."

My eye twitched and my temper sparked. "What'd he do?"

The phone rattled, and suddenly Jasmine's voice came over the line. "Hey, Evan."

"Jasmine, what's...what's going on? Did he...Is he...?"

My worst fear was that he'd start in on the degrading bullshit, the physical punishments that never ended, or ground her until she had no social life or friends. Tyler and I gladly took all those things as kids in order to keep her safe, because she'd been the one good thing in the house, the one person who'd taken care of us when we'd come home after the wreck. She'd been the one person who'd had nothing to do with any of it.

"Evan, I need you to stay calm. And I need you to listen. Faith is *fine*. However, she's grounded all to hell and back. He...took away everything—car, phone, makeup, clothes...Fuck, he went into her room and trashed her posters, her closet, her bookcase. He even yanked the home phone out of the wall."

My mouth fell open. I knew Faith was sassy. I knew she was braver than Tyler and me any damn day, but I couldn't fathom what she'd said or done to make him that mad.

"Why?"

"Because he found out about her applying to Edgewater...and about your Dani."

My chest squeezed tight, and I had to practically fall down into the porch swing. "Okay...and?"

The phone fumbled again, and Tyler's angry voice came back on the line. "I'm not going back, Ev. I can't. You have no idea how close I came to killing him when he called my fiancée a fucking whore. I refuse to let him control us anymore, 'cause that's why he's so pissed—he can't control us once we're spread as far away as possible. As soon as Faith is out of that house, he's shit out of luck, man, and he fucking knows she's the only fucking reason we're still in contact. I packed up what I wanted out of my room. I can't. I won't. I will go to jail, little brother, I'm not even kidding a little fucking bit."

"Shit," I hissed, and I nodded because I completely understood it. I couldn't bear the mere thought of our father saying something to Dani, to the one person who meant more to me than my own life. I'd also caught the word fiancée, but now wasn't the time to ask. My brother was too pissed.

"Okay, I'll deal with it when I go home for Christmas," I stated, simply because there wasn't much choice in the matter. There was a part of me that already felt numb at the prospect of it.

"Faith said you'd come anyway," Tyler sighed, and I caught movement in my peripheral vision. "You don't have to go back, Evan."

Glancing up, I saw Daniel standing there, a shoulder leaning on the porch railing post. His face looked worried as he tried to cover it up by running his fingers over his beard.

Dani had told me that she'd told her father about the wreck, my mother, my dad, so I rubbed my face and sighed. "I can't *not* go back, Ty. Not now. Now that he's aiming Faith's way. No. I can't do that to her. If I don't go home, he'll be ten times as pissed off. I'd rather just…face it. Maybe it'll take the pressure off her, yeah?"

"Damn, baby brother…"

"Just call me if you hear anything. Otherwise, I'll be back in Key Lake in a couple weeks."

Tyler promised he'd check on Faith as best he could. Even without the phone, there was still e-mail that Faith could access at school or the library. When the call ended, I sat forward on the swing, gripping my hair.

I felt the swing shake when Daniel took a seat next to me, and I glanced over at him.

"You okay, son?"

I shrugged a shoulder and then finally nodded. "I don't have a choice. I knew I was going back, and I knew I had to check on my baby sister…" I trailed off.

"We all have choices, Evan," he said softly. "Every choice we make affects everything and everyone around us. Then, there are things out of our control, like what kind of family we're born into or the members who surround us. You can't pick your blood relatives, son."

Snorting humorlessly, I nodded.

"However, you can surround yourself with people who treat you better than family. I've learned that family doesn't necessarily contain the family tree. You get what I'm telling you?"

"Yes, sir, but it wouldn't be right, wouldn't *feel* right abandoning her. He's pissed because she wants to come here to be near me. He's pissed because I asked my brother and sister to keep Dani a secret from him, for *this reason*. He's…"

"Your father is emotionally and verbally abusive, Evan," Daniel stated so firmly that my head snapped up to look at him. He was very clearly angry. "Maybe even a touch physical, but…He uses what you love against you. He's probably done that his whole life, maybe even to your mother, but I'm just guessing there. However, he's using your sister, using your brother's fiancée — sorry, he was loud enough I could hear him — against you."

"S'okay," I muttered, gazing blindly at the wood porch floor. "I don't know what to do. She's my sister. She…she took care of me and my brother a-after the car accident, and she was only ten then! She's always done it. I just…"

"Family—*good family*—is important. I'm not saying you're to abandon them, not at all, but there will come a time when those choices I mentioned will come into play. You have to decide what's best *for you*, son. You came to Florida for a reason, and I think that was an amazing and very intelligent first step of proving yourself to be a man, of separating yourself from something that in all reality could've made you a completely different person, but you are you. You're a good man, Evan. You're smart and kind. If you weren't, then I wouldn't have my daughter coming to me that first dinner saying she was keeping you."

Grinning, I shook my head.

"You've won her heart, which is saying something, but you've won yourself a different type of family too." He chuckled a little. "My wife wants to adopt you, my sister thinks you're the most adorable thing she's ever seen, and my nephew treats you like a brother. But it's my little girl who means the world to me, and she's decided that you're it. You're here, and you're not going anywhere, so that means you, your well-being, and even your siblings are now part of the equation." His lips twitched a little. "In order to keep *her* happy, I need to keep *you* happy, not that I wouldn't, Evan, because you're a damn good kid, despite what you've been told or what you've come to believe."

"I don't know what to do," I sighed. "I don't want to go; the idea makes me crazy, but I can't...I *have* to and..."

Daniel gazed out over the front yard for a moment, finally looking back to me. "No one said you had to stay the whole Christmas break. And no one said you had to face things alone. That guest room is yours whenever you wish, and Dani..."

Swallowing thickly, I nodded. "I know, but I...I..." I sighed, looking over at him. "I know she wants to go with me, but I won't...I *can't* do that. I can't bring her near him." Daniel nodded, but I went on. "I moved here to get away from him, but I...I also knew I had to be there for my sister *at least* until she graduated high school. I'm...I'm *hoping* this is the last time. I...I don't know what I'll do if he stops helping with school, or even what'll happen come summer, but I...I can't do it anymore."

"Good for you, son." He gripped my shoulder. "Stupid son of a bitch..." He shook his head slowly. "I'll never understand it. Your kids should be the people you treat the best, with the most patience, with the most love, because they're who will be taking care of you when you're old and pissing the bed."

Chuckling, I nodded, but then I shrugged a shoulder.

Both of us glanced in through the window when an explosion of curse words and name calling filtered out to us.

"Oh, hell," Daniel groaned. "Wes found the can of whipped cream."

"You asshat!" I heard Dani's voice snap and then the pounding sounds of footsteps and laughter.

Daniel chuckled again but stood from the swing, facing me. "When Dani brought you to dinner that first night here and told me she was keeping you, I asked her then about the holidays. It worries me to no end to send you home to a rough situation. I don't like it—as a father or a teacher. I don't see how a man could blame his child for something that was clearly an accident. But...I also understand your loyalty to your brother and sister." He sighed, shoving his hands into the front pockets of his pants. "I understand, too, your need to protect Dani, so..." He grimaced, shaking his head. "I would...really like it if you kept in touch while you were gone. I don't care if it's Dani, Wes, or even myself, but..."

"I'd planned on it, sir," I told him. "Dani made me make the same promise."

"Of course she did." Daniel laughed, and we both looked up to see a disheveled, grumpy-looking, slightly messy Dani step out onto the porch. "Oh, shit," Daniel mumbled, shaking his head. "Did you kill him, baby girl?"

"No, but he's currently taking a shower. An entire can of whipped cream may or may not have ended up in the back of his boxers."

Snorting to a loud laugh as Daniel squeezed his eyes closed and shook his head, I opened my arms for her. Her disgruntled expression was just as adorable as the rest of her, but I tried my damnedest not to laugh when I reached up to wipe away a smear of fluffy, white whipped cream from her cheek and her nose.

Her fierce expression didn't change as she glanced between us. "What happened? What's wrong?"

Taking a deep breath, I said, "Apparently Thanksgiving at the Shaw residence went...awry."

She narrowed her eyes, glancing again between me and her father. "That's it! You're not going! He's not going, Dad!"

Smiling, I shook my head. "I have to go, pretty girl," I stated as calmly as I could. "I'm the reason things went crazy."

She sighed impatiently, her nostrils flaring with her temper as I told her what had happened—about Dad finding out that Faith had applied to Edgewater, about Tyler and Faith keeping my relationship with Dani from Dad, and about how his temper was now focused on my little sister.

"Then I'm going with you."

"No." I shook my head. "I'd give you the world, Dani, that's no lie, but I can't put you in that situation. I won't." I was still shaking my head when Daniel shifted a bit behind her. "If I *don't* go, my dad will be even angrier, and who knows what he'll say or do...to any of us. If *you* come with me, he will..." I sighed, locking my gaze on Daniel for just a moment. "Dani, he'll use you against me. He'll focus on you to...Oh, God, if he said the things to you that he said to Jasmine, I..." I groaned, gripping my hair with one hand and touching her chin with my other. "Please, don't ask that of me."

Dani's sweet face was a mix of hurt and worry, her eyes watering a bit.

"Don't, please...Don't cry. You have no idea how badly I want to take you, but I know what's waiting."

"What will he do?" Daniel asked from his perch on the porch railing.

"Lots of yelling." I smiled ruefully, tapping my temple. "I've learned to tune it out. But I imagine the attic needs cleaning and wood needs chopping. I'm sure there will be things that need to be repaired."

"He's getting worse, Evan," Dani stated.

"He's losing them, and he knows it," Daniel sighed, standing up straight and folding his arms across his chest. "I don't like it, son. It feels wrong sending you back."

"It's a month—not even," I countered, shrugging a shoulder. I wanted to tell them a month was nothing compared to the seven years I'd endured, but Dani would most likely lose it.

Daniel let out a deep breath, pushing off the railing to go back inside and muttering about idiots raising good kids.

"Evan, please."

Looking back to her, I shook my head. "I can't, Dani. There's a part of me that...shuts down when he starts his shit, and I've learned to deal with it. It's a lot of hard work and a lot of yelling. If you're there, I…I can't…My brother almost killed him," I said, grimacing at the thought. "And honestly, my dad isn't worth the trouble that would bring."

Dani glared at me with a skeptical expression on her face, but she reached up to cup my face. "What's the real reason I can't go, Evan?"

Studying her face, I took a deep breath and shifted on the swing. "C'mere," I whispered, pulling her down onto the seat and wrapping my arms around her shoulders. I started to push the swing gently with my foot and pressed my lips to her temple, saying, "When I came here to Glenhaven, all I wanted…all I asked for was a new start. I needed to get away from my dad, from Key Lake, and from all the rumors and whispers I'd grown up with, but I also wanted to be someone different." Smiling against her hair, I chuckled a bit. "Problem with that is…I'm me. I can't change who I am. I came here anxious and afraid of water, shy and scared, running from my problems. I'm still all those things, but instead of an escape, instead of simply going to school, I've found…*more*. You…Jesus, Dani…You have no idea what you've done." I laughed softly into her hair, which was a bit sticky from Wes's prank, but I didn't give a shit. "You've given me… *everything*." I leaned on the last word, reminding her of our first kiss.

She turned to look at me, and I kissed her lips to keep her from saying anything.

"From the first time I saw you, the first time I spoke to you, you've shown me what things should be, *could be*," I explained, trying to brush her hair from her face, but I smirked when it wouldn't cooperate. "You, pretty girl, are my home now. This house, those people inside, and you…I need this to come back to, and I also need it to stay far away from Key Lake, Montana. I need the two polar opposites to stay separated."

Dani was shaking her head, tears welling up in her eyes. "I get that, baby. I do. Really. But if you…if you *need me*, then I can't promise to stay away. Could you?"

Smiling, I kissed her again. "No." Sighing deeply, I trailed my finger down her beautiful face. "You remember our first lunch after our kiss, after we became…more? When you asked me about going home? You were worried to even ask about it, but do you remember what I told you then?"

"That you have to appease your dad to keep him paying for school," she provided, but I shook my head.

"No, not that part."

Her brow furrowed as tears coursed down her face. "That he can't hurt you? That the only people who could hurt you are your s-siblings and..."

"My siblings and you. Exactly. It's true, Dani," I told her, shrugging a shoulder, but I wiped away her tears with my thumbs. "Please, trust me. I am well aware of where I stand with him. I know he blames me. I know that for a while, I blamed myself, but I also know that no matter what he says, does, or whatever, it can't touch what I've found here. Coming here, despite his anger and protests, has been the *very best decision* I've ever made." I smiled at the truth of that. "And I wouldn't have come here without my sister's encouragement, because I almost gave in to him. So...that being said, I have to go. I have to go home at least this last time until she's free of him. I owe her that...for...protecting my relationship with you..." I trailed off as my mind made a connection.

"Evan?"

I opened my mouth but shook my head as I realized something. "Wait a second..."

I pressed a kiss to her lips and stood from the swing. I started to pace, thinking back to the last conversation I'd had with my dad, when he'd told me not to weasel out of coming home for Christmas break. It was the same conversation where he'd told me I'd fall for the first girl who "got my dick wet." I narrowed my eyes because he'd already known. He'd been goading me then, but I'd ignored it.

"He knew," I whispered, turning to lock gazes with Dani. "He... He already knew about you. So...why's he pissed now?"

"Because he's an asshole?"

Chuckling, I nodded in agreement but knelt in front of her. "No, seriously. He had to have figured out...The phone bill. He's always saying he knows how much Faith, Tyler, and I talk, because he pays the bill, but he must've seen your number. He already knew."

"Which means he's baiting you, baby!" she hissed at me, her eyes welling up again.

"Maybe," I soothed her, "but it still boils down to this...If I *don't* go, he'll be even more pissed. I can't...I owe it to my sister to at least... *share* this shit with her. She's taken care of me since Mom died. I don't want to go, you know that—you saw that last night—but it's the right thing to do."

Dani kissed my lips hard, and she tasted salty and sweet with her tears and the remainder of whipped cream. "Okay, then...compromise with me, Evan Shaw," she commanded, and I nodded for her to continue. "You will talk to me or text with me the entire time you're gone. And...and...at night, we're still reading to each other..."

"Easiest deal I could make, Dani."

"And..." she added, raising an eyebrow at me. "You...Evan, I'm not kidding. If I can't...if I don't hear from you, I'm coming to you. And I'll bring Dad or Wes or someone with me." When I started to argue, she kissed me again. "That is not negotiable. Don't even argue."

I could see from her determined expression that she couldn't be swayed, so I nodded in agreement. It would be easy to keep in touch with her, so I didn't see a problem. I also knew that my dad's work schedule would give me time without any interruption.

"I won't argue, Dani, but I've got three weeks before I leave, and I'd...I'd really like to just...not worry about it. I'm gonna miss you enough as it is, and we've got tests coming and my shifts at the café, so can we just...be us, do what we've always done?" I asked her. It was as honest as I could be without begging her to run away with me, to hide from it all.

I wanted to tell her—in absolute detail—how much I loved her, but the words were too important, so I was pretty sure I'd have to write them down first. As I reached up to touch her face, I realized just how much she'd changed me. Maybe it wasn't change but just making me feel more...accepted, and I wasn't even scared of telling her; I just wanted to find the right words.

"Please?" I asked in a whisper.

Dani's smile was warm and sweet, as were those beautiful blue eyes of hers.

"Anything, Evan, but I need a shower first. Then I want to find out if Edmund and Faria escape the prison!"

"Yes, ma'am." Chuckling, I kissed her, loving that she was enjoying *The Count of Monte Cristo*, but in all reality, it was fun reading with her. It made every book—even that ridiculous yet sexy romance—that much more...Just *more*. And I'd take it, because I wanted as much *good* and *more* as I could get before I left Florida in three weeks.

Chapter Fifteen

EVAN

"Take your break, kiddo," Susan said, ruffling my hair on her way back to the front counter, but she stopped and cupped my face. "Gonna miss you when you're gone."

"Why? 'Cause you got more shifts?" I teased her, jerking when she poked my side, and I almost spilled the sugar I was refilling.

"Well, there is that, but..." She glared playfully. "You know, I'm old enough to be your...very awesome young aunt," she said, grinning when I laughed. "You're a sweet kid, Evan. I'd warn you all about being safe and being a good boy, but I don't think I have to. I'd warn you not to hurt Dani, but I damn well know I don't have to do that, so just...hurry back, okay?"

When I nodded, she kissed my cheek and ruffled my hair again, and I remembered her saying something about her own father being a problem. "Hey, Susan?" I asked, putting the lid back on the sugar. She stopped before heading out front, and I said, "You...Y-You said your dad was..."

"Toxic, Evan. He was bad news when I was a kid."

Nodding, I tilted my head at her. "You ever see him now?"

"See him? No. Though I do call him every few months or so to make sure he hasn't drunk himself to death or…forgotten to pay his rent, so…He's an asshole, but I'm all he has left, despite the fact that we can barely stand each other." She walked back to me, tapping my chin gently. "You can't pick your family."

Grimacing, I nodded. It seemed to be a repetitive statement surrounding me lately. "Yeah, Dani's dad said the same thing."

"They love you. Hell, kid, we all do, so if things get shitty, remember that. Remember who's in your corner here. You live *here* now, not back there. You're just going back for a visit. Home is where this is," she added, tapping my chest to indicate my heart. "And I am pretty sure you're leaving it behind."

She shot me a wink when I nodded. "Break, Evan."

I put the sugar away and restocked the back of the counter before grabbing my backpack. This was my last shift at Sunset Roast until after the new year. I was spending the weekend at the Bishop house, and Wes and Dani would be driving me to the airport Monday morning. The closer it came, the more nervous I was becoming, and I wanted to soak up as much of everyone here as I could, but the mere idea of leaving Dani had me pulling out my journal.

I lost myself to my words to Dani as the sun started to dip. I paused at one point, flipping through the filled pages from the very beginning and shaking my head at just how different things were from the start. And they were all to Dani—from that first letter to my Library Girl to my heart being scrawled out on the most recent page. So much had changed. *I* had changed. And I wasn't sure to whom I owed it all: my sister for making sure I came here; Dani for just being that sweet, beautiful thing she was; or was it me? I didn't know where to place the value, because everyone, all of it, played some sort of role in it. Despite how badly I didn't want to leave, I had no choice, but I had to figure out how to push through the next few weeks. I needed to cling to the good that was *here* in order to survive the stuff back home.

"You're not allowed in here," Meg stated, pulling me out of my head, my writing.

Glancing up, I narrowed my eyes at Brad's pompous grin as he shrugged a shoulder at her. Susan was pulling her phone out of her pocket, sending off a quick text, and it was most likely to Wes, who had left the café to pick up an order from the bakery. As I glanced

up at the clock and stuffed my journal back into my bag, I expected
Wes back any second, but I wasn't sure how this guy would behave.

I stood from the booth, shouldering my backpack, and stepped
behind the counter, coming face-to-face with Brad on the other side
of the register.

"You gotta go, Brad. Wes banned you from here," I told him
as calmly as I could, keeping my tone low because there were still
customers in a few chairs.

A slow, humorless grin spread over his face. "Well, if it isn't
garbage boy...How's Dani?"

The smile I gave him back was real, and I wasn't sure where the
words came from, but I said, "She's fantastic, and I'd tell her you
asked about her, but she doesn't really like you, so...she probably
won't care. You still have to go."

Meg and Susan giggled, and I waited for Brad to move, but he
shook his head. He tossed a look behind him, and I saw the two
girls from the library that day Dani had pushed Brad away—the
blonde and the redhead. I honestly didn't want to know how that
worked or even how they were possibly all together. Though I now
knew their names from class as Yvonne and Brigit.

"I'm just trying to get my girls some coffee, asshole."

"Oh, well...*they* can stay. You can't," I stated, shrugging a shoulder.

I wasn't sure what this guy's problem was with me, except maybe
his sour grapes over Dani, but he leaned forward. "Tell me, garbage
boy...Is Dani as freaky in the sheets as I think she is?"

There was movement behind him, and I smirked at who had
heard him ask that question. Wes sidled silently up next to him, a
heavy hand reaching toward his shoulder, but it was the smaller
figure I pointed to.

"Well, I'd say ask her, but I'm not sure she'll answer you," I ground
out through gritted teeth. However, my hands fisted at my sides as
I shook to keep from hitting him. I was used to people picking on
me, but *no one* disrespected Dani.

Dani's face was a gorgeous, heady mix between pissed off and
amused. When Brad saw that she was standing there, she laughed
outright in his face. "You'll never know, Brad."

Wes's hand finally landed heavily on his shoulder, making him
jump, and when he turned Brad around to escort him out, the two
girls had abandoned him. "Brad, the next time you show up in my

coffee shop, I'll have you arrested for trespassing. If you think I'm kidding, try me." Gripping him even harder on the way toward the door, he added, "And if I ever hear you talk about my cousin that way again, then fuck the arrest. I'll simply beat the shit out of you."

Snorting, I shook my head. I had to admit that Wes reminded me of Tyler more and more, but I looked to Dani. "Sorry, pretty girl. I tried to get him out of here before you got here," I told her, but my voice was terse and a bit harsh.

She grinned, leaned across the counter, and kissed my lips. "You're kinda sexy when you're angry."

Laughing, I shook my head and rolled my eyes. "Yeah, that's me." Turning to Susan, I said, "I'm back from break, but I need to file a few things in Wes's office before we start closing up."

"Yeah, yeah, kiddo. We're fine. We'll get you if we need you."

My temper was still a bit on edge as I walked to Wes's office. I knew Dani was behind me, and once we were inside the room, I heard the door clicked closed. After setting my backpack down in one of his chairs, I grabbed the stack of papers out of the inbox and started to file. Turning back to the desk, I found myself nose-to-nose with Dani. She'd moved the inbox and plopped herself up on top.

"Dani..."

"*Am* I a freak in the sheets?" she asked, and I could see her amusement, her teasing, and her warm gaze just about everywhere. "Only you would know..."

The laugh that escaped me came out like a bark, and I sighed deeply, the anger at Brad dissipating almost immediately. I walked into her embrace, her legs and arms enveloping me completely.

Inhaling deeply the scent of her, I nuzzled her hair, the crook of her neck, all while she dropped kisses to my cheek, my jaw, my throat. "I think you're beautiful in my sheets," I told her, grinning when her giggle shook us both.

She pushed back and cupped my face, kissing my lips. "Ditto, baby." Studying me with an adorably curious expression, she smirked when I raised an eyebrow her way. "I was just trying to remember if I've ever seen you mad, Evan. And I think that was the first time."

I shrugged, shaking my head and reaching around her for the next stack of papers to file. "He was saying disgusting things about you."

"He called you *garbage boy*," she argued, sounding affronted.

"He disrespected you. I don't give a damn about how he feels about me, but...*no one*..." I slammed a drawer of the filing cabinet closed after putting a page in its correct folder, spinning to face her. "No one can talk about you like that."

Dani tilted that gorgeous head of hers at me, beckoning me back between her legs, and I went willingly. "Well, I appreciate the...chivalry, Evan." She smiled, reaching up to rake her fingers through my hair when I chuckled, but her smile fell quickly. "This weekend will fly by," she whispered, wrinkling her nose when her voice broke a little.

My forehead dropped to hers, and I nodded against it when she asked if I had my things packed back at the dorm.

"Can we just...read tonight?" she asked against my lips, and I nodded again, smiling a bit. "Good. I just...I want to hear your voice."

"I'll read to you anytime, Dani. I swear it."

It really was my favorite thing to do with her. We'd kiss and make out, though we hadn't taken that big step, and that was okay because she was leading us. The physical side of our relationship was phenomenal, but to hold her in my arms afterward and read to her was the best feeling. She made me feel important, like I was taking care of her like she did for me. I could never find the words to tell her how I felt, so I showed her in every way possible—with my kisses and my hands and by reading to her.

And all of that reminded me of my journal, and a plan formed in my head. Pulling back, I smiled at her, kissing her softly, deeply, but ended it before we lost ourselves in her cousin's office.

"Dying to find out if Edmund finds the treasure?" I teased her because we only read together when we could, so we were slowly working through *The Count of Monte Cristo.*

"Well *yeah!* I hope he gets back at all those fuckers who screwed him over!"

Grinning at how adorable she was, I nodded, grabbing the last stack of papers. "Yes, ma'am." I chuckled and finished up the filing. "C'mon. I gotta help the girls clean up, and then I'm yours for the rest of the weekend."

"I want longer than that," she whispered, climbing onto my back, and I grinned over my shoulder. Dropping a loud, sloppy kiss to my cheek, she added, "I want always."

I sighed happily. "And you have me, pretty girl. I promise."

DANI

The flicker behind my eyelids and the deep roll of thunder quickly brought me out of sleep. I tried to remember how I'd gotten into my room, but I barely remembered Evan carrying me upstairs. I had to have fallen asleep watching the movie with him and Wes.

Rolling over, I frowned that Evan wasn't with me, but rubbing my eyes, I glanced over at the clock, my heart breaking at the fact that I'd be putting him on a plane in less than six hours. The weekend had flown by just as I knew it would. I'd lose him for a little over three weeks, which would no doubt crawl like molasses. Suddenly, the need to touch him, kiss him, hold him, was overwhelming, so I got out of bed and opened my door.

The guest room was wide open...and empty. I knew instinctively where to find him. He loved the library, in spite of its view. Curtains had recently been added to it—Aunt Tessa's and Mom's idea, which was really sweet. I padded softly down the stairs and through the living room, finding him in the chair by the window, his journal open on the table in front of him.

God, he was beautiful. The small lamp on the table lit up his face, but it also cast shadows along his sharp jaw and furrowed brow as he wrote. Even better was the reappearance of the sweet, wire-framed glasses. They made him look so smart yet a touch young, but it worked for him. Then again, I wasn't sure there was anything about him that I didn't simply love. From the top of his messy head to the bottom of his bare feet, I truly loved him. And I planned on telling him before he got on that plane. My hope was that he said it back, but I had no expectations. My Evan was shy and reserved, and he was dealing with stepping back into a shit-ton of drama at home, so I wasn't expecting anything. However, I knew he cared about me. That was something he was really, *really* good at showing.

I shifted in the doorway, and Evan lifted his head, the sweetest of smiles curling up his mouth as he sat up straight.

"Hey, pretty girl. What are you doing up?"

Smiling, I walked to him, and he sat back so I could curl up in his lap. "I could ask the same of you."

Warm, strong arms wrapped around me as I sat sideways on his lap. I wanted to ask about his journal, but I knew if he was writing in it, then he was sorting out some tough things. He was about to go home, so I could imagine there were heavy issues weighing on him. We sat in silence just like that, wrapped up in a cocoon of arms and snuggles as I slowly ran my fingers through his hair.

Lightning flickered again, followed by the low rumble of thunder, and I pulled my face from his neck to just look up at him. I wished I could run away with him, that I had a time machine to fast-forward through Christmas—a holiday I couldn't even find it in me to care about because the one thing I wanted under the tree wouldn't be there. And I wanted to protect him from anything and everything that could hurt him. The mere thought of someone hurting him, saying mean things to him, made me shake with anger and worry and the love that had slowly built into a ginormous feeling I couldn't control anymore.

"Cold?" he whispered, cradling me in his arms and reaching up to brush my hair out of my face.

I shook my head but smiled. "No. I just want to kiss you like crazy."

His smile was brighter than the next flash of lightning. It was boyish and beautiful, but it was deadly sexy too. It was something I'd learned he did when he just didn't believe what I was saying, which added a bit of embarrassment as well. It happened most often when I couldn't control my verbal vomit, just blurting out the crazy-honest shit I always said.

"We should probably go upstairs for that, pretty girl," he suggested softly, but his lips betrayed him, brushing across mine in the lightest, sweetest kiss.

"Probably," I agreed, kissing him back, and I chuckled at his smile but then forced myself to look away toward the table. "I'm sorry I interrupted."

"S'okay," he answered, lifting me to my feet and standing up. "I was just about finished."

He faced me, closing his journal and picking it up with one hand while cupping my cheek with the other. The expression on his handsome face was dark, heated, but his gaze raked all over my face with a warmth I wasn't expecting. I took his hand from my face and tugged it gently to lead him back upstairs and into my room, closing the door behind us. His gaze was still heated, and he dropped his journal and glasses onto my nightstand.

The room seemed to feel close, tight with how much I wanted him, how much I loved him, and I couldn't stop from staring. Blue plaid pajama pants, a plain white T-shirt, bare feet, and that handsome face with a touch of stubble to it — he was just gorgeous, and he had no idea. And that made him all the more beautiful because he only saw me. He'd said it time and time again, but as he gazed down at me with those warm brown eyes, I could see it wasn't a lie. It was that look that told me how he felt about me.

"I want you," I whispered out of nowhere, shaking my head at the truth of it. "I don't want to stop, Evan."

His face heated and his smile was warm, but he sat me on the edge of the bed before kneeling in front of me. "Dani, I..." He took a deep breath. "I...You have *no idea* how much I want that. None. But...I don't...I can't do that and then get on a plane in a few hours. I'll lose my mind. I know it's old-school or old-fashioned to say such things, but it's not about...sex for me. It's about you and me, and I don't want to do that and walk away from you for a month. It would kill me. I'd...I'd...I want something to come home to."

I reached for his face, palms flat on either side, and pulled him in for a kiss. "I love you," I whispered against his lips, and his gasp made me smile, as did the twitch of his fingers on the outside of my thighs. "I do. And I know I say a lot of shit. That I blurt out stuff, but Evan, I do *love you*. So, so much. And I need you to know that before you leave."

He kissed me stupid. It was deep and loving, sexy and almost harsh, but I felt it to my toes. When he pulled back, my forehead thumped gently to his.

"I...Dani, I don't have words to explain to you how I feel about you." He shook his head slowly against mine, his eyes still closed. "Saying it back seems trite because *I love you too* sounds unbelievably inadequate to me."

My eyes welled up because I'd gotten more back than I expected. "But it sounds *perfect* to me."

He grinned, a light laugh escaping him, and those long eyelashes swept up to reveal that sweet chocolate brown I loved so much. "Yeah?"

"Yes...The best thing I've ever heard." I swallowed nervously before I asked, "Evan, would you...We've only got a few hours left, and I'm gonna miss you so much. I just...Can we just hold each other?"

His eyes were a bit watery as he nodded and stood.

I slipped under the covers, holding them up, and he joined me, pulling me close and kissing my forehead. Snuggling as close as I could get, I inhaled the warm scent of him.

"As long as you want," he whispered into my hair.

I thought that with Evan leaving, I'd find it hard to sleep, but the comfort of his warm arms and heartbeat put me right back to sleep. The alarm a few hours later shocked us both. Neither of us said anything when I shut it off and sat up. Evan slipped from my bed, taking his journal and glasses with him.

Showers were taken, and I was dressed before him and downstairs pouring a cup of coffee that Wes had already made. I'd thought maybe I'd have to wake my cousin, but he was dressed and ready when I got down there.

Wes was quiet, sipping from his own cup, but his dark-blue eyes locked on to mine. "I bought the tickets…just in case," he stated, shrugging a shoulder when I gasped. "I don't like sending him home. He's practically been sick since Thanksgiving."

"I don't want him to go," I whispered, my voice breaking on the last word, and my gaze slipped from Wes to the steamy mug in my hands. I took a sip, focusing on not losing it, because we hadn't even gotten in the damn car yet.

The sound of Evan coming down the stairs caught my ears, as did the sound of his bags landing on the wood floor. When he stepped into the kitchen, I could see the wall starting to build up — the same wall he'd dropped inside my house…around *me*. His face was blank, indifferent, but everything he felt for me was in his eyes when his gaze met mine. He no more wanted to go home than we wanted to put him on the plane.

"Ev, you want something to eat before we go?" Wes offered, but Evan shook his head. My cousin stood from his stool at the counter and gripped Evan's shoulder on the way by. "I'll go put your stuff in my truck, okay?"

"Thanks, Wes," Evan and I said at the same time, making us smile at each other.

Walking to him, I offered him my mug, and he took a sip before setting it down and pulling me to him. A long, slow, heavy kiss landed on my forehead, along with the push of Evan's exhale. He smelled like soap and shampoo, like toothpaste and now coffee. I held him close, neither of us saying a word, until Wes called from the front door that we needed to go.

The hour ride to the Panama City Airport was just as quiet. As much as I teased my cousin, he was giving us space. Or maybe he simply didn't know what to say to make it better for anyone. By the time we'd parked, gotten Evan checked in, and made it to security, I was shaking with the effort of holding back tears.

I barely heard my cousin's request of Evan as he gave him a guy hug. "You keep in touch, buddy. Not kidding. If you need any-fucking-thing, just call us. Okay?"

"Thanks, Wes."

Wes grunted but stepped away, and I felt warm hands on my face.

"Dani—"

"Evan—"

We spoke at the same time, and I surrendered to the tears, falling into him. I couldn't help it. I loved him, I wanted to protect him and spoil him, and I very well couldn't do that when he was across the country. And I couldn't do that when he was with someone who had no fucking clue how unbelievably special he was. It made me angry, made me want to rage against Evan's father.

"Dani...Pretty girl, please stop crying," Evan begged softly in my ear. "You're killing me."

I sniffled and nodded, trying my damnedest to stop, but the tears kept coming. "I'm...I'm sorry."

His smile was warm, but he kissed my lips. "Don't be sorry."

"I'm just...I'm gonna miss you, and I love you. I wasn't playing around last night. I want you to know that. I wasn't just blabbering on, and I..."

"Shhh," he soothed against my forehead, and then he kissed me again. "You've never lied to me, Dani, so I know you meant it. You *show me* all the time. Please look at me," he begged, and when I met his gaze, it was sad but loving. "And you have no idea what it's like to hear you say you love me. I...I don't know what I did to earn it, but God, Dani...I'm...I...I love you too. And that doesn't seem like *enough* for what I feel. Or maybe I just can't say it right." He cupped my face and kissed my lips. "If you want to know how I really feel about you, I left you something in your room. I want you to keep it, hold on to it until I'm home. And I *am* coming home. I swear it. I know you're worried, and I know you want to protect me, but nothing will stop me from getting back to you. Do you understand?"

Nodding, I was crying in earnest when he kissed my lips, whispering, "I'll call you when I land. I'll text you all the time. Three weeks is *nothing*, Dani."

"If I don't hear from you…"

He smiled but glanced over my head. "It's not necessary."

"It is to us, dude," Wes argued. "Just…deal with it."

Evan grinned, his face heating, but then he looked up to check the time. He turned back to me, kissing me softly. "I love you. And *you* are reading tonight."

A sniffly laugh escaped me, but I nodded. "Love you."

Watching him walk away just about broke me, but watching his face go blank of all expression as he stepped around the corner toward security caused a sob to rip through me. Wes's warmth wrapped around me, and he guided me out to the truck. The ride back home was filled with the occasional sniffle from me and Wes's constant assurance that everything would be okay, though I wasn't sure he believed what he was saying. He just hated it when I cried.

The house was quiet when we got back home, but it was still pretty early, so I imagined Aunt Tessa was still asleep and that Mom and Dad were on campus for a few last things before locking up their offices for the next few weeks.

I rushed upstairs to my room, tears starting all over again at the sight on my pillow. Not only had he left the copy of *The Count of Monte Cristo* we'd been reading, but his beautiful, leather-bound journal was sitting next to it with a sweet flower sticking up out of it. The petals were a very pretty purple, and I recognized it from the flowers my mother had planted in front of the house.

Picking up the journal, I brought it to my nose, smelling its soothing scent. The leather smell had pretty much faded, but it smelled like Evan. Opening it to where he'd put the flower as a bookmark, I sniffled again at how much I missed him already. But the journal entry was addressed to me.

My beautiful Dani,

My mother once told me that falling in love was the easiest, most amazing feeling. She said it truly felt like falling...where your stomach flips, your hands sweat, but your face smiles... all the time. She also said that your heart just... knows. That it tries to break out of your chest in order to get closer to its mate. As a kid, I always thought she was talking about my dad, but now, I'm not so sure. But it doesn't matter. What matters is that she was right.

Pretty girl, that's how I've felt since the first time I saw you in the library. I didn't know you, but everything I'd ever held back, everything that kept me quiet, wanted to explode. Instead of wanting to stay invisible, I wanted to know everything about you...your likes, dislikes, your laugh, your voice. I thought you were the prettiest thing I'd ever set eyes on, that your eyes were the window to everything you were feeling, and that you had amazing taste in books. I kept telling myself it was that last thing that kept me coming back to the library, but it was you. Everything about you drew me in and stole my heart.

I think I've loved you from that first day we worked in Wes's office. You blew away every assumption I had of you. Everything in me shifted. I went from a crush on a pretty girl to getting to know the most amazing, giving, loving, and beautiful person. Never in my wildest dreams did I think I'd ever get the chance to TALK to you, much less become friends. And now we're so much more than that.

I love you, Dani.

I wanted to tell you that before I left, but every chance I had, the words simply didn't form. I couldn't express just how much you've come to mean to me. I wanted to. God, I've wanted to say it for weeks now, but I was scared. I wasn't scared of you but of me, of what it would mean, offering up my heart like that. However, I came to realize something my mother didn't tell me. That love makes you powerful. Yes, it can make you feel vulnerable, but my God, Dani, it makes me feel so strong.

I know you're worried, that your family is worried. You know my past, my family's history, and you know I came to Glenhaven to escape it all, but what I found was something more. I now know where I'm going in life. I now know I can survive a lot of things, knowing where I'll end up at the end of the day.

With you.

I'm leaving this journal with you for safekeeping. There's nothing I would hide from you, so this journal and I are open books. I'm leaving it to show you just how much you've changed me, what your love and gentleness have done for me. I'm leaving it with you because my dad (no matter what he says or does) can't touch the VERY BEST part of me. You showed me that, my love. YOU did. And you've already said the words. You said them first, my always brave girl, and they were beautiful. The very best part of me is what now belongs to you, pretty girl, so I need you to do me a favor while I'm gone.

Please remember that you mean everything to me.

All my love, all my soul,

Evan

A sob ripped through me. He was all things beautiful and sweet. And he loved me — really, truly loved me. But I needed more of his words until I could hear his voice once he landed. Settling back against the pillow that still smelled like him, I flipped to the front of the journal to lose myself in his writing.

Dear Library Girl...

Chapter Sixteen

EVAN

"And the fairy king knighted the archer boy so his daughter could marry him," I said, smiling when Faith squealed and clapped her hands.

"So they married and had a bunch of fairy babies, living happily ever after," she concluded, bouncing in her bed.

"Yo, Ev, that war was awesome, with the acorn slingshots and the fiery arrows! And then there was the hummingbirds they flew on...like horses!" Tyler proclaimed, tossing his baseball up and catching it in his mitt.

"Excellent job, baby boy," Mom whispered into my ear as she kissed the side of my head and wrapped an arm around my shoulders. "You should write it down, my love."

"Will you help me get it right?"

"If you want," she said through a soft sigh, raking her fingers through my hair.

"I do! I wanna be a writer like you, Mom," I told her but fiddled with the string of my pajama pants and then adjusted my glasses. "But... Dad says...Dad says writers starve."

My mother scoffed, rolling her eyes. "Do I look starving to you, Evan?" My siblings and I chuckled at her. "Your father is a very practical, *no-nonsense man, son. That's what makes him a good doctor. But when it comes to certain things, he's sort of lost. Everyone is different, Evan. Look at Faith and Tyler. Your brother is good at math, at sports, where your sister likes science and art. You…You can create a whole different world with just words. Being a writer can be tough, which is why I teach. Some writers have many stories to tell; some only have a few…or maybe just one. You know, Harper Lee only wrote the one book."*

Nodding, I smiled at her. "I like Scout. She's pretty cool. She always said what everyone else was thinking…or…or she pointed out what just didn't make any sense."

"She was a smart cookie." My mother chuckled, cupping my face. "I want all of you to listen to me." She glanced around at all of us just hanging out in Faith's room, and when we nodded, she went on, looking back to me. "Never, ever be afraid to follow your dreams, your heart. Don't be afraid to fight for what's right or for what you truly want in life. Anyone who tells you that you can't do something is merely afraid to try for themselves or they're jealous of you. What's right for Tyler may not be right for you, Evan, or Faith, and vice versa. Understand?"

"Yes, ma'am," we all answered her quietly.

"You ever gonna write another book, Mom?" Tyler asked her.

"No, probably not. I enjoy teaching, but more importantly…I wanted children. You guys. Being a mother was all I wanted, more than anything. More than writing or teaching or even money. I wanted you guys."

I grinned at her, but it was Faith who piped up with a question I hadn't considered. "And Daddy?"

My mother smiled, and I wanted to say it was a sad smile, but she kissed Faith's forehead. "I had to convince your father about children, sweet girl. He and his own father didn't get along very well, so he wasn't too sure, but he'd give me anything, so he gave me you guys. I couldn't ask for a better present."

I snapped awake, and the drone of the plane seemed loud in my ears. Rubbing my face, I wasn't surprised that I was dreaming about my mother. It had been a long time, but I remembered that conversation. Though, now I saw it in a completely different light. I saw what she *hadn't* said.

"Ladies and gentlemen, we're approaching Bozeman Yellowstone International Airport. The high today is a chilly thirty-eight degrees, and there's a chance of snow later on tonight."

Glancing out the window with a sigh, I ached for the Florida weather I'd grown to love. When I left, it was a gorgeous sixty-something and the sky was as clear and blue as I'd ever seen it. I also ached for Dani. Her tears had just about brought me to my knees. Her proclamations of love had almost broken me, because all I wanted was to stay. Turning away from her had taken every fucking ounce of strength I had in me, and I'd had to shut down a part of myself in order to board this damn plane.

Frowning at it all, I adjusted my seat belt, stowed my laptop, and put my tray up. It had been a long damn flight, with layovers in Atlanta and Salt Lake City, but at least I'd slept through most of it, which didn't surprise me any. I'd stayed up most of the night before, just holding Dani. I'd wanted so badly to make love to her like she'd wanted, but had I done that, hell itself couldn't have removed me from the Bishop home. Instead, I'd held her close, whispered to her over and over that I loved her, that she'd made me a better person, giving me back myself—something I'd thought had drowned with my mother. I'd pressed light kisses to her forehead, playing with her hair in order to keep her relaxed.

As the flight attendants helped everyone disembark, a sense of dread washed over me. I wasn't sure who I'd be meeting. All my father had said when I'd called him the night before was that "someone" would be there. Rolling my eyes, I stood and shouldered my backpack. I followed the masses down to get my luggage, but it was who was waiting for me that made me smile.

"Big brother!" Faith squealed, dodging a few people and hitting me like a brick wall.

Chuckling, I hugged her tight. "I missed you."

She pulled back, and I eyed her from head to toe—no makeup, her hair was up haphazardly in a long, dark ponytail, but at least she had her phone and car keys. She looked okay, just as strong and belligerent as always.

"Don't judge me; you're not the only one on break."

I laughed. "No judging. Promise."

Turning a bit, I watched for my bag and picked it up when it came by, pulling out my phone once I set it down at my feet. Faith waited patiently, twirling her keys, but I paused just long enough to call Dani.

"Evan!"

"Hey, pretty girl. I landed okay," I told her, my eyes closing at the sniffles I could hear as clear as a bell, despite the fact that she was across the country, but it was that honest, adorable rambling that made me grin like an idiot.

"Evan, baby…I got your journal, and you're just about the sweetest…I love you too. So much, and you left our book! What…How are you gonna read to me? I'm not doing all the reading! And I fucking miss you like crazy already."

I started to chuckle and couldn't stop. God, I missed that shit already. "Dani, slow down. I have a copy at my house. Just…relax. And I meant every word. I promise."

"Okay," she sighed. "Who picked you up?"

"My sister."

"Hi, Dani!" Faith squealed.

Dani laughed. "Okay, good. Tell her I said hi, and you call me later. We'll read."

"Yes, ma'am, but it might be late."

"I don't care how late it is."

"Okay," I sighed deeply.

"Love you."

"Love you too," I said and ended the call, but I flinched when a small fist landed hard on my arm. "Ow! Rylee Faith, what the hell?"

"You're an idiot!"

"Why?" I asked, rubbing my bicep and glaring down at her.

"Because you were happy and you came back here anyway!"

"Yeah, well, I wasn't going to leave you alone with Dad at Christmas."

She tsked at me, rolling her eyes and folding her arms across her chest. "I can handle Dad, Evan."

Glaring at her, I shook my head slowly. "You shouldn't have to, and I've talked to Tyler…I know all about Thanksgiving."

She grimaced, reaching for my hand. "C'mon. We'll talk about it in the car."

Faith's car was parked in the garage, and we loaded up in silence. I put my bags in the back seat before practically falling into the passenger seat.

"You hungry? 'Cause if you are, we should stop now. The diner will be closed by the time we get back home." If my dad had booked the flight to land in Missoula or even Helena, it wouldn't have been, but he'd gone the cheapest route — to no one's surprise — which just also happened to be the farthest from Key Lake.

"I had something to eat when I had my layover, but yeah, we can stop."

Faith didn't talk about anything in the car as she drove away from the airport. However, once she pulled into the restaurant just outside the city and we were seated, I raised an eyebrow at her.

"You gonna tell me?"

She grimaced but fidgeted with the straw wrapper from her drink. "I'm sorry! I didn't...I didn't mean for Thanksgiving to get out of hand. I didn't mean for Dad to find out about Dani, and I didn't want to tell him I applied to Edgewater until I knew for sure I was in...which I am." She wrinkled her nose.

I smirked her way. "Congrats, Faith. So he knows?"

"That I applied, not that I've been accepted."

I hummed, nodding a little. "And don't beat yourself up about Dani. He knew. He's known for a while now; he just didn't say it."

She raised an eyebrow. "What do you mean?"

I explained the phone call I'd had with Dad the day I'd told him I wasn't coming for Thanksgiving, how he'd baited me, goaded me, but that I hadn't given in.

"Fuck. The phone bill," she surmised in a whisper, frowning down at her hands when I nodded. "Shit...I'm so stupid. I fell into that trap."

Snorting, I shook my head. "He'd have found some other way to mess with you, Faith. That shit is aimed at me...and Tyler."

Faith groaned. "Jesus, big brother, you should've seen that whole thing. Jasmine don't play, for real! Dad was so rude — when he was around — and she merely smiled his way. When Dad called her Tyler's whore, I thought Ty would kill him right there on the spot. Honestly. He told Dad he could go fuck himself, that had it been him in the car instead of Mom, he'd have *let* the car sink. Tyler told him he couldn't control us anymore. He also told Dad that if he so much as looks at you cross-eyed while you're here for Christmas, he'll personally put him in the ground in the middle of the woods where no one would find him, not that anyone would fucking miss him."

Squeezing my eyes closed, I shook my head. "Ah, Christ…"

"Why does he hate us?" she asked in a whisper.

"I don't think he ever wanted us," I answered honestly, remembering the dream I'd had on the plane. "I think he *allowed* Mom to get pregnant because *she* wanted us. Which makes sense why he blames me, I guess." I shrugged a shoulder. "I don't know, Faith, and I don't care. He's been abusive and foul our whole lives, even before Mom died. This…I'm…I'm with Tyler on this. I can't…This is my last trip back, I think." I met my sister's sad hazel eyes. "I don't need him. He can threaten and take away shit, but I don't need him. I'm…I came here for you. I came to make sure you were okay and to make sure he lays off you until summer."

"Spring," she corrected with an evil smirk as the food was set down in front of us. "I'm trying to get Dad to let me come see you for spring break."

Grinning as I picked up my fork, I shook my head. "Good luck with that. Trust me, once you tell him you're going to school with me, he'll be sure to make your life miserable until you leave. Look what he did just before I left…My car, my school funding—all of it was held over my head. He'll tell you that you can't have both. Watch." I pointed the fork her way, raising an eyebrow at her.

She laughed and shook her head. "You're probably right. As long as I can get to you, I'm good. I can live without spring break. And Tyler and Jasmine said they'd help me move in."

I raked a hand through my hair. "So…all of you are coming to Florida?"

She laughed. "Yup!" Her laugh and smile faded quickly. "Jasmine's family is pretty great. They're sending her and Ty to Florida to visit you for the summer, so they're helping me move into the dorms or whatever."

Something about that made me very happy, but it also sent warning signals off in my head. "You know, Dad's just gonna flip the fuck out over all of this. It worries me to leave you until the summer, and we aren't even at the house yet."

She scoffed, shaking her head. "I got this. Trust me. He's…He barely speaks to me, Evan, so when I need something—like my car back to pick you up and the phone just in case and whatever—he gives in simply so he doesn't have to deal with it." She snorted a little.

"He blew up and took away my makeup, but he doesn't know me…I had spare stuff in my locker at school. I just dressed there. He pays no attention and is barely home."

"Lucky you."

I ate a few bites in silence, thinking she was probably right. Dad had always avoided her, so instead of enforcing the punishment with her, he'd simply give in to get her out of his face. And Faith had grown up learning that shit like the back of her hand. She was quick, she was smart, and she'd watched everything inside that house since our mother died. I just hoped stuff didn't escalate between my heading back to school and the summer when she left for Edgewater.

"Speaking of lucky…I wanna see your Library Girl," Faith segued beautifully, wearing the begging face I could never resist.

Laughing, I touched my phone and opened up the pictures, sliding it across the table.

"Oh, God, big brother," she whispered, scrolling through the innumerable amount of pictures I had of Dani, of Dani and myself, not to mention all my friends and people I now considered family. "She's gorgeous."

"I know, right?" I grinned proudly, shrugging a shoulder when my sister laughed at me. "She's amazing, Faith."

"And she loves you."

"For some reason, yeah."

Faith sighed, rolling her eyes. "I bet if I asked her, she'd give me a thousand reasons."

Laughing, I shrugged again. "Probably." When my sister held up another picture, I pointed to everyone. "That's Dani's parents, Leanne and Daniel. That's her Aunt Tessa, who is hilarious, and Dani's cousin and my boss, Wes."

Faith's eyebrows shot up. "He's hot."

"He's great. He's my boss, but…he's like my best friend down there."

She frowned, pushing my phone back to me. "You should've stayed."

"Maybe, but had I not come, Dad would've been worse. Let him think I'm doing what he wants, and it's over."

"You know…Mom would be pissed at how he's become," Faith said softly. "Don't you think?"

I sighed, setting my fork down and nodding as I reached for my wallet to pay the bill. "Yeah, definitely."

As we got back into the car, Faith looked over at me. "Hey, big brother…Can…Can we do Christmas like back when Mom was with us?"

Smiling over at her, I studied her face. "You want the tree, stockings, carols, dinner, and everything?" When she nodded, I asked, "What about Dad?"

She chuckled, starting the car. "Let's hope he's working."

Dad was home when we pulled into the driveway. Faith and I had chatted throughout the entire ride home, catching each other up on the little stuff. I told her how things were at school, at the coffee shop, and with Dani, and she told me all about how Key Lake never fucking changed. I'd asked her about the boy she went out with occasionally, Ron. She'd laughed, shaking her head, and told me he wasn't the asshole everyone thought he was, that they'd become good friends, just friends. According to Faith, Ron's dad, Dr. Lowe, was just as pleasant to his son as our father was to us, so they compared notes, not to mention used each other to avoid said fathers.

Dad's black Mercedes sat silently in the driveway like a warning beacon. My stomach knotted, but I took a deep breath, preparing myself for whatever mood he happened to be in. Sadly, my BMW was nowhere to be seen; he'd really gotten rid of it.

The sleek lines and stark angles of the house were shocking in comparison to the Bishop home back in Glenhaven. Dani's house radiated warmth and laughter and love. In fact, I couldn't think of a time I took the front steps where laughter didn't hit my ears as I reached for the door. But my house, this house in front of me, it was cold. It stood there surrounded by trees and manicured lawns like a tombstone in a cemetery. I felt nothing for this place but dread and hopeless, endless grief for my mother.

Tyler was right in his thinking…After this Christmas break, I'd most likely never come back here.

With that last thought, I got out of the car and grabbed my bags out of the back seat. I wanted to get seeing Dad over with so I could call Dani from the privacy of my room. I missed my girl too much already. I missed the pure, unadulterated love and happiness that floated around her like an angel's halo. Hell, I missed all of them—Wes's easygoing laugh, Leanne's hugs, Susan's teasing, Aunt Tessa's sarcasm, and Daniel. I missed Dani's father for his calming personality, for the fact that he'd never, ever said an unkind word to me, only praise, only good things — both in and out of the classroom. He was, in all aspects, the complete and total opposite of my own father.

As I stepped in through the front door, it finally hit me that Daniel was exactly how a father should be, not the hard-faced man draining a glass of caramel-colored liquid as he sat in the living room.

"'Bout time you got your asses home," he slurred, narrowing his eyes on the two of us, especially my sister, who laughed softly. "Thought you might've gotten in a wreck." He laughed at his own foul joke.

"We're fine. Thanks for calling," she stated wryly.

He hummed her way but locked sights on me. "Nice tan, Evan. How's the beach?"

"Beautiful," I answered without much emotion behind it. I was in no mood for his games or negative bullshit. I just wanted to call Dani.

That answer had to have shocked him, so he changed tactics. "Obviously you're doing something other than studying, since you're down to a three-point-eight."

Grinning, I shrugged. "That's still an A average, Dad, and it's well within my scholarship's requirements, so…" I shrugged again.

"And it's well within my rights to not pay for such shitty grades," he snapped, standing up in front of me.

Damn, I hadn't even put my bags down yet and he was in my face. Deep down, I could hear Dani's voice telling me that his problem with me was just that: *his problem*. As I stared at him a moment, I could see just how miserable of a human being he was, and he'd aged right before my eyes. There were dark spots beneath his eyes, his hair was graying at the temples, and his hands shook, meaning he was drinking just a bit more these days. He was in pure hell, whether from the loss of Mom or simply because he'd always been that way, but having been away from home for several months, I could see it all over him. But I also couldn't find it in me to sympathize. We'd all lost Mom, we'd all had to struggle through her devastating absence, and we'd all had to move on. He hadn't, and I found that I honestly didn't care whether he ever did.

"Then don't," I countered calmly, turning away from him to head upstairs to my room. "Don't pay for it, Dad."

"Don't you walk away from me, Evan!" he yelled, the ice in his glass clinking when he pointed at me.

Sighing, I turned around on the step and looked back at him. "Let's get this over with now, okay?" I said calmly. "I don't want to be here, but I came for her." I pointed to Faith. "I don't care about your money or your threats or anything like that. I'm here for her. I'm well aware of what happened here at Thanksgiving, and I'm not going to have a repeat of it. You wanted me here, told me not to... what was it? Oh, yeah... *weasel* out of it. So I'm here. But let's get a few things out in the open." I ticked off the next few things on my fingers. "My personal life—meaning my girlfriend, my grades, my job, and my financial issues...should you choose to stop paying—are *my* business. Legally, you have no say in any of it—mine or Tyler's." I glanced to Faith, who was smirking a little. "And soon, Faith's. Come next year, she'll move to Florida with me. And *she* got a full scholarship, so she won't need you at all. Now, I'm here for Christmas and we planned on actually celebrating it, so if you want to join us, which I sincerely doubt, then you can. If not, then point me in the direction of the shit you think needs to be done in order to 'adjust my attitude,' and we'll stay out of each other's face, okay?"

I'd never spoken to my father that way, but I'd lived since August without his foul words and insults, and I wanted to get back to my life. I'd witnessed what true family was, and this wasn't it. This was hatred. William Shaw hated every last one of us. He despised us for surviving when our mother hadn't. He despised how he had to care for three kids he'd never wanted in the first place. I suddenly wished he'd just walked away from us instead of punishing us for simply existing.

The glass in his hand shattered against the wall by my head. I felt the ice bounce off my sneaker. Faith ducked just in time, and I pulled her behind me.

"You ungrateful bastard!" he snarled, walking quickly to me, and I stood my ground, bracing myself for his barrage of degrading words.

He wouldn't touch me. He truly hadn't physically touched any of us since we were in the hospital after the wreck, and even then, it was only to save face around his peers. My father was a lot of things, and at the top of that long, twisted list, he was smart. To touch me at nineteen would risk me telling someone or pressing charges. Just below that, he was a coward. I could see it in his eyes as he glared at me from the step below mine. Fists balled up at his side and his face red with anger, he stared me down.

"Ungrateful for what?" I asked, trying to keep my voice even, while inside I braced for whatever he was about to do. "Nothing you've ever done for any of us was out of the kindness of your heart, Dad. Nothing. It was merely obligation and to save your reputation in this small-minded town." I almost asked him about the "bastard" part of that accusation, but I was pushing my limits with him already.

He glared at me like I'd truly struck the heart of the matter, but he didn't address that. Instead, he pointed his finger into my chest, and I flinched a bit but kept my eyes on his.

"She's not going to Florida to be with *you*."

"She is."

"I am," Faith piped up, coming to position herself between us. "It's a full ride, a good school, and I'm going."

His lip twitched. "Get out of my face. Both of you. Tomorrow, you'll have a list of shit that needs to be done around here. Your sister's been goddamn worthless since you've been gone. You'll show her how to keep some shit up, and you'll do it all or face the consequences." He opened his mouth to continue, but his phone sounded from the end table by the sofa.

The benefit of his job—for my siblings and me—was that he was constantly needed, whether on the phone or at the hospital. He snatched his phone up, answering with a loud, "Shaw!"

My nostrils flared in anger as I exhaled roughly, and I turned to head upstairs to my room. I could hear, feel Faith following me, and once I dropped my things down on my old bed, I turned to face her.

"Welcome home, big brother." She snorted at the sarcastic tone she let out, and I smirked, shaking my head. "Did you write down that shit you just told him?"

I barked a humorless laugh. "Some of it…and that was *before* I left for Edgewater."

"You're different," she whispered, walking to me and giving me a hug. "I *knew* getting out of here would be good for you. I can't wait to get down there and out of this house."

Kissing the top of her head, I said, "Soon, Faith. And I can't wait, either." Smiling, I hugged her closer and then let her go. "Speaking of…I need to call Dani before it's way too late. I just need to grab something out of the library."

"Tell her I said hello," she said, walking from my room to hers across the hall.

I smiled and nodded, rumbling down the stairs. I could hear my dad still on the phone, but he'd moved his conversation into the kitchen. The library—or really, it had been my mother's home office—was just off the living room. I stepped in, turning on the lights, and my heart constricted at the memories of this room. It was where my mother would grade papers, pay bills, and write. It was where she'd taught *me* how to write. It was this room my siblings and I would come to in order to talk to her. It was a lot like Dani's library, except the long back wall was nothing but windows facing the woods behind our house. There wasn't a lake, thankfully, but there was shelf after shelf filled with books.

I'd left Dani the copy of *The Count of Monte Cristo* because she'd checked it out of the school's library, but I'd also wanted my mother's copy. Actually, there were a few things I made mental note to take out of here before my break was over. Things I'm sure my father wouldn't miss—photo albums, my mother's journals, and the first editions of my mother's published works. Those things were important to me, and I wanted them before I left, even if I had to ship them to the Bishop house for safekeeping. But they were things I needed to do when my dad was at work and not after I'd just pissed him off.

My gaze, my fingers, trailed over the spines of my mother's most beloved titles—mostly classics, with a few more modern stories thrown in for good measure. The sight of them made me sad but made me smile too because Daniel had some of the same books in his own library. They would've been good friends. I was sure of it.

I found the old copy of the Count and pulled it off the shelf, jumping when my father's voice met my ears.

"Not even an hour in this house, and you're in here with your head in the fucking clouds."

Sighing, I held up the book. "Left mine back *home*," I stated firmly, leaning on the last word for a reason. "I need this one before I go back to school."

He narrowed his eyes, and I could see him debating on arguing, but he stayed quiet as I brushed past him in the doorway. I could've sworn I heard him mumble something about growing some balls and whores and my mother, but I was already hitting the steps and pulling out my phone.

"Hey, baby," Dani sang sweetly after only one ring.

"Hi, pretty girl. I miss you."

"Miss you too. So…my turn, right?"

"That's right. Get to readin', Dani," I teased her, smiling at her sweet giggle and falling down onto my bed next to my bags that I would deal with in the morning. "I need your voice."

Chapter Seventeen

Evan

As a little kid, I never thought to question my parents on certain things. Robyn Shaw had always been open and forthcoming with all three of us. She'd explained things, taught us things, and she'd done it all with patience and love and hugs.

Crack!

The sound of the splitting log was dull in the snowy late morning. I stood the next one up and swung again as my mind sorted through memories.

Crack!

I was trying my damnedest to remember if my father had ever hugged me — or any of us, for that matter. Other than the occasional medical issue, I was pretty sure he'd never touched us. Actually, I'd never really wanted to be anywhere near the man. I'd been perfectly content in my mother's presence.

I swung the axe again, simply to lodge it into the stump I was using, and it landed with a *thunk*. The crunch of snow met my ears, and I smiled at Faith as she grabbed the logs I'd just cut.

"You don't have to…"

She laughed. "I'm not a damsel in distress, Evan," she countered, setting them on the back steps in their bin. When she faced me again, she pulled her wool hat down a bit. "I'm not the fairy princess in your story." She picked up a few more logs.

Laughing, I shrugged. "Fair enough. What's left on his damn list anyway?"

"Way too much, but I guess he wanted to keep us busy until you go home," she stated.

The word *home* made me think of Dani. Pulling out my phone, I checked to see if she'd texted back. I smiled at silly pictures of her and Wes at Sunset Roast, multiple messages of her love for me, and a few stating how much she missed me. I sent one back after taking a picture of the snow-covered backyard, teasing her about her thin Floridian blood, along with the fact that I loved her and missed her more than I could explain.

I'd been back in Montana for ten days. Christmas was just a few days away. I'd kept my word to Dani about daily chats and messages, not to mention reading to each other just about every night. I'd also kept my word to my dad, taking his ridiculously long list of chores—punishments—and he'd kept his about staying out of my face. After each job was finished, I'd cross it off and move on to the next one. Faith helped most of the time, but chopping the wood was hard work and heavy, not to mention it left my hands sore and tender, even with gloves on.

"We should tackle the attic next," Faith suggested, grimacing.

"Well, if we do that, then we might as well decorate for Christmas, don't you think?" I asked, grabbing the axe to put it away in the now spotless garage—one of the first chores we'd done on his stupid list. "I mean, the ornaments are up there."

"The church is selling trees," she whispered, and I knew why she was tentative about it. Mom was buried in the cemetery across from the church. "Maybe we could...should..."

Nodding, I took a deep breath and let it out, and it plumed out of me like a white fog. "Okay, let me clean up. We'll go get the tree, stop at the cemetery, and maybe grab something to eat. When's Dad supposed to be home?"

"I heard him leave about six this morning. So we've got all afternoon. Why?"

"Because if I eat at the diner one more time, I may vomit," I said, rolling my eyes at her laugh.

"Spoiled to Southern home-cookin'?"

"Abso-fucking-lutely," I answered with a laugh, reaching for her hat and yanking it down hard over her face. "I may have even learned a thing or two. We'll stop at the market on our way home."

Once I was showered and in clean clothes, I walked down the hallway to open the attic door and pull down the ladder. Tyler and I had just cleaned it a few years prior, and no one really went up there, so I couldn't imagine there was much that needed to be done, except for maybe some sweeping. My brow furrowed at a few boxes that were open, but I didn't pay them much attention. I was looking for the Christmas ornaments my mother used to meticulously pack away every year. The last time we'd decorated was the Christmas of Tyler's first year at UM. He'd already met Jasmine but they weren't dating yet, and Faith and I wanted to celebrate having our oldest brother home for the holidays.

I found the box I was looking for and dragged it to the edge of the attic hatch.

"Here, big brother. Hand it down," Faith said, and I slowly lowered the box into her hands. It wasn't heavy, but the sound of bells shifting around inside made her smile.

Once I was back down in the hallway, I said, "There's not much to do up there."

"Thank fuck."

Grinning her way, I nodded. "There are some boxes that were opened after the last time Ty and I cleaned. You been up there?"

"Huh? No! Spiders, Evan! Are you fucking crazy?"

I laughed, holding up my hands in a surrendering gesture. "My bad!"

I wanted to tease my very strong, fearless sister about bugs, but I couldn't find it in me to do it, not when I still couldn't step near or even look at large bodies of water without cringing and breaking out into a sweat.

"So I'll be cleaning up there, I see," I did say teasingly, rolling my eyes when she looked up at me pleadingly. "Fine, fine."

Just before we left the house, I checked the kitchen to see what I needed, though I was expecting I would need just about everything.

I could see that Faith kept a few things in there for herself — cereal, soda, milk, eggs, some things for salads, and frozen dinners and pizzas. All of that was pretty standard in the Shaw house, since our dad didn't eat with us much. The cabinets were just about the same — cans of soup, boxed mac and cheese, and instant oatmeal.

"What are you making?" Faith asked, her eyes wide with amusement as we walked to her car.

"Um, I was thinking chili. Dani's mom taught me the last time she made it. It's pretty easy, and the weather's perfect for it since we're gonna get more snow tonight. I'll make enough to last through tomorrow."

The drive to the church was slow with the weather, but Key Lake wasn't all that big anyway. There was a tent set up in the front parking lot, and most people had already gotten their trees, though I was happy to see there were a few left.

"We don't need a big one, Faith, but you pick it," I said, getting out of the car. "Besides, you want to be careful about tying it down on top. A small one will fit in the trunk."

Pastor Sean greeted the two of us, hugging my sister. He was around our parents' age, and he'd always been very kind. He and my mother had known each other a long time. After she died, he'd tried to keep checking on the three of us. I sighed at the memory of that time. Mom's funeral had been a huge deal since she'd been a teacher at Key Lake High School. Her lady friends had dropped by with food, Pastor Sean wanted to check on us, and the rumors had started to spread like wildfire. It was that last thought that had me glancing across the street to the cemetery. I hadn't visited my mother's grave in a year — the last Christmas.

"Evan," Pastor Sean said softly, his hand landing gently on my shoulder. "It's good to see you, son. You've shot up an inch or two since the last time I saw you. How's college?"

Smiling politely, I nodded. "I'm good, sir. School's good too."

He studied my face for a second. "And your father? I only see him in passing when I visit the hospital."

Smiling ruefully, I answered honestly. "The same as always."

The man laughed lightly, if not knowingly. "I bet." He squeezed my shoulder, pointing to a table filled with potted poinsettias. "Just got these in…if you want to…" He gestured across the street to the cemetery.

Swallowing nervously, I nodded. "Actually, yeah, I would."

When I reached for my wallet, he stopped me. "Those are on me, son. Go on. I'll take care of Rylee Faith and send her over there once she's picked a tree. You can pay for it when you're done."

"Okay. Thanks," I muttered softly, picking up the bright red flower.

Crossing the street was surreal, and despite how long it had been, I felt twelve years old all over again. The funeral seemed like yesterday, not a little over seven years prior. I remembered everything — the tie around my neck that felt too tight, my suit that rubbed against my very sore stitches, holding Faith's hand but sticking to Tyler on his crutches like glue, the sound of sniffles and nose blowing, and the smell of impending rain. I remember following the broad shoulders of my dad in his black suit, but I also remembered he never uttered a single word to us.

Mom's grave was on the other side of the cemetery in the corner at the edge of the woods. It was beneath a small fir tree, which seemed fitting with the holiday and the snow that weighed down the branches; it was like she had her very own Christmas tree. Her granite headstone was a harsh reminder of the cold, abrupt loss of her. It seemed so fucking *wrong* for her to be there. I wasn't sure what I believed when it came to life after death. I wanted *so badly* to imagine my mother like the angel I knew she was on earth, but I'd never had a prayer answered, so all of it was confusing.

I removed my wool cap and knelt down, taking my gloved hand and brushing the snow off her tombstone. I also cleared a spot for the poinsettia, which was shockingly red and green against the white/gray of its surroundings. I brushed more snow off the words "Loving wife and mother," frowning at them.

As always, with the grief, the missing her, came the anger. I missed her to the point of pain, but then, I was mad at her too. She'd said she was right behind me, but she hadn't been, so it felt like a lie, no matter how hard I tried to rationalize it or let it go. And what she'd left behind was what made my anger that much sharper. Had she known what Dad was like? Did she realize what he'd become if she was no longer with us, if she could no longer protect us? All three of us had wondered about it more than one time, but not one of us had bothered to voice it to Dad, and there was an angry, bitter part of me that wanted to confront him about every damn rumor we'd had slapped in our faces. Maybe she had been leaving him. Maybe he really cheated on her…or she did on him. Maybe he'd never really wanted us, which was obvious with how he treated us, but then a few questions remained…*Why* would he give a shit about grades and colleges and personal lives? *Why* would he care what we did and where we went as long as we were no longer his legal responsibility? And if he never really wanted us, then why not just…walk away?

"You okay, big brother?" I heard behind me, and I nodded, wrapping an arm around my sister when she knelt beside me. She was quiet for a moment but finally said softly, "I wish I could talk to her just *one more time*."

Kissing the side of her head, I whispered, "Me too."

Faith turned to face me. "What would you tell her?"

Smiling, I stood, and Faith followed suit. "I dunno…Lots of things. I'd…I'm…I'd like to tell her about Dani, about school and Glenhaven. She'd love it there, with the warm weather and the beaches and the sunsets. I…I think she'd love Dani…and her family. I wish she could read some things I've written. I'd…I'd ask her why she said she was following me out of the car and she didn't." I shrugged a shoulder, shoving my hands into my jacket pockets. "But if I think that way, then I want to be mad and ask her about Dad, and not a bit of it would do any good."

Faith nodded, and despite how young my sister had been when Mom died and despite how strong she always appeared to be, her voice cracked a little when she said, "I miss her."

I pulled her into a hug, nodding a little.

"I miss the little things — hugs, cookies, back-to-school shopping, her laugh. God, her laugh was just…perfect."

Chuckling, I sighed deeply. "Yeah." I glanced around when fluffy white flakes started to drift down around us, and I pulled back to look at my sister. "Did you find a tree?"

"Yeah, it's cute. Like two feet or something."

"Cool. C'mon," I said, gesturing to the weather. "Let's get to the store and then back home before this becomes ugly."

"Okay, that needs to stay on low for a bit," I told Faith, jerking a thumb to the big pot of chili on the stove.

"Smells yummy," she said with a grin, looking up from behind the box of ornaments.

"Thanks." I smiled and pointed toward the living room where a fire was burning bright. "You got the tree? 'Cause I want to finish the attic before the chili's done and Dad gets home. That way I can call Dani from my room."

"Yeah, I need to call Tyler tonight, and I have to do that on the down-low from Dad. Ty wanted us to check in every once in a while… just so he knows Dad's not doing anything shitty," she explained with a grimace.

I barked a laugh, checking on my chili one more time. "Define *shitty*," I said with a chuckle, glancing over my shoulder as I stirred the pot.

She grinned. "I dunno. It seems since Thanksgiving, Tyler thinks Dad will get worse."

My brow furrowed, and I put the lid back on the pot. Facing her, I said, "You know, Daniel said the same thing after Tyler's call that day." I shrugged a shoulder. "I honestly don't know what pissed Ty off more—Dad picking on you or his calling Jasmine a whore."

"That's the thing," Faith agreed. "Tyler said to remember when we were kids, that Dad would at least pretend to be civil around friends and stuff. Now, it's like he's…"

"Desperate," I finished in a whisper. "Or maybe he just doesn't give a shit about pretenses anymore."

"Yeah. Or maybe both."

I hummed, tapping the counter. "Well, when you talk to Tyler, tell him he doesn't have to dig the grave just yet, but there's a perfect spot in the woods if he needs one," I teased her, which made her laugh wickedly before I walked back up the stairs to the attic ladder.

Snorting to myself, I climbed up to get to work. Despite how much I missed Dani, missed her family, and missed Florida, I was at least grateful that I'd had little to no interaction with my father since the day I'd come home and that my sister was out of the line of fire. I only needed to get through the next couple of weeks, and she only needed to make it to the summer.

The attic didn't exactly need all that much in the line of cleaning, and it wasn't exactly warm up there, but it was stuffy. I tugged my shirt off and dropped it by the hatch. Then I removed some cobwebs, discovered and squished the spiders Faith hated, and started to organize the boxes. Most of them up there were things that Mom had stored — baby clothes and blankets from all three of us, quilts and old bedding, not to mention different decorations for different seasons. There were a few boxes of Tyler's — mostly his sports stuff — and old games none of us played anymore. I shifted those around to allow more room, and I swept up. The last few boxes were the ones I'd noticed were open when I'd retrieved the Christmas ornaments for Faith.

I knew what they were, but in spite of my sputtering heart, I looked inside anyway at some of my mother's things. The first box contained some of her clothes, things that didn't get donated to charity after her funeral, and her box of jewelry. Most of the latter was costume stuff or things that matched her clothes. It was stuff Faith wanted, so we'd put them up there when one of our most severe punishments had been to clear Mom's things from my parents' room about four months after she died. Frowning at that old memory, I noted that those things had been rummaged through — and rather roughly, at that — but I rearranged them before closing the box back up. I stacked it off to the side.

The next box was just papers and such, it seemed, but again, the box looked like it had been ransacked. File folders were askew and lying on top, pages were ripped or just dropped back in there, and nothing seemed in order. As I tried to put things back in their place, I realized they were from my mother's desk in the library. It was just old files — utility bills, car payments and registrations, insurance papers, and her old bank statements. As I put things back in their folders, I noted that her bank was different than the one my dad used. He'd given Tyler and then me a card to use for school supplies, only depositing money into the accounts for books and supplies. Where his bank had a red and blue logo, my mother's was green.

My brows shot up high at the balance from the last statement that was filed away. I knew my mother had lost her parents — our grandparents — in an accident before we were born, but I'd never questioned any of it because it seemed to make my mother sad to talk of it. I'd also never thought to question money at all. Hell, I'd been just a damn kid. But I was looking at seven figures. Turning the statement over, I saw it was in a savings account, not a checking. Her checking account seemed to only receive her paychecks from Key Lake High School.

I filed that away, and I couldn't help but neaten the row of folders. It was just a part of me to straighten it up. I looked in the last file that had been pulled out and saw that it was my mother's life insurance policy, with my dad as the beneficiary, which made sense. I closed the box back up and stacked it on top of the rest along the wall of the attic. With one last sweep-up, I dumped the dirt into the garbage can I'd brought with me.

I grabbed my shirt and the can and turned off the light, descending back down to the upstairs hallway...coming face-to-face with my dad. He seemed surprised to see me, though he wasn't looking me in the eye but at my side—more specifically, my scars. I dropped the can, which caught his attention.

"What the hell were you doing up there?" he snapped.

"Uh, cleaning. It was on your list," I told him calmly, pointing to the garbage that had dust and debris on top.

When he had nothing to say to that, he scoffed, "Put your fucking shirt on, Evan!"

I huffed a laugh, glancing down at my scars, and somehow, I could hear my sweet Dani's brutal honesty coming out of my own mouth. "Does it bother you to see them?" I asked him softly. "Does it remind you of her?"

He sneered, stiffening as I snatched my shirt off the rung of the ladder, but he didn't say anything.

"Try looking at it in the mirror every fucking day," I muttered on the way by, pulling my shirt back on and grabbing the garbage can. Just before I went back down to the first floor, I added, "I made dinner, by the way. Feel free to join us."

I stepped back into the kitchen, setting the can back in its place and then washing my hands. My chili looked perfect, and the smell made me homesick for the Bishop house, for my Dani.

I pulled down some bowls from the cabinet, calling out to my sister, who was still decorating the Christmas tree. "Hey, Faith! Come eat!"

Just as she stepped into the kitchen, we both looked up at the ceiling when the sound of Dad's bedroom door slammed.

The day before Christmas Eve, I gave all the damn chores a rest, choosing to make the trip to Helena. Faith had simply wanted to get out of Key Lake, and I'd ridden along with her to get out of the house, but I'd texted with Dani pretty much the whole time. Even Wes piped in every now and then. Both were telling hilarious things about the Bishop house in Christmas chaos. Wes had called Dani a neat freak, and she'd dubbed him Scrooge.

When we pulled into the drive, Faith stopped so I could grab the mail. There were a few Christmas cards in there from various friends of my parents, one from Tyler and Jasmine to Faith and me, and various bills. But what caught my attention was an envelope from my mother's old bank. Faith pulled on into the driveway next to Dad's car, which was strange. He was supposed to be covering for a few doctors who'd wanted to take the holidays off.

"Faith, wait," I whispered, grabbing her hand before she could open her car door. I held up the letter. "What's this?"

"Dad's bank. Those come all the time."

"That's not his bank," I told her, pulling out my wallet and showing her the bank card he'd given me. "This is his bank. This..." I held up the letter again. "This was Mom's bank. I...I only know that because there's a file folder full of statements up in the attic. She had a checking and savings account. You know...money from when her parents died in one and paychecks from KLHS in the other."

"Okay, so?" she asked, but she focused her attention on it. "I mean...they were married, Evan, so it makes sense that they're addressed to him now. Maybe he just left it where it was."

I tapped the envelope across my knuckles, studying it for a moment. There was a part of me that wanted to know what it said, perhaps what the balance was, because deep down inside, my stomach was churning. Something seemed *wrong*.

"Did Mom have a will?" I asked her softly, glancing to the house for a second.

"Evan, I was *ten!*" she countered with a laugh. "I don't remember all that much."

"What *do* you remember?"

"Um, I remember staying home with Dad because I was watching a TV show, and I remember the phone call he got when you guys showed up at the hospital. Dad took me with him, and he made me stay with you after they'd stitched you up and Tyler was in surgery, but the nurses kept an eye on me. Dad was kinda all over the place. He was…dealing with police and the surgeons and the nurses. He told me that Mom wasn't coming." Her face looked sad. "I remember when you woke up, and I remember you crying. I remember Tyler waking up from surgery the same way. The funeral is blurry. There was that lady Dad brought in to watch us, but only until Tyler was like fifteen or so." Shaking her head, she shrugged a shoulder and looked my way. "He barely talked to us before, big brother, so he really wasn't going to come running to us after, you know?"

Nodding, I tapped the letter again. Glancing her way, I opened it. It was the same as the ones in the attic, a simple bank statement, with balances and charges. The significant difference was the type of account it was: a trust, with William Shaw as the beneficiary. The other significant difference was the balance.

"Jesus…" I breathed, shaking my head and turning the pages over in my hands.

"What?"

Shaking my head, I looked over at her. "I think we need to call Tyler."

"*Why?*"

"Because this account is like missing a third of what was showing up in the attic."

Faith narrowed her eyes and picked up her phone, scrolling quickly and putting it on speaker.

"Rylee Faith!" our brother answered. "What's shakin', midget? *Daddy Dearest* give you lumps of coal yet?"

I snorted but spoke up. "Tyler, listen."

Quickly explaining what I'd seen in the attic and about the statement in my hand, I asked, "Did Mom have a will?"

"I dunno, baby bro," he said grimly. "Do me a favor, you two… Just…keep that shit quiet for now. Okay? Let me see what I can find out. Jasmine's dad is a lawyer. Let me ask him a few questions, and I'll get back to you. Don't say shit to Dad."

"Okay," Faith and I said together.

"And keep that fucking statement."

I folded it and stuck it in my back pocket. "Done," I told him. "Merry Christmas, Tyler. We gotta go." I tapped Faith's arm and pointed to Dad, who was watching us out the window.

"Merry Christmas, guys."

Chapter Eighteen

EVAN

"Favorite Christmas movie?" I asked Dani over the phone as I flipped through the channels on the TV in my room.

The bank statement was still in my pocket, but Dad had left not long after Faith and I had gotten off the phone with Tyler in the car to come inside. He was working overnight, which meant he'd be back in the morning, sleep through the day, and go in again on Christmas Eve. It was that latter part that made me happy. That he'd be gone for Christmas Eve and Christmas morning. Gifts were not an important part of the Shaw household. They hadn't been since Faith had turned eleven and figured out that Santa was just a great big ruse. After that, no one bothered with any of it.

"Um, *A Christmas Story*," she answered. "You?"

"*Rudolph the Red-Nosed Reindeer*," I said, grinning when she laughed.

"Okay, then."

"What'd you expect? *A Christmas Carol*? Dickens and Scrooge?"

"Actually, yes!" She cracked the hell up, and God, I missed that sound, but more, I missed seeing her when she laughed like that. Her body would curl in on itself, her nose would wrinkle, and those blue eyes were just gorgeous when she laughed. Sometimes she'd curl up on me when she did it, and we'd end up kissing like crazy, like we couldn't breathe without our lips touching.

"Yours fits you, pretty girl," I said with a chuckle. "I can see you and Wes just…up to no good as kids."

"Oh hell yes. I always wanted to get his tongue stuck to a metal pole, if only to shut him up."

Laughing, I shook my head. "You mean you didn't?" I gasped in false shock.

"No, but that wasn't without trying. Yours fits too, baby. The different kid picked on by his peers."

"Huh…Yeah, I guess. Though, really, it's Rudolph's parents that fascinated me as a kid. The mom was cool, but the dad was all embarrassed of him, tried to change him, but in the end accepted him and corrected how he treated him." I huffed a humorless laugh. "And there's how you know it's fiction. It never turns out like that."

"Baby," Dani breathed over the line. "You said he was leaving you alone. Are you okay?"

Her voice softened, wrapping around me like her hugs. I dropped the TV remote onto the bed and raked a hand through my hair. One good thing to come out of being back in Key Lake was I'd gone to my old barber for a haircut. It had been needed.

"I…I guess." I sighed deeply. "You know, I never paid attention to some stuff as a kid. I accepted what I was told because I trusted my mother, and my dad…he didn't really tell us anything, but…"

I started talking, telling her everything I'd done and seen since coming back to Montana. I'd been keeping her posted on some things, but the bank situation was bugging the shit out of me. It wasn't even about the money, and I expressed that to Dani too. It was about the fact that the money in that account had belonged to my mother, and it was most likely that same money that my dad had held over our heads for *years*. I told her about every word Dad and I had exchanged and how he'd pretty much left Faith and me alone, except for the occasional run-in.

"I'm *so very proud* of you, Evan," she said softly over the phone.

I felt my cheeks heat with how firmly she'd said those words. "For what?"

"For not putting up with his shit but doing it in a way that makes you the better person, baby," she explained. "He's the one yelling and throwing shit like a fucking child, and you've stayed calm and honest. It's the honesty that's keeping him away. He doesn't want to hear it, and he's probably starting to see he can't get to you. I love you, and you're doing the right thing."

"I love you too." I uttered those words back so easily, and they still felt inadequate as to how she made me feel, but she seemed to cherish it every time I said them.

"The trust fund thing is a different story. If it's been changed from her savings to a trust fund, then your mom probably did have a will, Evan. You know, Aunt Tessa and Dad had a trust fund from Grandpa Bishop. I could…maybe ask them how it works."

"Do you mind? I'm a little lost here, Dani."

"Anything for you, baby. Aunt Tessa's here. I'll go ask her. Hold on."

I could hear Dani shift on the other end of the line. Doors opened, thumps echoed down stairs, and I could envision the whole house. And I missed it like the air I breathed.

"Hey, punkin'," I heard Aunt Tessa sing over the line. "What's up?"

Dani explained everything I'd told her as best she could, but Aunt Tessa interrupted her.

"Let me talk to him, Dani," she said, and her voice was clear over the line. "Hey, sweet boy! We miss you."

My grin spread over my face as I answered her back. "I miss you guys too. Um, Merry early Christmas."

She laughed. "Back atcha, kiddo. Now…let's talk about this trust fund thing." She took a deep breath and then started to talk. "Daniel and I were given a trust fund when our father died. He did have a will, and he had specific instructions on how things were to be distributed. Daniel was of age, but I was a minor when Dad passed away. So that made Daniel the executor of the estate…and my guardian. We didn't have any issues, though. I mean, it was just the two of us, so the house, the accounts, and everything my dad left behind were simply…split. Daniel and I were amicable about the whole business, like we always are.

"However, Evan, until I was of age, Daniel had to treat my portion of the funds delicately. Sometimes he had to show proof of what he'd spent, like a car or repairs on the house…whatever. That was just in case I decided to call foul play. Not that I would, you see. But you guys…Christ, buddy…this is a sticky situation. You're already on iffy terms with your dad, but you're all of age. All three of you. And your older brother…"

"Tyler."

"Tyler. How old is he?"

"He's about to turn twenty-one in January."

"Is he now?" she said slowly. "Some trusts are set up that the age of the recipient isn't eighteen but twenty-one."

"Seriously?"

"Yes, sir. It all depends on how your mother set it up."

"But…but…Aunt Tessa, wouldn't have someone told us?" I asked, swallowing nervously because this was starting to fall into place a bit — the money, Dad's sudden change in hostility, his desperate actions, even his leaving us alone the last few days.

"Yeah, your dad."

I laughed harshly, humorlessly. "Right."

My phone beeped, and I pulled it away to see that Tyler was calling me just as Faith poked her head in the door.

"Aunt Tessa, I gotta go. My brother's calling. Please tell Dani I love her and that I'll call her later. Okay?"

"Absolutely, Evan. And son?" she called urgently over the line. "Be safe, okay?"

"Okay." My chest filled with a warmth of her calling me son, because that's how she'd treated me the whole time I'd known her.

I answered Tyler's call. "Hey."

"Okay, the midget should be banging down your door any second," he replied, and as hard as he was trying to keep his voice light, he was failing. "Put me on speaker. *Daddy Dearest* isn't home, so I want to talk to both of you."

I did as he asked, and Faith and I sat on my bed with my phone between us. "Okay, we're here," I told him.

"Okay, so here's what I know, guys," he started and then let out a harsh laugh. "We…all of us…are so fucking stupid. That's first. Second, not one of us thought to look into public records."

Faith and I locked wide-eyed gazes for a second but didn't say anything.

"Look, before I tell you this, we need to talk about Dad," Tyler went on. "That asshole kept us in the dark. He banked on his...*discipline* to keep us scared or blind. But it's time to face facts. I'm not one for spewing psychological bullshit, but he's an abusive bastard. He always was, and he always will be. The fucked-up part is...there wasn't much we could've done after Mom died. I'm pretty sure no one would've believed us because he's got that whole community snowed that he's this...miracle-working doctor, never mind that nothing he ever said or did to us was illegal, just simply asinine."

"Ty, just tell us. We know all of this," Faith stated nervously. "Just tell us what you found out."

Tyler sighed on the other side of the line. "Mom had a will, which left everything to us. All three of us. However, she wasn't banking on dying before we were of age, so therefore, William Shaw became our guardian and the executor of said will. Mom's inheritance from Grandpa and Grandma Adams was supposed to be for us — for school, for our lives, but *not* for our father."

"Oh, damn," I breathed. "She left him nothing?"

"She left him nothing because she was leaving his ass, Evan. She'd fucking filed for divorce!" he practically growled. "Wanna know when he was served?"

Faith and I groaned, and my hand gripped my hair as I sputtered out, "Yes...no...Do we?"

"The day after the accident."

"Fuck," I breathed, squeezing my eyes closed.

"Yup! While you and I were in the damn hospital recovering from the wreck, while they were performing an autopsy on our mother, they brought him divorce papers." He laughed again, but it wasn't funny, just a nervous reaction. "I'd be willing to bet that the officers who were talking to him about the accident were the same ones who served him. From what I can piece together with Jas's dad's help, it looked like she was about to haul ass on Dad. She'd started with changing her will. After that, she filed for divorce, stating irreconcilable differences, and then she filed for sole custody of us."

I rubbed my face, chasing away the sting in my eyes. She knew. My mother knew what Dad was capable of, and not only was she trying to save us, she was trying to do it quickly and quietly.

"Let me guess," I mumbled behind my hands, finally pulling them away. "She would've picked us up from school the next day, and we wouldn't have gone home. She'd…she…Jesus, Tyler, she was acting like nothing was going on in the car!"

"I know, which makes her the most badass, the strongest person I've ever known," he said firmly, but there was a sadness laced in his tone. "Wonder what she saw or heard to make her do it…" he mused, but he trailed off.

"Okay, so…if she left everything to us, then why is Dad still in control?" Faith asked.

"Because the trust is set up for us to be given our share after we turn twenty-one," Tyler answered. "Knowing Mom, it was for *us*. Period. End of story. She would've wanted us to have it. Specifically, she didn't want *him* to have it."

"Oh, God…and you're turning twenty-one next month," Faith whispered, her gaze moving from the phone to my face. "No wonder he's been acting desperate. He's been keeping this shit secret the whole fucking time!"

"And it's about to come to a crashing end," I muttered, frowning down at the phone. "Dad has to know that as soon as Tyler was contacted, he'd tell us."

"I don't give a fuck about the money," Tyler stated, and Faith and I added our agreement. "But if Mom wanted something and he didn't fucking follow it, then I'm gonna be one pissed off motherfucker. His ass has blamed Evan and me for her this whole goddamn time, punished us, threatened us, denied us, and now I find out that she was trying to save us from the asshole? Guys, it's all I can do not to fly home and punch his fucking face."

"It won't change anything," I countered.

"What?" Faith asked, and Tyler sighed deeply.

"Evan, *come on!*"

"I'm serious," I said firmly, shaking my head. "Punching him won't do anything but give him a reason to have you arrested, Tyler. It's the reason he hasn't touched us all these years. I see it. He'd like nothing more than to beat the shit out of me, especially since I've been home, but he doesn't come near me because he doesn't know what I'll do, what I'll say and to whom." I glanced up to Faith and went on. "With Faith, it's a completely different situation, with her being a girl. That alone has kept him away from her. She's already fearless, so to touch her or overly punish her would cause questions at school, in town, that sort of thing, because I'm willing to bet he's pretty sure she'd get loud."

Faith giggled, shrugging a shoulder. "Maybe."

I sighed deeply. "He didn't want us. Mom did. And I wonder if he was only with her for the money, which pisses me the fuck off *for her*, but knowing she was trying to get us away from him…That's…" I groaned, my chest hurting a bit. "That's a question answered for me that I've been wondering for years. I wish I'd known that sooner. All those rumors, all that bullshit everyone spewed our way, it was true. Well, some of it…"

I kept going. "All I want—all I've ever wanted—is for him to leave me…us…alone. That's it. Honestly, that's still all I want." I met my sister's gaze and shrugged, but I was talking to both of them. "I just…I wanna go back to school and classes and my job. I want out of Montana. I just…I just wanna go home to Dani. I…I'm…That place is…No, *she's* my home now. I've finally found where I need to be, where I'm accepted, and where I haven't been this happy since before Mom died. Happier, actually." I shook my head slowly. "But I can't leave here knowing that he may completely unravel by your birthday, Tyler, because he thinks he's gotten away with something all these years. It's not fair to let Faith deal with it. Not alone. That's for damn sure."

"Shit, Ev…What do you wanna do, then?" my brother asked.

"I dunno." I sighed, gripping my hair, but shrugged. "What I do know is that the balance on that trust is significantly less than the last statement up in the attic. I know there is no way in hell it's due to college—yours or mine—or any residual medical bills or whatever from the wreck. It doesn't add up. I don't know what he's done with it, and I don't care. But if he keeps going, then by the time Faith is twenty-one, there won't be a damn dime left."

"See…that's not cool for me. At all," Tyler countered.

"Me, either."

"It's not about the money," Faith said softly, and she seemed uncomfortable with the conversation. "It's about what *Mom* wanted."

"Definitely," Tyler and I said at the same time.

"I think…" I grimaced at what I was about to say. "Shit, Tyler, I really think we need to consider getting a lawyer, though I don't know how we'd cover something like that. Technically, we're all broke students."

Faith and Tyler chuckled a bit, but it was the latter who spoke up. "That's the point of a lawyer, to fight so they can get paid too." He laughed a little. "My Jasmine, she's gonna make a kick-ass lawyer someday."

Grinning, I countered, "I can't see Dani being a lawyer. She'd tell every-damn-body to go to hell and how fast they could get there. Not exactly conducive to making deals."

We all laughed, though everyone went quiet for a moment, and eventually my brother spoke softly. "We can't do much over the next few days. I mean, it's Christmas, so not much can take place. I'll talk to Jasmine and her dad. And Evan, you might wanna go grab that other statement — the one in the attic. Do it now while the asshole is out of the house."

"I'll go." Faith got up and bolted for the attic. She wasn't gone a minute before she was back with the whole folder. "Tyler," she called, pulling out her phone. "I'm sending you pictures of these so you'll have them." She snapped the two pictures, including the recent one, and then handed me the last statement my mother had filed away. She left to put the folder back and close up the attic.

Once Faith was seated back on my bed, I said, "We'll have to tread lightly around him the next few days or at least until I leave, but…" I shot a look to Faith. "I'm really worried for Faith when I go home."

"Yeah, me too," Tyler muttered over the line. "I dunno, but we'll figure something out. Shit, Ev…She's eighteen, free to go if she truly wanted to. Faith, you're the one who'll be dealing with him. What do you think? Can you handle it? Or does Evan take you with him and you finish out high school in Florida?"

She huffed a laugh and locked gazes with me. "I have to finish here, don't I? I missed the cutoff for graduating early. I'd thought about it, and I had good enough grades, but it's just until May."

"Five months," I reiterated. "That's a long time to be stuck in this house, Rylee Faith."

"You guys figure it out and let me know," Tyler stated firmly over the line. "Jas and I will be back in Montana by the end of the week. I have no shame in coming to the house and packing up her shit."

Faith laughed softly. "Love you, Ty."

"Love you guys too. Merry Christmas," he sang gruffly, ending the call.

I looked to Faith, tilting my head her way when I could see the wheels turning in her head. "What are you thinking?" I asked her with a slight laugh.

Her brow furrowed as she toyed with her phone. "I'm thinking we need to maybe…watch our asses the next few days. I'm thinking we need some sort of…insurance or…or leverage against *Daddy Dearest*."

Grinning, I asked, "What do you mean?"

"I dunno, but I *do know* that he's carefully crafted this bullshit façade around himself in this stupid tiny town," she said angrily. "I think if he thought that could come tumbling down around his ankles, he'd shut the fuck up for once."

"Maybe." I barked a laugh at her evil grin and nodded, picking up *The Count of Monte Cristo*. Dani and I were just about finished with it. In fact, we'd have to pick a new book soon. It was her choice next. "I need to call Dani back. She's gonna want to know all this stuff," I said softly, picking my phone back up.

"Tell her hello," Faith said and then left my room.

As soon as Dani's sweet voice greeted me on the line, everything in me came spilling out, including a few tears at just how brave my mother had been. As I stayed on the phone with Dani while she read to me, all I wanted was her there. I needed her more than I needed anything. I craved her arms around me, her strengthening words that never stopped coming from her, and I needed her touch. I'd never understood how, in books I'd read, couples could ravish each other in the most stressful times, but as I read along with her, I truly just… got it. If Dani were in my room, in my bed, I'd have lost myself in her in order to drown in something completely and utterly *good*.

"Dani?" I said, interrupting her reading.

"Yeah, baby?" she asked, a yawn escaping her.

It made me chuckle. "Before I let you go to sleep, I just…I need to tell you…I love you. And I miss you. So much that it's painful today."

"Oh, God…Me too, Evan. I miss your hugs."

"Yeah," I said slowly with a grin. "I miss yours too. Night, pretty girl."

"Night, Evan."

Christmas Eve day was a quiet one. Dad shut himself up in his room to sleep, and Faith and I spent our time in either the living room watching Christmas movies or I read to Dani over the phone in my mother's library, finishing *The Count of Monte Cristo*. The best part was listening to Dani go on and on about how Edmund Dantes was probably the most patient character she'd ever read, that he'd waited until *just the right moment* to let loose his plan. Laughingly, she told me I should do the same to my dad. She told me that I should let karma kick his ass.

She was saying it again on Christmas morning. I'd gotten up to make French toast for Faith. We weren't exchanging gifts, and we were supposed to go to the diner later for their holiday special, just the two of us.

My dad's car was in the driveway, and I assumed he was sleeping after having worked overnight again, which was a schedule I was pretty damn sure he'd picked on purpose just to avoid us.

I stepped into my mother's library and turned on the light, grinning at Dani's adorable yet endless chatter on my phone. God, I loved that sound. She'd blurt out anything and everything she was feeling or thinking. It was pure and honest, not to mention so very missed, never mind that we talked every damn day.

"Hey, baby! You know what would be *awesome?*" she gushed over the line.

Chuckling, I shook my head. "What's that?"

"If…If…If one day, you're like this famous writer, then you could totally rub it in your dad's face!"

Cracking up, I fell even more in love with her. She had *way* more faith in me than I did. "You think so, Dani?" I teased her a little as I walked to my mother's shelves. "Okay, so…what are we reading next? My sources are limited, but are we re-reading something? Or are you doing what I did with Dumas?"

"I think," she sang, and I heard her get up from her bed. "I think we should read…*The Secret Garden*."

I immediately found my mother's copy, pulling it off the shelf. "Mom had it," I murmured softly. "But isn't this a girl's book?"

"Sort of," she hedged adorably, "but it's filled with a pretty interesting cast of characters, not to mention a touch of mystery. You picked the last one, even though you'd already read it. This one's on me."

"Okay," I conceded, flipping through the book in question. It wasn't a long book, but it would probably get us through until I got home. I set the book aside, gazing up at the bookshelf. "I need to grab a few of these before I come home," I said softly, and really, it was more to myself than to Dani, who was listening to me. "In fact, a few of these will come in handy for school."

"Do it," Dani said lightly.

There was a thump, a rattle of glass, and footsteps coming from the living room.

"Dani, let me…" I whispered and then paused, thinking I should end the call and then call her back once I was back upstairs. But something in my mind told me to simply pull the phone away from my ear. "Pretty girl, hang on."

I turned when the door opened. My phone was in my hand, along with the book Dani wanted to read. My dad leaned in the doorway, looking ragged, tired, or maybe even drunk. Either way, he was looking for a fight. I could see it all over his face as he gazed at me in pure hatred.

"Sweet Jesus, Evan…Can't you stay out of this room? Or are you always going to be this…this…weak loser?"

I shook my head and sighed deeply. "Merry Christmas to you too, Dad," I stated calmly, but sarcasm came shining through my words and tone. "I was simply looking to see if Mom had books I could use at school." My lie was smooth, and I supposed it wasn't technically a lie, but it was just enough to make him narrow his eyes at me.

He snorted. "God, you're so much like your fucking mother. Emotionless and cold. Nothing ever gets to you. Not even when you let her die."

I barely heard Dani's gasp on the phone in my hand, so I knew he hadn't. Leaning against the shelf beside me, I truly looked at him, and I wasn't sure if it was because my girl was listening or if I finally…*finally* understood what Dani had been trying to tell me from the beginning. I had been twelve years old when my mother had wrecked the car, when she'd accidentally taken herself out of our lives, but knowing what I knew now…I wasn't sure my mouth could be stopped if I tried.

"Is that what you tell yourself? Is that what you force yourself to believe in order to maintain this…this level of hate?" I asked him, setting the book down onto my mother's desk but keeping my phone in my hand. "You truly have convinced yourself that I was completely responsible for it all, haven't you?"

He stepped into the room, the ice in his glass clinking. "Aren't you, you little piece of shit? She wouldn't have been out in the rain... She wouldn't have—"

"I was *twelve*, Dad. Twelve. My fucking voice hadn't even changed yet, you asshole. I didn't drive the car; she did. You want to place blame, then let's start there. And I couldn't control the motherfucking weather! I also didn't push the goddamn dog into the road either."

"You let her drown!" he yelled, stepping closer.

"She told me to go!" I finally yelled back. "What more could I do! *What?* Tell me, because I guarantee you it's nothing I haven't told myself, so please, enlighten me as to what else I could've done. Because trust me, I've already come up with everything you could possibly spew at me now." My nostrils flared in anger as he stepped a little closer. "What I can't figure out is what pisses you off more," I mused, glaring his way. "That you *know* it wasn't my fault or Tyler's, but you can't blame her either. Tell me, Dad, what's worse? The fact that she's gone? Or the fact that even if she'd survived the wreck, she was still leaving you?"

He froze for a moment, his eyes widening a little.

I huffed a humorless laugh. "It must be pure fucking hell to have to raise three kids you never even wanted. But oh my God..." I gasped mockingly. "Heaven forbid the citizens of Key Lake find out that tidbit of information. Especially considering without those kids you detest so much, there would be no trust fund for you to bleed dry."

"The fuck did you just say to me?" he hissed, and I held up my phone unthinkingly.

"Public records and the US Postal Service are amazing and most helpful resources of information. Just what the hell are you spending it on?" I asked, not even caring about the answer, but I'd pushed too far.

The glass in his hand flew, shattering against the bookshelf by my head, but a heavier piece caught my face.

"You wretched piece of fucking shit..."

When I flinched, my phone was suddenly ripped from my hand, and I heard the telltale sound of plastic and electronics coming to an end on another wall, which made me panic because I knew Dani would be freaking out. A firm hand was at my throat, and he was in my face, shoving me into the bookcase behind me. He smelled like sweat and the hospital and the liquor he'd been drinking. Several books, not to mention a picture or two, tumbled to the floor.

"You should've drowned with her!" he snarled in my face. "Fuck, just looking at you…Your face…your fucking face. It's the same repulsion she had for me."

"Let me go," I wheezed, pushing him back. "Let me go, or I'll let the whole world know just what you are."

He shoved me hard before pushing away from me. "And what's that, you little shit?"

"An opportunistic, abusive thief," I panted, rubbing my throat, only to touch the stinging place on my forehead. My fingers came away with blood on them. "Jesus, Dad, did you even love her? Or did you just set sights on her inheritance? Did you fool her like you've fooled everyone else in this godforsaken town?"

His half smile was my answer. "Good luck proving it."

Faith stepped into the doorway, her phone in hand and fingers moving rapidly over the screen. "He doesn't have to, Dad. I just recorded the whole thing…and I've already sent it to Tyler."

He was in front her in just a step or two, and I tried to stop him, but he didn't touch her other than to snatch her phone as well. In a blur, it was thrown, and the sound of breaking glass as it went out the window met my ears. The damn thing landed in the snow in the backyard.

"Get away from me, both of you. Get out of my house."

Faith smiled, shaking her head. "No, see…I don't think so. I think we can work out some sort of deal. We'll tell Tyler to hold on to that video, and you will leave us — and what Mom left us — alone. No more threats, no more foul words from you. Otherwise, lawyers will be called, and I'm thinking the board of directors at the hospital may just get an e-mail. Oh! Not to mention Chief Clark. You know… his son Eric is in my class…" she mused dramatically. "He's a really nice boy, works with the audio/video department at school."

Dad was livid, but now he knew he was screwed.

"Blackmail," he muttered, shaking his head.

"Probably." I shrugged my shoulder. "Prove it," I said, echoing his repetitive threat as I walked over to pick up the remnants of my cell phone, sighing deeply. "By the way, I was on a call when you so rudely interrupted."

"No one gives a shit about what your college whore may or—"

I cut him off with a square punch to the face. "Call her that again, and everyone within a five-hundred-mile radius will know everything!" I turned to Faith as he slipped to the floor. "I've got to get out of here. I need some air." I pointed to our father. "If he tries anything, just…get in your car and head to the diner or something."

Faith nodded, wide-eyed and shocked, but she rushed to me. "Evan, your head…"

"I'm fine. I've…" I waved her off and walked to the front door, grabbing my jacket off the coatrack. Stepping out into the cold, snowy weather, I slammed the door behind me.

Chapter Nineteen

DANI

"Pretty girl, hang on," Evan said softly over the line, and I frowned at the change in his tone.

We'd just been joking, laughing, and we were trying to decide on a new book to read. Suddenly, he was serious, and if I'd had to guess…tentative, maybe even scared.

"Okay," I muttered back, but I didn't think he heard me because another voice came over the line. I grimaced at the sound of Evan's father. Jesus, could he sound more hateful and disgusting?

When I heard the words *"weak loser,"* I left my room quickly, practically skidding down the stairs to the living room, where my dad and Wes were watching TV. They both looked up at me as I shut off the flat-screen and put a finger to my lips for them to be quiet. *Someone* needed to witness this shit because the language and tone were so very foul. But more than that, if something happened to Evan, I needed my dad.

I put my phone on speaker just as Evan's dad said, *"God, you're so much like your fucking mother. Emotionless and cold. Nothing ever gets to you. Not even when you let her die."*

I gasped, looking to my dad in shock and hurt, and Wes moved to cover my mouth, touching the screen at the same time to mute our end of the line. Tears ran unchecked down my face with every foul word from William and every brave deflection from Evan. My sweet boyfriend was trying *so fucking hard* to maintain his temper. And he was doing a hell of a lot better than I would have.

"Daddy?" I pleaded with him, not knowing for what, but something needed to be done. I'd never felt so helpless and angry in all my life.

"Jesus," Wes whispered, narrowing his eyes as he shook his head slowly. "I think Ev's reached his limit. Uncle Daniel, we need to—"

"Yeah," Dad interrupted him. "Go get your mother and aunt."

Wes hesitated just as Evan completely threw every single thing he knew about his parents at his father—the divorce, the fact that William hated his own children and, finally, the trust fund.

"The fuck did you just say to me?" his father spewed.

"Public records and the US Postal Service are amazing and most helpful resources of information. Just what the hell are you spending it on?" Evan asked derisively, and I'd never heard him so mad, so angry, or so fucking *strong*.

However, it all came to a screeching halt.

"You wretched piece of fucking shit…" I heard, and a small sob erupted from me because the voice was closer to the phone, which meant William was moving closer to my Evan.

"Shh, baby girl," Dad tried to soothe me, wrapping his arm around my shoulders.

There was a loud rustling sound, followed by the sounds of crashing glass and a hard thump, and finally the beep signaling that the call had ended.

"No!" I wailed, scrambling to dial him back. "No, no, no! Pick up…pick up…Evan, *please!*"

The call went straight to voice mail, over and over, and I was losing my fucking mind.

"Shit," Wes said, standing up. "I'mma beat that motherfucker's ass." He faced the hallway. "Mom! Aunt Leanne!"

They'd been wrapping Christmas presents in my parents' bedroom, and both hurried into the living room. As soon as they caught sight of me, my mother was wrapping me up.

"Dani? Baby, what happened?"

Dad explained quickly and added, "I *knew* he shouldn't have gone home alone...or fucking *at all* for that matter." He rocked back on his heels, clearly thinking for a moment. "Wes, get on the phone with the airline about those tickets you have. I want to land in Missoula as soon as you can get us there. All of us, if possible."

Next, he took my phone from me and tried Evan again, only to get voice mail once more. He looked to me. "Dani-girl, calm down. Tell me the name of that town he's in?"

"K-Key L-Lake."

He nodded, swiping his finger over my phone and typing in a search. He found what he was looking for and called a phone number, putting the phone to his ear, murmuring that he was calling the local police. The tone my father took was the one he used in class or when he was dealing with some sort of business. He was normally so laid-back that to hear his no-nonsense voice was almost scary.

"Chief Clark, my name is Dr. Daniel Bishop, from Edgewater College in Glenhaven, Florida." He paused, nodding once, and then stood up to pace. "One of my students — Evan Shaw — is from your town, and he's home for the holidays. However, during the middle of a phone conversation, there seemed to be a scuffle of sorts in the home, an argument, and now, I'm unable to get him back on the line. Yes, sir, I heard some of it. It was pretty...ugly. He's my daughter's boyfriend, and we're just a bit concerned," he said, eyeing me as I tried my damnedest to stop crying. "I'm wondering if you could just...take a moment to send someone? I know it's Christmas, but... Listen, I'm about to head that way. I had plans to travel to Bozeman for New Year's, but I'm thinking I may need to move that up a bit..."

His lie was smooth but necessary, and he hummed a few times as he listened over the line.

"I'm...I don't have the boy's address...Oh, you know it. Okay, then. Is there any chance you could call me back, Chief?" Dad rattled off his cell phone number, glancing up at Wes when he gave a thumbs-up and a tap to his wrist to let us know we were now in a time-crunch. "I'm leaving for the airport shortly, sir, so just leave a voice mail. I'll get it when I can. Thank you, sir. I really appreciate this. I've got a very upset daughter, and the boy, he's...he's like family to me, so I'm just calling as a concerned parent."

Dad ended the call after thanking the officer again and then knelt in front of me as he gave me back my phone. Tears started anew when my eyes fell to the picture on my background. It was Evan and me, laughing and silly in a selfie we'd taken on my porch swing.

"Dani, I need you to calm down for me," he said firmly but gently. "The police chief said he'd personally drive to the Shaws' home himself. Apparently his son is friends with Evan's sister—they're in the same class or something. Okay?" When I nodded, he turned to Wes but didn't leave my side. "Wes, what'cha got, son?"

"Five seats for today in like two hours? Or four tomorrow? If we wait, not everyone can go," he told us, his hand over the phone. "What do ya wanna do? I'm sure as shit going, and we can't stop Dani, so…"

Dad sighed deeply, turning back to me to wipe away my tears, but before he could answer, it was my mother who piped up.

"Go…Everyone pack a bag. Keep it light and pack warmly. It's snowing in Montana. Carry-on bags only. If we need something, we'll buy it." She snapped her fingers to get everyone moving.

Aunt Tessa was on her own phone. "Susan, sweetie. I need you to run the café for the next couple of days…"

I started to get up, my temper flaring. "If…If he hurt him…If one fucking hair on Evan's head is harmed, that…that…*man* will have no idea what hit him!" I stated, pointing a finger to the ground.

Dad smirked but nodded, giving my forehead a kiss. "You make me feel almost sorry for the man, baby girl. *Almost*." He nodded again but looked around at all of us. "We pull out of here in as soon as everyone's packed. Go."

EVAN

My boots crunched over snow as I walked down my driveway. The cut on my forehead stung in the cold air, and my hand ached. I had no idea where I was going, only that I needed to get out of that house before I did more than punch that asshole.

I glanced back at the house, my nostrils flaring. I honestly didn't know what pissed me off the most—the vitriol that Dad had spewed my way or the fact that I'd completely lost my shit. I'd begged my brother to maintain his control, and I'd done exactly the fucking op-posite. In all reality, William Shaw could have me arrested for assault. I snorted at the thought, because what would the narrow-minded people of Key Lake think of that?

Still, I should've been the bigger person. I'd held on and held on the whole goddamn time I'd been in that house, but knowing what I knew about my father, I hadn't been able to bear to see the look of hatred on his face while he'd been the one damn thing my mother had been trying to escape. The fucker had wanted a fight, and I'd sure as hell given him one.

Shaking my head, I groaned as I gripped my hair in my hand. My knuckles were sore, and when I looked down at them, I saw two of them were split and already turning purple. I made a fist, sneering at it. So much for Dani being proud of me.

"Shit," I hissed, reaching into my pocket for my phone that had scattered all to hell when he threw it. "Fuck…Dani." I scrambled to put the battery back in, but the back was cracked and the screen was splintered in a spider web that started from the corner, which just happened to be the power button.

My one connection to Dani, to everyone outside this fucked-up situation, was completely destroyed. For a split second, I wondered if Faith's phone had fared any better. And it being Christmas, there was no replacing it, not until stores opened the next day. I needed to find a phone, even if I called the Bishop house collect, but I couldn't even see my contacts list on my phone. The only number I had memorized was Dani's cell.

My feet started to move, one in front of the other. I needed to think, and I needed to get away from that house. The crunch of snow was loud in the quiet streets. No one was outside, though I could imagine that most families were opening presents or still having breakfast or whatever the hell normal families did on major holidays.

When the black iron fence appeared in front of me, I came back to my senses. Gazing around, I realized I was at the cemetery across the street from the church. Swiping at my face, I could see that I was still bleeding just a little, but I ignored it and walked in through the gates. The snow on the graves was pristine, untouched, unsullied. I wandered slowly, noting names that had been here for decades. Dates went from the early 1900s to just last year. I saw names like Clark, Hill, Michaels, Wallace, and finally Shaw. Not for the first time did

I bitterly wish that the first name on that headstone read William instead of Robyn. And for a few minutes as I squatted down to clear snow off the cold stone and away from my potted flower, I allowed my mind to play the "what if" game. What if the roles had been reversed? What if Mom had lived and my father had died? How different would shit be? My siblings and I would've been loved, cared for, *nurtured*. Not hated, not forgotten, not beaten down with foul words, manipulation, and indifference.

But then there would've been no Dani. I'd escaped my hellish existence in this stupid town to get away from it all, and I'd found the most amazing thing. I'd found my true place, my heart, my soul…my *family*.

I was so conflicted, but I was still very angry, and that last thought caused tears to sting my eyes. The unfairness of it all slammed into me like a Mack truck. To wish for something different would change the now, and Dani was my *now*. And all I wanted was her. That was it; that was all I could hope for in life. I loved her, and I couldn't fathom anyone else owning my heart but her.

"Evan, son?" I heard behind me, and I stood up too quickly and spun, making myself a bit dizzy. "Whoa, easy, son…" Pastor Sean soothed, holding my shoulders. "You okay?"

I nodded, squeezing my eyes closed, but they opened when I felt a gentle hand on my face. He turned my head, eyeing my forehead, and then tilted my chin to look at my neck. I'd completely forgotten about Dad's hand on my throat.

"What happened, Evan?"

I was simply going to shake my head, but something in me was still bitter. My snort of a humorless laugh sounded rough in the quiet cemetery.

"Family disagreement," I muttered through gritted teeth.

Not for the first time did I see something akin to understanding cross his face. His eyes were as gray as the tombstones around us, but they were warmer, sadder. He sniffed once and nodded.

"C'mon," he said, pointing toward the church. "Let's clean you up. I'd just made a pot of coffee when I saw you through my window."

We walked back out of the cemetery in silence; the only sound was our steps through the snow. Pastor Sean was ahead of me, and I noted he was dressed in jeans and a sweater, completely different than the usual dress pants and button-down he usually wore. Once across the street, we bypassed the church, and he pulled out his keys for the small home next door.

His house was the rectory, something provided by the church while he was employed there. It was small, but the inside was warm, tidy, smelling of coffee and some sort of cleaner. I noted there was not a single Christmas decoration.

"Have a seat, Evan," he said, tapping the kitchen table. "Cream and sugar?"

"Yes, sir," I answered softly.

I wrapped my hands around the mug once he set it down in front of me, but he didn't take a seat. He stepped out of the room, coming back with a small first-aid kit in his hand, and he dragged the other kitchen chair over.

He pulled out some gauze and disinfectant, inhaling softly. "Bit early for whiskey, don't you think?"

I laughed, shaking my head, because I hadn't even realized the drink Dad threw had splashed on me. It had been the least of my concerns at the moment.

"Not mine. Trust me." I hissed at the sting as he started to clean my head.

"It's not as deep as I thought, and it's almost stopped bleeding. You want me to cover it?" he asked, but I shook my head. "Fair enough. Now, let me see that hand."

I lay my hand flat on the table, and he cleaned that up as well.

"Pastor Sean, is…is it possible to use your phone?" I asked, wincing when there was more stinging.

He reached into his pocket and pulled out a cell phone. I quickly dialed Dani's number, getting her voice mail instantly. Frowning, I dialed again, thanking Sean when he finished with my hand. The voice mail was immediate over and over, so I had no choice but to leave my girl a message.

"Pretty girl, I'm okay. Just…my phone is completely broken. I'll get a new one tomorrow and call you back. Just…don't panic, Dani. I *promise you* I'm okay, and I love you." I shook my head slowly, pushing the phone back to Sean. "Thanks," I whispered. I wasn't an idiot; I knew Dani would be freaking out. It wouldn't surprise me if she was on the phone with the damn airline.

When I looked up, Sean was studying me.

"You wanna talk about it? Anything you say to me stays in this kitchen, Evan. It's a perk of my job," he said, wearing a wry smile. He eyed my face, tilting his head before asking, "How long has this been going on, son?"

Something in his eyes, something in his calm, nonjudgmental expression caused something in me to crack wide open. Maybe it was because he'd known my mother, maybe because he'd been the one to speak at her funeral, or maybe something deep inside told me this man knew more than he let on.

I didn't say anything at first, and he let me be for a moment. I sipped my coffee, my eyes on the mug.

"This is the first time," I mumbled, frowning at the cup in my hands, but I gestured to the cut and my neck so he knew that I'd meant physically. I kept the fight and the facts brief, but I told him everything—the thrown glass, the trust fund, the punch, not to mention how badly I'd never even wanted to come home but that I'd done it for Faith.

Sean nodded, getting up for his own cup of coffee before sitting back down. "I can't say I'm shocked. Your father is a cold man."

I snapped my head up to stare at him. I was completely shocked that someone else in this town outside my siblings felt this way.

"What? You think it's a secret?" He laughed, but it wasn't really in humor. Shaking his head, he added, "This is a small town, son. Rumors burn through the members of this community quicker than a spark sets fire to dry grass." He sipped his coffee. "Some people see what they want, as long as it doesn't interfere with their happy, blissfully ignorant bubble. William Shaw puts on a good show, and he's done a heck of a lot of amazing work at the hospital. But see, you know the type of personality a man has with how they treat their underlings, their children, or even animals. It's something I've always noticed. Dr. Shaw can scare the nurses and assistants into quitting or at the least transferring away from him."

I sighed deeply, shrugging a shoulder. "We didn't exactly go see him at work."

"And *that* didn't go unnoticed either, kiddo," he countered, raising an eyebrow at me. "Your mother was my very good friend." He said it softly, sadly, smiling a little. "We were friends in high school—the same school you and your brother and sister went to—and your mom liked this town. She always said she wanted to raise her family here. How she convinced William to settle here is a mystery, but he had her..."

"Blinded?" I offered bitterly.

"Yes." His answer came so quickly and so firmly that my mouth fell open. "He was...perfect in every way, Evan. He was the doting boyfriend, the caring fiancé, and the flawless husband. What do you know about your father's family history?"

I shook my head. "Not much, just that his parents are dead. Mom said they had that in common. He moved here from Seattle after med school to marry her." I swallowed thickly, my brow furrowing as I tried to remember things my mother had told me ages ago. "M-Mom said that his parents were strict, that they'd demanded perfection from him. Sh-She said that his father was the reason he was in med school in the first place."

"All true. But add in the fact that his father would beat him to broken bones and bloody wounds before he sent him off to college."

I narrowed my eyes as my temper flared. "Are you telling me this to make me feel sorry for him? He...He blames me..." I tapped my chest. "He blames me personally for Mom's death. He has since I woke up in the hospital. He's told me and Tyler every day since then that we should have drowned with her."

Sean grimaced, but he shook his head. "No, son. I'm not asking you to feel sorry for him. I want you to know the truth. Your mother..."

"My mother was leaving him!" I snapped, starting to stand up.

"Evan, please..." he pleaded softly. "I know, son. I know she was. And I was trying to help her."

Those words made me freeze and then slowly sit back down. I stared at the man in front of me, my mind trying to wrap around it all. Every bit of it was rolling around in my head, and I needed someone to explain it all to me.

"Pastor Sean?"

"Just Sean, Evan...For this conversation, I am simply your mother's friend." His voice sounded so sad. "God, I miss her." He shook his head slowly. "In school, she was the prettiest thing I'd ever seen. In life, she was a damn rock," he said through a humorless laugh. "We were only friends, son. That's it. Like siblings, really. By the end of high school, I knew where I was going in life, that I was called for something higher. Robyn, though, she was brilliant. I knew she'd be a writer, and she was, but she was a phenomenal teacher."

He smiled sadly but went on. "She lost her parents toward the end of college. When she showed back up in town with William Shaw, I instantly didn't like the man, but he catered to her, he put in to transfer to the hospital here, and they got married." He met my gaze, shrugging a shoulder. "It's my…job to give people the benefit of the doubt, to not judge people on their pasts or mistakes. My job. My friendship with your mom, however, made me wary of him. But I didn't say anything. I knew if she needed me, she'd come to me, and eventually she did.

"Your dad didn't want children, Evan."

That fact being confirmed made me squeeze my eyes closed.

"Knowing his own past, the abuse at the hands of his parents, it was actually smart thinking, but Robyn…" He sighed, wearing a small smile. "Your mother wanted you guys so badly. Tyler was an oops, not really an accident, though I think William considers that pregnancy one, but still…Robyn fought for him. She was going to keep him, come hell or high water, even if it meant doing it alone. And your dad knew it."

My gaze shot up to see the anger in Sean's expression. "Something about your mother made your dad…possessive. And not in that protective, loving way but like he *owned* her. I honestly think that due to his childhood, she was the *first good thing* he'd ever had in his life, which made him selfish with her. He also was up for a promotion at the hospital, and being a family man would look so very good. So…he gave her what she wanted—Tyler, then you… and then eventually, Rylee Faith. It made for a picture-perfect life." His sarcasm did not go unnoticed.

Sean sipped his coffee, his eyes on his cup. "This is where things get touchy." He glanced up at me. "The older you got, the more you looked like your mother, which I'm sure you've heard." He chuckled a bit at my eye roll. "Yeah, well, to look at you, it's like William wasn't involved. And he started to accuse your mother of…infidelity."

When I narrowed my eyes, Sean held up a hand.

"You're his. Believe that, son. Your mother was faithful. Completely faithful. She didn't like her word being questioned, though, and she started to see that the knight in shining armor was starting to tarnish." He groaned, setting his elbows on the table and rubbing his face. "This...whole thing was a long time coming, because Robyn had to set things up slowly, in order to...keep you safe."

"She knew?" I yelled, and he grabbed my arm before I could stand up.

"Wait," he ordered, and his gaze was fierce. "Let me finish." Once I was in my seat again, he went on. "Rylee Faith probably doesn't remember, or if she does, then it didn't affect her much. She would've been about seven or eight at the time. You were about nine or ten. Robyn had a parent/teacher thing at the high school. She'd left you kids with William, something she tried to avoid at all costs because he admittedly had no patience, but she had no choice that particular night. When he agreed to children, she agreed that she would assume responsibility for you — babysitting, schooling, nurturing...

"That night, she came home to...raised voices and Rylee Faith in tears. Apparently she'd spilled something, and William was making her scrub the kitchen tile with a toothbrush. A child...with harsh chemicals and on her knees...and all the while standing over her berating her very existence. It was right then that your mother started to see what he truly was. She started to plan. And she came to me for help."

He stood up from his chair and paced a bit, saying, "I *should've* gotten all of you to a women's shelter in Helena or Bozeman, and I offered it to her, but she wanted to do it all on her own. She had the money, but she had to slowly change things. She shifted small amounts of cash around, she made a will, she...she changed the beneficiary on her insurance, and she started to plan. It took time! Too much time, if you ask me, but she was being cautious, so I understood that too. William may have been a busy doctor working his way up the ranks, but he was an observant man when it came to his wife and money." He stopped pacing. "Two years, son. *Two years* of protecting you guys, planning, seeing a lawyer outside Key Lake, and filing. She had everything set to go — a hidden bank account, an apartment in Helena, and a job too."

"And then the accident," I muttered, feeling my eyes sting. "I f-f... messed up. I...She had to drive me to the store, and..."

He sat back down. "Look at me, Evan. It's not your fault. That whole thing was an accident. The timing was terrible but not your fault. Your mother had to play the role all the way to the end, and even though she was going to be pulling out of this town the next day, she had no choice but to play the part for another twenty-four hours." He gripped my shoulder. "Son, I was there. I went to the scene because the chief of police called me. I saw the dog, the break in the railing of the road. I stood in the pouring rain as they rushed you and Tyler away. And I was still standing there when they pulled your mother's car out of the water." He squeezed my shoulder gently. "Evan, I saw the window you broke; I saw your mother's seat belt had jammed. All of it was just a foul and awful accident."

I shook my head, and I couldn't find it in me to care about my tears. I didn't care what he thought, because my grief for my mother opened up inside me like the day she'd died. It was painful, making me feel raw.

I could barely breathe in order to say, "She...Sh-She told me to get Tyler and get out."

"I'm sure she did, Evan," he soothed. "Her whole being was about the three of you. You need to know that. You need to accept that she loved you more than anything." He sighed deeply, shaking his head. "I tried my damnedest to watch over all of you, but your father wouldn't allow it. I came to see you and Tyler in the hospital, but he stopped me. I think William knew I was your mother's ally."

I rubbed my face, smashing the heels of my hands into my eyes to get control of my emotions. I winced at the soreness of my hand and my forehead. Suddenly I was just completely exhausted. I was tired of Montana and fighting with Dad. I was tired of cold weather and the holidays. I just wanted to go home to Dani. My whole soul missed her. I missed everything I'd left in Florida. However, I had a sinking suspicion that this shit would only get worse before I went home.

Once I had my voice back, I looked at him. "I punched my father."

He grinned, slapping my shoulder gently. "I'm sure he deserved it."

"No, no, no...You don't understand! He...He's probably gonna..."

"Gonna what, Evan? Clearly," he said firmly, gesturing to my face, "it was self-defense. And I have news for you, son. Chief Clark isn't exactly a member of the Dr. Shaw Fan Club."

"I should get back to Faith. I left because I didn't trust myself. I would've...The things he said about my mother and then my girlfriend..." I shook my head but pushed myself up from the table.

"Never mind that everything my mother had tried to leave to us is being wasted away…"

"Not everything, Evan." He stood up from the table and walked to a small writing desk in his living room. He came back with a file. "She needed an emergency escape, but she also needed someone as a contact who wasn't connected to your father. The account she set up for Helena and her insurance are all for you, Tyler, and Faith. I just happen to be the emergency name she gave. I've saved everything."

"What about the trust my dad controls?"

"There wasn't much she could do about that one. He watched it closely. Everything was supposed to come to you guys once you each reached twenty-one. She set it up that way in order to monitor it, and I'm certain she never expected to not be able to be here for you. She wanted you guys to have a comfortable life. That's all she wanted was to give you a chance to *live*. Is there anything left in it? Because your dad was sued for malpractice. He lost the case. He was probably using that to pay it. Though I have suspicions that he's got serious issues elsewhere. Highly unethical, but it wouldn't surprise me."

I snorted into a nasty laugh. "I'm pretty sure *unethical* is the least of his concerns."

"C'mon. I'll take you home." He pointed to the folder. "Keep that." He stopped me with a hand on my shoulder. "Listen, son…I'm *so sorry*. Your father forbade me from seeing you guys, especially after the accident, stating you were traumatized enough."

I snorted derisively and nodded. "I'm sure," I muttered, glancing down at the folder. "Hell, had he known, we might've lost this too."

Sean nodded, his brow furrowed. "Which is why I decided to wait, and then I tried and tried to approach you once Tyler and then you turned eighteen, but your father eventually threatened me with the removal of my position, which made me back down because I needed to watch out for all of you. It was what your mother would've wanted. And I obviously did a poor job of it," he said forlornly with a slow shake of his head as he eyed my face and neck. "All of you — you kids and William — put on a damn good front, not to mention I rarely saw any of you, especially when you and your brother went off to college. Finally I decided to wait until the accounts shifted to Tyler. If I'd known…"

"We…We didn't want anyone to know. Up until today, we had no proof," I told him.

He nodded, still looking a bit guilty, but I knew my dad well enough that he would've thrown his weight around to get his way.

Eventually he said, "Tyler's about to come of age, so I'm sure you guys can handle it. Get yourselves a lawyer."

I nodded, flipping through the pages in the folder he'd given me but not really seeing it. It was a blur of numbers and legal jargon.

The streets had a little more activity on them when we stepped outside and started the drive back to the house. The closer we got, the more nervous I became because I wasn't quite sure what would be waiting. When we drove by the diner, I didn't see my sister's car. However, I groaned aloud when we pulled into my driveway to see the chief's police cruiser parked behind Faith's car.

"Evan, self-defense, son. I'll tell him myself," Sean assured me.

Before he'd even shut off his car, Faith was out the front door and rushing to me. "Evan!" she called, wrapping her arms around my middle.

"You okay?" I asked her, hugging her close. "He didn't...Did you call..."

"No, that was Dani's dad."

"Aw, hell..." I groaned, shaking my head.

"They're on their way." Faith looked up at me. "Apparently Daniel called the chief, Wes called Tyler, and Tyler called me." She held up her phone, and even though it had a crack in the screen, at least it was still functioning. "They're all coming. All of them."

The front door slammed open, and my father burst out, yelling, "There he is. Arrest him!"

The chief was right behind him, narrowing his eyes at me *and* who was with me. "Sean," he greeted with a single nod, but when he reached me, he shook his head. "Jesus, Evan. You all right?"

I nodded, stepping back when my father rushed at us.

"Doc," Chief Clark sighed impatiently, placing a hand on his chest. "I saw the video, Dr. Shaw. Hell, I'd have punched you too, and Robyn would be ashamed of you, sir." Spinning my dad around, he took out his cuffs, and my mouth fell open at his next words.

"Dr. William Shaw, you're under arrest for assault. You have the right to remain silent..."

Chapter Twenty

Dani

Love, the boy in the library a few tables away

I closed Evan's journal for a moment, gazing unseeingly out of the plane's window. Missoula was coming into view, and I'd already put my seat belt back on and my tray up. I glared out into the night, my hatred and anger building into something ugly. My whole body shook with the force of it.

Opening Evan's journal once more, I lost myself in his words again. Since he'd left for Montana, I'd reread his entries a thousand times. They were beautiful and sweet, filled with love and adorable adoration for me, and they were Evan's pure, undiluted thoughts written down in black and white.

And they were all to me.

I loved the first one, his sweet initial crush on me, his curiosity over all I'd read inside our library. I loved the tentative decision to tell me about his past, his mother, his fears. My heart swelled with the one he'd left for me declaring his beautiful love for me before getting on the plane. But there were a few in between that were just…Evan.

Pretty girl,

It feels wrong for what I'm about to write, but I need to work stuff out. Everything about you makes me crazy...and in every good way possible. You're fun and sweet, sexy and alluring, and most days, I can barely see straight at the thought of you.

I've just told you about things back home. You asked about crushes, and I explained that I ignored everyone from home because it always seemed they had ulterior motives. It's all true, and I came to Florida not expecting to change that right away. I had no delusions that I was going to leave Key Lake and become like my brother, who is always so easygoing with members of the opposite sex. It never even entered my mind that I'd meet someone like you, but I did.

But now I'm nervous.

There are moments when it's just you and me, and all I want is to just...not stop. I just want to completely lose myself in you, Dani, but the reality is...I can't. There's a part of me (the bookworm/computer geek) that knows the basics of sex and what to do. However, the reality of it all is overwhelming. It's scary to place my heart on the line, not to mention a bit of ego too. I don't REALLY know what I'm doing, but I'm glad to know I'm not alone. I'm glad to know that we're both...ignorant (for a lack of a better word) about some things, that we're sort of diving into it all blind...together. That makes me feel better.

I've read so many books that describe sex and love like the universe shifted with the power of it all, and I know it's not TRULY like that. I've read romances with candles and flowers and beautiful words said, and I know it can't always be like that, either. But I'm a man too, so I've seen porn. I've even read some of my mom's old romance novels, which is probably the furthest from the reality of it all. But the daydreamer in me, the part of me that I've lost to you, makes me want all of the above and more. FOR YOU.

I want it all with you, Dani.

I'm writing this as you sleep next to me in my bed at your house. I look over at you, and my chest hurts with everything I feel. I want to give you all I just mentioned (the romance and candles), but I want the universe to move too. It sounds crazy, but it's true.

You're leading us, pretty girl. And I'm perfectly okay with that because each step we take is better than any book or movie. When we finally take that next step, Dani, I'm pretty damn sure it'll blow my mind.

Evan

I closed the leather-bound book again, wrapping my arms around it against my chest as the plane touched down on the runway. The book was a poor substitute for the real thing—the real, warm, strong arms that held me close, that always touched me like I was made of fine crystal or spun glass. It paled in comparison to his voice—that smooth, calm, velvety sound that made me melt into a puddle of goo no matter if he was just talking about school or reading from a book.

"You ready, Dani?" Mom asked softly, tucking my hair back. "We've got a bit of a drive…"

I nodded, looking over at her. "Yeah, I know. Evan told me he's like forty-five minutes from Missoula."

I pulled out my phone, turning it back on now that we'd landed. It took a minute to load up, but as soon as it connected, a voice mail alert bleeped. My hands shook as I looked at the number I didn't recognize, but I called to retrieve the message, sagging in my seat when my favorite voice met my ear.

After listening to the message, a soft sob left me, and I looked to Mom. "He's okay. He's okay. Thank God."

There was a beep, and another message came over as I took my bag Dad was handing me.

"Dani, it's me. I just…I needed to tell you. This is my sister's phone, and she's okay if you call. But I can't…Why aren't you answering?" he asked a little impatiently, but then I could hear his sister in the background reminding him that it was, indeed, Christmas Day. *"Oh yeah. Sorry. Anyway, I promise I'm okay. And baby, they've…they've arrested my dad. Apparently you guys called the chief, and…Wes called Tyler and…Are you flying here? Never mind. I just…I really need to talk to you…"* He sighed deeply. *"Dani, call me…please?"*

My mouth gaped because I'd thought I'd heard wrong, but no.

"Holy shit," I hissed, and my whole family stopped to look at me. Turning to my cousin, I asked, "You called his brother?"

Wes pulled me out of the way of all the people getting off the plane, saying, "Hell yeah, I did! I've had Tyler's number in my phone since Thanksgiving. It's the only contact Evan would give me on his application. Tyler said a bunch of shit was goin' down with their dad, but he and his fiancée were trying to catch a flight out of La Guardia as soon as they could. Why? What's Evan saying?"

Nodding, I had to lean against the wall and listen to the message again. "They…William's been arrested!" I whispered to them.

My dad stepped closer, his own phone to his ear as he nodded. "Yeah, Chief Clark left me a message. They arrested Evan's father on an assault charge."

"Good. Fucker." Wes grunted but then added, "Is Ev okay, though?"

"Yeah, but he sounds so…lost. I *have* to call him," I said, saving the phone number under Faith's name, just in case.

"Dani, wait until we're in the rental car, okay?" Dad requested. "You'll have better reception."

I gripped my phone like a talisman because as soon as I was able, I was calling Evan. We wound our way down to the car rental place, and my patience unraveled as the damned pimple-faced kid behind the desk took his dear, sweet time.

"Fuck this," I practically growled, stepping out into the very cold, very damp night. I dialed the number.

I heard a girl's voice answer, and she sounded relieved. "Dani!" I recognized Faith instantly from hearing her in the background of previous calls. "Oh my damn, Evan's been pacing the floor. I kept telling him to calm down, that it's Christmas or that you were probably already in the air... He's not believing a fucking thing I say until he talks to you."

I had to laugh. I couldn't help it. She rambled a little like me, maybe a bit more frantic.

But my laugh died quickly. "Faith, is he...Are you guys okay?"

"Oh God, he's...Dani, he just...snapped on our dad! Just lost it completely. Are you here? Because, fuck me, I think...I just...He needs you," she whispered.

Tears started anew at that statement coming from his sister — the same girl Evan called the strongest person he knew. So if she was telling me he needed me, then the cross-country flight we'd just flown was well worth it.

"Yeah, yeah, we just landed, and we're getting a rental car."

"Thank God!" she sighed with relief. "Who's with you?"

I snorted and sniffled at the same time. "My whole family, Faith."

"Why? What are all of you doing here?" she asked, sounding completely confused.

"Because we love him," I answered immediately. "Can...Can I *please* talk to Evan?"

"Shit! Yeah, sure...absolutely."

I heard the opening of a door, then the thump of feet on steps, and then finally a knock on the door. *"Big brother?"* she called to him, knocking again, and the phone shifted when the door opened. *"For you."*

"Is it Chief Clark again, 'cause I dunno..." I heard his voice, and my sweet Evan sounded so damned tired and lost. My need to wrap him up just increased by tenfold.

"No, silly…It's Dani!"

I heard his exhalation over the line and smiled.

"Dani! I'm sorry. I know I probably scared you. I'm okay. And…"

"Evan," I sighed in relief and worry and to get him to calm down. "Shhh, baby. We're here. We just landed in Missoula. Give us a bit, and we're on our way to you."

"You're really here?" he asked softly.

"Yes, handsome. All of us. I know it'll be really late, but…"

"I don't fucking care," he practically sobbed into the phone. "I don't give a damn how late it is. I can't believe you really came."

"I love you." It was my only reason to give, and it was a damned good one as far as I was concerned. And I'd *keep* giving that reason.

"I love you too, Dani. So much. And I miss you like fucking crazy. I…They…They want me to press charges, and I…I…I don't know what to do," he rambled, and I knew him well enough to know that he was probably pulling at his hair. "If I…Jesus, all hell will break loose if I do that, Dani."

"Is this something we can talk about when we get there?" I asked him. "What I mean is, baby, can it wait a few hours? Or does this decision have to be made like now?"

"No, it can wait. The chief said he's keeping him overnight, due to the holiday."

"Okay, then…First things first, baby. *Let me just get to you.*" I urged that last sentence, flinching when a warm hand landed on my shoulder. I looked up to see my dad silently asking to speak to him. "Evan, Dad wants to talk to you, okay?"

"Okay."

My dad took my phone, putting it to his ear. "Son, you all right?" he asked and then listened to Evan for a moment. "Damn, kiddo…" He groaned, rubbing his bearded chin. "Okay, well, we're heading your way. Give me your address, buddy." He scribbled down an address on the receipt from the car rental and then asked, "Evan, is there some sort of hotel or…or…" He huffed a laugh. "We didn't exactly plan, but we knew you might need us." He frowned a little. "What did I tell you at Thanksgiving, son? Exactly. That hasn't changed. And if you're sure you have the room…"

"We'll make room," I heard Evan urge over the phone, and I grinned.

"Fair enough. Here's Dani back, and we'll see you soon."

"Baby?"

"Pretty girl, it'll take you almost three hours to get here, but...I can't believe you all came," he mumbled that last part, and I swiped at the tears that fell. "Faith and I will get places for you guys to sleep."

"I don't care if I'm on the floor somewhere," I teased him, smiling when he huffed a light laugh.

"I'd never do that to you. I'll give up my room for you, and *I'll* sleep on the floor."

"I'm hugging and kissing you to pieces when I get there. We're leaving the airport now," I told him, glancing up when Aunt Tessa pulled the car to the curb.

"Please be careful, Dani. The snow is light, but it's still tough to drive in, okay?"

"Okay." I ended the call and dove into the back seat of the SUV they'd rented, my family already loaded up.

"How is he?" Wes asked, draping an arm around me.

I looked at him and then to my mother, who was waiting for the answer. "He needs us," I told them, and my aunt nodded and pulled away from the airport.

EVAN

I leaned against the door of my mother's office, my sister's phone still in my hand. Tears burned my eyes as I absorbed the fact that not only was Dani here in Montana, but her whole family had come with her. I knew they'd welcomed me into their lives with open arms — that was just the type of people they were — but knowing they'd shoved Christmas Day aside and jumped on a plane...There weren't any words.

Hearing Dani's voice telling me she was here was one thing, but hearing Daniel remind me of our conversation at Thanksgiving, where he'd essentially called me family, was something completely different. Despite how hard I was trying to stay calm, stay strong, I needed them. And the fact that they knew that enough to fly across the country meant more to me than anything.

"Big brother?" Faith asked, tapping the door tentatively. "You okay?"

I wiped my face on my shirt sleeve, taking a deep breath and pushing away from the door. When I opened it, she looked me over, but she didn't say anything, simply took her phone back.

"They'll be here in a few hours," I told her, swallowing thickly. "We need to get places for them to sleep. I dunno how long…"

"Okay, well…you know them best, so you tell me."

Nodding, I pointed to the stairs. "Leanne and Daniel can have the guest room. We just need to make the bed. Aunt Tessa can take Ty's old room. Wes can take Mom's office—either the sofa, or he can open it up. I…I don't know about Dani…Maybe in your room?"

Faith got a wicked gleam in her eye. "Why can't she shack up with you?"

Snorting into a laugh, I said, "'Cause her parents are here?"

"As many times as you've stayed at their house, they don't know about the two of you? I call bullshit, big brother!" she sang teasingly, poking my stomach. "C'mon. We'll get to work. I'll handle the guest room and Ty's room."

"Okay." I pointed to the shattered windowpane at the back of the library that had broken when Dad threw Faith's phone. "I've got to cover that up. And I'll build the fire. They won't be used to the cold, so…" I shrugged, and Faith nodded.

We got to work, which helped the time fly. As exhausted as I was, just knowing that I was minutes away from seeing Dani made me wide awake. Using some cardboard and tape, I sealed the broken windowpane and then set about cleaning up the broken glass my dad had thrown, shaking my head at the liquor that tainted a few of my mother's books. Quilts and blankets were taken down from the attic, sheets and towels from the hall closet, and more firewood was brought in from the back steps.

As I glanced out the window, my worries kicked up a bit as I saw a light snow falling, and I wondered if I'd ever be comfortable with cars and bad weather or if I'd always stress about everyone I cared about behind the wheel of a car. Hell, I hadn't driven a car myself since before I'd left Key Lake for Glenhaven.

I was stoking the fire when the headlights of a car flashed in through the front window. I tossed a log into the fireplace and stood up straight, brushing off my hands.

"Faith, they're here."

"Okay!" she called from upstairs.

I walked to the front door and opened it, shaking my head at the loud voices and teasing tones. Knowing Wes, he was doing it to give Dani something else to think about.

The back doors of the SUV opened before the front, Wes laughing as hats and gloves were thrown at his head. "That's it! I'm calling Santa. Only coal for you, little elf!"

"Shut up, asshat. That stopped working when I was like nine," she grunted, stepping out onto the snow. My girl shivered in the cold, giving a slow gaze around her, but she took off in a run when she saw me. "Evan!"

"Dani, don't run," I tried to warn her but then caught her at the bottom step just as she slipped. It took all I had not to collapse to the steps with her. I wrapped my arms around her. "You'll slip, baby," I whispered sarcastically too late, but the feel of her, the smell of her—I'd needed it and missed it so badly that all I could do was bury my face in her neck. "Fuck, I missed you. I can't…You're here and…"

"I was so scared for you," she mumbled into my neck. "I didn't know…I was just…I love you."

"I love you too, pretty girl."

I pulled back, cupping her face and kissing her briefly. Grimacing when her gloved hands touched my face, I let her look. I'd pushed the cuts and the bruises out of my mind for a bit, but watching my girl start to lose her shit brought the reality of it all back to the forefront.

"I'm okay, Dani."

"No, you are not! He did this?" she practically growled. "Then it serves him right that he was arrested. I hope he…he…"

"Dani-girl, that's enough." Daniel's calm tone always seemed to catch more attention than anyone yelling.

Seeing the rest of Dani's family standing there was surreal. My two polar-opposite worlds just came slamming together, and I felt awkward and strange, but God, I'd missed them all. I started to speak, my mouth opening and closing, but it was Aunt Tessa who broke the silence.

"Jesus, son," she whispered, pulling me in for a hug, and soon she and Leanne were wrapped around me.

It was the latter that I'd unknowingly needed. There was something about Leanne's hugs, something healing and nostalgic about them. I remembered the first time I met her, she'd hugged me, and I'd thought at the time that they weren't exactly like my own mother's, but I was so very wrong. They were identical, and I melted into it. I needed every second of it. After having been in my dad's home for two weeks, I needed to feel something besides anxiousness, fear, and hatred.

"Oh, my sweet boy," she crooned in my ear as she ran her fingers through my hair with one hand and wiped the moisture from my eyes with the other. "I'm sorry. We shouldn't have let you come alone—or at all."

"I had to come." I swallowed around the lump in my throat. "I had no choice," I told her softly, shrugging when I pulled back, and I looked to Daniel. "I found out things I never knew. C'mon in and warm up."

"No, no…don't mind me. I got this!" Wes stated sarcastically, slamming the back of the rental car, but he was draped in bags.

I couldn't help but laugh, and I walked to him to take a couple from him.

"All right, Ev?" he asked, the grin slowly slipping off his face as he looked at the cut on my forehead.

"I'm okay. Thanks for coming. You didn't—"

"Oh, hell yes, we did!" he grunted, and as I led everyone inside the house, setting the bags down in the living room, he followed suit. "You're lucky my cousin wasn't on the plane right after you."

Smirking at my girl who walked into my arms, I said, "Then it would be me down at the police station and not my dad." I shrugged again. "If he'd said what he did to her face, I would've done more than punch him." I held up my bruised hand, which made Dani gasp and take it gently.

Daniel narrowed his eyes. "Do I wanna know, son?"

"No, sir, you don't," I replied, shaking my head, and the sound of footsteps on the staircase caught my attention. "Faith, come meet everyone."

My sister stepped nervously into the living room, which made me smile. My very vibrant Faith was now suddenly shy, but as she caught sight of Wes, I understood why. Chuckling, I walked to her, pointing to everyone.

"This is Professors Daniel and Leanne Bishop. This is Theresa Harper, Daniel's sister—she prefers it if you call her Aunt Tessa. Her son is Wes." I held out my hand and pulled Dani closer. "And this is Dani."

Finally my sister found her voice, and she rushed at Dani, wrapping her in a fierce hug. "It's nice to finally meet you in person!" She pulled back. "All of you. I…" She paused for a second and then looked to me. "Ty's old room and the guest room are done, big brother. Did you find sheets for the pull-out sofa?"

"Yeah," I told her with a nod but looked at everyone else. "There's room for everyone." Then I looked to Dani. "My sister has a pull-out…"

"I want to stay with you. I don't even care if it's out here. I just… Please." Dani's voice was firm, and Wes snorted, but it also didn't seem to faze her parents or Aunt Tessa, either.

Faith giggled, breaking the silence.

Smirking, I hugged Dani closer, telling her, "We'll figure something out." Dani nodded, and I turned to everyone else. "Tomorrow, I've got to go down to the station. The chief wants my decision on whether I'm pressing assault charges. I don't…I have to…"

Daniel stepped forward. "Tell me exactly what happened today, buddy," he said, gesturing for me to sit down on the sofa, and I did, with Dani sticking to me like glue.

"My vote is yes," Faith snapped, holding out her phone. "Show him, Evan!"

Aunt Tessa looked to my sister. "Sweetheart, why don't you show us where we can put our things, hmm?"

Faith nodded, starting with Wes and the library, and then Leanne and Aunt Tessa followed my sister upstairs. I frowned down at Faith's phone, taking a deep breath and letting it out.

"I'm…" I started but felt my face heat. "I…I completely lost my temper." I glanced from Daniel's calm face to Dani's loving but worried one. "I just…I couldn't take it anymore. I'd bitten my tongue the whole time I was here, but…knowing everything my mother had gone through, knowing that he most likely was using her for so long…And then! *Then* he…he…He insulted Dani, and I just *snapped*."

I started the video for them, flinching at the sound of my father's foul voice, his hatred. Faith had told me she'd followed him. That she'd heard him leave his room. It was when he slammed his bedroom door that alerted her to his mood. She'd told me that she didn't want to take any chances. Her view was from the library doorway, and it started just before he threw his drink at me. The footage shook a bit because Faith wavered on whether to keep recording or step in, but she needed proof. Every bit of it was there—the insults, the destruction of my phone, the choke hold, every fact I spewed his way—even more the blood spilling down my face.

It cut off when I told him to let me go and he did.

"You didn't hit him here," Daniel noted, handing the phone back.

I shook my head, pulling Dani to me. She was a teary mess. "Pretty girl," I crooned against her forehead. "I'm okay, Dani. I'm actually sorry I let him get to me." I snorted a bit, shaking my head again.

"God, son…" Daniel sighed, frowning. "Jesus himself would've lost his temper."

"Right," I said with a chuckle. "To answer your question, I didn't hit him until after Faith had told him she'd already sent the video to Tyler, when I picked up my phone and told him that he'd been overheard. He then insulted Dani…I couldn't stop myself."

Daniel grunted and nodded. "What happens if you press charges, Evan?"

"I don't know. He goes before a judge?" I guessed, shrugging. "I don't…I'm not sure what to do, but I have to go down there tomorrow."

"I'll go with you," Dani offered.

"Yeah, me too, son," Daniel agreed, standing up from the chair across from us. "I think it's high time your father and I met." His lips twitched as he gave a wry smile. He pointed a finger between Dani and me. "You know, since our kids are…serious."

Dani's soft giggle shook us both, and I smiled a little, kissing the crown of her head. "That we are, Daniel," I promised him.

"Good. That's good." He winked at his daughter and then went upstairs, where there was laughter.

I collapsed a little to the back of the sofa, looking at Dani. "We are, right? Serious, I mean?"

"As a fucking heart attack," she breathed, her lips meeting mine almost roughly. And I kissed her back with all I had. Her forehead met mine softly, her breathing coming out in puffs, but I couldn't help but smile at her. "I really do want to stay with you, Evan."

I was nodding before she even finished that plea. "Okay."

"I missed you." She kissed me again.

"And I love you."

Her smile was sweet and adorable. "Here? Or your room?"

"My room," I told her, getting up to pick up the only bag left, which I assumed was hers. "Tomorrow...I...Hell, I don't know."

"Tomorrow..." she stated, taking my hand in hers as we walked upstairs. "Tomorrow, I'm gonna give your *Daddy Dearest* a piece of my fucking mind." As we stepped into my room and closed the door, my girl came to a stop at the sight of my bed. "Tonight, though," she said, pulling me down so that I sat on the edge of the mattress, putting her bag down beside me. Her lips met my forehead, the cut my dad had left, with a sweet softness. She tilted my head a little, leaning in to press a kiss to my throat.

"Tonight, I just want to love you, hold you, kiss you stupid, and remind you that you are amazing and strong and..." She stopped, trailing her fingers across my face. "Baby, you look so tired," she whispered, swallowing back emotions I could see her fighting.

I nodded, feeling completely drained. I'd ridden an emotional roller coaster all damn day, and it was now the wee hours of the morning. I pulled her closer to me as she stayed between my legs, laying my head against her chest. The sound of her heart soothed me as I wound my arms around her.

"You're not alone in this, Evan. I'll hold your hand through it all. We all will. Okay?" she whispered against my head, and I nodded.

"I'm sorry you missed Christmas," I mumbled, smiling when she laughed lightly.

"I'm not." Her smile was sweet when I pulled back to look at her as her hands cupped either side of my face, and she kissed my lips softly. "Nope. I was missing you too much to enjoy any-damn-thing. Now I wanna cuddle the shit outta you." She pointed to the bed. "Let's go, Mr. Shaw. I've flown a long way. You've been through hell and back...all today. You need spoiling. So severe amounts of cuddling must commence pronto, buddy."

A laugh escaped me, and I nodded. "Yes, ma'am."

I knew the next day would be trying at best, and I knew I'd be hearing from not only the police chief but probably Sean and Tyler as well. But for the moment, my wish of Dani in my room wasn't a daydream but an utterly perfect reality. And just knowing that they were all here to watch my back made me feel a sense of calm that I hadn't felt since I'd left them behind in Florida.

As she started to pull away, I stopped her. "I'm glad you're here."

She smiled. "I've got you, baby. Always."

Chapter Twenty-One

EVAN

I woke slowly in a cocoon of covers and legs and skin, surrounded by Dani's scent. We'd crawled into my bed the night before, completely and utterly exhausted. With all that I'd been through and her long flight, all we could manage was to curl ourselves around each other and a few very long, very deep kisses. Hell, I wasn't sure which of us had passed out first.

The gray, early morning light lit up my room, but it was the sight next to me, the perfect body alongside mine, that I couldn't take my eyes off. Dani was just beautiful. She always was to me—whether she was dressed for school or hanging out at home, it didn't matter... not to me. But watching her slowly wake, feeling her hands and arms against my bare chest and her legs entwined with mine, was the best thing ever, especially in my old bed. Having her here seemed to chase away the darkness that hung over this house.

Sleepy-sweet eyes opened up to gaze at me.

I trailed my fingers up and down her spine beneath her shirt—up between her shoulder blades and down along the edge of her pajama bottoms. I needed to touch her. Hell, if I was being honest with myself, I wanted everything all at once, but today, it wasn't going to happen. The trip to the police station was weighing heavily on me.

Dani smiled softly, raking her fingers through my hair as she eyed the cut on my forehead, but she continued trailing her fingers down my jaw.

"I want to wake up like this every damn morning. I mean, I know we've woken up like this before, but still…I mean it. I want this every day."

Smiling at that adorable rambling honesty of hers that I'd missed so fucking much, I let out a light laugh as I pressed a kiss to the middle of her brow. "Me too."

"We aren't the only ones," she teased, her body shifting. "Is this a morning thing?"

"It's a Dani thing," I said with a laugh, shrugging a shoulder. "You're so beautiful. I can't help it, pretty girl."

I tried to shift away, but she wouldn't have it. She gently gripped my side, holding me to her. Reaching for her face, I tucked her hair behind her ear. I still couldn't believe she was there, in Key Lake, Montana, in the bedroom in which I'd spent practically my whole life hiding. Absentmindedly, she traced my scars along my side, but I loved it. I loved that something that once made me dress for PE behind closed doors was now something I barely gave much thought.

She pushed at me until I fell back, and she climbed on top of me, making me grin up at her. "One day, there won't be just sleepovers at my house. We'll curl up and read together on our own sofa or bed. We can do ridiculously naughty things to each other and not worry about who's across the hall."

I hummed, cupping her face as she braced her hands on my shoulders. "I'm liking this plan."

"Which part?" she asked with a deliciously sexy giggle. "Our own place or the naughty bits?"

"All of it. Everything. Tell me more, Dani." I skimmed my hands flat down her back, cupping her bottom and giving it a squeeze to bring her closer.

Her eyes gleamed wickedly as she fought her smile. "We'll have our own library. A small one, but you'll have a desk in there, where you'll write the most amazing stories. I'll finally find out if the fairy princess marries her sweet, brave archer boy."

"She does."

"Does she?" she squeaked, grinning. "Oh, fairy babies…"

I chuckled at how she sounded like my sister when it came to that particular story.

"Well, you'll write and you'll be this famous author. They'll make movies about your fairy world." When that made me laugh out loud, she got serious. "I mean it. And I'll be your biggest fan, your best cheerleader. I'll make sure the gorgeous actress who plays the princess doesn't steal you away."

"Never," I whispered, gazing up at her in awe and wonder and head-over-heels love. "I've already been stolen, pretty girl."

Her eyes watered a bit at that, and she leaned down to kiss my neck, shifting to kiss the cut on my forehead. "And…And…I swear to God, I'll never, *ever* let anyone hurt you again."

"I love you," I breathed, shaking my head slowly at how I'd gotten so fucking lucky.

My life was a mess, truly. Outside the bedroom door we were secured behind, my world was fucked up. But everything in my arms, every inch of the beautiful girl who was draped over me, was pure perfection. From her adorable toes that were rubbing against my legs, to her sweet smile, to that smart mind — there wasn't a bit of her that I could live without.

"I love you too, Evan. I'm sorry he hurt you, and I know we have stuff to deal with today, but if you don't kiss me, I'm gonna—"

She didn't have to finish that sentence, and my lips met hers to stop her *and* to give her what she wanted. I gave in completely — at least for a few minutes. As much as I wanted her, as amazing as she felt pressing against me, touching me, kissing me, grinding over me, I was well aware of the sounds coming from the hallway. The house was waking up, which meant the chief would be calling, and Sean would probably stop over. There was a decision that needed to be made concerning my father.

Rolling her onto her back, I loomed over her, finally breaking our kiss. "There's something missing from this grand plan of yours," I teased her breathlessly, brushing my lips across hers lightly.

"What's that?"

"If I'm writing, what are you doing?"

She grinned and shrugged. "I dunno, but I'll let you know when I do. I just look forward to figuring it out with you."

"Fair enough, baby." I sighed, turning a bit when I heard my sister's phone ring. Turning back to Dani, I said, "I'd better get up. I need…and then you guys need breakfast, and…"

"Baby, baby…Evan…We here to help you, not impose. Just tell us what you need."

I pressed a heavy kiss to her lips. "Thank you. Let me shower first, and then we'll get with everyone downstairs."

Regretfully, I extricated myself from her arms, mentally preparing myself for the shitstorm to come. I shook my head at the sight of her in my childhood bed, trying my damnedest to keep my thoughts controlled. I definitely needed that shower—a cold one.

By the time we were both clean and dressed, we came downstairs to find my house filled with laughter and teasing…and food. Lots of food.

Wes grinned, slapping my shoulder. "That's one helluva diner you got down the street."

Grimacing a little, I shrugged a shoulder. "It gets old. Trust me."

"Apparently my big brother got spoiled by home cookin'," Faith teased from her spot at the kitchen counter.

"Whatever," I said as I waved her away. "Just wait until you've had Leanne and Aunt Tessa's fried chicken. That's all I'm sayin'."

Leanne kissed the side of my head. "You need to eat something, sweet boy, even though I didn't make it." When I laughed her way, she ruffled my hair. "Daniel'll be down in a moment."

Dani and I took the take-out boxes from her mom, and we sat down at the kitchen table with Aunt Tessa. I didn't think I was hungry until the first bite hit my tongue, but then I realized I hadn't eaten since breakfast the day before.

All of the bullshit my dad had said and done flashed through my head as I ate—the hatred he'd spewed my way, my phone, the threats. By the time I'd cleaned my plate and looked up at Faith, Daniel had joined us.

"Faith, have you heard from Tyler?" I asked, getting up to throw away the box and taking Dani's too.

"Yeah, he's in the air. And he told me to tell you to…and I quote, 'Nail the asshole to the wall.'"

My nostrils flared and I nodded, shoving my hands into the front pockets of my jeans. "He'll kill him," I whispered, mainly to myself, but everyone heard me. "He threatened Dad at Thanksgiving about you and me," I said to her. "I don't..." I shrugged. "I don't know what the right thing is here."

"Evan, he..." Dani started but then stopped, slumping in her chair at the table.

Smirking at her adorable attempt to keep her mouth under control, I simply said, "I know, Dani," against the top of her head.

Aunt Tessa turned to look my way, and in her hand was the long list of chores Faith and I were supposed to have accomplished while I was home. Most of them were done. Some of them had had to wait due to the snow.

"Has he always been this way?" she asked my sister and me, and when we nodded, she sighed deeply. "These aren't just...*chores*. Hell, some of this shit needs a professional...like the chimney and the gutters. Really? It's fucking snowing!"

Faith grinned, but she looked to me before she answered. "B-Before Mom died, he never bothered with us. But he really does blame my brothers for the accident. More Evan than Tyler, but Ty came to Ev's defense so much that he's just as hated."

I quickly explained all I'd learned from Pastor Sean the day before. How my mother had tried to leave my father. How he'd accused her of cheating because I didn't look like him. How it was a punishment against Faith that had truly kicked it all off.

"I remember that," she whispered. "Mom cried when she cleaned me up."

That caused a silence in the room for a moment, but then I continued, telling about all the money and accounts and even the file Sean had handed me. And finally, I ended with the fact that my dad had been sued for malpractice.

"Which means he'll have a lawyer at his fingertips," Daniel finally spoke, wiping his mouth with a napkin. He got up from the counter to throw his box away. "You should too, I suppose."

"I'm sure," I agreed, rubbing my face. "I need to talk to Tyler about that stuff. He's about to turn twenty-one, which means he's going to inherit his portion. I just...I don't care about the money, but it seems like my dad used my mother, like he's been syphoning from her this whole time, and it's *that* money he's threatened us with our whole lives. There's...There's a part of me that wants nothing more than to walk away from this house, him, all of it. But there are questions I want answers to, and I can't leave my sister here."

"Then let's go ask him, son," Daniel said firmly. "Maybe after you've given him a chance to answer, you'll know whether or not you want to press charges." He pointed to Faith. "And as far as your sister goes…we'll work it out, buddy."

Nodding, I sighed. "Okay."

"I'm still going," Dani said, standing up and taking my hand.

"Me too," Daniel added.

"Well, I'm not. I'll end up in a cell next to *Daddy Dearest*, and I'm way too pretty for jail," Wes added, his half smile making me laugh, but he squeezed my shoulder. "Give me your phone, Ev. I can at least go handle some business."

"I can't let you—"

"Oh, you'll work it off at the coffee shop. Don't think you won't." He shot me a wink, opening and closing his hand. "I'll get you something badass along with a new number because I think you're gonna need it."

Reaching into my pocket, I pulled out my poor, ruined cell phone. Wes's face darkened at the sight of the shattered screen and the broken back and power button. He muttered something about doing the same to my dad's face but tucked it into his pocket.

"I have to go," Faith piped up, wrinkling her nose. "They want a statement from me."

Nodding, I told her she could drive, and then Leanne was in front of me, cupping my face. "I want to spoil you—all of you," she said, glancing to my sister. "And if you've got your brother coming in, then we'll stay at the lodge in town, but I want to cook for all of you."

"You don't—"

Aunt Tessa chuckled. "Well, we are, kiddo. So…suck it up. And since you have such high praises for our fried chicken, the menu is easy."

Grinning, I nodded. "Yes, ma'am."

Faith drove us in her car after calling Chief Clark and letting him know we were on our way. Dani sat with me in the back seat, looking absolutely adorable in her wool cap, while Daniel sat up front.

Key Lake was so damn small that we were pulling into the station less than ten minutes after leaving my house.

I could see the chief's cruiser in the parking lot, and Sean was standing out on the steps waiting for us. His expression was curious as he saw all of us get out of the car.

"Pastor Sean," I greeted him.

"Son." He nodded once, reaching for my hand. "How's the head?"

Snorting once, I shrugged. "Fine. My hand hurts worse than anything."

He grinned, gripping my shoulder. "Ah, but that shiner you planted on William is quite the beauty."

"Good!" Dani grunted, which made me laugh. "Sorry."

"Don't be," I told her, pulling her to me. "Dani Bishop, this is Pastor Sean. Sean, this is my girlfriend, Dani...and her father, Professor Daniel Bishop."

"Professor," Sean mused, but he wore a small smile.

Daniel cracked a small smile, but he shook the pastor's hand. "Good to meet you. Evan's told us a bit about you and what you've done for him."

"It apparently wasn't enough." Sean sighed deeply, glancing over his shoulder toward the door of the station. "Listen, Evan, your dad is as mad as a wet hornet in there. His lawyer can't even keep him under control. And the chief seems to be enjoying himself."

Shaking my head, I let out a deep breath. "Faith and I have to give statements, and they're taking her video as evidence, but I'm...I have to decide whether or not to press charges. I don't know if I can... He'll want paybacks, and I can't...I don't..."

Sean studied my face. "God, you're so much like Robyn. No matter what advice I handed her, she only wanted to protect you three. She wanted no part of a fight. She was incredible at hiding her emotions."

I shook my head. "No, he knew. He knew she was repulsed by him. He accused me of looking at him the same way she did."

"I imagine the sight of you was a constant reminder," Sean murmured, shaking his head, but the door opened to reveal Chief Clark.

Introductions to Dani and Daniel were made again, only this time the chief smiled, patting Daniel's shoulder. "Smart thinking to call me. Had you not, there's no telling what he'd have done to these two. He was…Well, he *still is* rather pissed off." The chief looked to me. "C'mon in. You don't have to see him, but I will need those statements."

"I…I need to talk to him *before* I make a decision," I said, frowning a little, but Dani's hand slipped into mine.

"His lawyer's gonna love this shit," Clark said wryly, shaking his head. "Okay, I'll pull him out of the holding cell and put him in an interrogation room."

We all followed him quietly into the station. Key Lake Police Department was small—both the building and the number of officers. As we wound our way by the front desk, I could see one other officer sitting at a computer.

"Go get him, Dobbins," the chief said wearily. "Put him and that sleazeball lawyer of his in room three." Before the officer got up, the chief added, "Oh, yeah, and cuff that asshole to the table. I don't want him to move without my say-so."

"Sir," Dobbins grunted, leaving his desk for the side hallway.

Chief Clark faced us. "You sure you want to do this?"

"I have nothing to say to him," Faith said, looking to me with tears in her eyes. "Sorry, big brother. I just…I don't care what his reasons are. I want…Can I come with you when you leave?"

I pulled her into a hug. "We'll do whatever you want, Rylee Faith," I whispered to her. "You're eighteen, Faith. You tell me. We'll figure it out."

She nodded, looking up at me. "I'm…I'll just…write my statement. Maybe I'll listen in, but…"

"I get it." I sighed, glancing over at Daniel. "You still want to do this?"

"Oh yeah," he drawled, smirking a bit. "He needs to hear a few things."

It was Dani I turned my attention to next, cupping her worried face. "Look at me," I begged her softly. "I can't stop you from joining us, but…Do not speak to him, Dani. I *know* you're mad. I *know* you want to tell him where to go and how fast he can get there, but for me…for *my sake*, please just…wait on giving him a piece of that beautiful mind. Okay?"

Her smile was wickedly sexy, but she was still pissed. I could see it every time she caught sight of my cuts and bruises. Lifting up on her toes, she pressed a soft kiss to my lips.

"I'm here for *you*, so fuck him."

"Dani," Daniel chastised, but it was halfhearted at best. His amusement was clear in the smile that lifted his lips a little, and he muttered something about being just like her mother.

I heard my dad along with the sound of doors opening. His yelling was loud and foul; his threats about suing the station, the county, and the state were echoing out from the hallway.

Just as he was handcuffed to the table in the middle of the room, he snapped, "Why am I in here? I told you I'm not answering any more questions." I stepped into the room as he glared at a man in an expensive suit. "And you! How am I not bailed out yet?"

"Because technically I haven't charged you...*yet*. I'm simply holding you as a *person of interest*," Chief Clark told him as he led us farther into the room. "How you behave for this next part will determine whether or not I charge you with assault and, from what I hear, theft."

Dad paled at the sight of me, and his gaze raked over the people with me. He didn't know Daniel, so as far as he was concerned, I could've gotten a lawyer, but when his eyes landed on my girl, they narrowed.

"Don't do it," I warned him, taking the chair across the table from him.

"I don't have shit to say to you," he sneered. "In fact, I should have a restraining order put on you."

Shrugging, I said, "I'm just here because Chief Clark needs me to press charges. I haven't decided yet. Though, Faith is out there writing her statement, and I'm pretty sure the chief has the video by now, so..."

"Inadmissible," the man in the suit stated with a bored tone. "It'd be thrown out of—"

"I don't care," I cut him off with a harsh laugh. "I'm willing to bet you're the one responsible for all his...*legal* activities. So just...shut up." I turned back to my father. "This is a...*family affair*, isn't it, *Daddy?*"

"Then why are they here?" Dad asked, pointing to Daniel and Dani, who were leaning against the wall behind me and completely silent.

"*They* are my family now, so you'll answer a few questions for me with them here. Or I'll go write my statement and have a lawyer look into that trust fund you've been in control over for seven years..."

"What do you want, you little shit?"

I heard Daniel shift a bit behind me, but I looked at my father, saying, "I want to know *why*. Why you used Mom, why you blamed us, why a large chunk of what she left *for us* is gone, and why—if you hated us so much—didn't you just walk away? *All* of it. I want answers." When he didn't speak up, I added, "And while we're at it, I want to know if the rumors about you are true. Were you sued for malpractice? Did you cheat on Mom, because I swear to God…"

"What? What can you do about it if I did, Evan?" he asked, leaning forward on the table. The cuffs on his wrists rattled, and he only got so far, but he smiled. "Your mother wasn't innocent."

"Don't try me," I sighed, pointing to him. "You are a damned doctor, so don't sit there and tell me you didn't test me. It wouldn't have taken much, Dad. A bandage from a scraped knee would do it. And all three of us have had plenty over the years, so…what were the outcomes?"

He narrowed his eyes but sat back.

"Right." I nodded but then tilted my head. "Start talking, or I'm gone. And you'd better pray you're still in this protected environment when Tyler comes home."

Chief Clark chuckled, and I looked up at him and shrugged, but he said, "He *was* sued for malpractice, Evan. I can attest to that one. Should I tell him? Or do you want to do it?" My father glared at the table but stayed silent, so the chief continued. "It was a few years after your mother's passing, not long after Tyler went to college. There was a pretty bad rainstorm one evening. A van and a logging truck were involved in an accident. The truck driver had minor injuries; the family in the van, though, not so much. Your father was called down to the ER to help, and there was a missed diagnosis on one of the children. The little boy bled out internally. They didn't catch it in time. The parents sued because they'd seen your father send a nurse into tears. They'd tried to tell the good Dr. Shaw all about their son's pain, but he either didn't pay attention or he ignored them. There was concern that alcohol had been involved, but by the time it all came to a head, it was too late to test him. So rather than let the malpractice insurance investigate *and* in order to keep the hospital board happy *and* to shut the family up, he offered to pay it himself. Kid was only four years old."

The chief shook his head. "Personally, I think he'd be in some serious trouble had they dug deep enough. Wonder what the board will think with you sitting here in my station in cuffs, hmm?" he asked, bracing his hands on the table. "Wonder what they'd make of that video Faith was so kind to take of you. Evan here could seriously walk away, but honestly, I hope all three kids sue the shit out of you and leave you broken and alone. But that video—admissible or not—that's some pretty condemning stuff."

"What the fuck do you care?" Dad snapped.

Chief Clark grinned, shaking his head. "I don't like you. See...you forget yourself. You forget how small this fucking town is, Shaw. You forget that the nurses you drag over the coals on a daily basis have families and...*husbands*." He raised an eyebrow at my dad. "My wife would come home in tears, and she would tell me all the shit you said or did. Unfortunately, there wasn't much I could do, legally. An asshole boss isn't illegal, just an asshole boss...or father, as we're starting to see. She's head nurse over at the old folks' home now. She's damned happy too."

My dad was starting to see the shit was beginning to stack up against him. The only person on his side was his lawyer, and that was paid-for loyalty.

Dad's nostrils flared as he fiddled with his cuffs. "I never wanted children."

"I'm aware. Mom actually told us once," I replied calmly.

"Dammit, you—" he started to yell but then shook his head. "You really are just fucking like her. Nothing bothers you, does it? I could sit here and tell you that...No, I didn't want kids. I grew up with nothing, getting my ass kicked daily, so by the time I got to this fucking hole-in-the-wall town, I could finally breathe. I could tell you that your mother was a breath of fresh air, that she belonged to me. That I finally had something fucking normal. Your mother made all the bad shit better. But then...your mother, she started talking babies. She wanted children, and she finally trapped me with Tyler. And she'd have left then, but in order to keep her, in order to maintain my normal, I had to accept you three. Three!" He laughed harshly. "Fuck, I never wanted one."

He sobered and continued. "Your mother started acting funny just before the accident. She was secretive and distant. I was pretty fucking sure she was cheating. I was either going to kill her or the asshole she was fucking, but you had to..."

Daniel finally stepped forward, pulled out the chair next to mine, and sat down.

"What?" Dad asked him.

Daniel held out his hand. "Professor Daniel Bishop. I'm just…I'm trying to figure out if you could be a lower stain of scum, Dr. Shaw." His voice was low, even, that tone he took that caused everyone to stop and listen, but he lowered his hand when my father merely glared at it. "You might be the most selfish, most deplorable man I've ever set eyes on. Everything you've spewed at your children, at all of us in here today, is all about *you*." He leaned on his elbows, studying my dad. "You act like you're the only one who lost someone. You didn't want children, so their entire world was their mother—something *you* made sure of—and then when they lost her, you blamed them?" he asked, huffing a harsh laugh. "I heard you on the phone, you know. I heard you blame your son for your wife's death. I then see you wanted him arrested when clearly it was self-defense."

My dad's eyebrows shot up, but he glanced behind me to Dani.

"Say something to her, I fucking dare you," I ground out through gritted teeth.

"Then you shouldn't have brought her."

"What could he say, Evan?" Dani's voice sounded calm from right behind me, her hands landing on my shoulders. "He could call me names, like he did Jasmine. He could try to scare me or threaten me, but it won't work. He's a weak, selfish little man, and personally, I think asking him anything is a waste of time, but I hope you squash him like the cockroach he is. Thankfully you and your brother and sister are more like Robyn than him."

"Don't you dare say her name, you little—"

I grabbed my dad's cuffs, yanking so hard that his ribcage met the edge of the table, and no one in the room stopped me, not even his lawyer. "I wasn't kidding. Finish that sentence, and—what was it you always said to us? Oh yeah—you'll 'face the consequences.'"

He glared her way and then mine, sitting back in his chair.

"You know what gaslighting is, Dr. Shaw?" Daniel asked calmly, tilting his head. "C'mon, you had to take some psychology courses during med school, so…Do you?" My dad bit down hard on his bottom lip, staying silent as Daniel talked to him like a child. "Well, for those in the room who don't…Gaslighting is a form of verbal or psychological abuse, isn't it? You start the fight, but when the one on the defense fights back, it's *their* fault. The abuser—and truly, that's what you are—turns it on the other person over and over. It causes someone to question their sanity. I'm curious…Did that shit work on your wife?"

My dad lunged, but he didn't make it far. However, Daniel's hand landed on my shoulder.

"Son, I don't think you'll ever get the answers you're looking for. He'll never admit to anything. Hell, he probably doesn't see anything wrong with what he's done here. He may never see it, kiddo. You have to make a choice here, Evan. Remember what we talked about at Thanksgiving? About how choices affect everyone involved? He's made his, so now you have to make yours." He gave my shoulder a gentle squeeze. "Sometimes you have to make a tough decision and let the cards fall where they may. The *very best thing* you can do is to live *your life* and put him and all he's done behind you. I get the impression that's what your mother was trying her damnedest to do. I swear to God," he said, emphasizing the last part, "I will help you, son." He shot my dad a scathing glare. "If only to prove this asshole wrong."

I wanted to laugh, but nothing about this shit was funny. My dad scoffed, shaking his head and shrugging a shoulder. There was a scuffle at the door. I could hear Faith's voice rise, but it was the enormous, pissed-off form of my brother slamming open the door that caused everyone to jump. I pulled Dani out of the way before my hands landed smack in the middle of his broad chest.

"What the fuck did I tell you, motherfucker? I told you if you touched him, if you didn't leave them the fuck alone, I'd be back to bury you!" Tyler snarled, pointing a finger over my shoulder.

"Tyler!" I grunted, pushing him enough to get his attention.

When he looked at me, he was pissed off all over again. "That video...It's...Fuck, baby bro..."

Shaking my head, I sighed. "I'm okay." I looked up in the doorway to see Jasmine and a man who had to be her father, not to mention Faith too. "I'm not pressing charges," I stated, shaking my head at the outburst around me.

"Evan..." Tyler groaned.

"No, I hit him too."

"Fuckin'-A, you did," my brother muttered. "Grade-A shiner, *Daddy Dearest.*"

I looked to Tyler and then to my sister. "It's time to do what Mom wanted. We'll take what she left us, and we'll leave his ass. She tried to do it seven years ago. He's taken enough. I'm not pressing charges, but I am filing a restraining order. I'm done here."

"Excellent," Tyler said with a big grin. "Remember all those times you threatened us with money, Dad? Money that was really ours? Money that Mom tried to leave for us? We'll be starting the process to take it from you. And with the video and bank statements Faith sent me, I'm pretty sure there's not a judge who won't sign off on it." He leaned down to Dad's level. "Consequences, remember? Your turn, fucker."

Dad paled a little, and I studied him a second, finally saying, "You know, I don't care that you didn't want us. You weren't an integral part of our childhood. But Mom loved you — really, truly loved you — and you took that and smashed it in her face. For someone who claims she was the one good thing in his life, you sure had a shitty way of showing it. I can't fucking *imagine* what it felt like for her to find out that everything about you was a damn lie."

I let out a deep breath, and for a split second, I thought I saw remorse on his cold face, but I wasn't sure. Shaking my head, I finally turned away from him, smiling a little when Dani wrapped an arm around my waist and Chief Clark led all of us out of the interrogation room and back out into the office area.

"You okay?" she whispered, shifting to my front.

"Yeah, pretty girl."

I looked up to see my brother smiling at her. "Ty, this is Dani. Dani, this loud thing is my brother, Tyler," I introduced.

He grinned, shaking her hand. "You're as pretty as my brother said, Dani."

"Thanks," she said with a giggle.

"Let's finish this stuff up," I told them. "I'm ready for Leanne's cookin'."

Chief Clark gripped my shoulder. "Your mom would be proud of you, kid."

I nodded, trying to smile at him, but I really was just ready to go home. I was ready to be back in Florida. I knew that all of us needed to sit down at the house and talk. In fact, I could hear Jasmine's father introduce himself to Dad as our lawyer as the interrogation room door closed again. Nothing about this next step would be easy, but if we were finally out of Key Lake, then maybe we could start our lives the way my mother had wanted.

Chapter Twenty-Two

DANI

I sat near the fireplace that Evan had been so very sweet to build up to a roaring flame. The snow, while really pretty, was just too damned cold, and I smiled at the memory of Evan's teasing me with a picture of it not even three days ago. He'd said my thin Floridian blood would not be able to hold up. My handsome, silly thing was right. Whether it was from the nasty events at the police station or the extremely cold temperature outside, I was shivering once we followed everyone back to the Shaw home.

And I mean *everyone*.

Evan's house was full. Most of them were sitting at the dining table, the conversation ranging from what had happened over the course of the last few weeks, to Dr. Shaw's despicable behavior, to my mother's awesome fried chicken.

My dad was in deep conversation with Pastor Sean, who seemed to be a kind, patient man. He was a handsome older gentleman around my parents' age, and he spoke of Evan's mother with nothing but respect and love. Evan's brother, Tyler, commanded the head of the table. He was loud, like Evan had teased, but he seemed to be a great big lovable guy, and his fiancée was *stunning*.

Jasmine had to be the prettiest girl I'd ever set eyes on, and to look at her, I'd expected snobby or stuck-up, but she was neither. She was kind and strong and treated Evan and Faith really sweetly. Her father, on the other hand, was soft-spoken and extremely smart, if not a bit intense. Robert Lewis was at the opposite end of the dining table from Tyler—laptop open, cell phone to his ear, and a fierce look on his face. He was here for one reason—to financially destroy William Shaw, and I hoped to God he succeeded.

I gazed into the fire, remembering the night Evan had told me the story of his mother, of the wreck, and about his father's treatment. I thought back to how I'd been shaking with anger, how I'd never considered myself a violent person, but that night, I'd wanted to hurt the man who'd hurt my Evan. I'd been so mad that I'd had to tell my dad through angry tears that I was keeping Evan, that he'd almost died, that his father blamed him. And that came nowhere near how pissed I was after seeing the piece of shit in all his wretched glory.

The way he sneered at Evan, cursed his very existence, laughed at his son's questions, his pain, his threats…It was all I could do not to beat him to death right there in that room. When Tyler had burst into the room, there was a part of me that wanted Evan to let him go.

A steamy mug appeared in front of me, and I took it, gazing up to see my favorite person. Evan knelt in front of me, looking so damned weary, so sad. Leaning in, I pressed a kiss to the middle of his forehead.

"I thought some cocoa would help warm you up," he whispered, touching my fingers and then my cheek. "Better?"

"Much, thank you." I took a sip, smiling his way, but I trailed a finger beneath his eyes. "You look so tired."

"I'm okay. I think I need to take the contacts out."

"Well, I can't say I'd hate the reappearance of those glasses." I giggled at his pink cheeks.

"No? I don't look like a dork?"

I outright laughed, placing my hand flat on his cheek, and kissed his lips, whispering, "Oh, sweet *Lord*, Evan…" I giggled again. "You couldn't look like a dork if you tried."

His grin was that beautiful flash of embarrassment and disbelief, not to mention sexy in its crookedness, but it was his next words that made me tear up.

"I love that you see me that way, pretty girl."

"I love *you*. All that comes with you, baby." I kissed his lips but turned when the table got a bit louder. "Shouldn't you be…"

He snorted, rolling his eyes. "I'm so over it all. I just…I'm ready to go home, Dani," he said so softly and with a bit of a plea to his tone. "I'm tired of this house, this shit surrounding it, and I'm…" He sighed, looking down at the floor as he shook his head a little.

"What? You're what, handsome?" I prompted him, tilting his face up.

"I'm…I want…I just want you. I want all those things you said this morning." He shrugged a shoulder. "I'm ready to live my life without threats and hate. I'm ready for that 'always' you said you wanted before I came here."

"Oh, God, baby. Me too." I took a sip of cocoa before setting my mug down on the table next to me. "C'mere," I whispered, holding my arms out. His knees thumped to the carpet, and he hugged me close, his face in the crook of my neck. "I love you…so much, and I'm very, very proud of you, Evan."

He nodded against me, taking a deep breath and letting it out before pushing back just a little. My forehead touched his as I waited for those incredible eyes to open. When they did, I could see he was a touch better, a little more in control.

Brushing my lips across his, I smiled when he licked his lips adorably, just like our first kiss. His return smile was soft and sweet. However, his sister's laugh was loud from the library, and both of us looked over to see her and Wes trying to fix the window William had busted.

"I think my cousin is flirting with your sister," I whispered, grinning at Evan's snort and the slow shake of his head.

"I think my sister doesn't mind, pretty girl," he murmured back with a side glance my way, and we both chuckled.

He met my gaze, shrugging a shoulder. "I'd warn them both, but I'm pretty damn certain it would be like the pot calling the kettle black."

Giggling, I nodded. "Wes is a lot of things, but he's—"

"He's a good person. I know, baby." Evan kissed my lips and stood up. "And my sister can hold her own." His eyebrow quirked up, and I giggled again.

"Yo, baby bro!" Tyler called loudly from the dining room. "Get that folder Sean gave you. And get the midget…We gotta talk."

Evan nodded, and I stood up next to him, but he turned to me. "Will you…Can you…"

"I'm here to hold your hand, Evan. Remember?"

He smiled a bit but told his brother that the folder was upstairs, all while he rubbed his eyes.

"Baby, go take those contacts out if they're bugging you that badly," I urged him gently.

"'Kay. I just think they've been in too long," he muttered, rubbing again, but then he kissed me before heading upstairs.

I walked to the library door, smirking my cousin's way. "Wes, Tyler needs Faith for a minute."

I wanted *so damned badly* to tease Wes about the pink that colored his cheeks as he sealed the pane of glass he'd had cut today. Even funnier was the glare he sent my way, but I fought my smile as Faith walked by me. Once she was out of the room, my cousin's middle finger shot up.

I snorted into a laugh. "Is that your IQ, genius?" I asked him, smiling at his chuckle, but I took a quick moment to gaze around the room.

It was beautiful and obviously Evan's mother's room. There were shelves of books, like my own library at home, not to mention a pretty desk and view out to the snowy afternoon. On a small table was a copy of *The Secret Garden*. Tears welled up in my eyes because Evan and I had just chosen that book to read next before the bullshit all started. I picked it up and held it close.

"Dani?" Wes called softly. "You okay?"

Nodding, I glanced over to him. "Yeah. I'm just…worried for him, you know? All of them. This is…sad and ugly, and I wish I could make it better."

Wes closed the window he'd fixed and wiped his hands on his jeans. "You know…I figure they've kept each other sane all these years. That's good. I can imagine if it had been different, they wouldn't be as…I dunno…as well-adjusted as they are."

"Yeah, but I get the impression their mom was nothing short of amazing."

"No shit," Wes said through a soft chuckle as he picked up a bag from the sofa he'd slept on. "C'mon. Let's see what shit-storm is about to hit *Daddy Dearest*."

We walked into the dining room just as Evan came down the stairs. I couldn't help but grin at the sweet wire-framed glasses now gracing his handsome face. His smile was soft and shy, and his cheeks pinked as he shook his head. But his eyes didn't look so irritated.

"Better!" I praised him, nodding once.

He huffed a laugh. "Thanks."

Evan, Wes, and I all took seats at the table. I was between Evan and my dad. Tyler and Mr. Lewis were at either end, with everyone else in the middle or leaning against the wall. Evan set a manila file folder on the table in front of him, but it was Sean who spoke up first.

"Evan, I think in order to help you guys quicker and easier, those accounts, that insurance policy, can be shifted immediately to you three. I'll sign it all over to you." Sean set his elbows on the table, rubbing his face. "Maybe...maybe that's why your mother left me in charge of it. I don't know, but I'm following my heart, my gut on this one. I'm pretty sure she's looking down on all of this, urging me to just...*do something*."

"Let me see what you've got there, Evan," Mr. Lewis requested, and Evan slid the folder down to his end. He flipped through the papers, nodding, smiling, and looking up at Tyler. "Oh, she was smart," he praised. "This insurance policy alone is worth six figures, all in care of the good minister's name. The bank account, since no one's touched it in seven or eight years, is...right up there, also with Sean's name on it. And that's good. That'll help the three of you since you'll be severing ties with your father."

"I'd like to sever his head." Tyler's voice was soft but no less menacing, and I couldn't stop the snort of agreement that escaped me. He grinned my way, shooting me a wink when Evan slipped his hand into mine. "Spunky, Dani. Good! My baby brother needs that."

I laughed, as did most everyone else in the room, and when I looked to Evan, his smile was warm before he pressed a kiss to my temple, whispering, "Yes. Yes, he does." When he saw in my lap the book I'd taken from the library, he squeezed my hand but said nothing.

Tyler turned back to Jasmine's father. "Okay, so what do we do, Robert?"

Robert took a deep breath and glanced around the room slowly. "Well, since you've opted not to press assault charges on William but instead filed a restraining order against him, then we're in a bit of a time crunch." He took a sip from his coffee mug before setting it back down. "This house, understandably, is his. Completely and totally. With the passing of Robyn Shaw and with the timing of the divorce papers, he would've removed her name like any other widower. The only reason he's not here now is because his lawyer, Mr. Jenson, and I agreed that William should give Evan and Faith a chance to vacate the property without violating the restraining order. However, he's currently not out of the proverbial woods yet with Chief Clark."

"What do you mean?" Evan asked, adjusting his glasses and then raking a hand through his hair.

Robert smiled a little, and it was a bit evil, but he tented his fingers in front of him on the table. "Considering all that I've found out since Tyler and Jasmine asked for my help, I was able to show Chief Clark a few things. William is now being held on a pending fraud charge, not to mention resisting arrest, which I think was for the chief's personal shits and giggles." He chuckled with the rest of the table, but he sobered up quickly. "As of this moment, all of your father's accounts are frozen, and they'll be audited penny by damn penny. Everything he's done for the last seven years or so is about to come out into the open."

He held up a finger. "If we find that he's misappropriated funds from an account that should've been a trust, then he will be responsible for paying back all that he's taken from it. If he's unable to pay it back, then this house will have a lien on it, along with his income from the hospital."

"They'll dock his pay?" Faith asked, her mouth hanging open in shock.

"And then some," Robert answered calmly. "I will tell you three… This will get ugly. You'll hear things about your parents—both of them—that you may not want to hear. Your father, in all reality, may lose his position at the hospital altogether when they catch wind of his troubles, which will make getting anything paid back much more difficult. It's quite possible that he's doing something illegal with the money. The board of directors of any hospital is going to want to make this go away, but in a small town such as this? They'll crucify him. They'll want no part of any of it."

"What do you mean...*illegal?*" Tyler asked slowly, his eyes narrowing.

Robert tapped his closed laptop. "That's a lot of money missing, though it looks like some of it was your mother's doing. She moved small amounts here and there over the course of a few years." He held up the folder from Sean. "And it's here. But there are a few expenditures that don't add up as of yet. Not to mention he's been able to get into the account for some time now. I want to know who let him and how he managed to withdraw so much. Something about *that* sounds fishy or illegal. I wouldn't put it past that lawyer of his to have done something unethical." He sighed, sitting back in his chair. "Now, there were normal things that I could see. Expenses for the three of you—cars, education, food, clothing, medical and dental bills. All fine. Though, he makes enough at the hospital to have covered those things, so we're looking into his personal accounts as well."

"Cars," Evan scoffed, rolling his eyes. "He sold mine."

"Did he now?" the lawyer asked slowly, his eyes lighting up dangerously as he jotted down something on the pad in front of him. "Good to know, son. What was it?"

"A BMW."

Robert smirked dangerously. He wasn't exactly a small man, which made his powerful presence in the room even bigger. With every piece of information he was given, he seemed to expand.

"So he buys you a higher-end car but then yanks it from you... Damn, kids," he sighed deeply, shaking his head. "I...I don't know what to tell you that'll make this whole thing easier. I understand uncaring parents or strict ones, but I can't seem to wrap my head around this asshole."

Tyler chuckled. "Try living with the little fucking ray of sunshine, Robert."

Robert grinned. "Touché, son." He stacked his stuff up, nodding to his daughter. "I'm willing to take this one on pro bono...on one condition." He eyed Tyler, raising an eyebrow. "When you marry my daughter, you'd better treat her right."

"Without a doubt, Robert," Tyler replied instantly, his cheeks reddening.

"And...don't invite your father to the wedding," he added on.

"No shit," Jasmine sighed, but it turned into a soft, beautiful laugh.

"I'm pretty sure *Daddy Dearest* wouldn't come anyway," Tyler drawled wryly.

Robert stood up, loading his briefcase. "I'll keep you posted on everything, and I'll expedite these accounts of Sean's and set it so you guys can split it equally. You're all over eighteen, so it'll be easy to pay it out. No minors to file paperwork for. Your mother was probably advised to make the age twenty-one because she expected to be able to control the accounts herself, but considering the accident, it didn't quite work out that way. And for that, I'm truly sorry."

The room went rather quiet, but he looked to Evan. "Damn fine job you did at the station, Evan. Can't say I blame you for punching him." He smiled a bit. "Unfortunately, you can't lag on this. You guys have two days to vacate the house."

Evan flinched a little, but he spoke up before Robert left the table. "Sir, umm…" He swallowed nervously, glancing to his brother and then Faith before meeting the lawyer's warm gaze. "What are we allowed to take? Well…What I mean is…There are some things—some of my mother's personal things—that I…*we*…would like to keep. If left here, we may lose them."

Robert nodded. "Fair enough. I tell you what…Keep a list, maybe snap a few pictures with your phone, and send them my way. Do it quickly, and I'll present it to his lawyer before you leave. If your father takes issue with it, I'll fight for it. Perhaps I'll remind him just what he's taken from *you*." The man was dead serious about that statement too, but he gave everyone a nod and a smile. "It was nice meeting all of you. I've got a plane to catch back to New York, but I'll be in touch. Don't hesitate to call me if you have any issues or questions."

He kissed Jasmine's cheek, whispering something to her, and she nodded solemnly but pulled back to smile at him.

"I think I'll head out too," Sean said, standing up from the table as he thanked my mother and aunt for lunch. However, his smile was sad. "If there's anything I can do, just let me know. I'll be happy to help."

He followed Robert to the front door and closed it behind him with a soft click. Evan shifted nervously before looking to Tyler, but his brother spoke first.

"What'choo want, baby brother? What of Mom's do you want to take?"

A lump formed in my throat at just how gentle Tyler spoke to Evan, and right there, I saw their dynamic. Tyler may have been the loud, boisterous one. Hell, he may have been the one with the sharpest temper, but holy shit, did he love his siblings. And he treated Evan with love and respect and a gentleness I wasn't expecting. Suddenly I realized that Evan had saved Tyler's life during the accident, and Tyler had watched his brother be punished for it—all of them were punished for it—their whole lives. He knew what every damn bit of it had done to Evan; he knew what the scars, the hate, the fears had done to his baby brother, and he sheltered him as best he could. It was all I could do not to tackle-hug the big guy, but instead, I turned to Evan, who was playing with my fingers in his lap.

"Books, right, baby? You said you wanted some of her books," I answered softly for him, and he snapped his gaze from our clasped hands to nod my way. "What else, Evan?"

His brow furrowed, but he looked to Tyler. "There's...There are some of Mom's things in the attic—clothes and her jewelry. Those are for Faith. Remember? We saved them when we cleaned out their bedroom?"

"Oh, yeah. Okay, we'll get that stuff down."

Evan grimaced. "I...We...We need to take the photo albums. I doubt he'll give a shit, since he's hardly in them." That came out a little bitter, and when he realized it, he grimaced. "Sorry."

"Don't be sorry, baby," I whispered against his cheek.

"Damn, son...You've earned the right to be pissed off," my dad piped up, which made all of us chuckle at Evan's sweet, crooked grin.

My handsome thing cleared his throat, looking around the table, but focused on Faith. "Faith..." He trailed off, smiling warmly her way when he saw her shifting nervously with watery eyes. "You tell us what you want. We'll...I mean, whatever you want to do." I watched Evan struggle with what he was about to say next, but he took a deep breath. "I know you wanted to graduate from the same school as Ty and me...*and* Mom, but...you can't. I wish..." He sighed wearily. "We aren't leaving you here."

Faith, who had been a pretty strong thing throughout the whole damned ordeal, finally allowed tears to spill, and Evan gently let go of my hand. He and Tyler got up from the table. Tyler pulled her chair out, and to watch the two very tall men kneel in front of her was almost overwhelming with the emotions that were spilling from all three of them.

They looked at her like she hung the damn moon, and I imagined that in their world, she did. More than once, Evan had said that his sister was the *one person* who was innocent of the whole thing. She hadn't been involved in the wreck. She'd been their rock after the accident, taking care of them as best as a ten-year-old could.

"Tell us what you want, midget," Tyler soothed her. "We'll break our necks to get it done."

Faith crumbled, nodding as she swiped at her tears. "I know…I love you both…so fucking much."

Evan smiled, pulling her head down so he could kiss her forehead before making sure she was looking him in the eye. "And we love you, Faith, but it's your choice. You can finish out school in Missoula and stay with Ty, or you can come with me, but we'll have to figure out where you'll stay…"

"She's more than welcome to stay with us," my mother said gently, her voice thick with emotions — she and my aunt were teary messes, "if that's what you guys choose to do…at least until you figure out something different or Faith goes to the dorms next year."

When Evan looked to her and then my dad, who was nodding, he went back to his sister. "There's one option, Faith."

She wrinkled her nose as she thought it over, glancing around the dining room as she gripped Evan's shirt sleeve. "I…I'm already accepted to Edgewater, big brother. I…I might as well…I want to go with *you*."

Evan smiled sadly yet so warmly it was breathtaking. "I figured, but I just wanted to double check. It makes more sense with you starting school with me in the fall."

She quickly turned to Tyler. "But…but…Will you guys still come this summer?"

Tyler grinned, cupping her small chin in his large hand. "You just try to stop me."

Faith glanced up at Jasmine, who smiled warmly. "A whole summer in Florida? I'm in!" she teased, but I could see it was her way of lightening things up a bit.

"Okay, so we need to pack everything up for Faith and Evan, and we need to sort out the stuff to take pictures of for Robert," Tyler said, dropping a kiss to the top of Faith's head as he stood up. "Sean said he'd help, so I wonder if he'd be willing to ship things down to Florida for us. If not, I suppose I could do it."

"You're gonna need some boxes," Wes pointed out. "Where around here could I find some? I'll go."

Evan stood up from in front of his sister. "Um, the market and maybe the diner. And there's a sporting goods store on the edge of town."

"On it," my cousin stated, catching the keys for the rental car from Aunt Tessa. "Oh, and here's your new phone, Ev. They were able to move everything over, despite the condition your old phone was in. Number's written on the box."

Evan's eyebrows shot up, and before he could thank my cousin, Wes had left the house.

I stood up from the table, walking to Evan. "Put us to work, Evan. That's what we're here for, okay?"

Evan nodded, taking a deep breath and letting it out slowly. "We'll start with the library and then move on to Faith's and my rooms."

Tyler clapped his brother on the back. "You heard the man...Let's get to work. And maybe we can be rid of this place once and for all."

Chapter Twenty-Three

EVAN

"Evan?" Aunt Tessa called from the hallway.

"In here," I grunted, dropping the last full box from my bed to the floor and gazing around my bedroom for anything else I might want.

Those of us heading back to Florida were catching a very early flight, so we were staying tomorrow night in a hotel in Missoula. They'd asked my siblings and me if we wanted to celebrate New Year's Eve there, but we'd all declined. Tyler and Jasmine had to get back to school, and Faith and I…Well, we just wanted out of Montana.

Every item we'd wanted, we'd taken pictures of, which we sent to Robert. Personal items—like clothes, music, and our own books—were packed up without question. It was the items in my mother's office and the box in the attic we were waiting for the okay to take. We'd boxed them up, just in case he said yes. However, I honestly expected my father to say no just to be an ass.

I brushed off my hands and smiled when Aunt Tessa leaned in the doorway.

"How's it goin' in here, sweet pea?" she asked, glancing around.

"I'm done in here. I'd already taken most of the clothes I needed when I moved into the dorms, so…" I trailed off, shrugging a shoulder. "Really, I just wanted my old journals, some of my books, and a few framed pictures." I pointed to the two boxes at the foot of my bed.

"Then we're almost packed up. Sean's getting us a mover to ship the boxes to our house. They'll be here in the morning," she said, pausing for a second. "Well, once we get the all-clear from Robert, that is."

I snorted humorlessly. "Bet you five bucks he says no. And don't be shocked when he says to leave Faith's car behind."

Aunt Tessa's nose wrinkled, but she nodded in agreement, or at the very least, she suspected just about the same result. She pushed off the doorway and walked to me, cupping my face.

"Evan, I want you to do me a favor when we get home," she said softly yet decisively, tilting her head a little. When I nodded, she smiled softly. "I think…and just hear me out, buddy…I think you need someone you can talk to — your sister too. Someone who can listen to what you've been through. I have a very good therapist friend, and I can ask if she can see you. Both of you."

Frowning, I let my gaze drop to the floor, and I felt my face heat up. "You…Y-You…" I was going to ask her if she thought I was crazy, but then I remembered my fear of water, my sometimes-irritating level of OCD, and my fear of loved ones driving in poor weather. But I didn't voice it.

"Kiddo," she whispered, lifting my gaze back to hers with her fingers beneath my chin. "I'm going to tell you what I told Wes when I sent him to my friend a few years back after his dad left. Talking things out with someone *does not* make you crazy. It doesn't make you wrong or off somehow or even weak. It simply gives you a chance to get some ugly things off your chest that you may or may not feel comfortable telling a friend…or girlfriend."

My head snapped back up to see her face to see if she wasn't making fun of me.

"Ev, I know you love my niece. And oh my goodness, does she love you to pieces," she said through a soft, loving laugh, "but I also think maybe you might want to work out some things you may not want her to hear. Fears and anger and disappointment can be debilitating, not to mention *grief*, Evan." She brought my head down in order to kiss my cheek. "Just think about it. Okay?"

I nodded, and she started to leave the room. "Aunt Tessa?" I called softly, and when she turned to me again, I asked one question. "D-Did it…Did it…help? Wes, I mean."

She smiled softly and then nodded. "Oh yeah…most definitely. He went from a kid getting into fist fights on a daily basis, smoking weed, and skipping school, to the man you know now, the one who runs my café and the one who bought tickets for Montana before you'd even gotten on the plane in Florida, Evan. I'd say it damn well helped."

I opened my mouth but then snapped it shut, which made her chuckle.

"You don't have to answer me now, son. There's too much shit goin' on. But when you *are* ready, you come to me. I'll make sure it happens," she stated, reaching down to take one of the boxes downstairs to the living room.

Picking up the other box, I followed her down to see my brother pacing on his cell phone. His face was fierce and pissed off as he glanced my way and then to Faith, who had seemed a bit lost in all of this since the night before at the table.

"He's such a fucking prick," Tyler sighed, rubbing his face roughly, but he looked to me. "Baby bro, you get around okay at school without a car?"

"Let me guess," I muttered sarcastically, dropping the box I was carrying to the pile that was growing in the foyer and then folding my arms across my chest. "He's demanding Faith's car."

Tyler snorted but nodded. "Right in one, bud."

"Yeah, I get around fine," I answered him honestly. "The campus is small, but there are buses that cover just about everywhere. However, I've been saving up. I mean…I *was* saving, but coming here depleted that a little. Faith and I will figure it out."

"Fine, he can keep the fucking car," Tyler conceded into the phone, wincing when Faith stalked back upstairs. "But he'd better give us Mom's things…"

Dani stepped out of the kitchen, her eyes sad. I looked for pity and found none, just love and maybe a bit of anger.

She walked to me and stood up on her toes to kiss my lips. "This may be a bit of a shock for her, baby," she whispered, her nose wrinkling. "I mean, you and your brother have had a chance to move out, settle into college, and the two of you have lives and friends elsewhere. She's losing everything, and she's got two — now one day — to get out of the only home she's ever known, never mind she's got to finish school somewhere she won't know anyone."

"I know. And I hate it all for her." I sighed deeply before giving her a soft kiss. "I'll go check on her."

I trudged up the stairs to my sister's bedroom doorway, leaning against the frame as she threw clothes out of her closet.

"Faith," I called her, ducking when hangers were launched toward my head. "Rylee Faith!"

Her fierce, angry face popped out of the closet. "What?"

"Stop throwing shit at me and sit down," I requested, pointing to her bed. "Please?"

She did as I asked, sitting cross-legged in the middle of the mattress. I sat directly in front of her, mimicking her posture.

"I hate him," she whispered, trailing her finger along the seams of the mattress that had been stripped bare. "I hate him so much." She gazed up at me. "I…I used to dream of killing him in his sleep for the things he'd say and do to us. I used to fantasize about seeing his Mercedes sink to the bottom of that fucking lake."

Nodding, I gave her a weak smile. "Me too. I wrote stories about it."

"No shit?" She giggled at my nod.

"Oh yeah, I wrote a whole revenge, bloody massacre thing. I wrote a shark attack, but that wasn't satisfying enough. And I didn't use his name of course, but…" I shrugged, letting out a humorless laugh. "Funny, though…it didn't make me feel any better."

Her eyes stayed downcast to the trail her fingers were still making on the bed. "I thought I'd…I thought I'd feel different, knowing I was getting out of here…"

Frowning, I lifted her chin to make her meet my gaze. "Faith, I know it's scary, and I know it's sudden. I also know that getting out of this house and away from him was the *very best* decision I've ever made. And I owe you a thank-you for making me go, for not letting me give in to Dad's bullshit." I tapped her chin with my fingers. "Please trust me when I tell you that the car is one less tether to him. You don't need it. Glenhaven is small enough to walk or bus some-where — kinda like Key Lake, only without the assholes."

I grinned when she laughed a little. "You won't be alone in this. I promise. I think...Faith, I think you'll *really* like it. You...you're normal. You'll love the beach and the warm weather and the water. Hell, maybe Dani can take you. I sure as shit can't go with her, but..."

Faith gaze softened from the angry expression she'd been wearing. "Still?"

"You expect that to change?" I countered with a harsh laugh, sighing as I raked a hand through my hair and adjusted my glasses. "My scars are one thing, but I can't take my girlfriend to the beach she's grown up loving..."

"The girlfriend is perfectly okay with that," Dani said from the doorway, and I grinned her way while Faith laughed softly. "You're saving me from skin cancer or something, Evan. I'm sure of it." She stepped into the room, dropping a heavy kiss to the side of my head. "Tyler told me to tell the two of you that...you're clear to take your mother's things."

Faith gasped, gaping up at her, but I knew my girl, and I narrowed my eyes at her. "What aren't you saying, pretty girl?"

Dani's nose wrinkled, and she shook her head. "Your father's exact words were, 'Tell those ungrateful assholes to take it all. Otherwise I'll set fire to it.' He also said that if he sees any of you, it'll be too fucking soon. Though, he's kind of stupid because I'm sure there's court shit in his future."

Faith chuckled. "Robert said we might not be needed, and he said hopefully there are enough character witnesses to bury him, so..."

"Good. I'd hate to have to tell him what a disgusting slug he is in front of a judge," Dani stated, wearing an overly exaggerated sweet smile, which made my sister and me really laugh. "So...all that being said...You're packed, with the exception of whatever you were doing in here. Sean will be here first thing in the morning with the movers. They'll take all the boxes down to Florida for you. We'll store them at our house until you have a place to put them."

"Are you...I mean..." my sister sputtered, and I chuckled and ruffled her hair.

"Get used to it, Faith. When Dani or her family says something, there's no use in arguing."

"Damn straight, handsome!" my girl sang, kissing my lips when I stood from the bed. "Now he's getting it!" She shot my sister a wink. "Soon I'll have all of you over on the dark side..."

Shaking my head, I wrapped an arm around her shoulders, my lips at her ear. "I love you."

"Love you too, baby."

I gazed at her, my need to get back to Florida growing by leaps and bounds, which only served to remind me that this was most likely the last time I'd ever be not only in this house but in the town in which I'd grown up. As I gazed at the girl who was my future, I knew I needed to close my past.

"Feel like braving the cold, Dani?" I asked her.

"Sure." Dani smiled, though her adorable face was filled with curiosity.

"I wanna show you something," I told her, glancing over to Faith. "We won't be gone long."

My sister's face was sad when she nodded, which meant she most likely knew where I was going, but I didn't say anything.

I guided Dani to my room, where we put on coats and hats and gloves. We left out the front door, but I shot my brother a wave, telling him we'd be back in a bit. I reached for Dani, and she slipped her gloved hand into mine. The snow wasn't as pristine as it had been. There wasn't any new snow, so there were tire tracks and shoveled piles and footprints everywhere. I guided her down the street, where the houses became fewer and fewer. The woods were eerily quiet yet heavy with snow on either side of the street. Up ahead, the street narrowed, and my heart constricted at the place I hadn't set eyes on in seven years. Hell, I refused to look at it anytime I passed by it.

The railing had been repaired, of course, and the snow made it completely different, but as I helped Dani navigate the snow drifts, I could remember everything as plain as yesterday. The small lake the town was named after was partially frozen, but it didn't matter. And I didn't take my eyes off it as I started to talk.

"We were coming down this way," I whispered, my breath pluming out in front of me as I pointed to the street. "The... Th-The dog, it...Right there."

I frowned at the double yellow lines in the center of the small bridge where everything had been sent into a blurry spin. I swallowed back bile as I took in the lake again. The sounds of my mother's frantic voice, of rushing water, and of the car crunching were all coming at me. Dani's gloved hands met either side of my face, making me look at her.

"You're okay. And I'm right here. Evan, say something."

"I know, I know, I know," I chanted, letting my forehead drop to hers. "Her...Sean told me...Her seat belt jammed. That's why she...That's why..."

"Shhh," she breathed, pressing her lips to mine. "Evan...Baby, it wasn't your fault. Not a bit of any of it. Not the wreck or your mother or anything your dad has told you. Nothing. You and Tyler and Faith were all trapped in shit that wasn't your fault."

I nodded vehemently against her.

"Evan? Why come here?" she asked softly, her eyes only on me.

Gazing into the face that made me strong, that made me fight for what was right, I finally said, "Because I never want to come back here, Dani. Ever."

"Okay," she soothed me, reaching up to straighten my wool cap. Knowing her, I knew she'd rather rake her fingers through my hair, but it was too cold. "Fair enough."

I pulled back from her, eyeing the lake again, and I was nowhere closer to being over my fear of water than I was at thirteen years old. Swallowing nervously, I whispered, "Aunt Tessa says...She says I should see...a therapist."

"Dr. Costa." Her voice was soft and kind, without judgment. When I looked back at her, she smiled. "She's really nice. Wes loves her. And you'd like her too, Evan. She's...quiet and calm. She's really easy to talk to. And if you want, I'll go with you, but it couldn't hurt. Right?"

"No, no...I guess not," I murmured and shook my head a little. "Maybe..." As I remembered my sister's outburst just before we left, I sighed deeply. "Faith too."

"I think having someone to talk to isn't a bad idea...for any of you." Dani shrugged a shoulder. "But...I'll go with whatever you decide, Evan."

"'Kay." I gave one more glance to the lake, the railing, and the road. "One more place and we'll go back, okay?"

"Okay, baby."

I took the same path as the day of my fight with Dad, carefully guiding Dani around the slippery spots on the sidewalk, but when the wrought-iron fence came into view, I stopped us at the gate.

Taking a deep breath, I let it out slowly, and it plumed out again into the cold morning air. Frowning, I adjusted my glasses and then my wool cap before meeting Dani's gaze.

"Do you…Do you mind?" I asked her, swallowing around the nervous lump in my throat. I wasn't sure if Dani would want to set foot in a cemetery.

However, she was already shaking her head. "No, baby." When she held her hand out, I took it and led her toward my mother's grave.

I found it unchanged from the last time I'd been there, though I still knelt down and brushed the snow away from the poinsettia and off the top of her headstone. Dani stayed quiet by the small fir tree.

Glancing back at her, my heart hurt with how beautiful she was, how full of concern her face was, and I asked the one question I'd pondered the day Faith had picked out the Christmas tree.

"Do you…Do you believe in…in…something after this?" I waved a hand around, hating that I didn't have the right words at the moment, but my girl knew what I meant.

She gazed around with a thoughtful expression, taking a step forward and squatting down by my side. "I don't know, Evan," she stated honestly. "Despite my Southern upbringing, we aren't all that religious. I think some people have to believe in order to get through the rough stuff. I think that if anyone deserves something peaceful after all the bullshit, it would be your mother." She reached up to cup my face in her gloved hand. "I've never lost anyone I'm close to, baby, so I don't know what I'll feel when I do. I mean, I know it's inevitable, but that isn't something I have experience in."

She leaned in and kissed my cheek. "I could…quote books and movies or whatever, but…" She sighed. "My heart hurts at the thought of it. That one day I'll lose my family members, whether to old age or sickness or whatever. My need to wrap you up in my arms makes me crazy at the thought of something happening to you, so…That being said, I can't see you anywhere but a heavenly place after all the shit you've been through. Would I like to think that all those beautiful souls are somewhere happy? Sure. But I feel I'm smart enough to say I honestly *don't know.*"

She frowned a little. "That's probably not what you wanted to hear."

"I'd always rather have your honesty, pretty girl, than for you to say something you think I should hear," I told her, shrugging a shoulder. "I don't know, either." I huffed a laugh, but it fizzled out pretty quickly as I looked back at my mother's name chiseled artfully into the stone. "I just…" I swallowed back my emotions. "I just wish she'd had the chance to get away from here. I wish I could tell her…everything."

"You can, sweetheart. And if you believe she's someplace happy, then you have to believe she's watching over you." She tilted my head back to meet her gaze. "She fought like fucking hell to give you a chance to live, Evan. That's all she wanted — to clear a path for you and Tyler and Faith to flourish in life, and despite all your dad has done, you now have that chance. After all I've heard about her, about this place, I know all she wanted was for you to be happy. You can tell her now, here, or you can write it down, but I think…I'd *like* to think she knows, baby."

I nodded, feeling the sting of tears, because her honesty was sweet and really what I needed to hear. "I miss her, Dani."

"I know you do," she whispered against my cheek, wrapping her arms around me.

"I used to wish it was my dad's name on this stone, but I was angry at her and him and everyone. I just…I know you're right. I know all she wanted was for us to follow our dreams. She told us all the time."

"Angry is normal. I can't blame you for it at all."

I sniffled and laughed softly at the same time but looked over at her. "She would've *really* liked you," I whispered, brushing a lock of hair out of her face. "I know that much."

"You think so? I don't know…I mean, I'm crazy about her son, but I talk too much and say dumb things…" She laughed at my grin.

"I know she would…'Cause it's *you* who makes me happy."

Dani smiled, her eyes watering a little. "Good, Evan. I'm glad."

Chapter Twenty-Four

EVAN

"We'll be right behind you," Tyler told Aunt Tessa. "But if I don't stop at the diner for coffee, Jas'll kill me...or turn into the road-rage queen."

I grinned from the back seat at Jasmine's snort, but she nodded and shrugged too. "I resemble that remark," she muttered, grinning at Dani's soft laugh.

Faith, Dani, and I were all riding with Tyler to Missoula in order to spend a few more minutes with my brother, and he and Jasmine would go to dinner with us one last time before leaving us at the hotel by the airport. The two of them would then head back to the dorms to study and catch up on things they'd missed while in Key Lake. The movers were loaded up and gone with the few boxes we'd needed. Faith was packed and had already checked out Glenhaven High School's website, the school Wes had attended. She was nervous and quiet, but she seemed to be coming to terms with it all. She'd wanted to join me in Florida anyway. It all had just happened quicker than we'd originally thought.

"Coffee sounds pretty damn good, actually," Dani chimed in, leaning into me from the middle of the back seat.

She was between Faith and me, and just like I'd thought, the two got along perfectly. Jasmine too, for that matter. All three had very strong personalities, but they seemed to complement one another instead of clashing.

We shot waves to Daniel, Leanne, Wes, and Aunt Tessa as they pulled out ahead of us from my driveway, and I gave one last look to the house. As much as I missed my mother, I wouldn't miss that house. Anything good that I remembered was now overshadowed by Dad's hate. The house meant nothing to me. It was cold and sharp, with a darkness that hung over it. As I looked at it one more time, every anxious feeling about it melted away. I was going home, and I honestly didn't care what my father's fate would be, though I knew he was falling deeper and deeper into trouble—something for which he alone was responsible.

We pulled into the diner, and Dani and Jasmine went in for their coffee. Tyler followed to keep them company. I looked over to Faith.

"I won't miss this town," she said, meeting my gaze after rolling her eyes.

Chuckling, I reached over to squeeze her shoulder. "You really won't, Faith."

There was a rumble of a truck engine, not to mention a shadow cast over Tyler's car, and when I glanced to the parking space next to us, I groaned, shaking my head slowly. I'd gone the whole damn Christmas break in Key Lake without running into any former class-mates…until now.

Brandon Hill had once been a friend in middle school. He then turned into the biggest asshole. As he slid down from his ridiculously tall, oversize truck, he caught sight of Faith and me, a slow, evil smile creeping up his face. A petite blonde girl slid down from the passenger side at the same time.

"Ah, well…Looky here. If it isn't Slaughter Shaw!" he taunted, beaming like he'd just received an extra fucking Christmas present. "Rumor has it your old man is in deep shit."

I snorted, glancing to Faith, who looked like she was about five seconds from launching herself through the back window at him. But when I looked back at Brandon, I saw Dani, Jasmine, and Tyler emerge from the diner. My brother's face darkened at the sight of Brandon, but Dani's eyes narrowed as I opened the door to let her in.

"I got us a large to share, baby," she said, standing up on her toes to kiss my lips.

Brandon laughed outright. "You're Slaughter Shaw's girl?" he asked incredulously but flinched when Tyler stepped closer. "Hoshit! Tyler...didn't see you there..."

Tyler grinned, shaking his head. "Get away from me, Brandon. I've got more important shit to do today than teach you a lesson in history."

Brandon smirked, holding out his hand to Jasmine and then Dani. "Brandon Hill. I used to go to school with..."

Jasmine looked at him like he was a disgusting, slimy bug. Dani, however, eyed his hand, tilted her head to take in his truck, and then she looked to me.

"Did he really just call you...*Slaughter Shaw?*" she asked in a dangerously slow drawl, and I heard Faith's giggle, never mind the fact that Jasmine and Tyler were waiting for whatever my girl was about to say. When I nodded, her nostrils flared and her eyes darkened as she faced Brandon. "Is this your truck?" she asked, which wasn't what I was expecting, and Brandon grinned proudly her way.

"Hell, yeah...special mud tires, a lift-kit..."

"Aww..." she crooned sadly in a sing-song way, giving him a falsely sympathetic smile. "You know, in Psych class, we were just studying how men overcompensate for their shortcomings by going overboard with their...*hobbies*. It usually takes the form of status symbols—vehicles, gun collections, hunting trophies—all to make up for where they're *lacking*, which could be intellect, income, or penis size, so which is it?"

He looked confused, which only caused the rest of us to openly laugh.

"Tough call, huh?" She spun to face me. "Coffee, handsome?"

Grinning, I took the cup as she crawled into the back seat of the car.

Jasmine barked a laugh, mouthing *so sorry* to the blonde with him, and once everyone was back in the car, she turned to face Dani as we left Brandon and his confused girl and that stupidly ginormous truck behind us. "Oh, Dani...You may be the most perfect girl for Evan."

Dani grinned, glancing up my way as I whispered, "I know she is," against her temple.

The long drive into Missoula was a mix of laughter and music and conversation that had nothing to do with William Shaw, Key Lake, or even Brandon. Tyler and I traded college stories, the girls chatted about all sorts of different stuff, and for the first time since I'd landed in Montana, I felt normal, calm, but that could've been because I was about to leave the whole state behind.

My brother and Jasmine treated Dani to some of the sights of the city before we met up with the rest of Dani's family for dinner, which felt a bit like a celebration that some of the worst was over.

Once Tyler pulled up to the hotel, he turned to face us. "I'll keep you posted on Dad, guys. And we'll be down as soon as school lets out for the summer. Baby bro, watch over the midget…and vice versa."

"I will," Faith and I said at the same time.

"And guys…let this shit go. Forget about Dad. We're in the right, so we just have to wait out all his court bullshit."

We all nodded and got out, calling goodbyes and love yous before we walked into the hotel.

Dani squeezed my hand, looking up at me. "I…I got a room for the two of us to share, Evan, so I hope…"

Nodding, I kissed her temple. "Yeah, I'm gonna hate the dorms after this."

Her giggle was adorable. "Then my spoiling you is working!"

It turned out that Faith had her own room, where everyone else was doubled up. I honestly just needed to be back in Florida. I was ready to do like my brother said and put all of this shit behind me.

It wasn't until later that I realized how subdued Dani had been since we'd checked into the hotel. Throughout dinner, she'd been quiet, not to mention in the car as we drove around Missoula. Once we were settled in our room, I sat her down on the edge of the bed.

"What's wrong, pretty girl? You're so quiet. Is there…Do you…" I wasn't sure what to ask or even how to ask it, but something was making her nervous. I worried that I'd done something wrong, though I couldn't figure out what.

She reached up to trail her fingers down my face, her brow furrowing a little. "I love you."

"I love you too, Dani."

She got up from the bed to rummage around in her bag, pulling out something I'd completely forgotten about—my leather-bound journal. I chuckled a little, taking it from her.

"Did you read it all, baby?" I asked her, thumbing through it but looking up at the beautiful girl taking her seat back on the bed.

She nodded, leaning in to kiss me. "I did. And it was beautiful. All of it. I prefer the real deal, but I was missing you, so I was happy with what you gave me."

Grinning, I nodded but tilted my head at her. "So what's this got…You didn't answer my question. What's wrong?"

"Nothing's *wrong*, Evan," she spoke softly, fidgeting with my fingers in her lap. "I just…There was an entry in there." She finally met my gaze as she tapped the book. "You said…You…I don't need candles or…or beautiful words, but Evan, I'm ready for the universe to shift."

It took me a second to realize what she meant, and when I did, I gasped, gaping up at her with shock. "Dani, what are you saying?"

"I'm…I want to be with you…in every way, Evan. I'm ready… Shit, I was ready before you left Florida, but…I love you, and I want to show you."

I gave the room a quick glance as I set my journal on the floor. If I was being honest with myself, I hadn't seen it happening this way. Though, I wasn't sure what I'd expected. However, this was slowly starting to feel like the perfect place. We had our own room, not her bedroom at her house or my dorm room. It was ours and ours alone. It also seemed like perfect timing because I wanted to show her too. I'd thought I loved her before I'd gotten on the plane to come here, but as I gazed at the girl in front of me, I knew it was more, deeper, just everything.

Reaching for her face, I brushed the backs of my fingers across her cheek. "You're sure?" I asked in a whisper. "Pretty girl, I *need* you to be so sure…" My voice was soft, but the tone was pleading. I'd never forgive myself if she wasn't really ready.

"I'm sure I love you," she said back with a slight smile on her gorgeous face, but she tilted her head at me, brushing my lips with hers for a brief, light kiss. "Evan, we don't need candles or poetry or grand gestures. We don't need to plan a thing. We just need each other."

I grinned, kissing her again softly. "Plan…" I scoffed as I shook my head. "I never planned on you, Dani. That's for damn sure." I sighed, standing up in front of her and kicking out of my shoes before sitting on the bed with my back against the headboard. "C'mere," I breathed, holding my arms out for her, and immediately she was astride my lap. Cupping her face, I said, "We may not need grand gestures, Dani, but…This…this is important to me, not because it's the first time but because it's *you*. I want this to be…*everything*. You are everything to me, and I…Despite how badly I want you—and oh God, I want you so bad—I want this to be special. And I don't want to hurt you or mess up or…"

She smiled, leaning in to kiss me and raking her fingers gently through my hair to shut me up and most likely settle me down as well. "From the very second I met you, Evan Shaw, I knew you would *never* hurt me. I know it, deep down inside my heart. And at no time, no matter what we've done, have I regretted a thing."

I was overthinking. I knew I was. She'd once told me it didn't matter that I'd never had a girlfriend, and she'd placed her hand on my heart, telling me to follow it. As I gazed up at the girl who'd irreversibly changed my life for the better, I could feel myself completely surrender. She made me strong, she made me laugh, and she gave me peace in the stormy shit that was my life. But I could see she was my future too. All those things she'd said that first morning she'd arrived in Key Lake—I wanted it. I wanted all of it. I wanted to mesh our lives together into one perfect thing.

Slipping my hand into her hair, I brought her lips to mine. I kissed her softly, like our first kiss, taking my time, but I pulled back to meet her gaze. "I know we don't need…I mean…" I kissed her again, deeply, simply because I couldn't stop myself, but when I pulled back, I met her dark, heated gaze. "I want to make you feel good, Dani. And…and…"

Her smile was wicked and sexy and sweet—all at the same time. "We don't need anything. You know I'm on the pill, baby. You've seen me take it. Now…Finish that sentence, Evan."

I swallowed nervously. "I want to see all of you, and I can't wait to feel you."

"Yes," she hissed, reaching for the bottom of her sweater and tugging it off, only to reach for mine.

Something in us melted away. There was no more hesitation. When we were both shirtless, left only in our jeans, I sat up, wrapping my arms around her as we lost ourselves in the deepest kiss. It started slightly frantic and hungry, but slowly we both found a smooth, deep pace, with hands touching skin and chest pressing against chest. Rolling us, I melted into her, barely breaking away from her lips, but she wrapped her legs around my waist as hands started to pull and push and grip.

With one last brush across her lips, I pulled away, pressing my forehead to hers. "I love you, Dani."

"I love you too. Please don't stop."

"I can't," I said breathlessly, giving her a half smile when she cupped my face. "I can't stop. I need you, pretty girl. I need this and you and all of it. Nothing matters to me but you. Tell me you know that before we...before I..."

She was nodding before I finished that rambling plea, and I braced one hand by her hand, pushing up to gaze down at the beautiful thing beneath me. God, she was gorgeous, which I said out loud as I reached out with my free hand to touch — her face, her neck, between her breasts, and flat along her stomach. When I reached the edge of her jeans, I looked back at her face, and she nodded vehemently.

I pulled at the button until it popped open and then lowered her zipper. Dropping kisses to each peaked nipple and the soft skin along her stomach, I worked my way down to kneel between her legs. I grasped the top of her jeans, and we both smiled when she had to wriggle a bit to get out of them, but I was finally able to tug them off and drop them off the side of the bed. To see her sprawled out in nothing but a pair of tiny pink underwear was just about my undoing.

"Fuck, you're just...beautiful," I said in awe, reaching for the pale-pink lace.

I lost myself a bit when she lay completely bare in front of me, but her giggle brought me right back, as did her legs, which she wrapped around my torso to tug at me. I smiled back at her, feeling a little of my worries disappear as nothing about this felt wrong or too soon or too much. It was just us.

"I want..." I licked my lips at what I wanted to say, but my eyes betrayed me as I took in the apex of her legs.

"Oh God…" she whimpered. "Evan, please…"

"I've never…but I…Fuck, I want to…"

Skimming my hands flat along her thighs that were wrapped around me, I gently pushed them open. I'd touched her before—more than one time—but to see her spread out for me was better than anything I'd ever read, watched, or dreamed. I rubbed the inside of her thighs gently, finally trailing my fingers along her mound and then through her slit. I could feel her shaking, see her raising her hips up a little as I leaned down and kissed her stomach, the inside of her thigh, and finally her pussy.

Her reaction was better than any part of what we were doing. She was so sensitive, she shook as she raised her hips again. The flavor of her was heady, a salty-sweet taste, not unlike her skin when she was sweaty. She used her body to tell me what felt good; she barely breathed aloud not to stop when my fingers slid inside her at the same time my tongue hit the perfect spot and speed. And soon, my name, along with a few curse words, hit the air as her pussy fluttered around my fingers.

Ravenous for her, I lifted my head, still licking the flavor from my lips, and she sat up a little to reach for my jeans. She deftly popped open the button, and I kissed her briefly before slipping off the bed in order to kick out of them, tugging my socks off as well. She'd seen my dick before, but the way she was looking at me made me feel nervous and smug at the same time. She knelt on the bed, pulling me to stand in front of her, and I leaned down to kiss her.

We were hands and skin and heavy breathing, completely bare for each other, but as badly as I wanted her, I needed to slow down. However, it was Dani who took the lead this time, gently placing her hand on the back of my neck and guiding me back onto the bed over her. Her kiss was searing and needy. Her hands were everywhere. And we both moaned aloud when everything about us lined up perfectly.

Gasping, I squeezed my eyes closed for a second before opening them up to see her. "Dani…baby…I love you. I need…You have to…"

"Shhh," she breathed against the corner of my mouth. "I love you too." She wrapped her hand around my shaft and guided me to her entrance. "Please…"

My eyes rolled back and my mouth fell open as I started to push forward. It was unlike anything I'd ever felt and infinitely better than anything we'd done prior to this. She was warm and wet and heavenly, and I froze when she gasped a little.

Leaning down, I kissed her, slowly easing out and then back in, which was using every bit of my self-control. I wanted to feel all of her around me, and the urge to come was overwhelming, but slowly her muscles stopped tensing and her grip went from harsh to pulling me in, touching me everywhere as she wrapped her legs around me.

But it was her face I paid the most attention to, making sure I wasn't hurting her. The pinched expression faded from around her eyes, and the warmth returned as her lips met mine and her hips started to work with me.

"Damn, I...You feel so good, Evan," she moaned.

"Yes," I hissed, burying my face in her neck as I tried to keep from coming, but she felt too good.

I felt it building, creeping up my spine and tightening my balls. I was barely holding back, but it all became so much, *too much*. It was the feel of skin on skin and the smell of her hair; it was the sounds the two of us made together and the sight of all of that stuff combined into one single act. And it was overwhelming need, but most of all it was my overflowing love for her. Suddenly I was coming harder than I'd ever come before. Dani held me close, and my own curses, along with my love for her, were muffled against the skin of her throat.

My vision blurred a bit, and I was breathing heavy as my forehead fell to hers. She glided her fingers up and down my spine.

"Don't move," she pleaded against the side of my head as I buried my face in her neck again.

"I'm sorry. You didn't..."

"Don't be sorry," she whispered, and I heard her breathing hitch a little.

My eyes opened to see a tear escape the corners of her eyes, and I frowned, reaching to wipe one away with my thumb. "You okay?"

"I'm...perfect. I just...love you, and now...I may never let you go," she rambled adorably in a whisper, smiling when I chuckled a little.

"Good, then *my* spoiling is working," I teased her, brushing kisses all over her face. "That was...I can't...Thank you. I love you too, Dani." I laughed softly at my inability to speak, and her smile melted me completely. I trailed a thumb gently beneath her eye. "The universe *did* shift. I see...*everything* in your eyes, pretty girl."

There was so much truth in that statement. She was everything perfect and good and loving. She was everything I'd ever needed in my life. My life had completely changed since meeting her, and in spite of all the bullshit we still had to deal with concerning my dad, I finally felt, for the first time in my life, that I'd found my normal, my family, *myself.* Leaving Montana tomorrow would be the start of everything. I could do what my mother had intended for me...I'd truly live, seeking a future with my family—both blood related and hand-picked—and a future with Dani.

But some things I wanted to hold on to, things that were too important to lose, so with a smile and a slight grimace, I separated from her. After getting a warm washcloth and cleaning us both up a bit, I reached for the book I'd left on the nightstand before dinner.

"C'mere, pretty girl. I've missed this," I whispered, settling her under the covers, and she curled herself around me, wearing a beautiful smile, as I opened to the first page and dropped a kiss to her head before I started to read.

"*The Secret Garden. Chapter one. There Is No One Left. When Mary Lennox was sent to Misselthwaite Manor to live with her uncle everybody said she was most disagreeable-looking child ever seen...*"

Chapter Twenty-Five

DANI

The library was quiet as I strode down the last aisle at the back of the building. I scanned the shelf, reaching up high for the book I needed. My fingertips barely brushed the spine, and I grunted in frustration. However, I couldn't stop the smile from creeping up my face when a long, strong arm reached over me to effortlessly pull down the book I'd been struggling to obtain.

Turning around, I leaned back against the bookcase, giggling softly at Evan's sweet, crooked smile as he held out my book. He was in his contacts today, something he rotated on a regular basis. I loved the glasses because they made him look so sweet and smart. I also loved the contacts because they gave me an uninterrupted view of that deep brown and those long eyelashes.

"Better?" he asked, leaning in to kiss my lips as I hugged the book to me.

"Yes, thank you," I whispered, brushing my mouth across his a few more times. "I wasn't expecting you for another hour."

"Dr. Costa had to reschedule, so I told her I'd see her next Friday," he answered, shrugging a shoulder. "Which is fine by me; I have to study for finals." He reached out for my hand, and I laced my fingers with his as he led us back to our table. "I'll get some done now before work."

Our time in the library, even if we never said a word to each other, was precious to us, so we'd been determined to find a new meeting time once we returned from Montana. It'd been a new semester, so these last four and a half months had us meeting up in the library at the end of the day instead of the middle, like before Christmas break. Fridays were our favorite. Evan went to see Dr. Costa, met me in the library for a few hours, and then he went to work. From work, he'd come straight to my house to spend the weekend. Every weekend. It gave him time with his sister, who was coasting through her last few days of high school, and he and I would wrap ourselves around each other at night in my room.

That thought had me glancing up from my books on the table in front of me to stare shamelessly at Evan. He was different yet the same sweet, shy boy I'd first seen in this very library. He was still studious and smart, and he wrote amazing stories for me and for some classes he was taking. He still loved to read together, which was probably my second favorite thing to do with him. The thought of my favorite thing made me lick my lips and rake my gaze from his sharp jaw, furrowed brow, and set mouth, down to his broad shoulders, flexing arm, and those long, very talented fingers, which were innocently playing with his pen.

When he caught my stare, he raised a deadly eyebrow at me. "Pretty girl, you keep that up and—"

"Don't you dare finish that sentence at this table, Evan Shaw," I hissed teasingly, just to watch him laugh. Fuck, he was just stunningly beautiful when he laughed. "I will not be held responsible for my actions."

His grin flashed bright, and he nodded, reaching for my hand. He pressed long, soft kisses to my fingers, whispering, "I know, baby. I can't wait, either. I've missed you this week."

"Me too," I sighed, smiling at him because it was impossible not to just want to kiss him stupid.

Some things didn't change, but the dark, heated gaze he was giving me was something that had started since our first time in Montana just before coming home. Most of Evan's sexual shyness had completely dissipated. He was insanely sexy when he wanted to be, but usually he had no clue he was doing it.

"I'll make it up to you, Dani. I promise," he vowed against my skin, grinning again when I narrowed my eyes at him in warning.

I pulled my hand back slowly, mumbling about dangerously good-looking boys and their even more dangerous voices. I'd missed every inch of him this last week just due to homework, his shifts at the café, and everything else in between. However, I fought my smile as Evan pressed a chuckling kiss to the side of my head.

To say Evan was busy would be an understatement. The moment we'd returned from Montana, everyone just stayed...busy. A new semester meant new classes and a new routine. We'd had to figure out everything all over again. There was a shit-ton of homework, a new work schedule for him at the café, moving his sister into the guest room across the hall from me, and yes, Evan and Faith had started sessions with Dr. Costa. Add in the occasional conference call with lawyers and one weekend trip to Montana for the two of them to testify against their father, and it seemed like we never saw each other. It was the trip back to Montana that had made Evan decide to ask Aunt Tessa about her therapist friend—he and his sister had come back to Florida completely beaten down.

Everything William Shaw had ever done was now out in the open—and it was some pretty ugly shit. It started with fraud and embezzlement. William had forged Tyler's signature in order to gain access to the trust, and his lawyer had filed, not knowing it wasn't real.

He also owed or had paid several people a hell of a lot of money.

A woman in Missoula—who he'd been having an affair with *well before* Robyn passed away—testified that he'd been paying her to stay silent, which included an apartment and, later, Evan's BMW. Some of his patients and prescription history was being called into question. And a Dr. Lowe testified that he knew about all of it, and William had paid him a very large amount money to shut him up. There was even rumor of offshore accounts, but they were still investigating.

Charge after charge stacked up against Evan's father and not one of them from his children. He'd dug his own grave—several graves, actually—and not only had the board of directors at the hospital cut him loose, but he was now facing a few years in prison. The forgery of Tyler's signature alone was enough to get him three years at the least. The prescriptions, on the other hand, could cause the loss of his license to practice medicine.

Without income, never mind what he'd spent, William had lost everything financially. The Shaw home in Key Lake now had a lien on it, and the last I'd heard, it was up for sale. What was left of the trust — and the accounts that Pastor Sean had overseen — had now been equally distributed amongst Tyler, Evan, and Faith.

All of that bullshit weighed heavily on my Evan, which was why he saw Dr. Costa on a regular basis. Occasionally I'd go with him, but most of the time he'd go alone. I honestly thought he preferred it that way because he could rage behind closed doors. As sweet and shy and calm as my handsome boyfriend was, he was completely and utterly pissed off at his father. And I didn't blame him one fucking bit. My personal hope was that, while in prison, a large man named Bubba treated William like he'd treated his children, but I never voiced that aloud.

I glanced up at Evan again, this time reaching up to brush his hair from his forehead. There was a small, fine scar left over from the fight with his dad. It was the only thing visible, but it was the scars I couldn't see — the quiet, emotional scars — that made me want to wrap Evan up in soft pillows and that plastic bubble stuff to keep him safe and happy.

Evan met my gaze, the deep brown calm and soothing and curious, and I smiled, whispering, "Love you, baby. That's all."

His smile was warm and sweet, if not slightly teasing. "*Love you*, pretty girl. And you are the best of distractions today. You all right?"

"I'm sorry," I said, breaking out into a giggle I couldn't stop. His grin was beautiful as I shrugged a shoulder. "I dunno. I'm just…" I sighed deeply, taking in his patient face. "I guess I'm ready for summer. We've got one more week of classes. Your sister's graduation is coming up, and then Tyler and Jasmine will be here for two months."

Something I didn't recognize flickered across his face, but he nodded. "Yeah, I'm ready for the break," he said, tapping his books with his pen to indicate that he meant school, because I knew he'd continue to work and go to his sessions with Dr. Costa. He studied my face again and then reached up to drag the backs of his fingers across my cheek, finally pulling me in to press his lips to mine. "I picked a new book, Dani," he whispered against my lips before smiling wickedly at me.

Pushing away from me, he reached into his backpack and set the book in my hands.

My face heated, but I couldn't stop the soft laugh that bubbled up out of me. "There's a sequel?" I asked incredulously. "What more could those two get up to?" I raised an eyebrow, remembering the very first book we'd read together about the sexy, if not slightly asinine, CEO and his very pretty assistant who couldn't stop from wanting each other. It had led to some serious making out once Evan's voice had wrapped around the dirty parts.

Evan grinned and shrugged. "I don't think it's Jack and Sophia, just the same author."

The fact that he remembered the characters' names made me snort into the ugliest of laughs, but I loved him madly. I handed the book back to him, shaking my head.

"Fair enough, Evan," I told him. "I'll be kissing you stupid for that later, I'm sure."

He grinned but didn't even look up from his homework as he said, "I'm looking forward to it, baby."

I couldn't concentrate for shit, so I gazed around the library. Our new schedule brought new sets of eyes, people I'd seen in class and around campus and some I didn't know at all, but there were new girls who seemed drawn to Evan. As usual, he never even noticed them, or if he did, he didn't bother to acknowledge it.

Finally forcing myself to work, I lost myself in my English Lit paper. I was broken out of my concentration when Evan's lips pressed to the side of my head.

"Gotta go to work, pretty girl. You'll be by later?"

Looking up at him, I nodded. "Mmhmm. With Faith most likely. I promised I'd hit the beach with her after school and then get ice cream at O'Malley's." Glancing up at the clock, I closed my book. "I should go too."

He smiled and nodded, waiting for me to gather my things. We walked to the parking lot together, and I smiled at Evan's truck parked next to my car. The one thing everyone had encouraged him to do for himself was to buy a means of transportation. Evan, however, didn't go overboard or lose his mind with something crazy, though he had the money to do it. Wes and my dad had gone with him to make sure he got something decent, something reliable. He'd bought a simple used pickup truck—nothing humongous, nothing audacious, just a simple truck. It was black, and it seemed to fit him.

"See you later," I told him, smiling up at him when he walked me to my car.

"Love you," he said, leaning in through my open window to kiss me one more time.

Faith and I thanked the kid behind the counter for our ice cream, stepping back out onto the boardwalk. I slowly dragged my spoon through hot fudge, whipped cream, and cold ice cream, bringing it to my mouth.

The beach had been crowded with students from both Glenhaven High and Edgewater College. It was Friday, and most just seemed to need to blow off steam. Summer break was so close, the air seemed to vibrate with the anticipation. Faith had seen a few people she knew, and so had I—one of whom had been Brad.

"So...*that* was the asshole who threw a drink at my brother," she said, licking her spoon and smiling at my laugh.

"Yeah, he's...special." I sneered, shaking my head. "He's also not allowed at the café anymore. Wes banned him."

At the mention of my cousin, Faith's cheeks heated and she focused more on her sundae than anything else around her.

"Hey," I whispered, nudging her a little. "He really does like you."

Her sweet blue eyes locked on to my face, silently pleading with me not to fuck with her. I sighed deeply because I understood both sides. My cousin, despite his laid-back personality, was trying to give Faith a chance to settle in, finish high school, and heal a little from all that she'd been through with her brothers and father. He wasn't leading her on or teasing. He just wanted her happy. Faith, however, was running out of patience.

They flirted and laughed and got along better than I'd ever imagined they would, but my cousin was trying to be a gentleman. And he was Evan's best friend, which made him wary from the start. And even Evan had told Wes time and time again that Faith was quite capable of making up her own mind. My cousin, however, merely wanted to do the right thing because he *really* liked Faith—almost to the point of overprotectiveness.

"You think it'll change when I'm out of your house?" she asked hopefully. "Not that I don't want to be there...I just meant when I start Edgewater in the fall."

Grinning, I took another bite of my ice cream. "Maybe, but Faith, you need to talk to him. He's a dumb boy. Trust me, I grew up with him. As awesome and smart and silly as he is, he's just...Wes. He's busy, and he's trying to make sure you aren't..."

"I'm *fine*," she huffed, rolling her eyes. "I'm almost nineteen."

"And he's twenty-two, Faith. He's had relationships before — one was even serious for a bit — and he doesn't want to move too fast or hurt you. You...coming here...that was a big step that came out of nowhere. Even Evan worried about you, you know?"

At the mention of her big brother, Faith sighed. "I'm okay. It's been almost five months."

"And you're still dealing with your dad's shit, Faith. Hell, he hasn't even been sentenced yet, and he's still got to face the prescription thing. I'm hoping he'll plead out like Tyler said, but..."

She nodded, snorting a little, but looked over at me. "You know, Evan and Tyler...They guarded me, protected me after Mom died, even before that, and I love them for it, but I just want...normal. I want...I want to be treated like a girl, a woman, not someone's baby sister."

I laughed softly. "Maybe that's what my cousin needs to hear. I can't say I blame you."

We walked into Sunset Roast, and I smiled at the handsome thing behind the counter. His shyness was set aside when he was at work. He smiled and greeted the regulars, he joked with Susan — who was currently throwing sugar packets at him — and he worked his ass off in the back unloading the deliveries and keeping the inventory straight. He even continued to maintain the filing that my cousin still wasn't allowed to touch. He'd turned into Wes's right hand.

Evan's smile was warm, sweet, despite the fact that he was still batting away sugar packets. "How was the beach?" he asked, leaning over the counter to kiss me before I fed him a bite of ice cream.

"Sandy...beachy," I said with a grin, but I watched his mouth wrap around my spoon for one more bite, aching to have that mouth everywhere.

"Where's my ice cream?" Wes gasped in shock, coming in from the back.

"Down at O'Malley's, you mooch," I snapped back, looking at him like he was crazy. "Get your own sundae...or better yet...Next time bring your happy ass with us to the beach. Then you can get your own fucking ice cream. How 'bout that?" I smiled innocently his way as he narrowed his eyes at me.

"That's cold, dude," he muttered, eyeballing my spoon as I fed Evan another bite. "And you are distracting my employee with chocolate and whipped cream and…"

Evan snorted, shaking his head. "Here we go," he sang under his breath, wearing an amused smile.

"And you're seriously hogging my boyfriend, doofus, which means he can't go to O'Malley's, so I bring the ice cream to him." I pointed around the quiet café. "Don't like it? Send him on break."

Susan and Faith were in silent hysterics as they watched us like a tennis match.

"Meany."

"Slave driver," I countered, looking up at Evan. "Ignore him. Can you take a break before I head home?"

Evan's grin was adorable, but he shook his head. "I need to tackle the filing from this week."

"Ah-ha! Excellent. I'll keep you company," I said, turning to Faith. "We'll head home in a few minutes." As I walked by my cousin, I set the rest of my ice cream in his hand. "Here, you big baby. Maybe next time you'll man up and go with Faith yourself. Hmm?" I whispered to him, raising an eyebrow his way.

He shoveled a spoonful of ice cream into his face as we walked into the back, only to yell, "Don't do anything disgusting in my office!"

"Who says we haven't already?" I called back, grinning up at Evan. "It's best to keep him on his toes."

"Dani," he said with a laugh and a slow shake of his head as he shut the office door and clicked the lock closed. "Let's really make him nervous." He grinned, and it was deadly and teasing.

My giggle was loud, but I sat down on the edge of the desk as Evan picked up the stack of papers from Wes's inbox.

When the last page was tucked away and the drawer closed, Evan turned to walk into my arms, dropping a heavy kiss to my forehead. His lips met mine in a long, deep kiss, but he smiled into it, pulling back and licking his lips. "You taste sweet and chocolaty."

I smiled up at him, brushing my lips over his again. "What time will you be home?" Again, an expression crossed his face that I couldn't quite figure out. "What's wrong?"

He laughed, looking at me like I was crazy. "Not a damn thing, pretty girl. And I won't be too late. I promise. Susan's doing the closing tonight."

"Okay, good." I kissed him again, squeaking a little when he wrapped his arms around me and set me down to the floor.

Wes was on the other side of the door when we opened it, his hand poised, reaching for the knob. His eyes narrowed to me, then Evan, and finally around us to his desk.

"Good thing you got a sturdy chair, Wes," I told him, hearing Evan snort into a laugh when I patted my cousin's shoulder.

Evan walked me back up front, and we both chuckled when Wes muttered, "You know... I really don't like either one of you right now. Susan! Where's the disinfectant?"

My shower was long and hot, rinsing away the sea salt and sand from my few hours at the beach with Faith. I pulled on my usual shorts and T-shirt for bed, thinking I'd just work on some homework until Evan arrived, but when I stepped into my bedroom, I grinned at my handsome guy sitting on the edge of my bed.

"You're early," I said, shutting the door and locking it.

Evan was still in his work shirt and jeans, and he smiled up at me, pulling me between his legs as he nodded a little. "I was driving Susan bat-shit crazy. She kicked me out early."

"Aww," I crooned through a chuckle as I cupped his face. "Poor baby. Why?"

"I couldn't stop pacing," he replied softly, flexing his fingers on my waist, like he was trying to touch as much of me as he could at one time. "Dani... I... I want to... Dammit, I just need to ask you something, and I'm..."

He was so damned nervous that he reminded me of the shy boy I'd met in my cousin's office, and suddenly I was really scared.

"Did I... Is there..."

"Oh God, baby," he breathed, pressing his lips to mine as he cupped my face in his hands. "It's not bad, pretty girl. I just... I want to ask you something."

"O-Okay."

"I wrote this shit down, and still I'm nervous," he said through a humorless laugh, but he met my gaze and swallowed thickly. "Dani, I...I don't want to live in the dorms next year. I want...I want us to find a place...together."

I gaped at him, not because I didn't want it—I did, badly—but because he thought I'd say no. "Seriously?" I squeaked, unable to stop the smile from spreading across my face.

"Yes, seriously." He grinned, but it fell quickly. "Listen, Dani...I've talked to your dad, and I've weighed out dorms versus an apartment, but I miss you during the week, which sounds ridiculous since we see each other after school. I don't want just weekends. Pretty girl, I want those things you said when we were in Key Lake—our own couch and bed and library...a small one. I want to come home to you, not Brett or another roommate and not just here on the weekends. I want to hold you every night."

He shrugged and continued. "I've wanted it more and more since you said it, and I thought...I've talked to Dr. Costa about it because I don't want you or anyone else to think it's got anything to do with...I'm OCD and aquaphobic, baby, not codependent." He laughed a little when I giggled softly.

"Evan...stop. I know you love me and you want to be together because of that, not for any other reason." I trailed my fingers across his handsome face. "Yes...just yes. Like when? And how soon?"

He laughed, pulling me to his lap, and I locked my legs around his waist. "Well, I talked to Aunt Tessa too, Dani. She's actually got an idea. You know that empty store next to the café?" he asked, and I nodded. "She's thinking of expanding, but...But upstairs is a living space, and she's...Well, she thought it was kinda, sorta..."

"Perfect," I finished for him in a whisper, and he nodded, raking his fingers through my damp hair.

"For us. Yes." He nodded again, smiling up at me. "In fact, you and I were her first thought. She hasn't bought it yet, but she's working on it. It isn't big or fancy or..."

My lips met his roughly. He was too cute and too nervous, and I wanted it. Honestly, I wanted it all with him. Anything. Everything. There was never, ever going to be a single thing I'd deny him. He'd been denied enough in his life, and I wanted to be the one to spoil him, love him, keep him.

"I love you, and I love the whole plan. You just tell me when," I whispered against his lips, squealing into a giggle when he rolled us on my bed to loom over me.

His happy face morphed into something serious as he settled between my legs. Reaching up, I ran my fingers through his hair.

"I've missed you. This. I'm sorry I'm so busy and this semester has been crazy. It's why I want to live with you. I never want to be without this. I *need* this, Dani. I need you. *Always*," he vowed, pressing his lips to mine as I pulled him closer with everything I had.

"Always."

Our kiss became more — more heated, more frenzied, just more. Evan's hands roamed over me, beneath my shirt, along my legs. I pulled and tugged at his T-shirt, and he finally relented, pushing up on one hand as he reached back with the other to grab a fistful of fabric in order to tug it off. My pajamas were next and then his jeans, and when we were finally skin to skin, I moaned at the feel of him.

Since our first time, I wanted more of him. We couldn't get enough of each other, and we'd quickly learned how to drive each other completely crazy. He was beautiful, with heat in his eyes and his mouth on me — everywhere, just like I'd wanted when he'd taken the ice cream I'd fed him. And oh my God, he was so damned good at it. My head fell back as he kissed my sex like he kissed my mouth — warm, wet, deep, and with hums that made my eyes roll back.

Our bodies melted together as one as he slipped inside me. I wasn't sure I'd ever get over how amazing it felt, how perfect it felt to be one single entity. It was emotional and healing, it made me feel owned and loved, but it also made me feel powerful, because to watch Evan lose himself to me, to us, was absolutely stunning.

Pressing his forehead to mine, he reached between us to touch me in just the right spot to make me completely unravel. Between his fingers and his smooth, sexy voice begging me to let go, I shattered beneath him, pleading that he come with me, and he did, beautifully.

His eyes were closed as I trailed fingers down his back, rubbing my legs up and down his, finding his scars with my other hand.

"Evan?" I said softly, smiling when he met my gaze. "I don't want to read tonight. I just want…this."

He smiled, kissing me with the lightest of kisses. "Me too, pretty girl."

Chapter Twenty-Six

EVAN

"*B*aby boy," *Mom whispered as she pushed the grocery cart. "Isn't that the girl from your class?"*

I looked up from the comic book I'd been reading, pushing my glasses up my nose. I nodded slowly when I saw Katie at the other end of the store's aisle.

"Yeah. Katie." I frowned, going back to my reading when I felt my cheeks heat up.

I hated being shy. I wished I was more like Tyler, who got along with everyone—girls included. Though, at that very moment, I was glad he was at baseball practice, because he'd have razzed me something awful in the store, especially had he caught me blushing. I was just happy to have Mom to myself for an hour or so.

"You like her?"

Shrugging, I didn't bother to look up. Katie was pretty, with light-brown hair and bluish-green eyes. "She's okay. She…Sh-She likes Brandon 'cause he's funny and…and…can even make the teachers laugh."

My mother didn't say anything for a moment, but I felt her eyes on me. When I looked up, she only said, "Pick some cereal for you guys. Make sure to grab that fruity one your sister likes."

After setting my comic down in the basket, I spun to pick up three boxes. Tyler liked that chocolaty stuff, while Faith liked the fruit-flavored cereal. I liked the one with the marshmallows in it. Once I set them in the cart, I reached for my book, but Mom's hand covered mine.

"Evan, look at me," she said softly, glancing around to make sure we were the only ones in the cereal aisle. "One day, you're gonna meet a girl who won't mind that you're quiet and shy. It's okay that you are those things, son. It's what makes you…you. You're a smart, handsome, sweet boy, Evan. Don't change that. Don't try to be like your brother, who is outgoing and sometimes hot-headed. And you can't be like your sister, either, who doesn't particularly care about the opinions of others, just those she loves. You are my quiet, introspective one, and I love that about you. You're going to meet a girl who embraces those parts of you, who loves you for you. When you do, my sweet boy, then I want you to always be honest, no matter how hard the truth may be to say. It's easier to keep track of the truths than the lies.

"There's always going to be Brandons in the world, and there will be Katies too, those silly girls who are drawn in by the frivolous stuff. You, my baby boy, are not frivolous. You are deep thoughts and an old soul. You are the classic book, not the grocery-store drivel," she said, raising an eyebrow at me, which made me grin.

"You buy grocery-store books, Mom," I teased her, ducking when she reached out to ruffle my hair.

"I do, but it's the classics that I keep on my shelves, that I reread time and again. It's the classics that will still be around well after the grocery-store novel has long been forgotten." She grinned at my chuckle. "You'll find another classic, Evan, someone just like you. And when you do, hold on to her. Put her on a high shelf and love her and keep her safe and take care of her."

"I…I…can't talk to girls, Mom," I admitted softly.

She smiled, brushing my hair from my forehead and pressing a kiss to my wrinkled brow. "Trust me, son. The right girl will make you talk. But the right girl won't mind that you can't find the words, either."

Smiling softly at the memory, I glanced up to Dr. Costa. "She was right," I told her, shrugging a shoulder and laughing a bit.

"Your mom was a smart woman," she said, glancing up at the clock. "We're just about done for this week, Evan. Anything you want to discuss?"

I took a deep breath and let it out, raking a hand through my hair and adjusting my glasses. It had been a crazy semester, but thankfully it was over and summer was finally here.

"My..." I sighed deeply, picking at my jeans. "My dad is in jail. Some...some light-security place, but still...He got sentenced to three years." I huffed a humorless laugh, shaking my head slowly at how that sounded. "They said he won't serve it all, but when he's out, he...he can't be a doctor anymore," I added, meeting her warm, hazel eyes. I wrinkled my nose. "Is it wrong that I feel like it's not enough?"

Dr. Costa jotted something down in her notebook, but then she set it aside and leaned forward. Her dark hair was peppered with gray, and her demeanor was calm. "Are you upset that he's not being punished enough? Or are you still angry with him for things you think he evaded?"

Shrugging, I said, "I don't know. Honest. It's not about the money, and it's not about his hatred for my brother, sister, and me. We aren't going to miss him. I just...I feel my mother didn't get... justice. He...he *used* her and, in turn, us. But..." I shrugged again, not sure what I meant or how to say it.

"Evan, you have to accept that your mother wouldn't want you to dwell on justice or revenge against your father. She didn't. She could've caused a scene, dragged you and your siblings through a harsh court battle, and essentially exposed your father sooner. However, she tried to simply walk away. The choices she made were hers, and no one will know what she was thinking, but as a parent myself, I can almost understand. She just wanted you to have a good life, a happy one." She sat back in her chair, eyeing me for a moment. "And if you want to give your mother justice, then the absolute *best* thing you can do is to move on. Success, prosperity, happiness — those things are what would not only give your mother justice, but it would serve as revenge against the man who tried to keep you from achieving those very things.

"You aren't the damaged one, Evan. He is. And his guilt and past ate away anything compassionate he ever had. To live your life to its fullest would be the ultimate in payback. Be happy, follow your dreams, marry that girl you love *so much*..."

I grinned, my cheeks heating up. "I plan on it." I laughed a little when Dr. Costa smiled back at me. "Dani's...it for me. Just everything. She's that classic my mother told me about. I really do want to put her on a shelf, love her, take care of her. I'm hers until she says different."

"Having spoken with her a time or two, I'm pretty sure you're right, and I think she's in it for the long haul. Just make sure you don't put her on a pedestal," she said gently.

Nodding, I swallowed nervously. "We're moving in together."

"This weekend, right?"

"Yeah."

"Nervous?" she asked, smiling, and her dimples made her look younger than she actually was.

I thought about it for a moment but shook my head. "Um, no. I'm...I've fought anxiety and nerves and insecurity my whole life. Moving in with Dani makes me feel...*none of that*. In fact, I...I can't wait."

"It's hard meshing two lives together."

"I don't doubt that. But we're very similar. We're neat and tidy, we're quiet, and we'll be starting our sophomore year come fall, but as much as I appreciate her family and all they've done, I...I...I want to start doing things on my own — for Dani, for myself. I feel the need to prove Dad wrong."

"Prove him wrong...Which part, Evan?"

"Everything."

She let me be quiet for a moment, and I frowned at the table in front of me. "He was wrong. Everything he ever said to me was wrong — the wreck being my fault, that love makes you weak, that I...I was a loser.

"The wreck was an accident. And...and...love makes me strong; it made me stand up to him when I never did before. And...and...I'm not a loser." I shook my head, scowling at the memory of his rants. "I've busted my ass to maintain my scholarship. I'm working part-time at the café so I can pay for books and not spend everything my mother tried to save, but that may change when Aunt Tessa expands the new section into a bookstore." I grinned at the thought. "I have the most amazing people surrounding me, helping me, pushing me." I met her gaze again, shrugging one more time. "I used to want to be invisible. I wanted to disappear into the background. Now...I just want more."

"More?"

"Yeah, I want to finish school and write, maybe teach like my mother did, or...or run the bookstore Aunt Tessa is opening. I want to marry Dani and have a family. And I swear, I'll never look back."

Dr. Costa glanced at the clock and smiled, nodding once before standing. "Now *that* would be justice, Evan."

"I can't believe you're puttin' me to work on my vacation, baby bro!" Tyler teased as he dropped two boxes into the middle of the living room.

Grinning over at him, I set my own box onto the kitchen counter. "Sorry, Ty. You can hit the beach tomorrow with Jasmine, all while knowing I'll be unpacking all this shit."

He laughed but leaned against the counter, studying me. He and Jasmine had been in Florida since just before my twentieth birthday, which had been celebrated at the Bishop house with not only every member of their family but my brother, Jasmine, and Faith too. It had been the first time in *years* that I'd had a birthday party.

"Still can't go, huh?" he asked, and I shook my head without looking up from the box I'd opened. "You think...maybe one day?"

"I dunno, Ty." I sighed, resting my arms atop the box.

"It's not the scars anymore, is it? It's just the water."

Nodding, I raked a hand through my hair. "Th-The scars don't bother me. I mean the only person who sees them is Dani, and she's never...She doesn't mind them. I don't...I'm a fucking coward about the water, and that may never change. I don't think I'm missing anything, but still..."

"You know what I remember?" Tyler asked softly, a faraway look in his eyes. "I barely remember the dog or my knee hitting the dashboard...and...and I don't remember Mom in the car at all. But I remember *you*, baby brother. I remember coming to as you pulled me through the window. You ripped yourself wide open to get my ass up to the surface. You fought me like a tiger to try to help Mom, but you'd have died too. Evan...that's not a fucking coward. Without you, Ev, I wouldn't be here helping you move in with your girl."

He pushed himself up straight, shrugging his large shoulders. "*Daddy Dearest* told you too many times that it was your fault. You associate water with Mom, but…I can't look at it that way. I see water, and I see my kid brother saving my life. Dude, I was twice your size." He grinned a bit but shrugged his shoulders again. "You're right. You're probably not missing much, but I hate that you think you're a coward, 'cause you're far fucking from it." He raised a deadly serious eyebrow at me. "A coward wouldn't have punched the ever-lovin' piss outta Dad. And a coward wouldn't have looked him straight in the eye and told him what a piece of shit he was to Mom. But honestly, Evan…watching you our whole lives not give in to his bullshit, no matter what that bastard said…even in fucking court! You are the strongest man I know. You think Faith is strong?" He huffed a laugh, shaking his head slowly. "She is, but she ain't got nothin' on you, baby bro. Neither of us do. Got me?"

He smiled sadly, gesturing to the door. "Let's get this done so you and Dani can get your neat-freak on. Emphasis on the *freak*."

Snorting into a laugh, I shook my head at his salacious grin and eyebrows rising up and down. "Don't forget, we've got to get Faith moved into the dorms in a few weeks," I reminded him, still chuckling a bit.

"Yeah, I know." He reached for the doorknob, pausing enough to look back at me. "Jas and I…We're looking at transferring down here. She's looking at a law school just up the panhandle. Just…You've found something good here. Even Faith is doing well. We're gonna hold off on the wedding until she finds out, but I wanted to give you a heads-up. I mean, you are the best man and all." He smirked at my open-mouth stare, not because I was his best man — I'd already told him yes to that — but because I'd have both my siblings in the same state. "Jasmine likes it here, and my family is here. Plus, I honestly don't want to be in the state of Montana when they let *Daddy Dearest* outta jail."

"No shit," I sighed, following him down the stairs and out to the moving truck we'd rented.

The girls were sitting on the end, feet dangling, and I smiled at my beautiful girl, who offered me a bottle of water and open arms. I took the water, gulping almost half the bottle before setting it down beside her. I pressed my lips to hers, smiling into the kiss when arms and legs held me captive.

"You okay?" she whispered, pushing my hair from my forehead as I nodded. I honestly couldn't get any better. "Having second thoughts?"

Grinning, I dug my fingers into her sides just to hear her squeal into giggly protests. "Not a chance in hell, pretty girl." I dropped kisses to her cheek. "Though, the thought of unpacking scares me."

Her smile was brighter than the beaming Florida sun, but she leaned in and kissed me briefly. "We got this part, baby. We can be as OCD as we want because it's just us. No one can make fun of us because it'll be ours. We can do whatever we want, however we want. Always."

I fought my smile at her happiness, because it was completely and totally contagious. I hadn't been lying to Dr. Costa the day before in our session. Dani was *it* for me. Occasionally my dad's voice would enter my head, telling me I'd be used by the first girl I fell in love with, but then I'd look at Dani. I'd see the love she had for me, the warmth, the devotion that was all for me, and I'd push his voice away. He knew nothing, and Dani was everything.

I toyed with her long ponytail, tugging it gently. "Then I guess we'd better get our stuff in there, huh?"

"Yes!" she cheered, kissing me quickly and holding my face in her hands. "And we should have backup help soon. Dad, Wes, and Faith are coming to lend a hand. Mom and Aunt Tessa are bringing food."

Daniel was teaching a summer course, so it made sense he hadn't shown up yet, and my sister and Wes had been inseparable since Faith had graduated from Glenhaven High. I chuckled at the thought, at their age difference, but Wes treated my sister like a damned princess. As if Tyler and I hadn't spoiled her enough, Wes was a thousand times worse. But they were good for each other, even I had to admit that, though I was pretty damn sure I wouldn't be here without Dani and her small, loving, silly family, so I knew my sister was safe with him.

Dani grabbed my face again, squishing it to kiss me. "The more help, Evan, the quicker we're moved in. The quicker we're moved in, the faster we can finally have…we can have…"

I chuckled at her loss for words, but her honest rambling was still my absolute favorite thing. I kissed her lips to hush her.

"Everything, pretty girl. The quicker we're in, the quicker we have…*everything*."

I closed my laptop, glancing out the window. The rain had stopped, and I'd gotten a shit-ton written on the story I couldn't seem to get out of my head, so after discussing it with Daniel, who told me to just get it down, I found myself lost to my characters. Today had been the perfect day to work on it too. The rain had started early, Dani was working downstairs in Aunt Tessa's bookstore all day, I was off from Sunset Roast, and I was caught up on homework.

Tonight, though, was a different story. It was Dani's birthday. I snorted as I shook my head. A year ago, I was nervous as hell as Dani drove me to her house for the first time. I'd missed out on her real birthday last year, but I wouldn't this year. We would all meet at the Bishop house for dinner tonight. And this year, I had a present for her. The necklace I'd bought for her was hidden in the back of my nightstand drawer. I'd considered a promise ring, and I'd vowed to myself to buy Dani the real deal closer to our senior year, but damn it all if I didn't want something on her from me, something permanent and beautiful, which was exactly how I saw her in my life.

Gazing around our apartment, I sighed in contentment. My office was just like Dani had wanted — shelf upon shelf of books and a desk for me to use to write. My mother's books lined the shelves, with my own and Dani's added in. The bookcases were full to overflowing but neat and orderly, simply because Dani and I were that way.

I walked into our bedroom, another example of neatness, except for the bed. The bed tended to stay just a bit rumpled, which proved we'd lost ourselves to kisses and secret smiles, touches and pleas for more just this morning before Dani went to work. Personally, the bed was the only thing I liked messy. I pulled on a T-shirt, tied my sneakers, and then reached into my nightstand drawer for the little velvet box before I stepped into the living room.

Our place was small, but it was ours, and we loved it. We liked to cook in our small kitchen, stealing kisses and taste tests. We would read to each other on our sofa in our usual position, with Dani's back to my chest. And we'd loved each other on just about every surface in the place. There was nothing inside that apartment but good memories. Even small disagreements ended up with us laughing and kissing. Meshing our lives together had been a huge step, but after the last month and a half, I couldn't have been happier.

It wasn't perfect. We'd had to find a new schedule, and starting our sophomore year made us as busy as ever. I still worked at the café, but Dani worked with Aunt Tessa in the bookstore that was now a part of the coffee shop. Homework and classes, along with our part-time jobs, meant we only saw each other at the end of the day. The *very best* part was curling up with her every damn night.

I grabbed my phone and keys to head downstairs, locking the door behind me and making sure Dani's present was still in my pocket.

"Hey, sweet pea!" Aunt Tessa greeted when I stepped in from the back. "You just missed Dani. She ran out to the beach to get your sister and my son. We're about to head out to the house."

"Okay," I said softly, pushing open the bookstore door and glancing up. Chuckling, I said, "The sign looks good!"

"Well, kiddo, I owe *you* for the name."

I waved her praise away but glanced up again. "*As the Plot Thickens* was really Dani's idea."

"Well, both of you, then. Sweetie, she'll be back in a minute."

I smiled and nodded but stepped out onto the boardwalk that was still damp from the rain. The sun was setting on the beach. It was quiet—most of the patrons had found somewhere else to be—but there were a few caws from hungry seagulls and laughter coming from the beach. The soft crash of waves hitting the shore was calming, but I couldn't see the water.

Glancing up the boardwalk and then back toward the wooden path that ended in blinding white beach sand, I shifted nervously on my feet. Memories of the day I'd worked with Dani in Wes's office came crashing down around me.

Dani pulling me with her out to the boardwalk.

The smells of saltwater, suntan lotion, and people hitting me.

The sight of the water literally stopping me in my tracks.

Dani asking what she'd done wrong.

I took slow, nervous steps down the wooden path, thankful there weren't very many people around. I stopped at the end of the walkway, sitting down on a low post. Toeing the sand for a moment with my sneaker, I finally took a deep breath and gazed out over the beach.

Pinks, blues, oranges, and purples were splashed across the sky just above the endless ocean. Clouds were light and puffy, stretched over the sun. However, not one bit of it—not the water or the stunning sunset or even the splashing waves—compared to the beautiful girl who was teasing her cousin and my sister close to the shoreline. She was walking barefoot, her smooth legs deceptively long in her shorts, but it was the gorgeous yet slightly shocked smile that broke out on her face when she caught sight of me that steeled my resolve for what I knew I needed to do.

She rushed to me, leaving everyone out on the beach behind her. "Evan, baby!" she said, cupping my face. "Is everything...Are you okay? I was coming right back..." She paused, tugging my shirt. "C'mon. We'll get you off this beach."

Chuckling, I wrapped an arm around her, pulling her between my legs as I stayed seated on that low post. "Pretty girl, wait..." I took a deep breath, brushing my lips over hers softly, simply for courage. "R-Remember..." I frowned, toying with her fingers. "The...The day we after we met. You know, the day we worked in Wes's office?"

"Best day *ever*," she crooned, wearing a silly-sweet smile as she leaned into me, brushing my hair from my forehead. "My Library Guy was *way too cute* for his own good."

I laughed, unable to not wrap my arms all the way around her. "Yeah? Well, my Library Girl wanted to go somewhere that day, but I...I couldn't do it. I wasn't quite ready yet. Where'd you want to go, Dani? When you grabbed my hand, where were you taking me?"

She seemed to freeze for a moment, her big brown eyes wide but warm. "Oh God, Evan, I don't know. Maybe ice cream at O'Malley's or...or a walk on the beach, but I didn't know, and I was pushy..."

Cupping her face, I brushed a lock of her hair out of her face. "No, baby, not pushy. You just didn't know." I pressed a long, soft kiss to her forehead, gazing over the top of her head at the shoreline. "Pretty girl...I...I want...to try."

She gasped, her hands covering her lips, but then she leaned in to kiss me again. "Evan, there's no rush."

My forehead fell to hers. "I'm...I don't want water to mean bad shit anymore, Dani. There's absolutely *nothing* bad in my life now."

Dani's smile was warm and sweet as she pushed back from me a bit. "Sweetheart...are you sure? You have to be sure, because if it's too soon or you panic...I don't...It hurts me when you're hurting, baby." Her eyes watered a bit with that statement, and right then, I knew I was ready, because to hurt Dani would kill me, but I needed to let go of the past, the fear.

Nodding, I reached into my pocket, fiddling with the little black box. "Yeah, I'm…I'm sure, but before we do this, I want to give you your birthday present."

I held out the little black box, cracking it open for her. A small silver book and an even smaller key were attached to a thin silver chain.

"The book…It represents the library, and…well, us. Our love of books. The key," I said, huffing a light, nervous laugh. "Well, the key is you, pretty girl, because you…you're the key to…everything." Reaching over, I flipped open the tiny silver book, where inside was written: *Always.* "You…you asked for always, Dani, and I swear it's yours."

Dani's finger reached out to toy with the necklace, but when she looked back up at me, tears fell from those expressive eyes.

"Happy birthday, Dani," I whispered, reaching out to wipe away a tear from beneath her eye.

"I love you," she said back, suddenly wrapping herself around my torso, which made me chuckle. Pulling back, she cupped my face. "Thank you. And God, you make me want to kiss you stupid, Evan!"

"I love you too, baby." Laughing, I shook my head, taking the necklace out and putting it around her neck. "I look forward to it."

She fiddled with the book and key and then met my gaze with a shrewd expression. "Tell you what…You make it to the water, and I'll kiss you stupid in front of the whole beach and boardwalk."

I saw what she was doing; she was giving me an opportunity to make a new memory, a different one. A truly better one.

Glancing from her to the water and back again, I nodded, swallowing nervously. "Okay."

"Take your shoes off, baby," she said, pointing to my sneakers. "Leave 'em." She waited until I toed them and my socks off, and then she held out both her hands for mine. "C'mon, handsome."

I linked my fingers with hers, feeling the wet sand beneath my feet and between my toes. I honestly couldn't remember the last time I'd felt that sensation. The closer we got, the harder I squeezed her hand, but just hearing her steady encouragement kept me putting one foot in front of the other.

She stopped us just out of the range of the waves rolling in, and she stepped into my vision. "You're okay, and I'm right here. We can go back if you want to stop. But I will tell you the water's warm today."

Nodding fervently that I'd heard her, I held on to her hand as she stepped back while a wave slowly crept up with thin water and foamy bubbles and seaweed. I looked back at her face, meeting the gaze that had changed me, made me a better man, and I took that last step, splashing down into the water. Before I could panic, her lips met mine. Her kiss was pride and heat. It was squeals of happiness, and I couldn't help but kiss her back, smiling into it all.

As another low wave rolled over our feet, I wrapped my arms around Dani and lifted her up. Cupping my face and securing her legs around my waist, she laughed and kissed me again, and I heard cheers from behind us. I'm sure I heard Wes whistle and Faith cheer, but I only had eyes for the beautiful girl in my arms.

The first time I saw her, I was broken and invisible. I'd been nervous and alone. I'd thought I was escaping my past, my life that had been filled with hate, guilt, and grief, but really, I'd landed right where I needed to be.

I still wasn't sure what I believed about life after death, but if my mother was somewhere watching, then I was pretty sure she'd had a hand in some of this. Only my mother would have set the strongest, most perfect, most beautiful girl down in the middle of a college library just a few tables away from mine so I couldn't possibly miss her.

Glancing down at my feet in the water and then back out across the ocean, glowing in the low sunset, I felt lips on my cheek and whispers of love. Instead of panic and fear, I only saw my future.

Epilogue

EVAN

"Thanks for letting me know, Sean," I said softly into the phone, ending the call and dropping it onto the bed next to me.

I fell back, gazing up at the ceiling, my feet still hanging off the side of the mattress. I tried to figure out what I was feeling, but I wasn't sure I was feeling *anything*. If I were completely honest with myself, I had been expecting that call long before now, well before I'd entered into the first semester of my senior year at Edgewater.

I heard the door to the apartment open and close and then Dani's sweet voice calling out to me. "Evan, baby! Where are you?" she asked, entering the bedroom, and I couldn't help but grin when she was suddenly crawling up my body to loom over me. "Hi, handsome!"

Cupping her face, I pulled her in for a kiss. "Hey, pretty girl."

"What are you…" She paused, reaching up to brush my hair from my forehead. "What's wrong? Your eyes look…*tense*."

Snorting a little, I brought her in for another kiss. "Dad's out."

To say my girl hated William Shaw would be a complete and total understatement. She narrowed her eyes and sat up, still straddling me. "Out where?" she asked slowly and through gritted teeth.

"He was released, Dani," I sighed, sitting up and situating her on my lap. "He's at a halfway house in Bozeman, where he'll remain for another six months or so. He's…out."

Shrugging a shoulder, I tried not to dwell on it, but with Dani, it didn't work. We'd been living together above the bookstore since the summer before our sophomore year. We were now seniors, with Halloween fast approaching, and we'd blended our lives together better than I'd ever imagined it. Not only did we live together, but I'd moved over from the café to work in the bookstore in order to take some of the pressure off Aunt Tessa. Sunset Roast and As the Plot Thickens were one big consolidated storefront. We were busy, but for me, working in the bookstore was easier on my writing and my homework.

While Dani had finally chosen a major — business management, which was her idea to help not only Aunt Tessa but me as well — I'd still continued to turn to Daniel in order to be a writer. His guidance, along with his connections in the publishing world, had at least gotten my first book in the door. We were just waiting to hear back.

But the girl on my lap knew me better than I probably knew myself, and her gentle touch was soothing as she raked her fingers through my hair. "If he called you…I swear to God—"

I cut her off with another kiss. "No, no, baby, that was Sean on the phone."

"Oh," she murmured, her brow wrinkling as she waited patiently for me to find the words.

Toying with her fingers, I tilted my head at her. "It seems like I should be feeling something, but I'm not. Not a damn thing. I just…I don't even care. And…and…Apparently he was hurt or something while in there, but he's out." I sniffed a bit, wrinkling my nose. "Sean says Dad will be staying in Bozeman, even after the halfway house situation."

"Okay. Does Ty know yet?"

"Yeah, yeah. Sean said he'd call Tyler next. Though, I promised him I'd break it to Faith."

My brother and Jasmine had finally transferred last year to Florida State University just a few hours from us. They'd been married in a small ceremony right after they'd gotten settled in. I'd been his best man, and Faith and Dani had shared the duties of maid of honor. Tyler was working for a small architecture firm, while Jasmine was in her first year of law school.

As I remembered the intimate ceremony, I gazed at Dani, wanting it more and more. I was ready to ask her, though I needed to find the perfect time. The ring was already in my possession, hidden well in the back of my nightstand drawer. Reaching up, I fiddled with the necklace I'd given her for her twentieth birthday. We'd just moved in together, and we'd been busy with our sophomore year, but I remembered that day so damned clearly. It was the very first time I'd set foot in water since my mother had died. But it hadn't been the last. Dani and I went to the beach all the time—whenever we had a spare moment.

"I love you," I whispered, leaning in to kiss her lips. "And I'm okay. He can't contact me, and he's not allowed to leave the state. Even if he did, I can't imagine that he'd want anything to do with any of us, pretty girl, so stop worrying."

"You'd think so, but you never know with him, Evan," she stated, shaking her head. "Don't forget he tried to write letters and call."

"I know, baby, but he's got to learn to make a living now. No more medical license, so sleazy prescriptions are out." I grinned at her evil smile. "I do believe he's got enough shit to deal with besides angry, overprotective bookworms."

She scoffed, rolling her eyes. "He'd walk away with a limp. That's all I'm sayin'."

"Of that, I have no doubt."

She was right; Dad had tried to contact all three of us at some point or other during his imprisonment. All letters had been returned, and every last one of us had changed our phone number, though mine had been changed before we'd even packed up our stuff in Key Lake, thanks to Wes.

The thought of Wes made me think of Faith. "Damn, I really do need to tell my sister. Is she downstairs with Wes yet?"

Dani nodded. "Yeah, she just got there, actually. She's taking a break before the art show tonight with Mom."

"Gotcha." I kissed my girl's lips one more time and then gripped her waist and set her on her feet.

When Faith had told me originally that she'd applied to Edgewater, I knew in some ways it was to be closer to me and away from our father. I also knew that she'd really love it in Florida, and she did. What I never expected—none of us, actually—was that Faith and

Leanne would develop a fierce bond. My sister had always loved art but had never been allowed to do anything with it thanks to Dad, but now she'd not only surrounded herself with art classes, she'd learned to love the history of it, the showing of it, and the process of it all. Leanne fed it, built it up, and gave my sister the encouragement she needed. It had been amazing to watch. Faith had needed a mother more than I could possibly explain, and she'd found one. And Leanne had found another hyper daughter and an art student in my sister, who soaked up everything like a sponge.

I stood up from the bed, pocketed my cell phone, and turned to see Dani studying me. "What, baby?"

"He's…Your dad, Evan…He's not important. You know that, right? Anything that's happened since the moment he decided to lay a hand on you is his own doing, and whatever happens to him… he's earned it."

Smiling at her fierceness, I nodded. "I'm well aware, baby."

Her brow furrowed as she fidgeted in front of me. "I know — deep down — that one day he…he'll say or do the wrong thing at the wrong time to the wrong person and —"

I stopped her again with a kiss, but I was chuckling into it because I really did love that rambling honesty that never stopped. It was so Dani, and it flowed out of her adorably.

"Easy, baby," I soothed her, dropping my forehead to hers. "He no longer has power here." I gestured between us. "I'm not sure he ever did, Dani."

"Well, I'm just sayin'…I just can't wait until you're published and you're this awesome writer and you can prove to him that he didn't win."

Grinning, I kissed her again. "My pretty girl," I sang to her, shaking my head. "You seem to think there's some impending *Edmund Dantes* revenge moment still to come, but beautiful, I've already won. I've already had my say, and I've found everything I need…*right here.*"

Holding her face in my hands, I kissed her, smiling when she giggled at me.

"The Count was badass," she whispered.

Laughing, I linked my fingers with hers and led us out of our apartment and down the stairs. I kissed her once more before she went into the bookstore and I made my way into the back of the café and out to the front counter.

"Ah, hell, kiddo. What happened?" Susan whispered, leaning against the counter.

Grimacing, I pointed to Faith, who was sitting in a booth with Wes. "I need my sister."

"Shit, he's out," she breathed.

If anyone understood terrible fathers, it was Susan, whose own had just recently drunk himself to death. She'd barely batted an eye because their relationship had been so tense and she'd been expecting it for years. I nodded once and then went to the booth, sliding in next to Faith.

"Hiya, big brother," she greeted, but her smile fell immediately. "What? What happened?"

Wes started to get up, but I stopped him. "You...might wanna stay, Wes."

"Ev, you all right?" he asked.

Grimacing a little, I nodded. "Yeah, it's just that I got a call a few minutes ago." I turned to face my sister. "Sean called me. He wanted to let me know that Dad's been released."

The happy glow in my sister's eyes darkened. Her hatred for our father rivaled that of Dani's. The very moment Dad had been arrested by Chief Clark on that Christmas Day after our fight, my sister had washed her hands of him. She had no desire to hear his side, see him, talk to him, or even sue him. We'd had no choice but to appear in court the one time. I wasn't even sure she'd looked his way while on the stand.

"So...the fucker's free?" she sneered, her hands balling up into fists.

"Not free but out of prison. He's been released to a halfway house for the remainder of his sentence. He's in Bozeman."

"He'd better stay in Montana," she muttered, frowning down at her cup of coffee. "He...he can't call or anything. Do we need to do anything? Like another restraining order?"

"No, Faith, I think we're okay. He's not supposed to leave the state, and we've never allowed any contact since the trial, so I'm pretty sure he's gotten the message. If he hasn't, then Sean is happy to explain it to him."

Faith snorted, looking up at me. "I bet he will. He's been awesome."

"He has," I sighed, nodding in agreement.

Pastor Sean, our mother's old friend, had maintained contact with all three of us after Dad was arrested. He constantly checked on us all, had flown down for Tyler's wedding, and he'd teased me about mine being next. He'd also helped with the sale of the house in Key Lake, kept us posted on news about our father, and refused to let us thank him. He'd become a very good friend, almost family, stating it was what our mother would've wanted, and he'd admitted more than once to me that it was his way of making up for what we'd been through.

"You coming tonight?" she asked me, the glow in her eyes back to their happy sparkle.

"Hell, yeah! Like I'd miss seeing your work, Faith," I teased, leaning in to kiss the side of her head. "Tyler and Jasmine too. They were leaving after Tyler got off work. Dani and I will be at the art building as soon as she's finished next door."

I slipped out of the booth, but Wes's voice stopped me.

"Hey, Evan? You think…You think he'll try to contact you guys again?" he asked, and his gaze flickered to my sister. I could tell he was worried, already set on protecting her — us — in some way.

I thought about it, remembering the letters to all of us and the phone calls our father had tried to make to Faith and Tyler, but they'd stopped eventually.

Finally meeting his gaze, I said, "No, I don't."

The eerie cry of the sandhill cranes made me smile and glance over at the tall gray birds. That otherworldly call echoed out again, along with the mimicking baby crane that was with them. I had no way of knowing if they were the same two I'd seen the first time I'd set foot on the Bishop property, but the daydreamer in me liked to think so. Dani had said they mated for life, so my hope was that they were the same two, raising a new little one.

Gazing out over the small lake in the backyard, I tapped my pen on my open journal. Sometimes the sight of water made me melancholy, but the panicky feelings hardly rose to the surface anymore. I still saw the accident and I still worried endlessly whenever anyone was driving in poor weather, but I was working on it.

Right at that moment, though, I couldn't feel anything but hope and nerves. I hoped I was doing this the right way, but I was nervous about being able to pull it off. Rereading what I'd already written, I added to it. I found myself writing until the sun started to set. I still used the journal to write to Dani, and I used it to sort out tough conversations. This was both…and most likely the last tough conversation I'd ever have to work though.

When arms wrapped around me from behind, I closed the book and grinned over my shoulder at Dani.

"Dinner's ready, handsome."

I brushed my lips over hers, chuckling when she landed across my lap, and I couldn't help but cradle her in my arms. She gazed up at me with eyes that were happy, sweet, and curious.

"Now what's got you writing in this thing?" she asked teasingly, reaching for my journal—the same journal I'd left with her when I'd first gone home to Montana.

Laughing, I pulled it away from her. "Just some stuff I needed to work through. It's been a busy year, baby. I was just…Hell, pretty girl, we're almost college graduates."

She beamed up at me, cupping my face and bringing me in for a kiss. "And *you* are almost a published author!"

As awesome as that sounded, the words I'd just written down in my journal were more important than the book that had finally been accepted by a publishing house, even if they wanted more. The story I'd written so long ago with my mother's help—the same story I'd made up for my sister and the first story Dani had ever read of mine—was now going to be in print. Elven princesses and kings and archer boys would soon be out for everyone to see. Everyone wanted to celebrate, which was why we were having dinner at her parents' house.

Grinning, I kissed her again. "C'mon, pretty girl. Let's eat, and then I can celebrate with just you." I buried my face in her neck to kiss her just for the squeal into the giggles I lived to hear.

She stood up from my lap, and I tucked my journal and pen away into my backpack. When we stepped up into the back deck, I realized this was where we would've eaten the first time I'd ever come to this house, but they'd moved dinner indoors due to my fear of water. As I gazed around the table, I saw what real family was, what it should've been all along. It was my own flesh and blood—Tyler and Faith—along with the family who'd loved me from the moment the girl at my side said she was keeping me. Jasmine had become another sister, not to mention my sister-in-law. Daniel, who'd become the father I always needed. Leanne, who was the mother to us all. Aunt Tessa was strength and humor and a calm in the storm.

Wes had become not only my best friend but another brother — and most likely my brother-in-law because he'd already pulled Tyler and me aside to ask us for permission to marry Faith. We'd outright laughed at him because he didn't need our permission; Faith was quite capable of making that decision all on her own, and I was pretty sure she knew it was coming.

Then there was Dani. I gazed over at her, linking my fingers with hers beneath the table and giving them a soft squeeze. Without her, I had no idea where my life would be — not at that table, that was for certain.

Dinner was fun and loud, with teasing and the usual name calling between Dani and Wes, which now included Tyler. Despite the fact that it was in celebration of my book, I stayed quiet, absorbing every second of it, but I needed to watch my time because there was someplace I wanted to be before it closed.

The drive back was comfortably quiet. Dani's hand was in mine as I drove the roads back into town, and when I turned toward the library and not our apartment, Dani looked over at me.

"I need to grab a book before class on Monday. You mind?"

"No, not at all. I should probably return the one we finished."

We walked into the library and set our things down at our usual table. I knew we only had about thirty minutes before they closed, but it should work, and I was happy to see there was hardly a soul inside, except for the kid behind the counter and two girls who were packing up.

"You want that other book we talked about?" Dani asked after dropping off the one we'd just finished reading together.

Smirking, I shrugged a shoulder. "It's your turn to pick, baby."

God, I loved that we'd never stopped reading to each other. Sometimes we'd read for class or for ourselves, but we always came back to reading to each other. I needed it and Dani seemed to live for it, so we kept going.

"Okay," she sang, spinning around to make her way to the fiction section.

I waited until she was in the back before I pulled out my journal, setting it on top of her things. I left it just like I'd left it on her pillow the day I'd left for Montana—a bright purple flower sticking out as a bookmark. However, there was more inside than just a note to her. Before she could come back to the table, I stepped away. I did need a book for class, so I grabbed it quickly and checked it out, hiding behind the first bookcase to wait. She checked out a book and came to a stop at the table.

Dani gazed around, probably looking for me, but she slowly reached out to pick up the journal as she sat down in the chair. I'd reread the note so many times, I had it memorized.

To the girl who used to be a few tables away,

I remember the first time I saw you, there were tears in your eyes. I remember thinking that the book you were reading had to be something else in order to bring you to that much emotion. I needed to know exactly what made you cry, so I read the same book. And yeah, it was heartbreaking, which told me that your heart was as beautiful as the rest of you. I remember the first time I heard your voice. It was soft and sweet but filled with protectiveness and bravery, but there was humor and laughter in it, as well, which only proved to me that you were smart and funny and honest.

Dani, pretty girl, I remember everything about you from moment I first saw you. There's not a thing I ever want to forget. The first time I trusted you to let you in, the first time you told me you weren't going anywhere, and the first time our lips met. And my God, the first time you told me you loved me! All of it is stored away so I can remember it.

What started out as a shy, quiet, invisible boy crushing on a pretty girl just a few feet away turned into the best thing to ever happen to me. You made me strong when I thought I was weak. You made me feel things I thought were only in books. You forced me to see myself through your beautiful eyes. You gave me family and courage and a shoulder to cry on when life became too much. But mostly, my beautiful Dani, you gave me you. You offered up yourself with love and happiness and the sweetest smile I'd ever had the honor of seeing.

I'm a better man because of you. I told you once in this very journal that I know where I'm going in life, Dani. I know at the end of the day, it's only you I need. Nothing about that has changed. No college graduation or book contracts or whatever life may bring our way will ever change the way I feel about you.

My mother once told me I'd meet a girl who didn't mind that I was shy, who wouldn't mind if I couldn't quite find the words. She told me the girl would love those things about me, that she'd wait until I found the words. She told me that once I found her, I needed to be honest at all times; I needed to cherish her, love her, take care of her.

Well, I've found that girl, Dani. And all I want for the rest of my life is to love you. I want to spend the rest of my life with you.

Will you marry me?

Love, the boy who wants to always share your table...

Evan

I moved, sitting down in the chair next to hers, when my sweet girl sniffled. She picked up the red satin ribbon, which was the bookmark of the journal, but I'd used it to tie the ring to it. She pulled it off, finally meeting my gaze.

"I meant every word, Dani," I whispered, reaching up to gently wipe away the tears that were falling from her beautiful warm eyes. "I wanted to ask you here, in this place, because I never want to forget how we started."

She was up and out of her chair and in my lap before I could blink, which made me chuckle at her, but her lips met mine roughly.

"Yes! The answer's yes, Evan!" Her voice was a whisper, but there was an emotional edge to it too. "Oh, I'm glad there's no one in here, baby, because I'm really going to kiss you stupid."

And she did. She kissed me with love and heat, and I could taste the salty tears she was still leaking. I couldn't help but smile into it, and when I pulled back, I dropped my forehead to hers.

"Here," she said, holding out her hand, which was in a fist. When she opened it up, her ring was in her palm. "You do it."

The ring was simple and beautiful, just like Dani. And it fit, which I'd known it would, but that was a perk when I had a sneaky little sister who found out the size for me. Once it was on Dani's finger, I brought it up to my lips, kissing it reverently.

"Evan?" she asked softly.

"Hmm?"

"Can we go home?"

Smiling, I nodded. "Yeah, pretty girl. Home."

Three years later...
Dani

Dull, winter morning light filtered in from the windows, and I cracked an eye open. Seeing unpacked boxes and everything I owned in complete disarray, not to mention a way-too-early time on the clock, I burrowed back down into my pillow. I didn't want to get up.

Getting up meant that I'd be putting my husband on a plane soon, and I couldn't follow him for another four days.

Getting up out of bed also meant I had to at least *attempt* to unpack into our new home. A deep breath brought with it the smell of ocean air, fresh paint, and something altogether irresistible — coffee. God bless the damn timer.

However, none of that mattered when warm, strong arms pulled me back against bare skin and muscles. My whole body reacted to it. I simply couldn't help it. After being married for going on three years, I was still hopelessly head over heels for the man currently pressed against every inch of me beneath the covers of our bed.

"Evan," I breathed, my voice raspy from just waking up.

"Shh, pretty girl. Listen," he whispered in my ear, but I could hear and feel the smile against the skin of my neck and then my bare shoulder as he started to move his hands. "All you can hear is the waves."

I chuckled, rolling in his arms to see the face I adored. He pulled me closer, and I could suddenly feel just what was causing all the attention from where it was now trapped between us. I hummed in approval. Reaching up, I ran my fingers through his hair. Sweet, loving eyes gazed back at me, and not for the first time since I met him did I wonder how I got so damned lucky.

Evan was still the sweet, quiet-natured man I'd met in the library of Edgewater College. He was still the thoughtful, smart, unassuming thing he'd always been. It didn't matter that we'd been together since our freshman year, that we'd lived and worked together, or that we'd just moved to the exclusive Glenhaven Bay area of Glenhaven, into a new house his brother had designed and built for us. He was still my Evan, even though he was now a successful author — his elf book series had exploded in popularity.

No, staring at him now, I still saw the boy who looked at me like I was the best thing to ever happen to him, but he had that backwards.

"Just the waves, Dani," he reiterated against my lips, which made me smile, and it also made me reach out to touch.

Smooth skin, broad shoulders, even his old scars — there wasn't a thing about him I didn't love. At twenty-five, Evan was *gorgeous*. Women everywhere swooned over him. He'd lost a bit of that round, baby-face look he'd had in college and was all masculine beauty, with his sharp jaw, long eyelashes, and slight stubble. But *nothing* was as pretty as his smile. And he had so many versions of it—the polite one for the public; the slow, carnal one; the bright, happy one; the sweet, disbelieving one; and the knowing, crooked one. It was the latter I was receiving at the moment, like he knew exactly what he was doing when he pressed his hands to the small of my back, only to skim down to my bottom and squeeze, bringing me flush to him. No matter how handsome everyone told him he was, it was only me he saw—nothing about that had changed.

"I'm gonna miss you," I whispered, rolling onto my back, and he shifted with me.

"It's only a few days, and then we'll meet at the airport. I'm picking you up myself."

I nodded, trying not to dwell on it. Instead, I focused on how fluid and easy it was between us. Evan braced a hand beside my head, his forehead falling to mine. His hips surged forward a bit, causing us both gasp a little at the feel.

"Please, baby," he begged in a whisper.

I didn't answer him with words but with my hands reaching for his face. Years of learning each other's bodies allowed us to shift and pull and push just where we wanted, needed. There were kisses to lips, tangled legs, moans for more, and whispers to keep quiet.

Once he slid deep inside me, my head fell back to the pillows. He took advantage, pressing kisses to my exposed throat as he whispered against my skin.

"You feel so good, Dani," he breathed as we started to find our rhythm, hips meeting over and over, but we kept it deep, slow, languid. "I couldn't leave without this, beautiful. I just...I need..."

He wanted it to last—both our lovemaking and our small, quiet bubble we'd just woken up in—but we knew it wouldn't. Already the caws of seagulls started out on the beach, which meant the house would awaken soon, and the slow and steady had started to build into something faster with a purpose.

"So close, so close," I panted, my eyes rolling back when he pushed up on one hand and slipped the other between us to touch me where he knew I'd come completely unraveled.

"Yes," he hissed against my lips. "I love it when you come for me."

The shocks in my stomach crackled, causing everything within me to explode around him as I fell apart. Evan followed right behind, burying his face in my neck.

"I love you," he breathed heavily, dropping random, sloppy kisses to my neck and ear.

"Love you," I said, wrapping my arms all the way around his head and locking my legs around him. "Maybe I'll just keep you."

He chuckled, rolling us to our sides. "I wish, but at least we have most of the morning. My flight's not until this afternoon." When I nodded sadly, his eyes warmed. "Just a couple days and you'll meet me, Dani. It was the only way it could work—"

"Mum, mum, mum…"

We both grinned, glancing over to the baby monitor, where we saw movement on the small video screen.

"Dada…*Mum!*"

"Timing is everything," Evan teased with a deep, soft laugh. "I'm all over this. I need it before I go. Go back to sleep if you want, baby." He slipped out of bed, leaning back over me to drop a kiss to my forehead before pulling on a pair of jeans.

"If you go outside…" I started, but I broke into a wide yawn.

"I know. It's chilly. I've got this."

I chuckled low as Evan left the room. When I rolled to my side, my gaze was drawn to the baby monitor's screen again. I swallowed thickly at the emotions that seemed to overwhelm me when I watched my two very handsome boys. Robin Evan Shaw—though we called him Robbie—was fourteen months of chubby, happy, babbling goodness. He was everything perfect and healthy and loved. And he was probably way too spoiled, though I blamed aunts, uncles, and grandparents for that. Not to mention the man stepping into the room.

"Hey, Robbie," Evan crooned to his son, scooping him up out of the crib. "How messy are you this morning?"

Giggling, I shook my head. To watch Evan now, it was almost impossible to remember the brutal and heartbreaking panic attack he had when I found out I was pregnant. We'd been married a little over a year and had even discussed a family. Evan's book had taken off, and the second one was on its way. There had been talk of a TV show or movie, so it wasn't about the money or providing for his family. The heartbreaking part was when Evan was terrified of becoming like his own father. My soul had shattered that day because despite the fact that Evan had become strong and had overcome so many things about his childhood, the fear that had graced his handsome face had been hard to witness.

"Dani, I…" He glared at the stick in his hand, the two lines clear and bright and pink. "I…I…I don't…" He trailed off, shaking his head over and over.

Evan sat down hard on the end of the bed, his eyes barely leaving the stick in his hand, and my heart dropped to my stomach. Hardly a sound could be heard in our tiny apartment above the bookstore.

"Evan, baby…I thought this was something we were together on," I whispered, nervously shifting on my feet.

He was so quiet, so still, and his face was a bit red. When he finally met my gaze, those beautiful dark eyes were filled with tears.

"Dani, I'm…I'm gonna mess this up. I'm…I don't…What if I'm like my dad?"

The sob that ripped through me was loud and hurt my chest, and in a moment I was standing between his legs with his face cradled in my hands. "Not a fucking chance, Evan. Do you hear me?" I urged him to look me in the eye, and when he did, I pressed kisses to his forehead. "You are nothing *like him, baby. The entire time I've known you, you've never once said a derogatory word against me, even if you were upset. If anyone on this fucking planet knows what harsh words can do, it's you, sweetheart. And if anyone knows how to show love…Oh, Evan…that's really* you.*"*

My tears were flowing freely now because this was so very real and very scary. I wanted and already loved the baby we'd created, and if Evan didn't, or if he'd changed his mind, I would be in it all alone. I'd lose him, and that was terrifying because I loved him so much. That would never change.

"Evan," I pushed on, my vision blurry. "I need to kn-know if…If you don't want…" When I couldn't speak, something in Evan snapped, and I found myself in his arms and on his lap.

"Shit, shit, shit," he chanted, shifting us to the middle of our bed. His arms were shaking around me as he squeezed me almost too tightly. "Don't let me fuck up, Dani. Don't let me. I can't…If I mess up, if I hurt him…or her…" His hands pulled my now heated, tear-covered face from the crook of his neck. "I don't want to ruin our baby, Dani. I don't want to turn into him.*"*

Another sob escaped me, and I grabbed his face and kissed him. "You honestly think I'd let you?" I asked incredulously, sniffling when he froze for a moment. "Evan, no one loves as beautifully and selflessly as you do. In fact, the only way you'd ruin our child is if you spoiled the shit out of her...him..."

"Our child," he whispered, finally calming a bit. "We're having a baby..."

There it was. That stunning smile started to grow on his face, but it fell just as quickly as it started. "I'm sorry, baby. I just...For a second, I thought...what if, you know?" He swallowed nervously, but the tender touches to my face as he wiped away my tears told me he was calmer. "I'm scared, but..." He paused, his hand flattening on my stomach. His gaze was locked there as well. "I'm terrified, but we made this." His tone was awe and wonder, and he was still scared, but again, the smile started to curl up on his face.

"We did!" I giggled a little, sniffling at the same time. "We had fun doing it too," I teased him.

His laugh was loud and beautiful. "Yeah, we did," he whispered, looking back down at his hand on my belly. "What do we do now, pretty girl?"

Baby giggles brought me back to the present, and I smiled at Evan's deep chuckle as he changed Robbie's diaper, fought chubby legs to dress him, and tickled the bottoms of tiny toes. He was better at being a daddy than he ever gave himself credit for, because he loved with all his heart. And the very moment he'd held his son in his arms, he was a slave to our boy.

Once Evan got Robbie dressed, he took him downstairs, which meant I lost my ability to eavesdrop.

I had to have nodded back off, because I snapped awake with a quick inhale. Glancing over at the clock, I groaned at the hour I'd slept away, but I forced myself out of bed and into the bathroom. I had wanted to give Evan time with his son, not fall back asleep.

I showered, dressed, preparing myself for the trip to the airport. Evan was flying out to California today for a few interviews and a book signing. He'd be making his way up the West Coast and then into Montana, and it was in Bozeman that he'd be picking Robbie and me up at the airport. My husband may have come a long way with his past, but being back in Montana was unnerving for him, so I wanted to be there with him.

There had been no contact from William. Pastor Sean had tried to keep tabs on him, but after Evan's dad had finished his sentence in the halfway house, he pretty much fell off the face of the earth. Sean assumed he'd moved to Missoula to be with the woman he'd been with for so long, or that she had moved to Bozeman, but no one was certain. My guess was that William fell in with the wrong people or he was just mean and disrespectful enough to offend someone somewhere and had gotten himself into even more trouble. It was a guess, but as long as that abusive bastard stayed away from Evan, Tyler, and Faith, I was perfectly fine. They were my family—Faith being truly family when she married Wes. Everyone had moved on, and they were happy and prospering—Tyler and Jasmine were even expecting their first baby in the spring. For William to come in and sully that would piss me off to no end.

I poured myself a cup of coffee, smiling at the evidence of breakfast the boys had shared, but it was the squeal of happiness outside that called to me.

I stepped around boxes that still needed to be unpacked, which would wait until after I got back from the airport. Some things would wait until Evan was back home in a little over a week…if the chaos and mess didn't drive my own personal OCD to the brink of insanity.

Through the sliding glass doors, the beach stretched out to the right and left as far as I could see. There were houses close by on either side, but it was quiet, private. I stepped out onto the back porch into the chilly, overcast winter morning, giggling against the lip of my cup as I fell in love all over again.

Evan was in jeans and a gray thermal shirt, but he'd dressed Robbie adorably—little khaki cargos, a blue-and-white football shirt, and a blue-and-white-striped wool hat. Our son was an adorable blend of the two of us. He had big brown eyes and adorable dimples when he smiled, but his hair was fine—duck fluff, as Evan called it—so his little bald head tended to get cold. I loved that the color I could see coming in was dark like Evan's but had some light streaks to it like mine.

Robbie was squealing into laughter as Evan tried to hold him up to let him walk on the wet packed sand of the beach in adorable little sneakers. Our son was getting closer and closer to being able to do it, but not yet. Evan on the beach was a sight to behold, not because he was tall, handsome, with the chilly sea breeze blowing his hair but because he loved it now. When I first met him, the fear of water had a fierce grip on him, but ever since he'd taken that one giant step onto the beach when we'd first moved in together, he'd let that old fear go. Even our small wedding had been on the beach just off the boardwalk, and it was Sean who'd performed it. So yes, I was incredibly proud of Evan, especially when I saw him passing that recent love of sand and water on to Robbie.

When my son caught sight of me, he lit up. His smile was like Evan's, where it was a blinding flash of happy and sweet, making his whole face crinkle with it.

"Mum, Mum, Mum!" he called, one little fist opening and closing over and over.

Evan laughed, looking up from his stooped position as he guided our son, but then scooped the boy up into his arms. "There's Mommy," he crooned to Robbie, kissing the side of his head and walking to me. "Hey, pretty girl." He kissed my lips, chuckling when Robbie reached for me. He handed him over, trading me for the cup of coffee. "We wanted to let you sleep, so we came out here to be noisy."

Laughing, I smooched my son's face all over, down to his neck, just to hear him giggle uncontrollably. "Were you noisy, baby boy?"

"No!" he answered loudly in the laugh I loved, curling in on himself.

Evan set the coffee mug down on the porch railing, wrapping his arms around both of us. "I hate leaving you," he whispered against my forehead, pressing kisses there. "Don't overdo the unpacking, baby. Okay? If you need help, call Tyler or Wes. They promised they'd check in on you."

"We'll be fine. Mom and Aunt Tessa are coming tomorrow to steal Robbie for the day, and Faith too, I think. Though, I have to be at the bookstore to open for your book release." I smiled at him, cupping his handsome face. "I'm so very proud of you, Evan."

His grin flashed quick and bright, and he deflected the compliment by kissing the top of Robbie's head. "You take care of Mommy while I'm gone, buddy. I expect a full report when you land in Montana."

Grinning, I shook my head. "I love you both like crazy."

Evan chuckled softly, pulling us closer and hugging us fiercely. "We love you too."

"C'mon. I want to snuggle with my boys before you go, and you have to finish packing," I told him.

I knew dropping him off at the airport would be hard, but I also knew Robbie and I would be joining him in just a few days. We'd done it before when the first book took off unexpectedly right after the baby was born, so we could do it again.

Evan

I leaned against the wall at the airport, waiting for the conveyor belt to kick on. Damn, I missed my family. The last few days had been busy with interviews and book signings, but the closer I got to Montana, the more anxious I became. Some shit just didn't ever go away.

California had been fine, in spite of the meetings and interviews. My *Elves of Lenora* would end up a TV show, which I could barely wrap my head around. There were still contracts to discuss and more books to come, but I'd left LA in shock and humbled at the excitement my old story had garnered. I'd had to attend two book signings so far in Montana, in both Missoula and Browning. However, as I stood in the middle of Bozeman Yellowstone International Airport, I sighed deeply at the feelings coursing through me.

I'd told Dani a long time ago that I'd never come back here. And really, this trip wasn't by choice. It was business, but I couldn't help but remember some things from the past. I also couldn't help but continuously look over my shoulder. We were too damn close to where all the bad shit had happened. We were too damn close to my dad, and I was really happy that Dani had offered to meet me here for the next few days.

William Shaw had fallen off the grid. Sean, who occasionally would give me updates, had lost contact with him a couple years ago, not long after he'd left the halfway house. I didn't care; I was perfectly content with my life, with my wife and son, with my family back in Florida. He'd never been a real father to me, so the loss of contact wasn't a bad thing. Even if he'd tried to get in touch with me, he'd have been met with nothing.

The luggage carousel kicked on, and people started to drift in, and that was when the smile spread across my face because my beautiful girl stepped through the throngs of people with my boy in her arms. I met them halfway across the large room, meeting my wife's gaze over my son's head.

"Look, Robbie...Daddy!" she whispered to him, grinning my way, and my son's head snapped up off her shoulder to gaze around until he finally set his sights on me.

"Da-ee, Da-ee, Da-ee!" he called, reaching with stretched-out arms.

"Hey, buddy!" I crooned, taking him from Dani, but I leaned down and kissed her lips. "Hi, baby," I whispered. "God, I've missed you guys!"

"We missed you," Dani said, burrowing into my neck when I wrapped my arms around them both. "Apparently I'm not as good at storytelling as you are, Daddy, so bedtime the last few nights was...grumpy."

Laughing, I looked to my son. "Cut Mommy some slack, buddy."

My son grinned, all dimply and innocent, shaking his head.

"Tough audience, baby. Sorry," I teased my wife, unable to keep my lips from her one more time. "How was the release at the bookstore?"

"Biggest day we've ever had, Evan," Dani said with a laugh that was laced with pride and awe at the same time. "Not even kidding."

As we gathered Dani's checked bags and Robbie's car seat and stroller, I dropped repeated kisses to his head. I'd missed them both. I never thought I could love *this damn much*. It had been overwhelming and scary, but the very second I'd set eyes on my son, I was absolutely a different man.

Two things flew through my mind the day he was born. One was that my Dani was the strongest, most amazing woman I'd ever met and I'd never be able to thank her for the life she'd given me. And two...I was *nothing* like my own father, not one fucking thing like him. Where he hated the mere sight of his own children, I could barely put my own son down long enough for a nap. I couldn't stop kisses, tickles, revels in the littlest of things Robbie did or from the love I kept spewing at the two most important people in my life. No, I was not my father. Everything about being a parent I'd learned from my mother and then from Leanne, Daniel, and Aunt Tessa.

Once we were loaded up in the rental car, I turned to Dani before pulling out of the parking spot. "Baby, the hotel is right next to the bookstore where I'm supposed to be for the next few hours. If you want, you can avoid the chaos..."

Dani grinned. "And your overzealous fans," she teased, leaning over to kiss my lips. "Actually, that's sort of perfect. Robbie needs a nap, and I need a shower from being on this plane. We can meet you when you're done, Evan."

Smiling, I kissed her again. "Good, and then we'll get something to eat. Sean wants to see us when we're in Helena for the signing day after tomorrow—he's out of town today and tomorrow, so he'll make the trip to Helena when he gets back—so it's just the three of us tonight."

Robbie babbled excitedly as we drove through the city, but the chatter slowly settled down, and he was asleep by the time I pulled into the hotel. I carried bags and baby stuff upstairs to the hotel room as Dani carried a zonked-out baby boy. Once she settled him onto the bed surrounded by pillows, I kissed them both and then made my way to the bookstore.

Signings were hectic and sometimes crazy, but this one had been fun. There were pictures and tons of laughs, not to mention I signed my name more times than I could count. The line started to dwindle as my time was almost up. As one of the employees of the bookstore called an end to things, I glanced up to see who was left.

My wife was there with Robbie in her arms, and he was chewing on one of his toys. I smiled her way but signed the last three books in the line, finally standing up to stretch. They both looked like they'd had a nap and a bath.

Dani, who'd been gorgeous the first time I'd set eyes on her in college, was now just beautiful. She was older, and despite how she thought having Robbie had changed her body, she was still perfect to me. I'd teased her more than once that we now had matching scars on our stomachs, which always made her laugh, though I tended to do it while kissing every inch of her bare skin.

"Da-ee!" Robbie squealed, drool dripping from toy and chin and chubby fist.

I scooped him up out of her arms, holding him up and pretending to fly him like an airplane, just to hear him laugh. Shifting him to my hip, I leaned in to kiss Dani's lips and then forehead, glancing around. In the far corner of the bookstore by the storefront window, I saw what looked like a familiar face. Cold, dark eyes met mine, bringing with them a flood of feelings—inadequacy, hate, fear, and then finally indifference. For a brief moment, I couldn't understand seeing my dad. It had been so damned long since I'd been in the same room with the man that I almost didn't recognize him. Time had not been kind to him. But when I stood up straight, he was gone. Frowning, I walked to where he'd been, but I didn't see anyone.

"Evan?" Dani asked, joining me at the large window that faced the sidewalk and busy street.

"I swear, Dani…I thought I saw…" I trailed off, and on the sidewalk in the distance, again I saw who I thought was my father. "I think…my dad was here," I said in a whisper, "but maybe it's my imagination." I looked to her. "You know, being here and…"

Dani's face was fierce. "He'd better leave you alone, Evan. Knowing him, he'd want in all of this," she practically growled, twirling a finger around to indicate the bookstore and my signing.

I could see her thinking. He had been stripped of everything, and my name was out there now. "Eh, he can try, pretty girl, but we're leaving in the morning. C'mon. Your men are starving. Look, he's starting to eat his own fingers!" I gasped, grabbing Robbie's wrist and giving it a gentle shake. When I pretended to munch on his hand, he broke into hysterics.

"My silly boys," she sighed, smiling warmly. "Let's go eat."

"Thanks, Mr. Shaw," the woman said, waving as I handed her book back after scrawling my name inside the cover.

Another copy landed in front of me, but it was the voice that made me smile. "Your mother would be mad you outsold her."

Grinning, I tilted my head up at Sean, and no matter that there were a dozen more people left in line, I stood up to shake his hand and hug the man.

I couldn't help but laugh again when he added, "That's a downright lie, Evan. She'd be out front with signs."

"True," I agreed easily, pulling back to look at him. "It's good to see you, Sean."

As I sat back down, I really got a look at him. He'd aged, of course, but he looked well. There was more gray at his temples and he was dressed casually, but his eyes held something hard in them.

"What?" I asked him.

He glanced around but then leaned over. "I have some news, son."

"Okay, well, can you hang out for this last bit? Dani should be here soon."

"Sure," he conceded, pushing my book closer. "My goal is to have the whole set signed, kiddo."

Grinning, I shook my head. I did as he asked, writing a personal thank-you inside to him. The rest of the line was getting antsy, but it went pretty quick once Sean stepped away to pay. I was signing the second-to-last book when there was a tug at my leg. Glancing down, I chuckled at my boy pulling himself up into a standing position, using a fierce grip on my jeans.

"Da-ee…"

"Hey, buddy. You're late to the party."

I had to laugh at the coos from the women in the room, some standing around waiting, others just shopping, but when I set my son on my lap, he slapped his hands down on the table, beaming that dimply smile at everyone. He stayed content on my lap for the next couple of autographs, and then I stood up with him in my arms when the line was finally empty.

I found Sean and Dani off to the side, and I kissed Dani's lips. "Thanks. I needed an assistant there at the end."

Her laugh was beautiful as she reached over to adjust Robbie's wool cap and jacket. "Once he saw you, it was like trying to hold a greased pig, baby. He just wouldn't stay away."

"That's one beautiful boy, you two," Sean praised, shaking his head in awe, but he chuckled a little when Robbie reached out to grab his finger. When he met my gaze, there was a touch of sadness there, but he seemed to shake it off. "We need to talk, son."

"Okay. There's an Italian place right across the street."

Once we were settled in a booth with Robbie in a high chair at the end, Sean leaned on his elbows and rubbed his face. "I got a call yesterday, guys."

"From?" I barely asked aloud because I was afraid it would be my dad, since I was pretty sure he'd been in the bookstore in Bozeman.

"John Jenson. William's lawyer," he stated with a finality, wrinkling his nose. "Jenson knew your father wasn't allowed to talk to you or your siblings. And he also knew I'm in contact with you pretty regularly, so most of the info I've ever given you came from him."

"*Wasn't...*" Dani noted the tense of the word before I did, and I glanced to her before looking back at my mother's old friend. "What happened?" she asked, dropping a handful of Cheerios onto Robbie's tray just to keep him happily busy.

"Your father, Evan," Sean began slowly, eyeing Robbie for a moment. "Your father's body was found yesterday morning." When my eyebrows shot up, he nodded. "He was...beaten pretty badly, had two gunshot wounds to the chest, one to the head, and multiple broken bones — mostly fingers."

"Wha...Umm," I started, frowning at the table as I adjusted my silverware for a second. "Why? How? I'm not even sure if I want to know this, Sean," I finally blurted out, and then the memory of seeing him hit me. "I just...I swear I just saw him in Bozeman a couple of days ago. He was at the bookstore."

"Did he approach you?"

"No. No, he left."

"I *knew* he'd end up with the wrong people," Dani whispered, shaking her head. It wasn't as if she was saying it to anyone in particular, because her focus was on our son.

"That he did, Dani," Sean concurred, nodding a little. "From what Jenson can piece together from his connections at the police department, William left the halfway house at the same time another man did. They'd followed the rules, worked at a grocery store together, but once they left, they dropped the job and the façade. The guy was head of a pretty big gang or crime family, and he needed an under-the-table/off-the-books doctor who could fix up his members should they need medical attention. William was perfect. I can imagine the money was big; drugs and prostitution and gun sales are always going to be big money. Apparently he pissed them off."

"Jesus," I whispered, raking my hands through my hair. "How? How'd he piss them off?"

Sean smiled ruefully, shaking his head slowly. "William never really respected anyone, and he never could shut up when he should.

He picked the wrong girl to mouth off to and rough up a bit — just about killed her — and she happened to be the leader's cousin. He was barely sober or dressed when they dragged him out of the motel room."

"So…wait," Dani pleaded. "He goes to see Evan and then runs off to do…*whatever* with this woman?"

We both looked to her, neither of us answering, because that seemed to be exactly what happened. It was as if seeing me set him off on some sort of downward spiral. Sitting there in that booth, I could remember every single foul insult the man had spat my way, including how badly he hated the fact that I looked just like my mother.

"Yeah, he probably did, baby." I sighed deeply, linking my fingers with hers under the table. Looking back to Sean, I merely said, "He did that to himself."

Sean smirked. "He did. Though, they need someone to claim him."

"It won't be me. And don't bury him next to Mom," I said firmly as an afterthought.

My old friend smiled. "I figured, and I didn't. He's being cremated."

Before he could ask, I added, "And I'll tell Tyler and Faith. They won't care either, so…" I shrugged a shoulder, remembering Susan's words to me so long ago. "Some people are just…toxic. He was one of those people. I understand that he came from an ugly childhood, but instead of overcoming it, he allowed it to swallow him up. He treated each of us like we were to blame for what he'd been through, and he made *my childhood* ugly.

"My worst fear was becoming him, but instead, I made it my life's goal to love my son, my wife, give them what I lost after my mother died. And I couldn't have him in my life anymore. There's absolutely nothing toxic in my life. I did what my mother wanted for me — school, career, a beautiful wife and son. Tyler is opening his own architecture firm soon, and Faith is working her way up at the museum. Both are married, happy, and Tyler will have his own little one soon. No. Just…no."

I shook my head, looking over at Robbie, who was playing with a Cheerio before putting it in his mouth. To say the things to him that my father had said to me would make me sick. But I also finally understood why my mother had wanted to simply walk away. I couldn't fathom putting Robbie in a situation where all the ugliness could surround him, bear down on him. I also knew I'd never need to make that decision because Dani was the epitome of love, home, happiness. Leaning over, I pressed my lips to the side of her head, whispering that I loved her.

Looking back to Sean, I said, "Thank you for telling me, but we all wiped our hands of him when we packed up the house in Key Lake. That hasn't changed."

Sean nodded, his gaze raking from me, to Dani, to Robbie, who was chugging from his sippy cup. "Robyn has to be beaming with pride right about now," he whispered, his brow furrowing a bit. "This... *This* was what she wanted for you, for Tyler and Faith. And I'm happy to see it."

I gazed over at Dani, thinking about how my mother would've loved her, how I was pretty sure if Mom was watching, she had to have been responsible for my Library Girl, but if I believed that, then deep down, I had to believe that she might have had a hand in my father's fate. Maybe it was seeing her in my looks that set him off after all this time. Maybe it was knowing that we had erased him from our lives, moving on with good things, prosperous things, that nothing he'd done to us had held us back. Maybe guilt and hate and everything else in between just hit him all at once, taking over. Or maybe she intervened, stopping him from trying to approach me one last time. I'd never know, and I didn't really want to know.

"Evan, you okay?" Dani asked, tilting my face a bit so I could look her in the eye.

Nodding, I kissed her lips. "Yes, ma'am. I'm okay. I'm better than okay. I'm..." I trailed off because the word "free" came to mind, but I was already free of my father long before he'd gotten himself killed. "I'm just ready to go home, pretty girl."

She smiled, glancing at Sean when he chuckled at us. But when she looked back to me, she nodded. "Me too, handsome."

I smiled at her and then at my son, who was babbling innocently around his fist as he watched us with big, curious eyes. They were my home. Home was our new house that still needed unpacking, that would see a huge Christmas this year, and that held everything that was precious to me. Home was Florida, with warm weather, sea air, and friends and family I wouldn't trade for anything. Home was what I'd unknowingly found the second I set foot in a small college library years ago.

I smiled at my wife, nodding once. "Yeah, definitely ready for home."

Acknowledgments

I would like to thank Jenny Rarden, because nothing I do is possible without her. Much love to my husband, John, and thanks to my friends, who are my hand-picked family.

About the Author

Deb Rotuno was born and raised in central Florida, where she currently lives with her husband and four cats. She's worked in retail for almost seventeen years, but if she were able to do anything she wanted, she would be a full-time reader, writer, and fur-baby mom. She has always been a big reader, and writing was something she started late in high school, but she began to dabble in it again once she discovered fanfic in 2009. Since then, she's read and written plenty in her spare time, especially since she cannot watch a TV show or a movie without thinking about how she could write a story like it.

Website: www.debrotuno.com
Twitter: @Drotuno
Facebook: Facebook.com/drotuno
RR Books Website: www.rr-books.com
RR Books Twitter: @RR_Books
RR Books Facebook: Facebook.com/writers.at.rrbooks/

Other works by Deb Rotuno:

Rain Must Fall (Rain Must Fall book 1)
Sun Still Shining (Rain Must Fall book 2)
High Heels & Hard Drives

Made in the USA
Lexington, KY
14 December 2019

58588546R00181